OUR CITY THAT YEAR

A NOVEL

GEETANJALI SHREE

TRANSLATED FROM THE HINDI BY DAISY ROCKWELL

HarperVia

An Imprint of HarperCollins*Publishers*

OUR CITY THAT YEAR. Copyright © 1998 by Geetanjali Shree. Translation copyright © 2024 by Daisy Rockwell. All rights reserved. Printed in the United States of America. No part of this book may be used or reproduced in any manner whatsoever without written permission except in the case of brief quotations embodied in critical articles and reviews. For information, address HarperCollins Publishers, 195 Broadway, New York, NY 10007.

HarperCollins books may be purchased for educational, business, or sales promotional use. For information, please email the Special Markets Department at SPsales@harpercollins.com.

Originally published as *Hamara Shahar Us Baras* in India in 1998 by Rajkamal Prakashan.

FIRST EDITION

Design adapted from the Penguin Random House India edition designed by Manipal Technologies Limited.

Library of Congress Cataloging-in-Publication Data has been applied for.

ISBN 978-0-06-338570-2

25 26 27 28 29 LBC 5 4 3 2 1

Remembering beloved Ma,
who taught us to love motherland, religion and
humanity, in generosity and mutual respect

Author's Note

There are seismic moments that will not let a writer be away from the immediate. It becomes imperative to engage with it even if, in being bang center of things flying all around, sights get blurred and confusion is created. If literature is about subtlety, deflections, and detachment, can there be literature in such moments? When the "outside" turns so invasive that it is as if no "inside" space remains for the writer? The moments so fraught, so overwhelming that the distance between thought and feeling shrinks to the point of vanishing. Could I possibly write anything meaningful without solitude, without a modicum of distance?

That is where the witness-narrator came to my rescue. Recording, even if not understanding. Picking up bits from here and there, letting a collage emerge where continuities crack up, stories turn upside down, dismembered objects fly, clarities are cloudy. An act of faith that all this would make sense later in a quieter moment.

That is how *Hamara Shahar Us Baras*, the Hindi original of *Our City That Year*, got written.

I live in a country that is home to all major religions of the world. This makes for an organic pluralistic society marked by both nurturing and rupturing, cooperation and conflict, camaraderie and competition. Leaving out the Partition, which is the one big traumatic fall-out of rupture between the two major communities, Hindus and Muslims, intercommunity friendships and hostilities have been more like in a family—the whole range from silly bickering to serious quarrelling but a general acceptance that we all belong here.

This phenomenon changed around the 1980s as relations between the two communities went on a precipitous downward curve and in the '90s a new stridency surfaced, particularly of the Hindus. Religious identities sharpened, and mobs came out on the streets. Conversations acquired sectarian undertones. Even the "educated" began speaking a language of intolerance. What, until now, had seemed a problem among the poor and illiterate "out there" spilled into middle- and upper-class localities and homes "in here."

Many questions arose. How, why, and where did we, the progressive secularists, fail? Are we pretending to be progressive but veering another way? What is it in societal junctures that makes unities dominate at one time and divisions at another? Is one or the other the more real and innate character of the phenomenon?

The novel searched on, looking at the fast-spreading intolerance all around. It was easy to call out the familiar villains—the fanatics and the intolerant insulars of either religion. But what of the shadowy figures living within us who did not know their own narrowness and prejudices? They must be drawn out as well. To face ourselves, look for subtle bigotries and not just the loudest ones.

"That year" of *Our City* is not yet over, and the "city" has sprung up everywhere. Not just in the "backward" East, but also in the "forward" West. More and more communities are asserting their separate identities, seeking to subjugate, even annihilate, the "other" community.

This novel and its Hindus and Muslims have become a metaphor for what's happening in much of the world.

Despairing though that is, there is still hope. The novel is read and cared for by so many, and the translator and publisher care to bring it forth. We have a voice, and it will not be silenced.

Given that *Our City That Year* is an invitation to look beyond our smug certitudes and think anew, it will help to recall that extraordinary, consistently unheard voice of our times, Gandhi. Just two months before he was assassinated by a fanatic in 1948, he had warned:

. . . About 137 mosques of Delhi have been virtually destroyed in the recent riots. Some of these have been turned into temples. . . . To despoil mosques in this manner is to put Hindu and Sikh religions to shame. In my opinion, this goes against every tenet of religion. . . . The magnitude of this act cannot be mitigated by saying that Muslims in Pakistan have also despoiled Hindu temples or turned them into mosques. In my view, any such act would destroy the Hindu religion, the Sikh religion. and Islam.

—Geetanjali Shree

So this is the place. Our city.

Into this city the three of them came forth. Panicked. Determined to bring everything to the fore: the crime and the criminal; the wounded and the dead. All of it. They would see clearly, and clearly they would reveal whatever they saw. Sharad, Shruti and Hanif, who had resolved that they would write. That this time they could not remain silent. That everything must be brought out into the open. That the blowing wind was no breeze but a gale. That they could not allow it to uproot them.

It's raining. Shruti has stepped off the train and stands on the platform. A vibration. A trembling agitation passes beneath her feet and departs with the train. People run stumbling, soaked, searching for passengers outside. The city's cows and dogs have ambled in to laze on the flooded platform. The water flows towards the tracks. A wasteland.

There was a time that year when such rivers flowed in the streets, but they didn't come from the rains. They came from the neighbourhood water tanks that were emptied into the streets for fear they'd been poisoned.

Sharad recognizes her from afar and approaches. She stands alone, waiting. They come face to face; their faces bound in an inhibited silence. They exit with measured steps.

The three of them understood that everything making us restless and frightened was right there, outside. They faced the same fear that filled me. I, too, began to panic. They'd try to write, then stop midstream. They'd find their writing hollow and say, all these words have been written before, nothing will be accomplished by recording them; the words have become utterly useless, grown empty, like government slogans.

It was then that I realized I'd have to do something, somehow or other. I'd have to write, whether I understood or not. If it couldn't be the three of them—a professional writer and two intellectuals—it would have to be me. Me, who knows only how to copy down words.

At that time, it was barely possible to string together two words of sense. Nonetheless, I, who had neither the experience to string words nor the tenacity, could write. If you call copying down writing, then that's what I was doing. That's what I could do. I would pick up the fragments that flew up in their wake. Whatever caught my eye, wherever.

Before my eyes is that house, that gate, that letterbox. The flap of the letterbox hangs open, shivering in the rain. Shruti hesitates at the gate. Her sandals are soaking wet, as are her feet, up to the ankles. Sharad opens the gate. The front yard is overgrown with wild grasses.

Once a madhumalti vine had climbed here, and the sight beneath that vine, of a row of white teeth in pink gums, had sickened me. The pen had slipped from my hand, ink splattering. Later, I'd wonder why I hadn't recalled the pink and white blossoms of the madhumalti vine when I saw the teeth and gums. Instead, madhumaltis now always remind me of those gums and those teeth. They nauseate me. Nor do I recall the rest of that face that used to blossom with laughter. That beautiful, hearty laugh. Instead, the face becomes a repulsive shape lying in the dust, its individuality erased, defiling all the beauty of the laughter, wiping out the entire existence of the person to whom it had belonged. Daddu used to say that if you recognize a thing by only a fragment of the whole then it becomes trapped in its own contour, a useless, lifeless caricature. True recognition bursts forth, spreading and wandering about in the open, enveloped by all things, melting into everything. It is light. If you trap it within a single fragment to purify it, you'll simply extinguish the light. The shape will be rendered lifeless. A repulsive lump of flesh.

But I kept picking up the fragments. I didn't have the time, let alone the ability, to fill in the middle parts, to search for fitting links. There was no time to act deliberately. Fearfully, quickly, I simply copied it all down. I wrote of here or there, scribbled down unnecessities, pasted the fragments willy-nilly. When life itself had become a collage in which slivers and scraps floated about, sticking hither and thither as in the aftermath of an explosion, forming and deforming shapes, how could we escape the incomplete, the scattered, the broken?

Who's ever heard of a cauliflower crop growing in a field of corpses?

But listen:

There was such a crop in our city, that year.

Who's ever heard of a crop of fresh plump white cauliflowers that can't be sold for even a handful of cowries?

But that, too, happened in our city, that year.

There were many such things that made no sense at all, and I was incapable of gathering all the bits and pieces to create the true picture. For they were mere scraps, whose proper worth I could not gauge, nor did I have to. It was none of my business. I just had to copy.

I am copying down from the beginning.

From the beginning . . . or maybe not? I don't really know; because no one knew where the beginning was. But from the moment, whenever it was, that I jumped up, frightened of their panic, grabbed paper, uncapped pen, and set to work in that dusty smoky season; because if you won't, then I will; I'll write it myself, that is, I'll copy down whatever you say, whatever you see, whatever I can grasp; and if I don't grasp, I'll write anyway, I'll write without comprehension.

Because someone had to write about that year, and that city.

Someone had to bear witness.

And who knows, there could be some essence to be distilled from the unhinged language of incomprehension, and who knows, there could be other years after that year.

For example, the year in which Shruti stands, and Sharad pulls her inside and locks and chains the door.

'Come in. Do look,' he says.

'No, no need,' she refuses.

'Look.'

'No need.'

But Sharad walks ahead and opens another door. A bundle lies on the bed inside, its back to them. Two skinny stick-like things protrude from under the sheet.

Shruti does not walk through the door. She stares from a distance at the items set out on the small table next to the bed and turns to enter the hall directly. He who used to bask in the light that radiated from his body has shrunk to a tiny bundle. His spark has gone dark. Now all that remains is a contour, a shrunken caricature.

Sharad wishes to mention Hanif.

'Hanif . . .?' He falters and falls silent.

'He's writing,' Shruti tells him. 'And you?' she asks.

Sharad shrugs.

I open my bundle of writing paper. Flip quickly through the sheets. Then slowly lay them out like rummy cards. But who will become the pairs here and who the sequences? The cards lie scattered, my pen uncapped.

No one's listening.

They sit quietly, gazing at the rosewood divan from that year.

That year, in our city, Hindus abandoned their pacifism. *We've run out of other cheeks to turn*, they proclaimed. *We're helpless!* they screamed. They climbed atop mosques and waved the flag of Devi affixed to their tridents proclaiming, *What was done to us will be visited on them! Wrong shall be answered with wrong!* Holy men abandoned their meditations, and angry cries echoed in place of prayers: *They killed our progeny, dishonoured our daughters! Sons, are you cowards or men? O, descendants of the heroes Shivaji, Bhagat Singh, Rana Pratap; O, sons of Arjun and Bhima, rise! Transform the neighbourhoods of your enemies into graveyards! Enough with your gentlemanly behaviour! Even the deities rage when the crimes of demons are on the rise.*

Arise.

Awake.

Save us.

And out poured gangs upon gangs to tear the mosques in our city down to their foundations and erect the idols of goddesses and gods in their place.

The air in our city began to pulse. It echoed with their feelings of helplessness: *boom boom*. The gangs emerged with a clamour, raising clouds of ash which could turn to dust at any time and sting our eyes. They released fountains of Ganga water which could turn to blood at any time and splatter our eyes.

It was like a rollicking festival. So many hues, it could have been Holi in a storm of coloured powder. They held sacrifices and threw into the flames the cowardice that had been nurtured in the name of dispassion. They marked their brows with a tilak of ashes, hurled sharp bits of metal at the sun, slicing it to ribbons, skewering the brilliant sun-scraps and waving them in the air as they fanned out into the streets, over the moon to discover in their clutches the joyous sun.

We shivered when we saw how the sun danced in their hands.

'Should I write from the perspective of a child?' Shruti asks. Her hands drip red from peeling beets. 'Of our unborn child? Who will see this, hear this, tell this?'

'No,' Hanif vetoes the idea at the outset. 'For one,' he says, 'that narrative style is very old, it's been going on since the time of the Mahabharata. For another . . .' his voice is severe now, 'we don't even want a child. Who would want to inherit these times?'

Even the glancing thought of an unborn child's testimony fills me with dread. But why?

If I just shadow them and keep copying, what do I have to fear?

'Why should we be afraid? We live over here. Your friend has no right to spread the psychosis of fear. He enjoys it even,' frets Shruti.

They sit in the flat upstairs. Dirty dishes piled before them. Sharad has just gone home, downstairs. Earlier, the three of them had been eating, drinking, gossiping, and I'd been standing nearby, wondering if I should listen, if I should copy everything down, if I should just ignore. The three diners had pushed bay leaves, cloves, cinnamon sticks, black cardamom pods to one side on their plates. Sharad's final utterance still lingers in the air: 'The city's on fire, and you're laughing?'

That's where I'll start, I resolve; that's where I'll begin to record.

'You're humourless.' Hanif ribs Shruti. 'Sharad was teasing you because he knows you'll blow up.'

'That wasn't teasing at all. Your friend is the completely humourless son of an overly humourful father.' Shruti was angry when she started to speak, but by the end she smiles at her own mention of Daddu.

'But the fire's been lit.'

'But not here, over there,' Shruti objects.

'But the fire can't burn us. Sati is still in practice, tender-hearted women watch as their own kind are set aflame, fingers burn daily turning chapatis on hearths: fire is our familiar! Why should we fear it burning us?'

'Arre, are you waxing philosophical or just telling tasteless jokes like your friend?'

I am not omniscient. I write about wherever I am, whenever. I cannot weave things together. I wouldn't know a warp from a woof. But I cannot escape writing. Will any witness survive this horrifying tongue that flickers about devouring our city? Because, who knows, tomorrow this tongue could find us . . . and you? And if we are no more . . .

And who knows if by some simple coincidence we survive, or you survive, then perhaps we'll be able to understand something when we look back. Or preserve something.

But now, just write. Write without comprehension. And if not you, then I will write down whatever you say, write, see; whatever can be expressed in ink.

Daddu begins to laugh. The divan bounces. His eyes narrow to slits and his wide-open mouth makes the rest of his face shrivel like a raisin. His ears stick out even further than usual. Truly, he begins to look like a chimpanzee, or a *chimp-ahn-jee*, as he pronounces it.

Sharad's also bouncing on that same divan, but he isn't laughing. The springs of the divan, Daddu always says, are 'ancient, like me'. Daddu might be a bouncing raisin or a jumping chimpahnjee, but the sight of Professor Sharad bouncing up and down while reading a book like *The Philosophical Discourse of Modernity* with a grimace on his face would make any observer burst out laughing.

Daddu's laughter gathers force with the chuckling of Shruti and Hanif. Any moment now, Sharad will surely bounce up and hit the ceiling reading his book, like a ball!

'Write, write,' says Daddu, his eyes shining. 'You're young, you'll keep working. Fools! You'll never grab hold of the sun.'

'He's laughing on purpose,' whispers Shruti. 'He's got in the habit of bouncing violently. It must help him digest his food. It must help him sleep.'

'Habit is a nefarious thing,' says Hanif. He kicks Sharad in the leg to get his attention. 'There once was a young fellow just like this one, who would nod off reading about modernity and such. Then a drunk moved in downstairs. Every night he returned home late and fell on to his bed with a *thud*. He unfastened one heavy boot and flung it up at the ceiling with a *thunk*, following which, he laboriously removed the second one and flung it up with another *thunk*. Then he fell into a blissful slumber. But our fellow's sleep had been ruined. He went downstairs and gave the drunk a stern talking-to. And the decent drunk . . .'

Daddu screams. With laughter.

'. . . grabbed both his ears and promised *never again*. But now listen to what happened next. Night came and so too the drunk. He sat down with a *thud*, removed one boot and . . .? Threw it up with a *thunk*. Took off the second one. When he remembered his promise, he bit his tongue. In slow motion he placed the second boot silently on the floor and fell fast asleep. But our fellow? He sat there waiting and waiting and waiting . . .'

'For the second *thunk*!' Daddu begins to bounce.

'The third!' Shruti laughs. 'First he falls on the bed with a *thunk* . . .'

'Falls with a *thud*,' Daddu corrects. 'Now he was waiting for the second *thunk*.'

'Which didn't come, nor did sleep . . .' Hanif continues.

'And why would it?' Daddu has transformed into a ball, bouncing all the way to the ceiling.

'Then our Sharad-esque fellow went downstairs, and pleaded, "For God's sake, have mercy, toss the second boot, please, I beg of you!"'

Daddu laughs and laughs. He stands up, adjusts his dhoti and heads to the bathroom. In the meantime, Hanif jumps up and pours a couple of decent pegs into Sharad's and his own glasses from the whiskey bottle that always stands by Daddu's feet. The liquor effervesces, and all blandness disappears.

'To decent drunks.' Sharad raises his glass.

Shruti bursts out laughing. 'See, see? There's the habit! When the divan stops bouncing, he can't seem to read.'

Everyone's eating dinner downstairs again. At Daddu's full-length dining table. The hall is sparsely furnished, but everything in it is huge: there's the divan where Daddu sits, the long sofa across from him where guests sit, and a tall floor lamp. So, so huge. There's a cabinet that covers an entire wall on one side of the room, full of books behind wooden doors. Within the cabinet there's also a niche for the television and the liquor bottles.

On this side, there's a large glass door, which Daddu doesn't open, and beyond that are the gate and the street.

On that side are the dining table, a stone fireplace and the old radiogram. So, so, so huge.

Besides these things, there's only the heavy black telephone that sits on the floor wrapped in a metres-long cord, like a tail.

Sharad keeps eating raw carrots.

I sit at the ready with pen and paper.

I'm no researcher that I would quote my own original research, nor am I a creative writer that I would write a draft, scratch everything out in the next draft, then write again, then meditate on it, then write again, then edit again.

Are such things really editable, anyway?

I don't have the leisure to go back and re-evaluate my writing. If I had the time, I would certainly want to do that, just to know what I'd written, and try to understand what it turned out to mean, or if it meant anything, or if it was just what it was. But who has the time! We belong to that cursed class of beings that has run out of time.

It would appear that Sharad wants to eat only carrots. He bites into a raw carrot with a *crunch* and Daddu watches with surprise, then smiles.

I can hear the *crunch crunch* all the way from here.

But first, the part about how I'm not a researcher. And I'm not a creative writer. Nor yet am I Ganesha that I would jot down the Mahabharata as Vyasa speaks. Or should I put it this way: I could have been Ganesha if I were able to comprehend as I wrote, but in this case, I forgot even my own words, and the people whose words I had to record didn't know what dictation was; so if there was no Vyasa, and no one who knew what the Mahabharata was, how could I possibly have been Ganesha?

So how should I describe myself? A copier, one who copies without comprehension, because who has the time? (And if

I did have the time, would I comprehend? Are such things comprehensible?) But whose words? Their words, the words of those who cannot even claim to understand themselves. I'm busily writing as I gaze at them like a detective under orders from an undisclosed source: *Don't assess; just keep copying.* If something floats before their eyes, or I catch something that pops up in their speech, I write it down; if they write something down on paper, copying is especially easy: I simply peer over their shoulder and note it down. Their scattered bits and pieces.

Sharad picks up another carrot. Then he sees it's the last one and puts it back.

A single carrot stays put, for the sake of appearances. No one claims it.

There are many riots in our city. Cross the bridge and you'll encounter madmen.

Our city is just like other cities. The station building is old, and back in the day, during the times of the English, there was a huge reclining armchair in the waiting room. I can't say if it's there now. There are shops for food and drink.

There's a university too, with old domes occupied by pigeons. Pigeons and crows abound in this city. People too.

'You'll do it too,' teases Daddu. 'Once I crumble, this building will crumble too. And then a skyscraper will be built here. And it will be called Sharad Shruti Hanif Apartments.'

'Stop it.' Sharad smiles. 'We're telling you about beautiful old buildings. Beautiful old homes. This house is actually new . . .'

'It's not that new, kid,' chuckles Daddu, pleased. 'And I am, after all, ancient.'

'And beautiful,' chuckles Hanif.

'Name it after me then . . .'

'Daddu Apartments!' shrieks Shruti.

Through the latticed window, Hanif and Sharad watch the white dome of the ashram, atop which flies a saffron banner.

The ashram has been visible ever since the brush was cleared.

There are few people in the department today. They're all from this side of the bridge.

They all form a line, the university, the ashram and the field that's currently subject to a lawsuit. The field that runs alongside one of the main streets of the city.

On one side are the university and the ashram, and down the middle runs the dry ravine that only fills with water in the rains but is called a river year-round. Across the river is the bridge, and on the other side is the entire confounded city.

'Good morning, sir . . . sir . . .!'

'Arre, bhai, why are you people wandering around outside? Stay home.'

'No, Sharad Sir, we actually live here, not over there.'

Daddu taps the divan and recites rhythmically:

Khari baat saidullah kahen
Sab ke man se utare rahen

Truth was what the wise man said
'Twas dismissed from every head

'What now?' asks Shruti with a laugh.

'Yeeesss,' Daddu replies in rhythm with his recitation. Tap-tap-tapping on the divan.

The staffroom is fairly empty, but the department head sahib is worked up, so he's just lecturing at whomever is left. He's got one sandalled foot up on his chair, and he holds a cup of tea while resting his elbow on his knee. He has a habit of nibbling and snipping at the edge of his moustache while speaking.

'It's horrendous! Children used to play—*nibble*—hide-and-seek—*nibble*—and now they play Hindus—*nibble*—and Muslims. We intellectuals have to do something. Yesterday my—*nibble*—granddaughter—*nibble-nibble*—said, "We know why you've gone quiet. You're"—*nibble*—"talking about Muslims." Six years old. We intellectuals feel very upset. We should write, we should speak. Did you see today's paper? We're being told there was a temple there before! Amazing! *Nibble*. So what! Before that there was a Buddhist temple, and before that there was something else. Once it was tribal territory. So what? We intellectuals are guilty of remaining silent . . .'

'Wow, Head Sahib, what's this outfit you're sporting?' Sharad whistles.

'Black corduroys, yellow T-shirt; looks new . . .'

'It is,' Professor Nandan admits, but he's displeased at his speech getting nibbled off in the middle.

'Listen, this reminds me of a story,' Hanif begins jovially. 'Someone we know once put on a yellow T-shirt and black corduroy pants just like these and went to the bathroom. Suddenly there was a loud sound . . .'

'Must have been a *thunk*,' teases Sharad.

'A *thunk* indeed. "What happened?" called out his wife. "My T-shirt fell!" our friend shouted back. "With such a loud *thunk*?" The wife was amazed. "I was inside it!" our friend clarified.'

Everyone laughs.

'Do be careful, Head Sahib,' says Sharad.

Professor Nandan is silent. His habit, when silent, is to tug at his moustache with two fingers and nibble on it . . . *nibble* . . . *nibble* . . . *nibble* . . .

Our city became both an inspiration for and a reflection of the rash of riots in our country.

The Devi Ashram is here, and its branches were shooting up in other cities.

If you wander about here, rest assured you are getting a proper tour of India—Bharat bhraman!

When I realized they'd decided to write, I found some peace of mind.

Peace of mind, in our city, that year!

Where peace of mind came to mean reading in the newspaper about riots arson looting breaking out in some neighbourhood and after a frisson of terror, breathing a sigh of relief because: we were far away, on this side of the bridge.

Birds chirp on the branches of the neem tree.

'Maybe I can write here.' Shruti sits down in Hanif's office.

Hanif leaves to teach a class. Today he has a class, so he'd better teach it.

The din from the department reaches his office.

'No talking, no talking.' It's Shorty Josh's voice. The sound of chairs being dragged.

Shruti stares out the window, paper spread out, pen uncapped. Forehead wrinkled. She's pushed Hanif's papers and books to one side. A light breeze ruffles the pages. She keeps glancing at them from the corner of her eye and starting. She has the sensation that they're not papers, but a white kitten that suddenly darts by, tail held high like the tricolour.

It's morning. Hanif has come downstairs to open the front door. He stands in the doorway. There's no one there. He looks back and forth at the deserted street as though it's busy and he's about to cross. He bends over quickly and searches for the rubber-banded newspaper. Doesn't see it anywhere. He looks up at the sky, then out at the street. Has it rained? It doesn't seem so. Nonetheless, he glances at the letterbox.

He opens the flap and is standing there when Shruti calls out to him from the balcony above: 'It hasn't come.'

Hanif stops. He looks up angrily. 'Why didn't you tell me?' he asks.

No, this isn't anger, it's alarm. The city doesn't feel normal without its quota of reported murders.

Sharad glances out of Daddu's hallway.

'Come in, the news is about to come on TV.'

It's a cultural programme. Meerabai and her girlfriends are performing a rippling water dance. Their hair is braided with yellow garlands, and they're surrounded by pointy lotus-shaped flowers made of cardboard or plastic.

Hanif calls out to Shruti, 'Come down if you're coming.'

The news is on. They'll hear of killings, beatings, bombs, fires. They learn there's a curfew on.

'But let's listen to the radio.' Sharad turns the knob of the large radiogram. 'Maybe we'll get more details.'

The phone rings. It's Babu Painter.

They start to breathe more easily. Something's happened far away in the city, over on that side of the bridge. Four youths of one community pushed an ikka driver of the other community to the ground and gouged out his eyes. A crowd gathered, and the police had to spray tear gas. Two dead in total, six wounded, but now the situation is under control. A precautionary curfew has been imposed, and the police are on high alert.

A song plays on the radio, and all three of them talk at once.

'O, bade miyan divane . . . O, mad teacher of mine . . .'

'Oh hell, the market will be closed for today then.'

'I'll go to the department anyway . . .'

'Hasina kya chaahe yahi to . . . What women really want is . . .'

'Class will be cancelled too . . .'

'I don't know . . .'

'Humse suno . . . Listen to what I have to say . . .'

'Uff, turn that off.'

Click.

And I'll write this too: Daddu is asleep right now, and if he gets up, he'll drink chai and laugh.

Nothing appears clear or under control when the ashramites call for everyone to plant saffron flags on the domes of mosques. Not to the government, nor the uniformed, nor the administration, nor the wrestlers, nor Shruti, nor Hanif, nor Sharad, nor anyone else, because by then the stamping feet of the ashram's procession have thrown dust in everyone's eyes.

Such dust swirled that year.

'So what should we do?' The cleaning lady sounds angry. 'It's not like we set the curfew!'

Shruti is seated in her writing pose.

The cleaning lady sets down the phenol-soaked rag by her feet and grumbles, 'It's a disaster for us. In all the houses, they say, "You didn't come for three days, the clothes and dishes are piling up, finish them, then go." What am I, a machine?'

'Arre, baba, just do as much as you can. Why are you scolding me? I don't set the curfew either.'

'No . . . of course I'm not scolding you . . .' The cleaner reddens. 'I'll do it all tomorrow, okay? Truly,' she assures Shruti. 'You soak all the clothes in Surf tonight, and I'll wash them. Truly, tomorrow.'

'Okay,' said Shruti. 'We'll see what happens tomorrow.' She closes the door and returns to her writing pose.

Daddu's divan.

Today, the divan becomes a kite.

When Daddu speaks of the wind, his feet rise slowly, and as he continues, he slowly rises until he's suspended in the air, swinging lightly.

Sharad and Shruti gather up food and clothing, and deliver them to some of the camps for those displaced by the riots.

They return before curfew, and Daddu has chai made when he sees them.

'Nankau!' he calls out to his servant.

Shruti sits alone upstairs. Papers scattered about, pen uncapped. She sits on the bench, leaning against the wall, resting on rainbow-hued cushions. She leans over the low table, supporting herself on one elbow, her neck—like a bird's, she thinks—outstretched so she can see the balcony in front and the street beyond the railing. The sliding door between the room and the balcony is open.

From downstairs comes the sound of Daddu's laughter.

Someone must have come.

He laughs again.

His laughter can be compared with that of a bird or an animal, thinks Shruti.

'Why do I keep dredging up birds and animals?' she mutters to herself.

What must Sharad and Hanif be doing over at the department?

Who knows? It's not feasible for me to be in both places at once.

But I breathed a sigh of relief when I heard they'd decided to write—a cowardly sigh, as when I hear about the riots.

Because they weren't writing; they couldn't write at all.

Events and time proceeded apace and would not wait for them.

Write, brothers; write, sister! I wanted to urge them on.

But I couldn't come forward. So, I lost my mind, lost my cool, stared from one to the next to the third then the first again.

They themselves stared at one another, fretting speaking tangled words getting tied in knots and falling silent.

They couldn't figure out what they'd seen or what they'd said. Everything was happening so fast it seemed impossible to untangle, but things were such that as impossible as it was to untangle one's understanding, it was even more impossible to do anything else. All other reasons for living had run out.

'In terms of truly being a writer, you're the only real one among us,' points out Sharad, urging Shruti on.

'Explain *truly*,' says Shruti with a laugh.

'And all you do is scratch your head,' Hanif scolds. 'Go wash your hair with shampoo.'

'It's dandruff,' Shruti explains.

But it was paralysis: the thing that seized her after writing just one line. Every time I looked, she was doing it again, writing another first line.

'Look at this one now, this one will work out. How is this for an opening?

It feels like something happened this year.

Daddu's radiogram, as ancient as he, is playing, but the strains of the sarangi are not enough to drown out the noise of the procession.

Daddu gets up and pulls the curtain across the glass door.

Shruti, Sharad and Hanif go out to the veranda to watch the ashramites and the crowd that accompanies them. They cry out:

Hindus awake, our country's at stake! If you sleep, injustice against us will only grow. Our blood already flows in rivers, and it will only get worse. Temples and gurdwaras are being destroyed, and

it will only get worse. Our honour and wealth are plundered, our
daughters are openly abducted, and it will only get worse. Hindus
wander about getting beaten like stray dogs and cats, and it will
certainly get worse.

'Hindus are getting beaten all over the world, because they're too
tolerant!' A scream rises from the crowd: 'Stop being cowards or
drown in the ocean of Hind, the Indian Ocean!'

'Don't say Hind,' comes a growl. 'Hindu. Say the Hindu
Ocean. That's the Hindu Ocean. Stop being cowards or drown
in the Hindu Ocean, because there won't be anywhere else for
you to die. You are second- and third-class citizens in your own
country. For others there are scores of countries, but for us there's
only Hindustan, only India.'

'Say *Hindoo-sthan*! The land of the Hindus!'

'Hindoo-sthan!'

'But Hindoo-sthan has become a refuge for all, and the
Hindus are the ones being chased out.'

'How long will this go on?' the leader asks through the
loudspeaker. 'We won't put up with it any longer!' comes the
response, the cries increasingly sharp.

Two of the ashram leaders look over at the veranda and
approach the gate.

'Can we have a bit of water?' they ask.

'No,' Daddu tells them. He motions for them to be on their
way and goes inside.

No one knows when he came outside in the first place.

'Beat the bastards,' he mumbles. 'Now you come in, too,' he
calls. 'If you listen too much this will start sounding sweet to you,
like that sarangi.'

Furthermore, in all this disturbance, I can't afford to worry about ink. But what if the ink runs out? Which could happen, because anything could happen. And what if, who knows, ink becomes unavailable? Bread, milk, kerosene, are all unavailable from time to time these days, no?

'We intellectuals . . .' Professor Nandan is in an excitable mood today. Nearly all the teachers stand in the veranda of the department, from where the spire of the ashram is visible. The sounds of the aarti and *Jai Jagadambe!* recited in unison mingle and rise, launching an assault on the department.

'They must have installed loudspeakers,' explains Shorty Josh, aka Dr Josh, four and a half feet tall.

'As intellectuals . . .' the head continues.

Hanif shrugs. 'We intellectuals must and will do something,' he said. 'But for now, allow me to break into this lament with a tale. Attend well, if you please. Four handsome horseback riders have set off on a journey. They are passing through a village when a pony rider joins them. Four handsome horseback riders in front, and our little ponyback rider bringing up the rear. As they ride through yet another village, the people cry out, "My, how smashing! How dashing! Where could these handsome horseback riders be going?" To which our tiny rider replies, "Sir, we five horseback riders are travelling to the capital." And now let us intellectuals go and teach class.'

'Bastard's going to get smacked,' chuckles Sharad outside the room.

'What can I say?' laughs Hanif. 'Nowadays, everyone's an intellectual.'

This is what Shruti is thinking as she sits in Hanif's office with her pen uncapped: Uff, it's a hard wind blowing, but it blows in one direction only. What a strange sight. It flows in one direction with all its might and only progresses that way. The trees and all their leaves have bent with it, as though they'll never grow straight again or lean in another direction. As though thousands upon thousands of people are reaching out, fingers outspread, performing calisthenics.

Uff, the ink is drying, she thinks.

How careless she is, and in these times particularly!

'Is it a laughing matter?' Shruti's expression is haughty, but secretly she feels comforted. She's getting anxious sitting upstairs alone. When she stands on the balcony, those far-off things are just the lights on the bridge, and she fixes her eyes on them as though this will help her see something over there.

'Arre.' Daddu holds out his hand to touch her chin and winks. 'Today our Dole truly seems upset.' He calls Shruti *Doll* but pronounces it *Dole*. 'Those two have gone together, and they're both hearty young men.'

Shruti's jaws hurt from laughing. She's had this relationship with Daddu perhaps since the first day they became tenants in the upstairs flat.

'You, too, have turned out to be a first-class loony,' he teases her affectionately. 'Why couldn't you have chosen some nice village idiot with a pious Brahmin braid? If you'd told me, I'd have come and picked one for you from my village. I'm a villager. But, of course, you know this.'

'Yes, yes.' Shruti glances at him adoringly. 'Ever since I've known you, you've not gone once to that village, but you're always claiming to be a villager.'

'Arre, Mousie.' He also calls Shruti *Mousie*. 'You people think you must actually go to a place to be called a thing. For me, I can concentrate on a place as I sit right here, and that's enough to take me there. And look at those two weaklings: they've gone off to the city because they think that's the way to get to know it.'

'Should they have gone to the village, then?'

'They don't have the guts to go to the village. Only I can go there. There's still time. If you want, I could grab you some nitwit, and you could travel cheerfully to your wedding in an oxcart with a long veil pulled down over your face; but instead, that wood-sniffer has carried you off. Know what a wood-sniffer is?'

'Hanif?' Shruti laughed.

'A wood-sniffer makes you sniff his magic bit of wood. He does it to lure small children and carry them off. Reap what you sow. Your Daddu cannot save you now.'

The divan bounces along cheerfully like an oxcart transporting a bride.

Just then Sharad and Hanif return.

'A crowd stopped a truck over there and beat the driver, and . . .'

'What! Were you two there?' Daddu's alarmed.

'We weren't there, we'd already gone to the university. Some of the students passed that way; they were telling us. We heard many . . .'

Shruti's listening.

The divan bounces along, absorbed in its journey. Daddu sticks out his hands and feet when he laughs.

'Arre, you people! What are you crying about? It's all about overpopulation. People have to die, some way or another. And truck drivers are a vile breed, they drive all night in a drunken stupor with their eyes shut tight, sending untold numbers to Allah's durbar. Just consider it one scoundrel less in this world.'

We were wretched. We'd begun to feel useless. When we fought, we were full of bravado and bluster. If we remained silent, we were martyrs. Speaking became mere sentimentality. We felt as though the sentences we spoke walled us off from our surroundings: all were useless. It wasn't even a matter of the sentences between us and them. There were sentences inside of them, and there were sentences inside of us. What did emerge made no difference between them and us; they simply reached the surface like boils, hollowing us out in the process. We felt alone and wished someone would keep us company.

It didn't feel like a dream. It was true, those two had gone stamping by me.

They wore tall leather boots, marching *left-right left-right*, chests out.

No, they weren't human, so I couldn't tell you what they looked like. They were two words: *Hindu* and *Muslim*.

The lamp glows. And Daddu glows, like a second lamp. He's talking to himself. Or maybe to the divan?

A far-off explosion. Could it be a firecracker?

The Hanif–Sharad–Shruti band are out and about, visiting the narrow lanes of the city. It's a landscape of uneven rubble, of burnt roofs and walls. The rioters have looted all the fans. Wires dangle like the tangled legs of a spider from the blackened broken ceilings. The people living there have either been burnt alive or fled.

'Those with somewhere else to stay have gone,' Babbu Khan the tailor tells them. 'Our livelihood has been destroyed, but those with nowhere to go will stay here. Prepared.'

Sharad is gathering information for a newspaper report, and I'm copying.

'Prepared! Everyone has learnt to be prepared; to live in a state of preparation. Prepared to examine one another's faces, prepared when they open the newspaper, prepared whenever the phone rings, and Babbu Khan has had his broken window replaced and is prepared for it to break again.'

'Don't write that,' says Shruti, 'there's no need to embroider your language.'

'This sounds like embroidering to you?' Sharad is ready to fight, right there in the gali.

'Don't start this argument here,' scolds Hanif. He turns back to Babbu Khan and asks, 'This didn't used to happen, though?' At which Babbu Khan replies that it has happened before, too, but now it's come out in the open.

'Look, Hanif, it's that yellow bird,' Shruti points to the peelak sitting on the neem. 'It's a very common bird, you know. But doesn't this one seem unique? It comes every day. But doesn't it seem as though it's only flown in today? It's called a golden oriole in English. Yellow feathers with lamp-black eyes.'

'Do you come here to write or to learn about birds?'

'To write.'

Shruti makes a face and turns off her inner ornithologist. Her inner Sálim Ali.

'Great writing going on,' jokes Hanif.

Shruti again opens the page, where she has written very clearly:

It seems to me that something happened this year.

Our memory of the ashram only starts from that time, although the ashram had been there before too. Like that year. Right next to the university since the beginning of time. Before that time, it had sat there peacefully, or else no one had noticed it. Rapt in its yogic austerities. Behind the shrubberies.

It crouched among the brambles. And next to it, there was that large field, the maidan. Beyond that, the domed buildings of the university with their latticed windows. But in those days, it wasn't visible from the windows. Children used to come to play in the maidan, Muslims to pray and dogs to pee.

Then, one day, from out of nowhere, came a rock—or was it a ball?—tossed by the playing children into the shrubberies. At which the ashram was disrupted, as was the beehive hidden in the brambles. They say the angry buzzing bees stung innumerable children, and great welts broke out on their faces. Then the whole business of the pruning began, which led to the incarnation of the ashram from behind the hedges. The maidan was put in the custody of the courts and has yet to be released. It has simply been announced that no one may consider it theirs until the matter is settled.

But it did not become deserted.

The dogs still showed up to do their business. A sympathetic ashramite might even throw them a bit of leftover prasad. The children continued to raise mayhem there. Well, not just the children, adults too rambled about the ashram fairs and melas that started popping up in the field. But one thing did stop happening there: namaz.

That year, the ashram fairs really took off.

Sometimes nothing happened for days. If nothing special happened, we would get nervous and hold our breath. The city feared quiet. Like the Japanese, who, for many days after a small earthquake, feel anxious if no further tremors shake the earth. The earth regularly doles out its tremors, and too few tremors can only mean that the tremors are percolating underground, banding together and growing larger, in preparation for a powerful earthquake. A series of small tremors means a big one has been avoided, its power has dispersed; otherwise, the entire city could be destroyed. And us? We feared the next explosion would not confine itself to the small lanes over there, but spread over here, to this side of the bridge.

And then what?

Shruti and Hanif are out for an after-dinner stroll. The street is deserted.

'What will happen to your image, Professor Sahib, when people learn you jump like a mouse if someone makes the slightest attempt to tickle you?'

Shruti digs her fingers into Hanif's side.

'No, stop!' Hanif writhes.

A woman watches them through the window bars of a nearby house, her face covered. In the faint light of the room, she appears as a shadow, but she believes herself to be completely invisible.

'Did you see her?' asks Hanif.

'Why don't we know the history of our own country?' Hanif asks his students. 'This makes it possible for uncivilized souls to lift whatever they want from the pages of history, pulverize it, fit it on to poisoned arrows and shoot it out continuously. And we, in our ignorance, continue to believe them. Think about what sort of history we're making!'

He's referring to the sort of history that has no relation at all to lectures like this one and has only a superficial connection to the writings lifted from history books. This history is being created and circulated in homes, on the streets, in dhabas, in restaurants. Its authors are partly sinister and partly lost souls.

Hanif is attempting to link the discussions cropping up in his classes to the ones at the dhabas and restaurants, to demonstrate their inherent emptiness, to untangle prejudices linked with history books and point out the obvious bigotry therein.

'There was an era of feudal values, not completely bygone either, of kings, zamindars, nawabs, whose methods included seizing the assets of others to increase one's own power and land. They looted freely: money, women, slaves. They were both Hindus and Muslims, and there were others too. And in that age of feudal power, religion too became a rationale for looting; religion too became a tool for governments; religion too became an excuse for everything. But there were also peaceful times, when the rulers of both communities rewarded the people of all religions with knowledge, safety and honour.'

'You are students of history,' resumes Hanif. 'Don't just look at the Mughal records. Put aside the likes of Emperor Akbar, examine the records of small cities. There, too, you will see many such examples that demonstrate togetherness and goodwill.

'And where did our mixed culture come from? It exists in every field: music, literature, architecture, philosophy, dance, cuisine, clothing. It's everywhere!'

'Where does it not exist?' he asks again.

'This is our past, one to which we are bound, which is intrinsic to our being: there's no so-called "pure, unmixed past", even when there was only one Vedic culture, and before that, Mohenjo-daro. Even in those eras, there were various bits and pieces that mixed together and continuously evolved. Our ancestors at that time were beef-eaters. Is that a problem? Do we have anything in common with them?'

'Questions.' His voice carries all the way to Professor Nandan's office. 'Ask questions, because that's how you'll contribute to the thinking of our society. Why don't you ask why we hear only of oppression and only of Muslims during time periods when there was actually a mishmash of three factors: mutual oppression, comingling and peaceful coexistence? Politicians will be dishonest as they struggle for power. But why do we let them delude us? Why do we nod our heads in agreement like idiotic flunkies?'

'What about me?' he asks, practically shouting. 'Do I belong here any less than you?'

His voice is shaking.

Hanif's question rises on a wave of pain and anger, and spreads in every direction.

'Hmph.' Shorty Josh grimaces. 'Of course, he's talking about himself,' he remarks to Professor Nandan.

Downstairs, the students answer, as do others, as we ourselves always do: *Oh, but you're different, Hanif, you're special, and you and we are something else entirely.*

The problem is with *them*, with those who are not us and not you; it's those people, the ones on the other side of the bridge, the ones that riot: those people.

'Look.' People in the lane are showing Sharad around. 'If we aren't getting any help from rich countries, should we just sit around

and do nothing? We'll help ourselves. We stuff paan zarda tins
with sulfur and potassium nitrate. They're bombs.'

'These, too, they ignite and stick to people's bodies.'

Babu Painter has asked Sharad to write for his newspaper
regularly.

Sharad writes:

*In this district, there's a shoe factory. The solution used to fasten
the soles on to shoes is highly flammable and sticks to the skin. They
have filled earthen pots with it; the pots are covered with fabric
and sit ready for use.*

Ah, the rain has come, and the dust abates.

Bang bang.

'What's that, Daddu?' asks Sharad.

'It's nothing,' Nankau responds, sticking his head out from
the kitchen. 'That Bose Sahib with the four-storey? He's chasing
away pigeons.'

'*Bang bang bang,*' says Sharad and sinks back into his book.

Rain.

Shruti and Hanif sit on their balcony upstairs, drinking tea.

'At our place nowadays, days are green and nights are damp,'
observes Shruti.

Hanif smacks his head. 'You and your literary flourishes!'

'And you, and your theatrical flourishes!'

'Listen, Shruti Begum,' says Hanif, 'I've started to like this bird-watching idea of yours. There are no trees here, but if we train a fragrant vine up to the balcony, we'll get less rain and more birds.'

'Yes,' says Shruti. 'And then I'll stop coming to the department, and I'll write here.'

'Just as Sálim Ali wrote, but better,' laughs Hanif.

'It should be a dense vine. Sun birds will come. The lal munia will come. The waxbill.'

'Only sparrows will come.'

'Nightingales will come! But we'll have to talk to Daddu. If we train a vine up here, it will hang down below as well.'

'Will you discuss it with him, Dole?' asked Hanif. 'There's an empty space right in front of the house, so we don't have to plant it outside the gate.'

'Aha!' Shruti's dreaming now.

Hanif smiles affectionately. 'And now I, too, have green longings.'

Shruti sings: 'Our days here are oh-so-green. Our nights here are oh-so-damp.'

'If a poor soul passes by wanting to observe his festival, this too offends you modern folk?' says Daddu with a laugh.

'But did you see how aggressive he was? He can go ahead with his festival. But why is he asking us for money?' demands Shruti with annoyance.

'Do you intend to wipe out all the old traditions?' Daddu enjoys her annoyance. 'We used to wander from door to door with our begging bags, and the women of the house would come out and put whatever they wanted in them. Alms! We respected them and they us.'

'Okay, enough with all the *we we we*,' says Shruti. 'And whatever he wanted, he didn't come to receive it, he came to seize it. That's not how alms are done. It's started to seem like, whether you agree or not, the kingdom is ours, we will observe our festivals and you will support us, you'll give us all the money we want.'

'Festivals . . .' Daddu sparkles and prepares to tease some more.

'Not festivals. Noise. Loud music in the streets. Rude screaming. Disturbing everyone.' Shruti babbles more and more as she goes on.

'But did you run him off or not?' asks Daddu, suddenly turning the tables. His laughter teasing everyone and everything, absurd but apt at the same time.

Everyone is always going upstairs downstairs back and forth. Sometimes Sharad comes upstairs to eat, sometimes Shruti and Hanif come downstairs. Daddu, in the meantime, goes nowhere. He has only to sit on the divan!

Sharad and Hanif keep their scooters locked up in the garage downstairs. When the sabziwallah comes to sell vegetables, he never asks Shruti who's who; he just assumes Sharad and Hanif are brothers when he sees them driving their scooters down the street, and says, 'The brothers said for you to get some sweet potatoes.'

'Who said they were brothers?' Shruti laughs loudly. 'If they were actually brothers, would they go everywhere together?'

Yoga classes are held at the ashram, so foreigners start showing up.

Babu Painter likes to say that most of the yoga swamis are people who have run away from their villages and learnt yoga on the job. 'And then, their devotees, have you noticed? There are more and more of them all the time.'

'Okay, but what caste does Karmath Baba belong to, do you know?'

'Well, where we come from,' says Sharad, 'there's plenty of evidence that at some point, lower castes, or sometimes even people from other religious communities, used to create religious art for upper castes or other communities, like they would paint tales of the gods or sculpt idols, and so on. Just think. What would that interaction be like, what emotions could come up? It's a fascinating puzzle!'

Sharad goes on and on, and Babu is left bewildered.

. . . but today, if we muster all our powers of mental resolve and anti-communalism, we'll defeat reactionary thought. We cannot ignore the fact that this fight is going on right now; and whether we sit at home or take to the streets, we're all fighting on one side or the other . . .

Sharad's reading his report aloud from the newspaper. Daddu's on the divan with another newspaper spread out, reading and drinking tea. There's a group of noisy children outside at the bus stop.

'The bell's going to ring!' screams one child.

Just then the phone rings. Sharad jumps up.

'Okay . . . all right? Yes, exactly . . . a daily report? Look . . . thanks . . .'

He picks up the phone off the floor and places it on the wide sofa arm, and proceeds to talk at great length.

In our city that year, four hundred people were counted as dead during the communal riots in the official governmental tally. The non-governmental estimate was over 500.

And these three were as determined as ever to record the details they'd seen with their own eyes and heard with their own ears.

'But I've never seen a corpse in my life,' Shruti blurts out suddenly. And then, 'Oh no, the toast is burning. Is anyone there?'

They don't get loaves of bread every day; and anyway, it's careless to burn food and throw it away. But Shruti doesn't care as much about toast as about what's going on around her.

'Writing is very important,' she says, flopping her loose flip-flops back and forth.

'Write, Shruti, short story author and novelist!' commands Sharad.

Shruti has given this same command to herself, *Write!* But not everything happens on the strength of commands.

Hanif begins to laugh. 'She did write last week. A love story. In which the days were green and the nights were damp. Your writing feasts on the sensual, Begum Shruti.'

The flop-flop of the flip-flops stops suddenly.

'I don't want to write all this to fatten my writing. I don't do it so I'll feel clear and refreshed once I write. No, that's not why I do it.'

Sharad also laughs at her outburst. 'Writing love stories is what refreshes you, and you're knocking them out one after another.'

'This trolley is going to run over my foot.' Hanif smiles as he pushes it away.

'And you're laughing?' asks Shruti, picking up her teacup.

'That's why you're having trouble writing.' Hanif smiles. 'Laughter's important, otherwise you'll end up writing something scrawny and malnourished. Well, you can't help it. Why would you laugh now if you couldn't before? Each to his own. Have I told you that story already? The one where a Bengali and a Punjabi go to see a film? When they come out, the Bengali is weeping and the Punjab is laughing. *Boo-hoo, sobs, tears, boo-hoo, bhishaun bhaalo fillum, what a wonderful film*, weeps Mr Bengali. But here's our Punjabi slapping his thigh and endlessly guffawing, *vah vah hahahaha, sohndi, ekdum sohndi film, what a fantastic movie!'*

Sharad laughs. 'Must you always come up with ridiculous tales?'

'What we need is a writer like Renu or Premchand,' says Shruti.

If Renu and Premchand had made an entrance at that historic moment, they would have ably captured our history in their writing and left behind precious gems for the researchers of the future. But did our city need precious gems? Or a huge rock to hurl at people's skulls so they could examine the blood and pus flowing from their wounds and understand how we'd changed?

Shruti feels furious. She hasn't the slightest interest in producing precious gems that will make people touch hand to heart and cry, *Vah-vah, wow, how beautifully you've written, I have tears in my eyes!* How could she possibly fashion the horror all around her into a work of art? How could she beautify such coarse things? But wouldn't it also be coarse to present it stripped bare for all to see? How could she consider our city and this year a windfall for a writer and make use of it?

Is this a contest for good writing? Or rather a time when we must think hard and get everything just right: the tone, the tightrope walking and the responsibility, in order to ensure our words don't get accidentally used for ill, and don't fall on this or that side of the tightrope and transform into weapons? This is the blade of a sharpened knife: it can cut me but also anyone else.

The sharpness enters Shruti, and I note it down sharply.

'Who cares about love stories?' cries Shruti angrily. 'They're so irresponsible. If they came splashing down and washed away centuries-old traditions, then maybe the writer would kiss her pen in gratitude. Who cares about love stories and where they end up?'

'That's why they say all's fair in love and war,' says Sharad with a wink.

'This is no joke.' Shruti's eyes fill with accusations. 'I can write a love story but . . .' She stands up and walks over to her desk. 'Now it's wrong to write about anything besides this.'

She writes:

'I have never seen a corpse,' she said.

She shows the line to Sharad and Hanif, and then sits down foolishly.

'Does it work?' she asks.

Under the circumstances, it's the wrong question. All three of them bow their heads.

Sharad comes running up the stairs.

'When's Hanif getting back?'

'Why?' Shruti panics when she sees his tense expression. 'Tomorrow, on the morning bus.'

'By bus? Oh.' The lines of worry on Sharad's face relax.

'What happened?'

'Shruti,' says Sharad in a serious tone, 'two bombs exploded at the railway station. There's still no word about any casualties, or . . .'

'Hello.' Daddu is squatting, talking on the phone, which is on the floor. The long fat cord lies densely coiled.

Ring ring.

'Hello. No, bhai, your voice isn't clear.'

Ring ring.

'Hello. Yes, now I can hear you . . . How long will it stay this way? Hahahaha! If you people won't tell me, who will? And, by the way, who are you? You're at the telephone exchange, that I know, but . . . all right . . . so, Mr Jadeja, it sounds clearest when the call comes from you . . . hahahaha.'

He continues to squat for a while after replacing the receiver, his knees peeking out from the sides of his dhoti. Then he stands.

Hanif has only just arrived when Shruti starts quarreling with him.

'What's the point of giving so many speeches? The smaller the city, the smaller the college, the quicker you are to rush off. Are you the only one left to educate everyone? Giving speeches like a politician: "We're all one, all brothers, bhai-bhai."'

When the phone rings downstairs they both jump.

'Is it . . .?'

Ring ring. Ring ring.

Ring ring.

'Plant away, plant away,' twinkles Daddu. 'This is all that was wanting: for your Daddu to become genteel in his old age. Plant a garden. Let's plant foreign roses!'

'Not foreign roses, a vine! It will grow quickly, with lots of flowers, and wrap around our windows spreading fragrance everywhere . . .'

'Oh, my dear,' a light breeze begins to waft from the divan, 'don't you folks know what to buy if you need more fragrance? Perfume!'

He pronounces the word *perfume* as though it's huge and cumbersome. Like this: *paaarfyooom*.

'I'm talking about the fragrance of flowers. In the garden . . .'

'The garden!' Daddu growls with laughter.

'Flower bed?'

'Well, I'm a country man, you know. How could I have a garden, you loony girl? We're plow-wielding folk. Fragrance for us is stagnant drain water . . . Yes, yes, there actually is a drain in our village . . .'

'No mere village, you make it sound like paradise, that's what you do!' Shruti bursts out laughing.

Daddu also shrieks with laughter, and the divan fills with air. So much air it bounces back to the ceiling the moment it deflates.

And now Daddu's reciting, or rather laughing out, a couplet by Ghalib:

Hum ko maloom hai jannat ki haqiqat, lekin
Dil ke khush rakhne ko, Ghalib, ye khyaal accha hai

We know the truth about heaven, but,
Ghalib, this idea soothes the heart

Hanif is out 'farming' every day now. One day he removes large rocks with a pickaxe, another day he breaks the earth, and another day he mixes in the manure. Now he must go get the plant.

'The curfew has great advantages.' Daddu is laughing inside the house.

'Now he's a plougher, like you,' teases Shruti.

'Flower? Already?' Sharad looks up from his reading.

'Why are you asking about flowers?' asks Shruti.

'How should I know? You tell me.'

'How should I know . . .?'

'You were the one saying it . . .'

'Sharad, your ears are ringing. Read your book.'

They can see Hanif outside, on the other side of the glass door. He's softly patting the soil.

When there isn't a curfew, the three of them come out into the open to chase history, to see it face to face in those neighbourhoods and lanes where the stagnant drain water has now begun to flow with blood, and where people have left their braziers cold and wandered off with the coals to start fires elsewhere in the void, and the stench of burning chafes our nostrils and fills our insides.

All three are in a hurry. They have something to say. There's no time for a detailed flowery speech in such a hullabaloo because everything has come out in the open. Somehow or other, very quickly, they must tell everyone the sad news about what's come into the open, and that it must be stopped, and that you must do whatever you can.

Sharad's upset the whole way. 'Yaar, they'll stop you from entering, and it'll be offensive. I'll be offended. You'll be offended.'

Hanif laughs. 'Why should I be offended? I'm definitely going.'

'But those people . . . they . . .' Sharad looks worried.

'Let's see if anyone stops me.' Hanif is unconcerned.

At the door of the ashram, where there's a cut-out image of the goddess so high it nearly touches the sky, the kind they stick on the bonnets of the ashram vans to make them look like chariots, Hanif addresses Sharad loudly enough for the priests to hear, 'Yaar, Hanif, have you ever been here before?'

And thus, it is Sharad whom the priest stops!

'Come, Sharad,' Shruti says to Hanif quickly, hiding her laughter, and pulls him inside.

But inside their laughter becomes subdued.

The ashram has already spread into the maidan by now, expanding over the area of the cleared brush. There's plenty of land on all sides of the temple. On the side that faces the university, there's an akhara for wrestling and calisthenics, and an array of festive shops for the mela. A queue of devotees stands at the front of the temple near the marigold garlands, the small baskets of laddus and the pile of sandals. On the other side is a huge tent where a speech is being given.

On the pillars of the tent are mounted short-circuit TVs, so that the ashram leader, the Mahant, remains in close proximity to every portion of the crowd.

Hanif and Shruti spend quite some time peering behind the pillars for the true Mahant.

Even if you just stand in one place and only swivel your eyes, the clusters of saffron-clad devotees pop up as orange splatters everywhere. And nothing but heads. And little piles of discarded sandals.

'If you threw a plate or a thaali, it would hit all the heads,' whispers Shruti.

'But why would you throw a thaali?' Hanif whispers back.

'That's what Umrao Jaan said,' says Shruti.

Hanif doesn't understand.

'She went to the fair in a pale green muslin dupatta.' Shruti is still whispering.

Hanif smiles slightly.

'At the Aish Bagh Festival . . .'

'In Lucknow . . .'

'Yes, so Umrao Jaan . . .'

'Okay, quiet.' Hanif elbows her.

Shruti jumps when she feels someone touching her. A woman in orange is pinning a brooch with a portrait of the Goddess on to her clothing.

'No. No, no, thank you,' says Shruti, startled.

The sermon is about Devi bhakti, about worshipping the Goddess. The ashram officials pin the brooch of the Devi—depicted with wavy black hair, wearing a sindoor-coloured sari and mounted on a saffron lion—to their orange clothing as they wander about the crowd like security guards. Many other devotees—children, the elderly, youths—are seated in the audience, all wearing the same brooch.

The sermon about the virtues of the Goddess continues. The tent echoes with cries of *Jai Jagadambe! Victory to Devi Mata, the Mother Goddess, victory to Mother Sita, victory to Mother Lakshmi!*

Victory to Mother India!

Bhagwan Lord Krishna, Prabhu Parameshwar Ram, O, Vishwanath, brave Hanuman, victory to all of you!

Victory to the eternal dharma, victory to the Vedas!

Victory to Mahavir, to Lord Buddha, to Guru Gobind Singh!

Victory to Swami Dayanand, Lokmanya Tilak, Veer Savarkar, Swami Vivekanand . . .

Rana Pratap, Chatrapati Shivaji, Rani Jhansi, Sukhdev, Bhagat Singh, Lala Lajpat Rai, Netaji, victory victory victory!

Victory to the Hindu martyrs, victory to Hindoo-sthan, victory to the Mother Goddess, Jai Jagadambe!

On the TV appears the serene countenance of the Mahant, speaking gently:

The politics of our country today are an insult to us. We are forbidden from cultivating our own religion. We do not have the freedom to express joy at our own festivals. What is this freedom our country has won? Is India truly free? If we demand our land for ourselves, it's not out of greed for wealth, but only our fervent wish to gather up our lost scraps once more. If someone burns the national flag, will you say he is squabbling over a piece of fabric? Or fight him for the protection and respect of the nation?

Will the TV screen break? But no, the same serene personage is sitting there, only his serene tone has changed. And then turned serene again.

. . . be virtuous, respect your elders and your gurus, respect your guests; for us, a guest is a form of God, and for centuries we welcomed foreign guests into our country with respect; our philosophy is Vasudhaiva Kutumbakam—the world is one family—but politeness is not cowardice . . .

I start. Again. Has the speaker changed as I write? The tone has changed again. Is this the same being speaking, or did someone else take over when I was looking down?

O, Goddess give us the power never to tolerate the disrespect of our motherland due to our considerate natures . . .
Jai Jagadambe!

The Mahant raises his hand.
Jai Jagadambe!
The pandits punch their fists in the air and voice their pledge in warlike tones.
And this pledge begins to spread throughout the city.

'Out of my way. I'll water it.'

Shruti stands over Hanif with a mugful of water.

Hanif pats the soft earth around the plant.

'The gardener says the madhumalti's a fast-growing vine.'

'Let it take root first.'

'And then the nightingale will sing on it.'

'Actually, that's not a nightingale, it's a guldum, a shrike,' says Shruti, showing off her knowledge.

I have no pretentions. I'm not under the delusion that I have the capacity to understand. I simply copy.

The entire department gathers in the seminar hall. The students, the teachers and all the rest of the workers as well. Professor Nandan has called the meeting. He is seated between Shorty Josh and Urmila. Sharad takes a puff by the window, sticks his head outside and exhales. He's taking long drags in his hurry to finish the cigarette.

Professor Nandan reads a paper out loud:

> *What is happening in our country is hidden from no one. A battle has been stirred up between democracy and communal fascism, and we all know what side we're on. This struggle will be widespread, but we must all make an effort in our own circles, and in this way a strong collective voice will arise in our society. All patriotic citizens have this duty today . . .*

Should I just copy down what was written in the paper?

But now he's not reading from the paper.

'. . . this department has on every occasion shown its progressive, liberal, committed face. We must work together again today, each according to their own capacity. We're intellectuals, and whatever we can accomplish by reading and writing, we'll do. That's why we're gathered here now. Why don't we all come together and prepare a joint project? Everyone can offer suggestions as to what we should do and how we should do it.'

Everyone's silent.

'Speak up.' Professor Nandan looks towards the students, who had been squirming a bit but now are silent.

'But what can we do?' asks one girl softly. She looks down, then up again.

My pen has stopped . . . but it's ready.

Hanif looks up. 'Students come here to do a BA, an MA, and the curfew has already thrown a wrench into their studies. Where will they get the time to write lengthy reports?'

'Who said anything about lengthy . . .?' objects Urmila.

'One minute,' interjects Sharad. 'Hanif hasn't finished.'

'Thanks, Sharad. Head Sahib is correct: we're intellectuals, not street fighters. But sometimes it's necessary to join a fight, come what may. The question is, how to do it without harming the students' work?'

'But it's already being harmed.' The girl student speaks up again and looks down, and then up again.

'I believe,' Shorty Josh says, 'that we should work towards the goal of preparing a handbook.'

'Good . . .' Professor Nandan turns to him.

'Good,' Hanif agrees. 'Just as we did with the AIDS project, when we told people the underlying facts about the illness, explained the misinformation to them and shared their fears with doctors . . .'

'After all, the thing that's spreading now is a type of illness,' interrupts Sharad.

Head Sahib begins to nibble his moustache.

'Let's prepare the report so it can be made available immediately,' suggests Shorty Josh.

'A first-aid handbook,' clarifies Urmila.

'Simple firefighting,' suggests the Head.

'But what can we do? It's a very bad time. We're all upset.' Urmila seems upset.

At this, everyone begins to speak at once. The typist, the chaprasi, the driver, the students.

'Our milkman says such-and-such . . .'

'But there's always fighting among brothers. It's a sign of love.'

'But now we're giving it so much importance.'

'Isn't it important?'

'No . . .'

'It is, but . . .'

'Shall we prepare the project?' asks Professor Nandan. Silence spreads. 'Hanif, you're good at this, you tell us.'

'No, no, we'll all do it together. Some people have already started writing, such as Sharad . . .'

'I'd like to repeat that our department has always been vigilant about current events in the city and the country; we're not an ivory tower, intellectually.'

'Let's prepare some headings, such as the role of the police, challenges for doctors, the role of rumours, the responsibilities of newspapers . . .'

'And then we'll form eight or nine groups, and research each of these a bit. If we want, we can even start in our own neighbourhoods. When do the police show up, what are their prejudices, how difficult is it for the wounded to reach the hospitals, what is the procedure, what are the shortcomings, the camps that have been set up for those who have fled, what's going on over there, etc., etc.' Sharad's interest is growing.

'We need to know what's happening, but we also have to explain what's really going on.' Shorty Josh is also enthused.

'And we have to distribute the report to the government, to the newspapers, wherever possible, to help them with riot management,' says Urmila.

'To those wanting to manage the riots!' laughs Hanif. 'But for those who want to make things worse . . .'

'They will be exposed,' announces Professor Nandan, as heads bob excitedly around the seminar room.

Daddu, seeing them standing sadly by the vine, opens the glass door and says: 'Fools, that's what they're like. At first, they're all yellow and shrivelled. The new soil is making the plant dry. If you don't leave it alone, how can it breathe? Leave the poor thing be. It'll blossom on its own.'

Sometimes I copy so much, I'm out of breath. I leave things out or repeat them. The words fall in my ears only to fly off. The scene gets cut off in the middle. My pen moves, stops, moves again, then pauses. Hopping about sideways and crossways saying God knows what as the ink blots grow.

'Oh ho! Slowly, slowly. I said to make tea, not to run and catch a train,' accuses Daddu.

'Why are you knocking things over?' asks Sharad, looking up.

'I didn't knock anything over, he did,' Shruti tells Daddu, pointing at Sharad.

'Wah! Are you seeing this, Daddu? And poor me, I'm just sitting here reading . . .'

'But that's just it. While reading you don't notice when you kick something or elbow it.'

'This Dole of yours is very quarrelsome, Daddu,' complains Sharad.

Daddu is only waiting for an excuse to laugh: the divan begins to bounce.

When Hanif gets up to turn on the news, Daddu cries out, waving his hands around, 'Of course she'll be quarrelsome if you insist on listening to all this! Play a wonderful song, show her a dance, then she'll do the same. She'll become a great dancer or singer, a Rukmini Arundale, an Indrani Rahman, a Kesarbai, a Gangubai Hangal!'

The sugar bowl in Daddu's drawing room tips over, scattering its contents everywhere.

The three of them return despondent. In their hands are copies of the cassettes playing in every lane. They put one in the player and sit down silently.

We have given you equality, but what have you given us? Pakistan. Enough talk of kindness and mercy. These are the days of heroism and severity. If you insist on living here, you should be like Rahim and Raskhan, dissolving gently like sugar into milk. But no, you insist on being a lemon instead. Then what happens? The lemon is squeezed into the milk, which splits and turns into paneer. Then prices go up! But what happens to the lemon? It's been squeezed dry, and thrown into the trash . . .

The speaker delivers his tirade in a single breath, like a scream. His voice is gravelly; it grates as he goes on and on, with no commas, no pauses. Sometimes the voice rises to a threatening pitch in the middle of a sentence, like a warrior pulling out a large dagger with a *clang*. Then the one-note scream continues. But suddenly he'll change again, as though the speaker's a follower of the Goddess, spent in his ecstatic devotion, and he's entered a trance, swaying back and forth, jerking his head up and down.

> *We are the descendants of Rana Pratap Shivaji. We are the descendants of Arjun and Bhima. Whoever deceives us or our community will never receive forgiveness. Clang!*
> *Nine hundred thousand years ago, there was a demon called Ravana. He abducted our revered Mother Sita. Even today (clang!) we haven't forgotten. Every year we burn Ravana in effigy . . . and now you'll have to learn a lesson . . . we've given you your Pakistan. So why do you insist on staying here and creating a second one?*

The three of them sit together, avoiding eye contact. Listening to the cassette with their heads down. They wish they weren't listening to this in front of one another. They act as though they're not listening to anything at all, or like nothing is playing, or like only one of them is hearing it, the rest are not. They wish these things were so, but they're not.

Clang! Clang! The ringing of weapons cutting through the air in the ashram akhada pours from the cassette. It crackles in their ears.

> *We've had enough of your tricks—this practice of yours of doing everything backwards. If we write from the left, you write from the right, if we turn east, you turn west, if we worship the sun, you worship the moon, if we say god, you say dog (clang)! If we eat with our mouths you . . .*

The atmosphere in the room has grown heavy; it feels like it's suspended above them by fine threads. Shruti picks up her cup of coffee, but then she fears she, too, could be swallowed up with the coffee and puts it back down.

The air's grown so tense they feel the need for humour. For acting casual.

'The coffee's gone cold,' says Hanif.

'All thanks to the Mother Goddess.' Shruti clenches her fist ironically and punches it in the air. *Jai Jagadambe!*

Hanif echoes *Jai Jagadambe!* and swallows down the cold coffee.

'Yaar!' says Sharad laughing, 'I've had enough of these circumcised katua Muslims!' He says the slur inside the house, but in an affectionate tone.

And yet such slurs are also being said outside the house, out in the open, on the streets, in the clear light of day.

The madhumalti has finally sprung to life. Hanif and Shruti stand gazing at it.

'That spray really worked its magic. It lifted its spirits,' says Hanif, deeply satisfied.

'Give it some more water,' suggests Shruti.

Daddu, seeing a mug of water in Hanif's hand, teases, 'If you give it too much love, the poor thing will suffocate.'

'Daddu!' Shruti calls from the veranda, 'I know you've vowed never to come outside, but do take a look. It's grown two new leaves!'

Daddu peers through the glass door.

'I cannot tolerate this "outside". I, a simple village dweller. I'll be crushed by a car or something. Staying inside and sitting is best. The fun's in here, you can dream and sing devotional songs, like bhajans or kirtans.'

'Please don't do that Daddu.' Shruti comes in laughing. 'Now the mere mention of bhajans and kirtans nauseates me.'

'This is what's wrong with you people. You don't even know what they are. You just think they're whatever those psychos say they are.'

He goes and gets a record to play on his ancient radiogram. He lifts the edge of his dhoti and leans over to carefully wipe it off. In this same crooked pose, he turns his head to look at them: skinny legs below, round body in the middle, and on top, the head, sideways, as though swivelled on an axle.

A cup with two handles on a stand, thinks Shruti.

The record plays:

Vaishnav jan to taine kehiye je peer parai jaane re

You call those people Vaishnavite who recognize the pain in others.

There's a discussion taking place in the department about the phone call that came today. Our State Education Council has announced Hanif's book as this year's winner of the prize for best work in the field of sociology.

'I'll catch tonight's bus,' says Hanif in reply to someone.

'What a great council! Inviting you today to receive a prize tomorrow! Why didn't they send a letter . . .?' jokes Professor Nandan.

'Many letters are disappearing,' observes Sharad.

'They called to find out why I hadn't sent a response,' explains Hanif.

'You should definitely go,' says the head, nibbling at his moustache.

Sharad smiles into his beard.

'Your book is coming ahead of his! Betrayed by his own state's education council!' he whispers into Hanif's ear only.

The ashram fairs begin to swell, with the entire city in attendance. In the festival shops there are Devi bhakti sermon cassettes and books, colourful Devi calendars, Devi lockets that swing from pink-and-green necklaces, hair ornaments bearing the image of the Devi, combs, pens and all sorts of sundries with images of the Devi printed on them.

The fairs used to pop up occasionally, but now there's a permanent mela in the field. The grounds are festooned with colourful chains made of kite paper, and tube lights have been hung from the pillars.

In one shop, in a brass dish, there are several varieties of the lizard family, alive and writhing in piles.

'Eek!' shrieks Shruti, recoiling.

They extract oil or something from them and make medicine, which they then bottle and sell. In this same shop there are also various medicinal herbs and Taakat brand medicines for increasing stamina. Images of the Goddess astride her saffron lion, with her hair streaming down, are printed on the boxes. These medicines are guaranteed to attract women, make weak men virile and give couples a satisfying sex life.

Shruti is looking through the books in the bookshop: *The Haraam Harem*, *The Trickery of the Mullah's Wife*, *The Poison Tree of Islam*.

Professor Nandan has taken permission from the police chief. Everyone will meet at four o'clock, across the bridge, by the clock tower in the old bazaar, where an interfaith meeting will take place, to which religious leaders from all communities have been invited: Parsis, Jains, Hindus, Muslims, Christians and Sikhs.

An ad for the meeting is printed in the paper.

'What a large shield they've given you,' laughs Shruti. They're drinking chai on the upstairs balcony.

'Nandu will be very sad.' Sharad looks half serious and half joking. 'Until now it was merely foreigners who invited you, but now it's his own people!'

'Oh, then should I turn it down?' Hanif hands him the ashtray. 'I didn't ask them to give me a prize.'

'Who knows?' Sharad smirks and gives him a wink.

Shorty Josh is arguing: 'But some people believe true research weaves in theory. Everyone else is just doing substandard empirical research.'

'Mere data collection!' teases Hanif.

'But how can one do research without data collection, Dr Hanif Zaidi?' asks Shorty Josh sarcastically.

'It's Jaidi, Dr Josh. Please do not ruin my name. Where I come from, we pronounce Z's as J's,' announces Hanif grandly. 'It's Jaidi, and I can.'

Shorty Josh stares at him in bewilderment.

Sharad chuckles. 'He's saying he can do research without data collection!' Then he, too, begins to jest. 'Data collection is a separate matter. Our Head Sahib has gathered data from all over, but substandard empirical research is another matter.'

Shorty Josh is both angry and confused.

Seeing him silent, Urmila says, 'Those who aren't using theory—it's not like they're just writing newspaper reports.'

'But now a report is what we want. Riots. A report on riots.' Sharad changes his tone. 'We don't need theory right now,' he says.

The head is silent. He's not laughing.

'A one-hundred-fifty-one-page book: it's become a book!' Shorty Josh sneers, but then he laughs.

'Are we going to make this report five hundred pages? What say you, Urmila Ji?' Hanif is enjoying himself.

'And no theory. Right, Josh?' Sharad, too, continues to tease.

'What, yaar, Josh?' says Hanif, standing up. 'You get driven mad when you hear the word *theory!*'

'Here's a story,' says Sharad, Hanif-style. 'I was saying something or other to Head Sahib, and then he said, "Oh, that's cheery," and Josh Sahib became enraged because he heard *theory.*'

Shorty Josh has to smile. 'Sure, sure, go ahead and tease me,' he says. But now he stops smiling. 'This is not the moment to spout theory. You'll be busy with that, and in the meantime, the world will change.'

'All right, I would tell a story, but this is no time for stories; it's time for direct action. So let's go straight to the classrooms, where the action is.' Hanif salutes and departs.

A police van drives about the city sounding the warning: *Curfew in an hour!* There will be a siren, there will be whistles. Schools, shops and offices are closing. The sound of shutters falling, speeding cycles, scooters, rickshaws, busloads of people: this chaos takes a bit of time. It's clear from people's faces who are parents, as they race to get their children home.

Young men wander about with Sten guns during the prayer meetings.

Daddu has picked up an Urdu book. He riffles through it, reading, '*Ye ye ye ye Allah Allah ye ye ye ye Allah Allah.*'

Everyone starts laughing. 'How can we learn if you just read it to yourself?'

'But only I can teach it.' Daddu laughs too. 'No one else here knows Urdu. I studied in a madrasa, and that put me out ahead of the rest of you. First Urdu, then Hindi came later. I also know Farsi.'

'How many people could imagine that our Hanif Zaidi doesn't know Urdu,' says Sharad with a laugh.

'Not Zaidi, Jaidi! We are the Jaidis of Jhunjhunu. We don't put nuqtas under every letter. All those z, kh, q sounds are affectations of the denizens of Lucknow. We don't do all that,' laughs Hanif.

'His people don't qut their ququmbers, or make zam of their zackfruit!' Daddu's laughter awakens the divan.

'But I want to learn Urdu,' says Shruti with a laugh.

'Learn Hindi first. Okay, hang on, just learn English properly,' jokes Daddu.

Everyone's turning somersaults with laughter: this is what my pen thinks, so I write it down.

A special report on rape begins on the TV. Daddu gets up and turns it off.

'Those were women, Daddu,' laments Shruti.

'*In 712 AD, Muhamad bin Qasim attacked the kingdom of Sindh.* Blah blah blah.' Sharad fills in the parts that don't need to be read with blah blah blah. '*This should not be surprising. Islam itself was created by smashing 360 idols.* Blah blah . . . *Then Qasim divided the Hindu women amongst the soldiers, and their honour was openly violated. They treated the children inhumanely and looted the wealth of the Hindus and . . .* Wow, amazing, listen to this . . . *They established socialism and destroyed the Hindu temples and erected mosques in their place, and in this way sowed the seeds of secularism.* Did you hear that? They're up in arms about both secularism and Islam! Blah blah blah . . . *With the help of greedy secularist Hindu traitors this nation will become not Hindustan, but Islamistan.* Unbelievable!'

'Read it properly. Why do you keep saying *blah blah blah*?' interrupts Shruti.

'Listen to this . . . amazing!' Sharad flips the page. 'Statistics, dates, everything. As though they've done thorough research. Shorty Josh will be happy: no theory, just hard standard empirical data! What? Blah . . . sorry. Okay, listen to this. The seventeen attacks of Mahmud of Ghazni are described the same way. The secular traitor Hindus are helping out everywhere in this book. There are statistics here too: *30,000 horsemen attacked Somnath . . .* What? *A secular Hindu gave the suggestion to attack the Rajputs by positioning thousands of cows before their army. Thus, the Rajputs would not attack the cows, for if the cows died, the Muslims would gain religious merit by eating cow meat.*'

'What's going on?' asks Shruti.

'My eyes are bugging out with astonishment,' says Sharad, his eyes bugging out.

'Eyes are opening. And Hindus and Muslims are appearing,' says Hanif.

'That may be what people think!' Sharad's eyes bug out again.

'What happened next?' asks Hanif, pointing towards the book.

'*Mohammad Gori . . . et cetera, et cetera . . . Look at these* figures: *Tamerlane had a 92,000-horse army . . . Babar built a stupa of Hindu heads in Chanderi . . . they call Akbar the Messiah of Indian unity, he's praised for his respect for all religions . . . but . . . when he attacked Chittor, 8000 Rajput women self-immolated and flung themselves into the flames of Jauhar. 30,000 Hindus under Akbar's protection were killed. The newly-wed brides of Hindu kings and thakurs were forced to spend their first night of marriage in Akbar's harem.*'

'Uff, show me!' Shruti snatches the book from his hand: *Our True History.*

There are lines of pseudo-poetry on the cover advertising the book:

This Hindustan will soon be gone
Destroyed completely by Islam
All Muslims will await that dawn
When all is ruled by the imam
Awake, friends! Awake!

'It's a whole industry,' says Shruti, who's holding the book now.

'This industry didn't just appear out of nowhere. Where were we? When did it begin?' asks Hanif.

'Arre, just drop it.' Sharad has become impatient. 'Let's not quibble over anything right now; that will weaken our task.'

'Then why did you bring it up?' asks Urmila, turning suddenly.

'To explain, madam, that this favourite topic of yours— research with or without theory—is meaningless. Good research is good research, and emerges from a variety of working styles,' says Sharad quietly.

'Who doesn't agree, Sharad?' asks the head.

'All kinds of work are important. When you embroider a kashida you use many different types of threads. Society isn't just under the command of those who take to the streets. Even those who sit and work alone have a minute effect on the changing or turning of the direction of the wind. The wind has its own rhythm, which is the rhythm of life, and society has a rhythm, which is made up of all different melodies, and each twist and turn shifts the wind, which in turn shifts life and society . . .'

'This jerk is getting carried away,' Hanif mutters to himself with a smile.

'Bastard,' Hanif laughs as he gets on his scooter.

'Your book is 151 pages of idiocy,' jokes Sharad.

'You're saying this to me?' retorts Hanif. He sees Sharad is peeved. 'Yaar, you get carried away too.'

'The times are such.' Sharad chuckles.

Shruti has written another love story, which she's not showing to anyone. In it, there's love and marvellous grass, which feels soft when you sit on it. But when you get up to leave it feels prickly.

She wants to write something else, but she loses her nerve when she sits down to write. I hear her say so to Hanif.

I reach out my hand to copy, but then I worry about the ink. It's all just crazy talk. I'm copying down furiously, but it's not easy to sort through it all. And then, who knows when some crazy talk will turn useful . . .? But should I knowingly waste ink?

A love story!

'Sir, we've come to congratulate you.'

The entire group stands around Hanif.

'Sir, this book will get even more prizes.'

'You people insist on calling me sir!' rebukes Hanif.

'Sorry, Hanif, Professor Hanif.' The students laugh. 'Now you must give us a treat in celebration.'

'Here you go, have these.' Hanif picks up two apples from his desk and chuckles. 'But how will we divide them?'

One student promptly produces a knife.

'Where's the lemon, son?' asks Hanif with a chuckle. 'Oh, wait. How have I not told you this story? Listen. One gentleman, wherever he goes, he carries a lemon and a knife in his pocket. Whenever someone brings out something to eat, he promptly cuts his lemon and squeezes it over their food. It is clear etiquette requires that he then be served the food as well. So this is how he goes about feeding himself. Now, one day, on a train journey, he finds himself in the company of an elderly man. When the old man brings out his food, this fellow takes out his lemon as usual, squeezes and has only just broken off a morsel of the meal for himself, when the elderly gentleman rewards him with a tight slap. Upon which the young man responds politely, "My respected father also used to serve me up an affectionate beating with my meals!"'

Hanif gives a low bow with a flourish, at which several students laugh and imitate him. All the students and Hanif are now bowing low with exaggerated politeness.

The siren is about to sound again. Metal shutters clang shut at all the shops.

When Sharad drives by the Buttercup School, he sees a little girl standing alone by the gate. She's tiny. Even her bag is larger than she. He continues on, but then turns back. Suddenly the girl sees a scooter, runs out, holds up her large bag to the driver and climbs on the back.

I keep dreaming it's curfew and I've run out of ink.

Loudspeakers have been installed where the shrubberies used to be, and their sound echoes through the university. Sermons shoot out night and day, and fall crashing into the classrooms, intermingling with the classes and the teachers and the students.

Right now, we have Sharad on one side, the loudspeaker on the other. And me.

'In the Middle Ages, attacks on religious sites were an aspect of military strategy . . .'

They are being coddled, we are being obstructed . . .

'The Mongols, who were not Muslim, mind you, despoiled the mosques and libraries of Central Asia . . .'

We never said that if you won't put bhakti into the Upanishads and the Gita then . . .

'There's a long history of religious wars in Europe . . .'

We'll cut off your heads and place them at the feet of the Goddess . . .

'Protestants smashed the idols in Catholic churches and defaced the artwork . . .'

Our race is not low and ungenerous. It is honourable . . .

'You've all read about the cruelty of Mary, Queen of Scots, already . . .'

We are the Hindu race. Say 'We are Hindu!' with pride . . .

'The Spanish Inquisition is another example . . .'

The messengers of ungodliness are corrupting our education system . . .

'The Pilgrim fathers fled to America because of religious persecution . . .'

They are misleading the students, telling them this race is polluting . . .

'The Muslim armies that caused destruction were nomadic, and nomadic peoples have always created shelters for themselves in this manner.'

Open your eyes, look, this is not right . . . consider the Banjaras of Rajasthan . . . *the Hindu population is diminishing, Musli—. . .* fighting, looting, killing, destruction, these are the cycles of history, no one race . . . *believe that it is increasing . . .* not the eternal nature of . . .

I try to write it all out on separate lines, but it's becoming a tangle.

'What was happening in the Ramayana and the Mahabharata? In the history of the Magadh Raj, what was . . . ?'

Three words: talaaq talaaq talaaq; I divorce thee, I divorce thee, I divorce thee, and then they're free, or they run off with someone else, this is how they satisfy their desires . . .

'Was this happening? The Guptas, the Mauryas, Harsha, who wasn't doing exactly the same things with the aim of expanding their empires? And yet this accusation is being lobbed at the Muslims only. Ashoka . . .'

. . . astonishing levels of cunning! But we must learn one thing from them, and that is, when it comes to one's own religion . . .

'. . . with great sorrow he renounced war and attained enlightenment!'

. . . for everyone in your religion, both large and small, to make sacrifices and the destruction of other communities, other races, your one goal in life . . .

'Shaivites took an aggressive approach and attacked Jain temples and Buddhist viharas. All over the world it happened that . . .'

. . . Muslims are praiseworthy. Blessed are the Muslims!

'Those who finished off kingdoms and began new ones erected new buildings atop old. This was the manner in which they announced their victory.'

Protect the Devi.

'Shiva temples appear atop Buddhist and Jain holy sites. On top those and around them, we find Islamic minarets.'

Jai Jagadambe!

Sharad stops.

'Why are they shouting Muslim Muslim?' he exclaims.

Some of the students laugh, and Sharad also smiles.

Daddu's always seated on his large divan in his large room. Large room, large divan, small himself. He's always talking to himself. If someone visits, he's pleased.

'Come in, come in. Where are you coming from?' He pats the spot next to him. 'Come, sit!'

Daddu doesn't go outside, and Daddu does not lock the door.

Daddu also never complains if you haven't visited for a long time. Each to his own. Come twenty-five times a day, don't come for weeks, leave after one minute or sit for ages.

That's Daddu for you.

The department is built in the old style. There are latticed windows made of carved wood and stone. The dome on top is studded with a mosaic of blue glass. The pigeons have this whole area firmly under their control. Just as what goes on below is under the control of Professor Nandan, who started working here as a youthful researcher. They say back then it was just a department in name. Really it was Nandan who built it. That's why the department is also called Nandu's baby.

An attempt has been made to burn down some of the large mansions of Swaroop Nagar. Photos appear in the newspaper.

'The violence is not sated by huts alone,' sneers Hanif.

'Now we'll have to do something,' jibes Shruti.

'Like what?' Sharad glares. 'We see a picture of an airconditioned home, and suddenly we're moved. And this will turn into the biggest story. But it's happening to poor people even now. You've seen Babbu Khan—that stoic look settles on his face; he calls the carpenter yet again. Have bottles of acid been thrown at your windows?'

'Have they been thrown at yours?' Hanif is annoyed.

'Don't speak of ours and yours,' scolds Shruti.

'He's saying it, not me.' Hanif rolls up his sleeves and goes into the bathroom.

'He's going again?' asks Shruti.

'Seems the canteen cutlet has caused more damage. Didn't I say the potato tasted rotten?' Sharad has begun to mutter to himself, '. . . *Muslim, Muslim*, everywhere you go, you hear the word *Muslim* . . .' Suddenly he turns to Shruti. 'How many Muslims do you know?'

Shruti starts to recollect and name them all. The entire list.

Hanif's name is not on the list.

Shruti begins to tell him her memories. Scattered. From childhood. Once she was sitting in the picture hall, and she and her brother saw a woman in a burqa and started laughing.

'Look, look!'

'Help! Help! A ghost!' they chirped. They didn't even whisper.

Mummy had a classmate named Sughra Bi. Shruti recalls her Dhakai parathas with their countless folds, and her kabobs and egg halwa, and every year on Eid, she sent over sevaiyan from her house.

Sughra Bi's son, Jamal, was Shruti's brother's friend. They visited on all the holidays: Eid, Bakrid, Holi, Diwali. One time, he'd mischievously dragged Shruti and her brother to see their goat slaughtered. The maulvi recited a verse from the Quran, and the goat wore a garland of marigolds. The strangled bleating seemed to come not from the goat's mouth but from its throat, where the knife slowly sliced. Shruti's brother was silent all the way home. Then he said, 'How cruel, Shruti.' Shruti came down with a fever, but Mummy and Sughra Bi laughed uproariously. 'She's had a fever for two days,' said Papa, '. . . but she's eating heartily!' When the cook would come for a big party, he'd pull a live chicken flapping from his bag, hold it upside down from its bound legs and take it under the tree where brother and sister would run about excitedly, watching him pluck the feathers and remove the skin, as though it were a game.

How to untangle this knot? The three of them sit lost in thought—about how Mummy and Sughra Bi had laughed together, and how the kids had felt nothing for the chicken, but the bleating of the goat had gone to their heads and brought on fever.

Hanif and Sharad's students are sitting everywhere in Daddu's room: on the sofa, on the ground, on dining chairs they've pulled over.

'No ifs, ands or buts,' says one boy excitedly. 'We're among those taking their side, but it's starting to seem even to us that what they're doing will destroy their entire community. Their mullahs are going crazy everywhere they live. In Iran, Bangladesh . . .'

'In the countries you don't mention, this isn't the only thing happening,' corrects Hanif. 'In places like Indonesia, Morocco, Malaysia, there are progressive Muslims, but that's never discussed.'

'This is the media narrative, especially in the West. The new enemy is Islam; they label Muslims as violent, conservative. After the Cold War they needed a new Satan . . .' adds Shruti.

'That's the scapegoat theory, sir. But for how long will that be valid?'

'Let's say what you are saying is correct,' begins Sharad. 'Mullahs, pandits, priests, politicians in many countries are creating havoc and giving a bad name to their entire communities. But we'll have to look at what the reality is where we ourselves live: who's being beaten here, who's lying . . .'

Daddu isn't looking at anyone. He's sitting right at the edge of the divan, his face distorted with seriousness, his mouth coming to resemble a beak.

'So you're saying Muslims aren't doing the beating? They aren't lying?'

'Doubtless they are. But where? Hiding in their neighbourhoods and mohallas, closed in on all sides. We don't even know what they're babbling about in there, and it doesn't make much of a difference, because we don't let them come out.'

'Why are you saying "we"?' asks Shruti angrily.

'That's a different discussion,' retorts Hanif, looking her in the eye.

'In those closed mohallas, despite the money they receive from Arab countries, people are ignorant. They're poor, they fear coming out of their galis and lanes.'

'And those who do manage to get out are no longer ignorant, nor poor, nor are they the type of Muslim that announces what they are by . . .'

'. . . looking different from us.' Sharad finishes Hanif's sentence. 'Out here, they don't look any different from us . . .'

'You're still saying "us".' Shruti gets annoyed again. 'Why are you still saying "us"?'

'Do they look any different? Look at Hanif.' Sharad continues to speak, heedless of Shruti. 'This is a Muslim whom those penned up in their mohallas would probably refuse to acknowledge as such.'

Daddu slides back a little on to the divan. He smiles faintly. 'Let them stay locked up in their ghettoes. In their holes. Like frogs in a well! Let them shout in there to their hearts' content. If they come out, then Muslimness will heal on its own. If some fine imam makes a cockamamie announcement from the Jama Masjid, what harm does it cause?'

'We're less afraid of them, Daddu. We're scared of the fundamentalist Hindus, who aren't shut up in their homes but dancing about in the streets,' says Shruti.

'Shameless, like they're dancing naked.'

Daddu guffaws. How sad the divan had been till now. 'Not even the gods can shame the naked!'

Everyone laughs.

The divan lurches. 'Yes, yes, so naked not even the gods will cause them shame. They'll dance, bhai, oh, how they'll dance! As long as they have breath, they'll dance. Then they themselves will fall lifeless and die.'

'But after killing how many?' asks Hanif.

'How many?' The lurching of the divan ceases momentarily. Then it resumes. 'How to get rid of poverty? How to create more jobs? God won't give us these things; let the Naked Maharaja give them!'

In the akhara of the ashram, youths in loincloths are trained in wrestling and the use of traditional armaments, such as spears, tridents and maces. They slice the air with their weapons. At night, the breeze carries the swishing and clanging of the weapons into our houses, and wakes Shruti and Hanif and Sharad from their slumber.

I follow them, but when Shruti goes to the library, I don't, because she sits in her cubicle and writes love stories and then hides them. Instead, I follow the two men to the department.

Usually, they park their scooters under the overhang of the tin roof outside the canteen, then cross the dried-out drain via a rickety wooden bridge. The bridge is almost completely obscured by trees from above and from the sides as well, so they inevitably encounter amorous couples there. As you ascend the hill from the bridge, the department building comes suddenly into view. This is the shortcut.

The department had received a large grant, under the auspices of Special Assistance Programme, from the University Grants Commission. It is one of the most highly reputed departments in the university. Professor Nandan is proud of both the department and himself.

'Daddu, tell me,' asks Shruti turning towards him, 'how many Muslims do you know?'

Daddu's beak has emerged again. He's sitting at the edge of the divan with his legs crossed.

'In our village, there were many Muslim families. Okay, today I'll tell you something. You people eat in dhabas and restaurants all the time. You have no idea what caste your servers and cooks belong to, and you have no qualms about eating the food served and cooked by them. On the train, on the bus, you'll buy pakodas-kachodas from any community. You'll sit down with anyone; you don't believe in untouchability. On top of that, you even arrange Hindu–Muslim weddings. In our village there was never a question of any of that happening. There'd be joint holidays and festivals, and there were always meetings, and people would sit together, but all the food and drinks were served separately. I'm talking about the entire village. I parted early from this world of everything being cooked and served separately, but even then, when we went to a Muslim home, a Hindu boy from a Hindu halwai shop would bring food for me and my father in a leaf bowl. My father, and the entire village, did things this way. In our home we kept china dishes just for Muslim guests! And none of us was offended by any of it. You don't do casteism, but we did. And yet, there was so much more affinity between Hindus and Muslims in those days.'

I've already said what I'm not. I'm just a copier. The process is eccentric and possesses me like a spirit: it descends in an instant! I stop in the middle of writing and avert my eyes. I start to write something else, and then it seems as though what's happening in front of me has already taken place and I'm reporting on the past. As though what's occurring before me becomes, in my mind, a part of the past as it bursts from my pen! I keep copying, but I don't understand if it's the present me or the past me who's doing it.

'Oh, my, Daddu!' Shruti picks up one more piece of sesame brittle. 'You go on and on about the village, and now, when I've brought you a real village thing, tilpatti, I'm the only one eating it!'

'In the village,' laughs Daddu, 'we didn't get it packed in polythene. There'd be piles of tilpatti sitting out like this, which were consumed by both us and the flies.'

'Ah, the flies excuse,' notes Shruti triumphantly.

'Well,' says Daddu, 'nowadays you won't get them any more real than this in the village.'

'You're right.' Shruti's mouth is filled with the sweet taste of gur. 'If you go there, you'll get these same plastic packets. The city shows up in the village as well. Like when Hanif and I went, remember, to a tribal village? And we were given mutton and brandy.'

'Ha ha!' laughs Daddu cheerfully. 'Tell me, tell me, what happened to you . . .'

'We'd thought we'd be given traditional dishes, like mahua and rotla, but special arrangements were made for us . . .'

'. . . for mutton and brandy!' Daddu and the divan are getting their desired dose of humour. 'And when you said you'd take a photograph of that tribal woman, she disappeared, and when she returned, she'd made her face up with two maunds of powder and wore a nylon sari she'd purchased in the city.'

'With ulta pallu draping! I sent her the photo.' Shruti is telling the story for the thousandth time, and Daddu has it memorized. They laugh and laugh.

Then Daddu says, wiping tears of laughter from his eyes, 'No, no, I won't be going to the village any more. It's changed too much, there's no connection any more.'

'Now you can just hang a picture of the village on the wall and gaze upon it,' suggests Shruti, Daddu-style, and laughs.

'Totally.'

'And never ever go outside.'

'Totally.' Daddu enjoys her teasing. 'And this glass door is still here, so whenever I feel like it, I can just turn my head and look outside with the Mousie and note that going outside isn't worth the bother, that I'm safest right where I am.'

'And that we feel happiest when we're inside.'

'Yes, and you too, Mousie, don't you go outside. The Mousie is better off in her hole. If she goes out in the open, she'll be so confused: "Should I run this way or that?" she'll ask herself!'

'Truly, we are mice,' agrees Shruti. 'Beings that crawl about secretly underground. The animals leaping about above ground are of a different sort.'

'But you're no mouse!' Daddu widens his eyes and puffs out his cheeks. 'You're a feminist after all! You're a pluralist . . . a secularist . . . goddamn it!' he intones theatrically.

'Police state?' Professor Nandan's face is red. 'You don't know what a police state is. You are the children of tomorrow; if you think this looks like a police state . . .' He unclenches his fists and holds out his arms. 'I poured my blood, sweat and tears into this. I built this department brick by brick. I've given you all perks, free rein in your research. I established the Centre for Excellence. Go ahead and show me another department with such freedom! Whenever you want, you just get up and leave for whatever seminar, whichever study tour.'

'What are you going on about, Head Sahib?' Hanif's taken aback. 'I'm speaking out against the new attendance register. I completely agree with everything you've said. Let's not ruin the environment here. Forget about the teachers, if you force the students to attend daily, you won't get them to do better work. That's fine in a police regiment, but let's keep the free atmosphere we have here . . .'

'You people go to seminars, win prizes, make the students arrogant, so you think all that's department work,' exclaims Shorty Josh irritably. 'This is a democracy! There's a limit to everything.'

Urmila's also spoiling for a fight. 'Head Sahib brought in a reading room, an archival cell, microfiche and microfilm readers, the department has quite a reputation . . .'

'Of course,' Hanif agrees. 'Because we're different from others.'

'What we're saying is that maintaining an attendance record is the wrong direction,' says Sharad. 'We're not insulting Head Sahib.'

'If the students use our names instead of saying *Sir*, that's democratic.' Shorty Josh piles on. 'You grow a beard so you're the saviour of Muslims!'

After the meeting, Sharad's cursing everyone, complaining about the new demands being made of them—all the rules, discipline, control.

'You've grown a beard, so you think you've become a Muslim,' laughs Hanif suddenly. 'Now go!' He points theatrically at Sharad's trousers. 'Do that, too. Why are you neglecting that misery?'

'Oh, that.' Sharad smiles. 'I had that done as a child!'

'What?' Hanif is surprised.

'Many Hindu children have it done. If they have an infection or something. Why are you acting so surprised? But what do you know? If you had free time from going to seminars, you'd become more familiar with the customs here!'

'No, this is not a complaint about seminars.' Hanif begins to walk again. 'It's about not being able to go abroad. Now I've started getting invitations from Paris, one hears constantly that some people have turned the pure profession of teaching into a form of vagabondage and made it an excuse for decadence.'

'And now there's this prize, which means your book will be translated, and not Nandu's!'

'Shall I write to the authorities?' laughs Hanif.

'No, no, wait. Wait for the new attendance registers being created in the name of discipline and competence,' jests Sharad.

My copying is disorganized. Sometimes I just copy along. Because nowadays, who knows what will come up?

'The leaves are sprouting now. This one's new, too.' Sharad stands with them by the madhumalti. 'But the flowers should also bloom. Until then, where's the fun in it?'

'You're ridiculous,' snaps Shruti.

'Come, come!' Hanif touches her cheek softly.

'He's badmouthing our vine. Your friend.'

Sharad laughs and gives her a friendly punch.

The mahant of the ashram is speaking sweetly, the very picture of benevolence. He no longer has teeth, nor even a mouth; or maybe they've melted into his beard and moustaches. Only the eyes remain beneath thick brows, and below his nose, a huge white banyan of moustaches tangles its roots in his matted beard. There's an unseen point behind the banyan from which his voice emerges, causing his beard and moustaches to flap like the wings of a bird.

The wind is blowing, and a tiny leaf is caught in the mahant's beard. A disciple steps forward, pulls it out and tosses it away.

'What's this you've done?' A compassion floats in the mahant's eyes. He speaks in the soft tones of a guru. 'My child, birds and beasts used to nest in the matted locks of our forebears;

they laid eggs and brought forth their young there, yet you have been disturbed at the sight of a single leaf.'

Jai Jagadambe! someone calls out.

'We have drunk the wine of goddess–devotion,' intones the mahant pleasantly. 'That is the only intoxicant for us. Hers is the only name we continuously chant! *Jai Jagadambe!*'

The echo returns from every corner of the ashram: *Jai Jagadambe!*

'Why do you refuse, my sons?' The mahant extends his feet for the new devotees to touch when he sees them draw near. 'Here, try this, my son.' He picks up a piece of fruit from a pile and tosses it towards the crowd. 'This sin has grown too heavy. Now repent. Does hearing the name of Devi create an obstacle in children's studies? Oh, forgiveness, forgiveness, Mother Jagadambe!'

The wings of his moustaches flutter.

'There is a need for gurukuls, for Hindu schools. Our civilization is in trouble! What is this we've taught our children? That Akbar was great? Akbar was a cruel foreigner. He was Angrez.' *Flap-flap* go the wings.

'You say our gods and goddesses are false? Forgiveness, forgiveness, forgiveness!'

Flap-flap.

'Reading about the irreligious religions of others: that's what democracy is. Forcing us to remain silent: that's democracy. Allowing the country to be divided. What? No! We shall recreate undivided India.'

Flap.

'Silence is cowardice . . . fill yourselves through and through with love for your motherland. Hamara Bharat Mahan . . . Our India is great . . . It's ours, all ours . . . We can no longer be patient. The torment of our children is a challenge to us. The voices of ordinary people will burst forth.'

Jai Jagadambe!

There's no time to fill the pen with ink. I just dip the nib in the pot and keep writing.

Gusts of wind keep throwing the reflection of the tree on to the glass of the cabinet. Hanif jerks his head up. Is someone coming? But no, it's that same tree standing at attention.

The head's denial of his request for leave lies on the table. Why a refusal right at the last minute? Why couldn't the request have been considered earlier?

Hanif pulls his chair out and puts a hand in his pocket. He comes out of the office, walks about, then returns and picks up his scooter key from the table. He drops it in his pocket and walks down the corridor. He lifts his hand in salaam when he sees someone below, on the stairs.

He walks straight to Professor Nandan's office.

'Head Sahib, what's all this?'

'Please come in, Hanif. I was about to come myself,' says Nandan.

'My application for the Berlin seminar?'

'Look, you gave me no time. You're telling me today that you have to go tomorrow? How do you expect me to respond at the last minute?'

'I didn't ask for a response, Head Sahib. I sent in a letter as always.' Hanif's face reddens.

'What if the vice chancellor doesn't agree? Shouldn't there be a notice period?' Nandan begins to pull at his moustache.

'But the VC has always agreed until now . . .'

'Hanif, I have to advocate for you so frequently . . . to others, this looks like favouritism . . .'

'It's favouritism if you don't stop me from attending a seminar?'

Each of them is starting his sentences before the other can finish.

'Before it was up to the VC, now people . . .'

'Sorry, Hanif, everyone's against leniency because people take advantage . . .'

'Professor Nandan!' Hanif's tone contains a note of warning.

'If you go away all the time, why can't others? This leads to conflict. As the head, I must put a stop to jealousy. If you apply ahead of time, there will be more time to . . .'

'In front of everyone—you too—my trip to Germany has been discussed. We've talked about the eastern and western sides of the Berlin Wall. For so long. If your system regarding leave was going to change, why wasn't I told to apply sooner? Why did you wait until today to write your refusal so the VC would read that along with my note?'

'Dr Hanif, are you imputing a motive to my actions?' replies Nandan loudly.

'If someone's jealous tomorrow because I'm publishing my book, will you calm them down, or stop me from . . .?' Hanif is furious.

'Who's stopping you? Who's stopping you? But will you follow any rules, or will you just do whatever you want? This is a university department, not someone's personal estate!'

'Do whatever you have to do!'

Hanif takes out his scooter key and walks outside.

'Sir, I checked. In this one the same pages are missing, and the third copy is missing.' A student is showing Professor Nandan a library book. 'These IAS–civil service aspirants should be debarred from the library, that's for sure.'

The Central Reserve Police have been removed from the city, and the Border Security Force have been installed.

Right inside the gate of the ashram begin the rows of potted marigolds, roses and hibiscus. A spear-bearer at the entrance suddenly shouts, *Jai Jagadambe!* at which all three of them jump. His muscles ripple.

The ashram has begun to echo yet again with the refrain.

Shruti says it's like when a jackal's howl sets off a succession of howls from one field to another to another into the distance. As the echo returns, it feels as though all the jackals are about to descend upon you.

Shruti and Daddu sit downstairs, but they can hear everyone speaking upstairs. Hanif is saying, 'Why are you attempting to pull a single thread from the entire weave of history?'

'But, sir, if people ignore inconvenient truths in order to prove their secular theories . . .'

'Who's saying that?' yells Sharad. 'But you must understand there are many other factors. You'll find wherever people are inspired to fight by the call for jihad, they're also fighting over wealth and the spread of commerce. This is why the Arabs established themselves in Europe, Africa and Asia! And where there was jihad, there was also infighting. And where there were mixed coalitions of Hindus, Muslims, Jews, Parsis, everyone, all different groups were formed for all different purposes.'

'Just ponder,' says Hanif, 'how our thinking has been hijacked, and by whom, to make it so that wherever we turn our heads, we see destruction at the hands of Muslims, broken Hindu temples and Hindu corpses? They want to draw a veil over different aspects of . . .'

'And the veil,' growled Sharad, 'was here before the arrival of the Muslims. So why do we only think Muslims brought the veil? Sati existed before. Why is it being blamed on them alone?'

'Yes, and who decided we'd only count this or that and forget the rest? And why did we agree to it?'

'What sort of satisfaction are people getting from this? Think about it: How satisfying can it really be?'

Shruti wants to go upstairs, but she sees Daddu is silent, so she stays. Daddu sits cross-legged on the divan. His elbows rest on his knees, and his head is in his hands. As if his entire body is focused on some point inside him, and that point has shaped him.

'That's so true, isn't it, Daddu? How can people feel satisfied with so much one-sidedness?' asks Shruti, trying to connect with him.

Daddu begins to unwrap his body, as though he's straightening and separating tangled branches.

'My dear,' he begins.

But then the voices from upstairs grow louder: 'Why do so few of us know? If you ask people—yes, yes, the situation becomes perfectly clear—when did the Muslims come to Hindustan? People will say: in the eighth century, from the north, through Sindh and Multan, cruel Arabs, destructive Turks, 712 AD, Mohamad bin Qasim, Muhammad Ghori, Mahmud Ghaznavi, Khilji . . .'

'But in the north, the Rajputs were fighting among themselves. Jaichand aided Mohammad Ghori. The Meend and gangs of Jats were making one attack after another. The exact same pillaging, abduction of women . . .'

'But let me finish . . .'

'Oh, sorry, yes, speak . . .'

'Why doesn't anyone know that Muslims first entered from the south, not from the north, for trade with the Malabar

Coast, and without attacking? They settled in the south with no
bloodshed, and there the Rashtrakuta and Chalukya kings, who
were Hindu, welcomed them. To the point that there were mixed
marriages, and their offspring became a new community called
the Bayasaras. This was a convergence, not a battle. Why has
such information not reached ordinary people? Why have people
forgotten? Why are they made to forget? Do they themselves wish
to forget? Think about it . . .'

'Sorry, were you saying something, Daddu?' asks Shruti.

Daddu smiles gently. 'Let the class continue upstairs. Amazing,
these students. They're not satisfied with their university lectures,
they must come here too . . .!'

'They mostly just come to these two,' says Shruti.

'Star professors!' laughs Daddu. 'We were made of different
stuff. We took joy in life. We read good literature, sang great
songs. Once, I heard Uday Shankar had opened a dance academy
in the hills, so I went there to learn.'

'You learnt how to dance?' Shruti finds this hilarious.

'No, I didn't. I wasn't good enough. I lacked the flexibility.
But there were beautiful girls, gorgeous hills, dance and drama.
What more could you want? Pure joy! But you people have taken
all the fun out of life. Dry academics! Now don't make the mistake
of going upstairs. I'll keep you protected here.'

'Oh, I was thinking I'd go listen and see where things
stand . . .'

'Where can they stand? Empty words. The sound and fury of
empty vessels. Yes, yes, go, if you want things to be dry, go.'

'They must be sitting on the balcony; that's why the noise is
coming down here . . . I'll send them inside . . .' Shruti stands
up. On the stairs she begins to mutter to herself, 'I'm going to
dry off!'

'It'll just become a government office.' Sharad glares.

Shorty Josh glares too. 'Get them from the office and read them. They're the rules made by the syndicate . . .'

'Such rules were always there, Josh Ji. The question is, how were they carried out exactly? According to the culture of enlightened educational institutions or . . .?' asks Hanif as he sips his tea.

'. . . or government offices?' Sharad puffs on his cigarette.

'Are seminars so very important? Are we responsible for children's education, or are we just supposed to travel around the world?' asks Urmila.

Hanif laughs, 'You, Urmila Ji, are extremely innocent. Here the curfew has upended our teaching, and you're unjustly cursing seminars.'

'Since when have seminars and lectures become sworn enemies?' asks Sharad.

'Well said!' agrees Hanif.

'We are completing our courses despite the curfew, but we also take part in seminars.' Sharad pats his chest with pride.

'If we're not strict, people will take advantage,' frets Urmila.

Nandan is silent.

'I've heard these things somewhere before,' remarks Hanif, looking bored.

'If we have liberal rules, then some people will take advantage of them, but it's better to take the risk than stifling free inquiry and good research. Will good people do good work?' asks Sharad.

'Don't waste your breath, Sharad.' Hanif smiles.

'Strict rules, conspiracies, backbiting, flattery, toadying, sycophantism, all are intimate companions . . .' Sharad mutters.

'This is all because he couldn't go abroad,' Urmila whispers to the woman next to her. That's what I hear.

'Nandu is silent, but the others are speaking,' Hanif whispers to Sharad.

I note it all down.

In the story there are Muslims, and they're surrounded by the din of those blaring cassettes that play everywhere in our city. One Muslim youth raises a burning torch and throws it, another speaks of leaving for Pakistan, because these cassettes aren't playing there.

'But what does that accomplish? It's all a way of forcing us to think of Pakistan as ours. There won't be any room for us there either, only slogans.'

Those listening to the cassettes knew this place was all they had.

But was it? There was so little space, penned in by all the cassettes, their neighbourhood surrounded by Hindus. Behind them, a wall riddled with bullets; before them, a window shattered by a bulb full of acid.

Karamat Miyan held a knife in his hand, concealed in the folds of his kameez. He'd only just changed his stance, when . . .

Hanif stops. He puts the story down.

'What happened?' Shruti doesn't look confident.

'Jai Jagadambe!' cries Hanif.

Jai Jagadambe! Sharad punches the air in the combative manner of the ashramites. Hanif stares at Sharad with annoyance. Shruti feels anxious and gives Sharad a kick.

'Why are you making crude gestures? Is this a new habit?'

Sharad looks stunned for a moment, then clarifies, 'No, it's not. Hanif was just annoyed at the cassette, not at me.'

'It isn't working, is it?'

'No,' says Hanif, reluctantly.

'How about the style . . .'

'I don't want style. It should be straightforward, so what's said is plainly understood.' 'But besides that,' says Hanif, 'you're making Muslims the sacrificial goats. You're doing away with their human dignity.'

'But not completely,' Shruti argues.

Sharad smacks Hanif on the back. 'If you're annoyed with me, I'll tell you, yaar, you're becoming so humourless, a proper miyan bhai!'

Hanif thinks, weighs his words, speaks slowly. 'Don't write on this topic. Don't write a short story or a novel. It's fine for a newspaper. The problem is with trying to dress it up as fiction . . .'

'But so what?' objects Shruti, though she also seems uncertain. 'Must every genre have a different style? If it works for a newspaper report, then why not write the story the same way? There's all different sorts of literature.'

Sharad slaps Shruti on the back.

'This is my best friend; you showed up later. Don't tell me how I should behave with him!'

The three of them burst out laughing.

'This one was already half Muslim,' says Hanif. 'After hanging out with me, the other half went Muslim too. I was half Hindu; the rest of me converted in his company, and I became more Hindu. So which of us is Hindu and which is Muslim?'

He looks pleased.

'Which of us wears a braid, and which is circumcised?' asks Sharad.

'Hush!' Shruti laughs. 'Obscenity in front of me?'

The lights of the fair twinkle in the distance. Everyone's all dressed up. There are sweet shops, chaat shops, an abundance of toys, cheap flashy things, rich and poor, something for everyone. Sermon books.

'Do you need to buy a few more?' Hanif is pointing to *Our Blood-Stained and Horrifying History*.

'Stop it.'

Before them is the ashram temple. Diverting devotions. The three of them stand in front of a calendar shop. I examine the calendars before the shopkeeper wraps them and hands them to his customers.

I take note. On the calendar they've purchased is a picture of an Englishman, hat in hand, placing a bouquet at the feet of the Goddess. He's bowing down. The flowers look like lilies or some such thing. In the pictures that hang in front of the shop, there's a Jain mendicant, a Sikh and all sorts of other people prostrating themselves before the Goddess.

'Did you see, beta?' the devotee standing next to them explains to his child, who's going about the fair on his shoulders. 'That Turk stopped being a Muslim; such is the splendour of Jagadamba.'

The picture shows a warrior in a tasseled fez bowing his head in devotion.

'Then why is there fighting?' asks the child loudly.

'Not with him, the fighting is with the descendants of Babar.'

'You wrote well.' When Hanif says this to Shorty Josh, he puffs up with pride. 'Don't just tack it to the notice board,' he suggests. 'Turn it into a letter to the editor.'

'Arre, how can I write the sort of language you people do? I just wrote whatever came to mind.'

'Wah wah, Dr Josh! You're not calling it jargon this time,' teases Hanif.

'And too much theory!' Sharad jokes too.

Shorty Josh laughs and extends a hand of friendship. 'You caught me. All right, I admit it.'

'It's not just a matter of language,' says Hanif, becoming serious. 'And there's no evil in language, Dr Josh. But these are powerful words. Everyone knows that. All the same, not all are aware that people's historical and geographical circumstances create who they are and form their religion as well . . .'

'. . . and the part about how nationalism has raised its head wherever the colonial empire engendered a sense of existential fear in various peoples and in Muslims too,' Nandan joins in. 'In countries where the identity of Muslims isn't in danger, conditions are more relaxed.'

Sharad picks up what Shorty Josh has written and begins to read aloud:

> . . . we can neither state that the underlying nature of Islam is always strict nor that it is always liberal . . . that Muslims too shape their attitude to Islam according to their circumstances . . .

'Okay, I always thought that the Quranic verses revealed in Medina were intolerant and aggressive towards non-Muslims, such as Jews and Christians, since Islam had acquired political and military power by then. Before reading this, I didn't realize many of these verses provided a framework for a pluralistic society, allowing for religious freedom to all communities, as well as coexistence, mutual respect and understanding between Muslims and non-Muslims. Hey, did you know that?'

Some research scholars nod their heads.

'Yaar, I've never seen a crazier bird than a pigeon.' Shorty Josh jumps up and shoos a pair of pigeons away from his bookshelf. 'Even if you twist their necks, they'll be back again the next day.'

'And they make everything so dirty.' Urmila wrinkles her nose and laughs.

'So it's not useless?' Shorty Josh asks, cheerful now. 'I still have so much to say. Just give me some help with the language. A bit of jargon will give it personality!'

'Tell them to start bringing air guns tomorrow. Our neighbours have discovered the secret to attaining freedom from pigeons. *Bang bang*!' Hanif tells them.

'They kill them?' asks Nandan.

'No . . . no . . .' Sharad shoots a fake gun into the air and bursts out laughing.

The riots have started again.

'It's a flowerpecker,' says Shruti, pointing out a tiny bird hopping on the madhumalti.

'A wren!' cries Daddu.

'But aren't they all flowerpeckers?' laughs Sharad. 'Give it a flower and it comes to peck!'

'Are you criticizing again?' scolds Shruti.

Hanif calls out from upstairs, 'Come, you should listen to this. Babu Painter has brought news.'

'I'm asking you, little wren,' Daddu touches Shruti's chin. 'Why are you getting caught up in all this mess? You're different from them. Those people are a different breed.'

'Oh, look, its beak is longer than its body!' Shruti peers out of the glass window. 'Aah, it flew away!'

'Here you all are, crying with your beaks out again. Why are we separate, over here, why are we on this side of the bridge?' Daddu chuckles. 'This, too, is a bird, which I have caught! It's called a secularist!'

The echo of his laughter follows her all the way to the staircase.

People are fleeing the city. One hears the station is jam-packed, and due to a shortage of tickets, they've resorted to stamping them on people's hands.

There have been deaths. Many have been wounded. The department's team has curfew passes, and gathers medicine and money to take to the hospital. They've also prepared notes for their report. The doctors say, 'Look at the register. Either the list of names will be equal parts Hindu and Muslim, or there will be more Hindu intakes.' Then Nandan has another survey done that looks at separate lists of the wounded and the dead, and another of the Muslim wounded. Whose heads are more bashed, whose fingers more cut?

They pay careful attention to who can be admitted to the hospital as soon as they're wounded or dying (Hindus), and who lies rotting in the streets and lanes (Muslims).

Shruti cuts *this* and adds *that*. Now what is written on the page is this:

It seems to me something happened that year.

'He's an especially bright man, but when it comes to writing he drags his feet,' Hanif is saying.

'Who? Shorty Josh?' Shruti asks.

'He just spends all his time hopping around Nandu,' says Sharad.

'Have you noticed how Nandu's always silent? These people just speak his mind for him!' replies Hanif.

'Why do you have to be so negative about Nandu? They're simply his friends who sit around waiting to speak his mind for him!'

'But Shorty Josh is not an owl—he's no idiot,' says Hanif.

'What are you two talking about?' asks Shruti.

'He's not an owl, he's an egret—deceptively meditative but always ready to pounce.' Sharad makes a face. 'We're talking about Nandu and his buddies, Shruti. When Nandu enters a meeting, I'm reminded of a mud-caked buffalo. *Squelch, squelch.* With egrets hopping on his back and around his feet, and mynas too, pecking for worms!'

'Ew, Sharad!' Shruti laughs.

Anyway, I've learnt to make my pen act as a suction pump. I'm not sure if this is an insult to it or an expression of respect. But I am aware of no other way. It's they who are racing this way and that, not me. I'm the one spilling as much ink as my pen can suction on to these pages.

I wasn't the one stirring; it was they who were doing the stirring, as when Daddu would send a spark to the person sitting quietly before him, so that when it reached them, they would fall under the delusion that they were the source. So, too, I would tremble from the shuddering that arose in them. Even the suctioning was perhaps not done by me, but by the pen. Or they were themselves becoming the suctioned ink and flowing from the pen. The tragedy was that no matter what happened, I felt like I'd left something unsaid. In the city, in the department, in the ashram, on the divan! Perhaps all of this would actually seem so to them, and it would only seem to me that it seemed to me!

People insisted it was more important to know who said it, who wrote it, who did it, than simply to know that it was said, written, done. Everyone's names suddenly held deep importance. Although the newspapers never stated a person's community, this too was an aspect of the insistence that names held deep importance.

That's why Shruti becomes silent on the train, swallowing her anger along with her hunger.

The train seems like an extension of our city: uniformed, at attention, finger on the trigger, seconds from pressing down.

In those days, the police stopped the riots, but they amplified them too; so nobody trusted the police when it came to policing.

The authority bursting from the bayonet of the Sten gun-bearing guard swells his chest like a balloon. His forehead is smeared with a sandalwood tilak.

Majestically looking this way and that, he stops to stare straight at Shruti and Hanif. Shruti, as is her habit, has wrapped her dupatta round her hair to protect it from dust and tangling. She wraps it tightly across her forehead, pushes it behind her ears and drapes it across her neck.

The bayonet advances swiftly to ask her name and business.

Shruti is livid. Her self-respect is wounded. My name is Saira Begum, she nearly says, what are you going to do about it? But . . . but suddenly she remembers Hanif's name.

When I write *suddenly* I recall Babbu Khan: 'None of this is sudden; it happened before too. Only now it's coming out into the open.'

She calms down. 'Why are you asking? What's wrong?' A controlled voice, mentally preparing the next line.

But now Hanif looks angry, and Shruti gazes into the policing eyes and begins to fear.

'What do you do?' the policeman barks in a *hands-up!* tone.

Shruti says quickly, 'I'm a writer, Shruti, and this is my husband, he's a professor at the university.'

'He teaches, oho, then go in,' says the policeman, who goes in himself.

Shruti thinks she'll write down her own name when buying a ticket in the future. She glances over at Hanif, a bit distraught, wondering how she'll get him to agree to this.

So many are wounded: one has a busted head, another a broken hand, a third has been stabbed in the stomach. Medicine has been applied to the gashes, and the blood has coagulated. Yellow, red and purple. At the hospital, our eyes fill with the colours of wounds.

'You didn't like it either. Hanif's already given it a zero. Should I just stop writing stories altogether?' Shruti is complaining to Daddu.

'A story is not in the details of an incident, silly. It creates a new and distinct world. If that doesn't happen, then you've got nothing.'

'Okay, I'm going to say I've stopped writing stories now.' Shruti is acting childish.

'Start writing stories. But don't call this a story,' suggests Daddu. 'Look, little wren, how can it be a song without a tune? Don't fight it, don't fight it. There's a tune to this, I acknowledge that, but it sounds more like a speech!' he adds, narrowing his eyes until they look like raisins. The divan will now perform a new dance tune.

I've heard they're also getting rid of the Border Security Force and calling in the Gorkha regiment.

Truly, much dust flew that year. Our eyes filled with it. Our sight grew hazy. We walked about, eyes red and squinting. We rubbed our eyes till they watered. They felt full of gravel. At one point, rumour had it that this was a horrifying form of conjunctivitis that had spread into our city along with the bombs and weapons from the other side of the border. Wherever it came from, it upset us, and we wondered if we should open our eyes at all now. But how could we see? And if we couldn't see, how would we know who was attacking and from where? How could we bear witness? And how could we escape? Sometimes there'd be such clouds of dust, a fine layer would collect on my copied pages, obscuring the ink. I had a terrible fear that this would make the ink disappear altogether. I shook the dust from the pages to make the ink come alive again.

It's all true. All this happened. It was our city, and all those people were there: the people in the department, those of the old city, the ashramites, the people in Daddu's house, everyone. If anyone was absent, maybe it was me, because it was in me that their souls trembled, their storms raged.

If that's what they call existence, then I exist. Doubtless, I exist. I'm still alive.

Daddu massages his body every day with mustard oil. What ink is for me, mustard oil is for him. He pays great attention to his health. If you ask him his age, he'll say a hundred, but Sharad says he's probably about seventy. Everyone's been instructed to bring back oil if they go to the bazaar, so it always remains in stock. He spends a couple of hours in the bathroom every morning. He massages himself, he bathes, and then emerges shiny and clean.

'Hire a masseur,' suggests Hanif.

'I left all those feudal luxuries behind in the village,' replies Daddu.

'The village is your cure-all!' laughs Hanif.

Daddu doesn't laugh. First, he sits down on the divan, then he laughs. As does the divan!

'But it is a cure-all. My illness is the village, and the cure is also the village. What the village is for me, the riots are for you!'

He bounces.

'It's a good joke,' observes Shruti, marvelling at the revelling divan.

'No joke! I sit here far from the village yammering on and on about it. You people sit over here yammering on and on about the riots. And thanks to the gods of every religion, it's got nothing to do with you. What I'm saying is, don't make life boring, read and write good things, eat and drink. What need do you have for all that killing?'

'Wow, Daddu!' Shruti glares.

'Wow, Shruti, wow, Hanif,' says Daddu, imitating her. 'She's saying, "Wow, Daddu!"'

A fourteen-year-old girl is getting stitches. She lies on her back crying.

'Abbu, these nurses have saved my life. Abbu, they're very nice,' she says.

'Yes, daughter,' says the man standing next to her. 'Think of these people as parents and thank them well.'

'Abbu, the police beat you. Where did they beat you?'
She weeps.

Today, Sharad's reminiscing about an incident from his
childhood, when he was in class four. For the annual school
festival he had to act in a dramatic adaptation of Premchand's
short story 'Eidgaah'.

'We had a rehearsal. It was Eid, so there would be namaz. The
group of children was to shout *Allahu Akbar*! But none of us was
willing to say that. We didn't consult one another, but somehow,
we all stood silently together in quiet agreement. No one had
said anything to us at home; we weren't thinking anything in
particular, but none among us could bring ourselves to say *Allahu
Akbar*,' recounts Sharad, looking from one to another.

'*Allahu Akbar* means *God is great*!' observes Shruti, staring up
at the clouds floating about in the pink sky.

'We feared this God,' says Sharad.

'But why?' Shruti stares at him.

'I don't know. You tell me.'

Sharad gazes off in the distance, over there, from where they
could hear the call to prayer.

'Due to some unspoken agreement, without any forethought,
who knows?' Hanif is like a detective searching for clues to a
murder. 'Some children refused to say *Allahu Akbar*. Was it fear?
How? Why? Where did all this come from in the subconscious
minds of children?'

'Two teachers made the call to prayer at the mic, and then
Mohsin and Kidwai and Hamid hopped onstage,' continues
Sharad.

'The fears of children are like this,' says Daddu. 'Look at this
girl. How fearful she is. Say it. Can you say *Allahu Akbar*?'

'Of course I can!' Shruti makes a face, like a small child. 'I love
the sound of the azan early in the morning. It's divine. It comes
from far off, from where the sun is rising, and beyond even that.'

'Let it come from nearby, then we'll see what will rise here
and what will sink with fear!' parries Daddu.

'I'm not afraid.' Shruti acts like a baby for him.

'Are you afraid?' Sharad asks Hanif suddenly. 'Why are you
afraid?' he asks. 'You should be,' he adds, before Hanif, taken
aback, can respond.

'What are you saying?' asks Shruti, flustered.

'You,' Sharad is saying to Hanif, 'should stop taking the
shortcut to the department along the drains.'

Hanif looks angry at this pointed 'you'.

When Shruti sits down to write, she sometimes scratches her legs
with the pen, sometimes her head. Nothing comes from the pen,
but what pours from Shruti is smoke. Which isn't visible but fills
the air. It's growing denser. Finally, she gets up coughing and goes
out to the balcony.

This happens again and again.

The ashramites say Shiva himself bowed his head before the
Goddess in this very place, and they remind women that in our
religion they're goddesses, and everyone knows how high their
status is.

That place where the lotus feet of Lord Shiva alighted upon the
earth is inside the ashram temple. A sign written in red proclaims:
We are Hindus! Say it with pride! There's an image of Lord Shiva,
and his body is purple.

'Bhaiya, I went into a stupor—I felt a tingling in my legs when I came out. Like I'd touched a live wire,' one devotee is saying. *Victory to Lord Shiva, victory to the Devi. Jai Jagadambe!* He holds yellow flowers in his hand.

'Look, you're only making everyone more alarmed. We know what's happening and where. You people see one place and then generalize about the entire city in your account. You're escalating things with your writing; you're making people think every Hindu is a communalist.'

The women from the society sit before Trivedi, the plump district magistrate, who's flanked by two subordinates behind a plump table, sipping tea and chewing paan zarda continuously.

Shruti and the other women are getting angry. Why shouldn't we visit those districts, the ashram, the camps? Why shouldn't we tell people what the mahant is saying, and how the people harmed in the riots are being helped, how they're not? One thing is promised, another is done.

'The outcome of the information you're spreading is the daily letters of complaint that appear in the newspapers. Do you want to give people hope or the opposite . . .?' With a flourish, he unfurls a string of paan zarda packets, tears off a corner of one and tosses a bit of masala into his mouth. 'We know our work.' A voice heavy with saffron emanates from his mouth.

'And we ours,' Shruti retorts.

'What do you do?' Trivedi lifts his face as though it's a pot, and he must be very careful not to spill its precious contents. 'Then go ahead and write stories and novels. Deliver flour, clothing, medicine, of course. We're all in this together.'

At his signal, the men by his side get up to escort all the women to the car.

The steps of the collectorate are completely coated in paan stains, as are the walls.

'Why are you people doing all this?' asks Trivedi's junior. 'Why do you only look at one side of things? We've been beaten for so many centuries. Where were you then? Now one guy gets beaten on the other side and you're all up in arms?'

It used to be that people visited our city because of the university. But that year it became a pilgrimage site. People came from afar, crammed into buses and cars. Then the ashram vans, with the Devi cutouts astride the bonnets, picked them up all over the city and brought them to the temple.

Shruti stops climbing the library steps. She turns. She sees Hanif walking to the department via the shortcut. She watches him for a long time.

It's an old jalopy of a bus. It's headed for the place where the ruins of a mosque have been taken over by devotees of the Goddess.

'The Breakdown Express', Hanif has dubbed it. People of all ages are going there for a darshan of the Devi. The bus's engine hiccups, then it jerks *clunk-clunk-clunk*, and shuts down.

There's silence for a few moments. Then people begin to speak. They seem contented, completely unworried.

'What happened?' asks one man.

'The bus stopped.'

'Oh, stopped, did it?'

'Hey, Driver Sahib, what happened?' asks the same man.

'The bus stopped,' answers the driver sitting back comfortably.

'Oh, so it stopped?'

The driver sits in his seat, key in hand. The lad seated by his side jumps up and gets out. He's circling the bus. He's kicking the tires.

'Will it start?' someone asks.

'Did it start?' asks another.

Clunk-clunk-clunk, the bus hiccups again. It doesn't move an inch.

'Pull a bit more, bhaiya.'

'Kick it a little harder, na?'

The lad smacks and whacks at the bus.

'It's not an oxcart, bhaiya,' the driver announces proudly from his seat.

The crowd of devotees bursts out laughing.

Another bus hurtles by, churning up dust and smoke.

A child sticks its head out of the window and calls, 'Stop! Stop!'

The passengers begin to stir. Everyone gets out and stands in the road. Some stroll about. The driver has fallen asleep in his seat.

'She's coming! She's coming!' they cry, and everyone starts running. The cutout of the Goddess is approaching.

'Stop! Stop!'

They wave. The van is empty.

'Shall we get in?' asks Sharad.

'No,' says Shruti.

'Quick!' Hanif pulls them inside. They get two seats.

An ochre flag flutters atop the dome of this mosque-turned-ruin. It's stuck on askew.

'O, Bhagwan!' Sharad presses his palms together and addresses a man with a tilak on his forehead: 'The authorities say no one can climb on to the dome without a ladder, but didn't they need a ladder to get up there?'

'Why is he suddenly acting like a pandit?' Hanif asks Shruti with annoyance. 'We don't speak this language!'

'Bhagwan' is playing a small pair of brass cymbals.

'The devotee monkeys came to fly the banner of Devi from the dome,' he explains. '*Jai Bajrangbali! Jai Jagadambe!* All is the desire of the Devi.'

He becomes lost in his devotional song.

The ruined mosque is completely surrounded by barbed wire and armed soldiers.

'Strategy,' Sharad says softly to Hanif. 'Act like you're one of them; then they'll talk.'

'It was a festival of the Goddess,' the priest explains. 'Hindu hearts from all over filled with a signal from the Devi. People crowded in the thousands to this pure spot: from Kanyakumari, Dwarka, Puri, Kashmir. What was it? Yes?' He seems less like a priest and more like a schoolmaster at this point. 'The Devi festival. What was it? Yes?'

'The Devi festival,' all three answer in unison.

'The Goddess signal arose in the hearts of the devotees. To come where? Yes, yes, to come here. Where?'

'Here,' the three parrot.

'And why come? To make the sacrifice.'

I keep writing, but in my mind I hear this schoolmaster voice intoning the letters of the alphabet: 'Ka is for kabootar, kha is for khargosh. Yes? Yes?'

'The authorities say six died?'

'No, six thousand were sacrificed.'

'But . . .'

'A bullet flew through the air. The group of devotees was standing in a straight line. The bullet ripped through all of them and came out the other side. Yes? See, here are the bullet marks on the walls.'

'But . . .'

'They were heroes. There was some powerful force at work; it was shakti, the divine power, that caused the flag to erect itself. The irreligious Muslims shot through the chests of all the devotees.'

'But there weren't any Muslims here,' says Hanif. 'The Hindus who came had threatened from the start that they would turn the mosque back into a temple on the feast of Devi. And the bullets came from the police.'

A crowd has gathered, and they all cry as one: 'They were Muslims!'

Shruti nibbles on the chain around her neck. She's not even writing love stories, but at least the madhumalti is growing.

'It has branches, twigs. What should we call it?' she asks Hanif. 'Look, look, how they're plaited like a braid.'

'Let's call it Gunjalka, because it's plaited,' says Hanif.

'It's a nice name.'

'But when will the flowers come?'

'They'll come, they'll come,' Shruti hushes him. 'Don't be critical like Sharad.'

Shruti spreads out some sheets of paper, uncaps her pen and gazes at the madhumalti.

'Our madhumalti, by the name of Gunjalka,' she says, leaning over.

And she's writing:

News came of wounding, news came of killing, news came of burning, news came of looting, news came of breaking walls, news came of mass rape. We heard, we heard again, we didn't hear, then panicked about what news would come next, scoured the newspapers through and through, grew accustomed. Then at some point, felt a shock, which came like a flash, that all these things we read about from time to time in other places, at other times, were all happening at once, and right here!

A small child is sucking on a lollipop and people are asking it, 'Tell us, what did you see, what happened in your home, tell?'

'They beat everyone. I ran away,' says the child without removing the lollipop.

'It's the builders' doing,' Trivedi tells the department people whom he had sent for to tour these areas with him in a car. 'They got these riots going and then cleared out all the huts and shacks.'

The burning stench coats their breath in soot. One acid bottle, one wheel, one burnt-out busted Hero Honda, one Reebok shoe, a child's tricycle, a mirror, a comb, a cassette trailing a long, dusty, tangled tape, a ruined settlement. I am making a list.

'Every district has caused riots for different reasons,' Trivedi explains. 'We're attempting to identify the perpetrators correctly. Please help us.'

Outside the police tent, Trivedi is serving everyone chai and grandly presenting them with strings of paan zarda packets.

'You're important intellectuals. Please give us your reports. They'll help us search for causes. We only request you not make anything public in haste. These days, just one spark will start something.'

Everyone shakes hands in turn and says thank you.

'An entire community is lying?'

'Both communities are lying.'

'People's brains have emptied.'

'People are not empty compartments that you can just throw in anything and rattle them about.'

The three of them sit in the university canteen.

'These are frustrations of all kinds let loose; trying to get free of the tensions of life today . . .' Hanif can't finish his sentence.

'Enough of these arguments; the same things come up over and over again,' says Sharad, disgusted. 'Economic constraints, political tensions, vote-bank politics, the frustrations of young people . . .'

'Then make a new argument,' responds Hanif, annoyed.

'Why have people become so alienated, why are they searching for this kind of satisfaction?' Sharad feels combative.

'Why? What Hanif's saying, how is it wrong? These are the same reasons, the ones you're calling tired, which make people act like this.' Shruti's also ready for a fight.

'So their feelings, their beliefs, all that's artificial? These are just excuses to overcome exterior conflicts?' retorts Sharad.

'We're not getting anywhere with theory.' Is Hanif joking or arguing? Because just then he jostles Sharad's hand and upsets his glass of water, and all three of them rush to protect their books.

That year there was frequent news of work transfers. There was a riot, and one left. There was another riot, another left. If one newspaper accused someone of being a communalist officer, the other would say he fixed the hooligans of the city, and then the hooligans met with the MLA and had him thrown out.

'Oh, look, Kapadia's come. Isn't he that fellow, Sharad, you studied with?' asks Daddu, glancing at the newspaper.

'Yes, Daddu,' replies Sharad.

'You forbid us from reading the news and then you read it yourself, don't you, Daddu?' Shruti smiles mischievously.

'What do I matter?' asks Daddu laughing. 'I'm already done with living. I've had my fun. What does it matter to me if I accidentally read something crazy now? But you're dying before living at all. Such joyless people. Worthless, too. How is life worth living for you?' Between his guffaws and the bouncing divan, his face is turning red, and he's squinting.

As soon as Daddu gets up to go to the bathroom, Hanif and Sharad quickly pour a bit more liquor into their already-full glasses.

'But Daddu is old,' he says when he returns. He fills his glass and asks Sharad and Hanif, 'Well, shall I give you more?'

'I still have some,' says Sharad, wrapping his hand around his drink.

'I have some too, thank you.' Hanif hides his glass behind the sofa.

'Daddu's getting old,' says Daddu, taking small sips. 'To be honest, I don't understand anything you all say these days. I watch the TV, read the newspaper, but all those new things don't make it into my brain at all. Your academic language, your literature . . . the mind of an old man is old too. How can you cram in the new stuff?' He bounces at his own words.

I'm writing all this down: that the divan is jumping up and down like a child. What to say? Daddu's turning into an old man, but the divan is turning into a child.

The pages flutter.

'This is the list of the dead. Okay, one must admire the fact that in this case, the Muslim camps are much more organized than the Hindu camps,' observes Nandan.

'There's no unity among the Hindus.' Urmila is bent over her work. 'They just make a lot of noise, that's it. Muslims systematically prepare lists of their wounded, dead, missing.'

'Now do it quickly, Hanif Sahib,' says Nandan.

'How can I do that, Head Sahib! We'll have to sit down and go through all the notes we've been given and try to make sense of them. You people are taking a lot of shortcuts. If you write clearly and systematically, it'll be much easier, but this is all scrawled in private diaries,' complains Hanif.

'But, for you, it comes naturally to untangle tangled writing,' laughs Shorty Josh.

'Sure,' snipes Hanif. 'No one has time for useless tasks. Just quickly throw a bunch of nonsense at that fool, Hanif; he'll polish it and your name will shine. A report must be given to the University Grants Commission: call Hanif Sahib. A proposal must be sent to the Indian Council for Cultural Relations: Hanif, where are you? We need a write-up for a seminar: get cracking, Hanif . . .'

'Look, man, what's the point of all your seminar experience? Will you do something for this department or not?' Sharad asks with a wink.

Daddu has taken a pill. Now he lies sprawled on the divan with his eyes closed.

First Daddu stares at it. Then he gets a cloth and begins to dust. Still dissatisfied, he dampens the cloth under the faucet, wrings it out, then returns to polishing the telephone smartly. Wipe here, wipe there, stick the corner of the damp cloth into the

holes of the dial. Now he's uncoiling the cord, wiping as he goes.
A long cord. If you wanted, you could grab the phone and run
a great distance!

An extremely narrow lane, and even so the rickshaw can squeeze
through! Shruti panics and tries to stand, but Hanif pulls her and
makes her sit back.

It's amazing the rickshaw can move at all! The driver sticks
out a foot and pushes along the walls of the houses that line the
lane, then switches sides, just to get through.

'Our heads are spinning from all the listening,' says an educated
youth. 'See how aggressive they are when they are so few. Imagine
how it'll be when their numbers grow! We've endured their
deceit since 1947. We were better off with the British Raj. You
understand what I'm saying, right? We've started to believe even
slavery would be better. Think about it, how afraid we'll be when
there are more of them!'

'So what do you do otherwise?' asks Shruti.

'I'm in my BA final year.'

'At our university?' asks Hanif, astonished.

'Look, my dear.' Daddu's beak has come out, and he's not
laughing. 'When did I ever say what's happening is good? It's very
bad. I'm saying, life's not bad, you're not bad, live happily, far
from all this. Eventually, I won't be around, and neither will you.'

Not a trace of laughter. Shruti is surprised.

'All this has happened before, it will happen again, then it will stop. These ones protesting are part of the process, so are those ones creating the uproar; but these voices won't die, nor will those.'

'And those who stay silent, what about their voices?' Shruti makes a face.

'What voices do they have?'

Now he's smiling a little, Daddu, but only for a moment.

'Some voice must be drawing strength from their silence,' insists Shruti.

'Everyone will go along maintaining the balance of suppression and exposition. Today, this one enjoys, tomorrow, that one. But...' Daddu's beak is completely out now. 'Why are you squandering your quality of life on this? It's all a superficial game; reality is some other emotion that keeps us alive.' He's glowing splendidly, but he's not laughing. 'Now look. I'll show you.' He reaches far into the cupboard and feels around before pulling out some leaflets. He dusts them off and returns to the divan. 'Back then, these leaflets were distributed in our village. This is from Bakrid, 1917.'

Shruti comes and sits beside him on the divan.

Victory to Lord Rama!

The following is imperative for Hindus: As you well know, there are hostilities between Hindus and Muslims due to Muslim cow slaughter. You must also know they hanged a Hindu from a tree and left him to die, and then took his cow and paraded it about the village before slaughtering it. This has brought shame upon Hindus, and, indeed, our continued existence after such a disgrace is a curse. Because of this, know that you must loot Muslim homes, kill Muslims and spread this message to 500 villages. If you don't spread the word, and don't loot and kill the Muslims, then you are a daughter-fucker, a sister-fucker and a drinker of your wife's urine. You might as well marry your own mother off to a Muslim! I have written only a little, but you must understand.

If you're not capable of killing as many Muslims as possible, send news to the raja of Dumraon, and he will come to your rescue with his gun-equipped armies.

'Oh dear.' Shruti looks at Daddu.

'It's true, my dear, that among Hindus, too, there's never been a shortage of communalist feeling. Sometimes it bursts out in the open; the rest of the time, it stays peacefully inside.'

'What did you do?' Shruti looks curious.

The familiar smile spreads across his lips.

'We did everything. We boasted. We behaved as young louts.'

Then the smile leaves. Daddu sits silently.

Now he speaks angrily: 'Does life exist only for us to destroy it? Those crazies make life so limited, so barbaric. I left it all and came here. Those people destroyed the village!'

What side were you on, Daddu? Shruti wants to ask. Instead, she says, 'You're always singing village, village, my village, but you left and ran away!'

He smiles slightly again. 'Okay, now let's quickly lock it up in the cupboard again, otherwise those two intellectuals of yours will devour it greedily.'

Today he's rationing his sprinkles of laughter.

If I wanted, I could pick them up, but they'd fill only a tiny box! Shruti thinks to herself.

As though to prove her wrong, the divan finds a reason to be cheerful again. Suddenly it begins to bounce.

'You think by hammering away over here, you're fashioning a life, while they, over there, presume they're refining it, and you gaze at one another with contempt, saying, *Ew, you! Ew, you!* Meanwhile, life stands to one side enjoying itself and laughing mischievously! Arre, if a mosque was demolished, if a temple was demolished, what of it? Did they manage to kill Bhagwan or Allah? Or did only humans die? But they must die anyway!'

Sprinkles of laughter cascade everywhere, enough to fill not just a tiny box but an entire drum.

All the teachers agree that many copies should be made of the poster two students have tacked to the noticeboard and pasted up everywhere—on all the university noticeboards, at the bus stop, on the walls of the cinema hall—so that people walking by or waiting will see them.

'Poster war.'

On one side of the poster there's a list of statistics commonly used in the ashram sermons, and on the other are facts proving them to be false, with additional context.

Hanif comes outside when he sees Nandan yelling at the chaprasi under the department neem tree.

'Did you speak with Australia?' he asks.

'Oh, yes, I forgot to tell you,' recalls Professor Nandan.

'But I was right here in my office.'

'No, you were in the reading room, and the peon had gone out. I was feeling very tired—I have a heart condition, you know that—so I couldn't come, nor could I call out for you. I wrote down their number. Here you go . . .'

'Head Sahib! Now I'll have to call Australia! Is that easy, or is it easy for them to phone?'

'Oh, no! So they haven't called again?' Nandan asks with feigned sympathy.

Hanif shakes his head and leaves.

Perhaps I hear Nandan telling Urmila, 'It looks like Hanif Miyan is dreaming of crossing the ocean again!'

Hanif is angry and Sharad is laughing. Their dialogue goes like this:

'I won't tell him that this phone call would've made him happy. They were requesting permission to print the department project report there.'

'He gets jealous at the mere mention of abroad.'

'It's not like he never goes.'

'But not like you, right!'

'Yes, yes, his students say so, and they are themselves the children of such doctors,' says Shruti, sitting on the divan with Daddu. Sharad is on the sofa.

'Really?' Daddu's enjoying himself immensely.

'These quacks are openly giving medicines for three or four illnesses at once.'

'All strong allopathic medicines,' adds Sharad.

'Then they'll ask: Do you want silver or gold?'

'When he fears death, even a poor man will reach for his purse.'

'And one is just calcium, and the other is only vitamin B!'

'So that's what they mean by silver and gold injections!'

'The moment you get the injection you feel a surge of strength . . .'

'A slight change . . .'

'A false change!' cries Daddu.

'It gives the poor man the will to live.'

'The poor man gets poorer.'

'No, re!' Daddu's eyes widen; they are shining but also shot through with worry. 'Such cheating?'

'Absolutely, Daddu. All this is happening.'

Today, even my kajal box will remain empty, thinks Shruti as she gathers up the wispy bits of Daddu's laughter in her imagination.

People began to say there's no discipline any more, and our liberal ways are responsible for that. They said, go to other places and see how everything has been black and white from the very start. No one had the courage to utter a peep. If you must stay, recognize your place and stay in it, and don't try for equality.

People began to say that democracy had been terribly misused. It had become a weapon for spreading anarchy. Defiance was growing in the name of rights. People were getting more selfish. And loyalty? Loyalty was nowhere to be seen.

That year, people were saying that those being harmed in all this were the ones who were too generous and egalitarian. That we Hindus were losing our rights because of them, we were the ones getting beaten, while others took advantage of us; they wanted to dominate us; they were making progress in leaps and bounds, and becoming liberated from all their duties.

People had started to complain that the rules didn't even seem to have been made for them.

'They stroll in, they stroll out,' says Shorty Josh animatedly, 'like this is a garden or something, not a department! If you need to get something typed up, where's Type Babu? Why, he's drinking chai at the Shalimar. When you have to send something to the post office, where's Dagdu? "Oh, no idea." Is this acceptable?' he complains hotly.

'The peons and the typist have seen the ways of the scholars, and now they've all started disappearing,' suggests Urmila, wiping off her spoon with her pallu, before placing it in her tea.

'Then they must be instructed that their work is like that at any other office, and they must stay here from ten to five. They're administrative staff. Or must we be bound by the same rules and regulations as them?' asks Hanif, peeved.

'What does it really mean for a scholar to sit here from ten to five? Should we sit around and talk nonsense? Idle away? Lectures, libraries, field trips, seminars, those are all places for a scholar . . .' Sharad frowns.

'You must crack down on that typist, Sharad,' says Nandan. Hanif glares at him suspiciously.

'But what's left to write about all this? Everything's already been written. All the same things.' Shruti is depressed.

'Isn't that what I've been asking? What's left to write about this!' agrees Daddu.

'Isn't that what I just said?'

Shruti continues to feel depressed.

This, too, has begun: processions of ashramites parading past the university. At the moment when a bit of sunlight remains, yet the sky darkens with a scarlet tinge, dust swirls and everything is clouded in a purple haze.

'Daddu, this is Kapadia,' introduces Sharad. 'Do you recognize him? He's gone bald.'

'Absolutely, I recognize him. Come, come.' Daddu pats the divan.

'This is how I've stayed young!' chuckles Kapadia. 'So what if you kept your hair? It's turned gray, and everyone can see how old you are!'

'What's more, he's grown a beard to further announce his age!' Daddu enjoys Kapadia's joke. Shruti isn't there to count how many buckets they fill with their splashes of laughter.

Thus far everything has been about the ashram temple, but now there's fresh excitement. Devotees arrive from far and wide to bow their heads before the ruins of the mosque at the edge of the city—on to which, it is said, a monkey army climbed and planted the ashram flag, transforming it into a temple.

We've already been to that mosque, no, that temple, or, actually, that ruin that stinks of bats.

We had to go in the ashram van, because our bus broke down along the way, and everyone joked it was hardly an oxcart that it could be started up with a bit of pushing.

'Yes, it's true.'

Sharad's voice has an impressive ring to it, so it has a great impact when he's giving someone a scolding. Hanif is correctly pointing out that Nandu hides behind Sharad.

'It's true,' agrees Sharad again. 'What to do? Even if I speak normally, it sounds like I'm shouting.'

'But more than you, Nandu is annoyed at the typist's waywardness,' explains Hanif.

'So?' Sharad is in a quandary.

'So, my friend, he wants you to do the scolding, so you can be the bad guy; you'll be the unpopular one . . .'

Sharad stares back at him like an idiot.

'Listen, yaar, are you empty up top?' admonishes Hanif as a squirrel leaps out of his way. 'Nandu's fatherly image, of being a sympathetic character, won't be ruined. And who wants to be strict? Who wants to put a stop to things?'

'Meaning we . . .' Sharad stares.

'. . . meaning we're idiots!' laughs Hanif.

'Yaar, he's a genius!' says Sharad.

'No, ji, crafty like a fox!'

'Look, ji, you are a university type. That's not real life. The rest of the city is running on a different type of petrol. Aji, those people don't let you play Holi. The things that are getting stirred up in Hindustan are hair-raising.' Kapadia feels combative.

As does Sharad: 'It's possible,' he says sternly, 'that one particular mohalla may have tried to put a stop to the hubbub of Holi in their area, but investigating the rest of the city on that basis . . .'

'You're the one investigating the entire city, my boy, you and your so-called university intellectuals. The city is something else, something completely different.' Kapadia waves his hands around.

Daddu appears detached from the entire debate.

'But tell me, Daddu, is this Hindustan or Pakistan?' asks Kapadia.

Daddu begins to pay attention.

'And the part of the city I'm talking about, over there, Bhai Sahib.' He bows to Sharad with excessive politeness. 'Over there, for years . . .' At *for years* his eyes bug out as though they've become a pen and thickly underlined the phrase. '. . . Holi was not observed. I'm telling you. I was posted there.'

'What's it to us if you were posted there?' Sharad sulks, lighting a cigarette.

'Now, Holi is an outdoor festival, with joyful dancing and singing under the open sky.' Kapadia sways as he speaks. 'So I resolved that since I'm the police captain, it's my job to tell you whether Holi's going to take place here, or Muharram.'

Daddu stands up and opens the glass door, not completely, just enough to give the smoke a pathway out of the room.

'I put a stop to the bastards' Muharram procession. They've had their fun.' He stops, thinks a moment, looks pleased. 'So I killed two birds with one stone, and clipped their wings!'

Sharad is exasperated.

'One by one, the VIPs in their community came and said, "Sahib, what's this outrage? How did you make this happen?" Wah, why can't I make it happen, Bhai Jaan? Certainly I can! It's a question of law and order, it's my duty to prevent riots. The situation's delicate, I'll take no risks. But, they said, "Captain Sahib, you've only done it for our ritual mourning." And I said, "You got that right, just for your ritual mourning!"'

Kapadia's laughter pushes Sharad to sit on the divan with Daddu. He stubs out the rest of his cigarette and throws it away.

'To hell with mourning! This is a festive country. We engage in boisterous feasting when someone dies! Even when we're carrying the corpse, we swing it around and bounce it up and down!'

Daddu begins to laugh and bounce up and down himself.

'Down with mourning!' cries Kapadia, seeing Daddu happy. 'Tell me, miyan,' he adds, turning towards Sharad, 'is this Hindustan or Pakistan? Should there be Holi or Taziya?'

Sharad doesn't respond, but his silence isn't devoid of content either. So should I write *Sharad* and then, after that, draw a line indicating an empty space? Like this: 'Sharad —'?

When holidays came, we both observed and feared them. That year, there were fireworks, but also bombs and guns. We trembled at every explosion: Was it this or was it that?

When Daddu goes off to the bathroom, Hanif does two things. The first one is . . . yes, that: he augments the shimmering liquid in his and Sharad's glasses. And the second? He tells a couple of stories.

'". . . this is truly the Kali Yug!" cried the elder. "And here we'd been living by all the rules. The whole world knew I was having an affair with the low-caste Chamarin, but I followed all the rules of purity and pollution, kept my food separate and uncontaminated, and never, ever kissed her on the lips." So you see, bhai, there are principled people out there!'

'And romances!' laughs Shruti.

'But,' says Sharad, lost in thought, 'all the same, in truth, he's not a communalist.' Seeing Shruti start, he quickly adds: 'Don't get me wrong, but Kapadia's bark is worse than his bite. All the same . . .'

'Get you wrong how? I haven't understood you from the start.' Shruti looks disgusted.

'Some of it . . . I can't understand either . . .' replies Sharad.

'Did you see this?' Sharad shows a circular to Hanif. 'Starting next year, there'll be a rotation of the headship.'

'I saw. Want to try some?' asks Hanif.

'What are they? Give me one. A bit of achar, that's good—enough, enough. So that's why Nandu has been irritable. If the VC had waited two years, Nandu would simply have retired as head. Yum, this is delicious with the white radish.'

'It makes no difference. No matter who becomes the new head, Nandu will hold on to the reins. Only he knows all the needs of his "baby", and he has all the connections, so no one will oppose him.'

'You, sir, are up next. Be prepared.' Sharad licks his fingers.

'Me? Never.' Hanif wipes up the oil with a paper napkin. 'I couldn't tolerate a headship even in name with his constant interference. All the signatures would be mine, but . . .'

'Like, take him away, put him in jail, off with his head!' giggles Sharad.

'People will come begging for refuge and justice of Emperor Jehangir. Save us from this evil Nadir Shah!' says Hanif.

'Babur. Make it Emperor Babur. Babur is the cool Mughal these days!'

'But I said . . .' Kapadia is back on the same subject again. '. . . only two things can happen—either a legal case or martyrdom. Either file a lawsuit or die a martyr. Now there's already been a lot of martyrdom. People have run out of patience. So sometimes we go too far. But then, both sides go too far.'

'Kapadia, what are you talking about? I must take you to task,' objects Sharad. 'When you were about to elope with Nusrat, I remember it well, you . . .'

'Shh! Shh! Shh!' Kapadia puts a finger to his lips. 'Never bring up the Nusrat saga in front of the wife. Nusrat was such an amazing debater.' He punches the arm of the sofa. 'She knocked me out cold. Totally! Daddu, the way Muslims express themselves is just wow. What can I say? When Nusrat spoke, she was so articulate. Our girls are taught to speak softly; they're taught to speak with their mouths closed. One moves her lips, the other merely mumbles.'

'And then?' interrupts Sharad.

'That's it! We couldn't get married. My father set me straight. In this entire world you only found this one girl? Fool, said my father, have you ever seen a wasp's nest? If one wasp flies out alone, will it change its nature? Who will tell him,' he gasps, 'that my wife is not from that nest? But she's a wasp for sure, and oh, how she stings!' He begins looking merrily back and forth, as though fearing she could be hiding nearby and listening. 'She's not listening, is she?'

Even Sharad sneaks a glance at the door, as though someone might be there.

'I'm telling you the truth, Daddu.' Kapadia prattles on. 'I don't believe in all this, but we can't pull the veil of idealism over our eyes like these intellectuals. I'll tell you the truth and nothing but.'

'In the police profession, do you see many Hindi films?' jokes Sharad.

'It was police work that pulled the blindfold from my eyes. Then I saw things for what they were: Dhritarashtra was dhattrashtra, and blind justice was for the birds!'

'Kapadia!' Sharad reprimands him.

'Listen, first,' roars back Kapadia. 'I have seen such bullying. In one place, they wouldn't even let Hindus burn their corpses. People put clay lamps on the chests of their deceased and floated them down the river.'

Sharad is getting angry.

'Do some research, Kapadia. In this country, there are separate laws for burning and burying. Both communities have influenced one another. In Gujarat today there are still Hindu graves . . .'

'You people keep looking all over, but you ignore what's right before your eyes. Actually, my dearest wish is to once, just once, shoot straight at the enemy and quench the fire in my soul.'

Sharad maintains his silence.

'They themselves are frightened now, the fools! But my goddamn desire to shoot at them has remained a fantasy. The fire in my heart still burns,' Kapadia practically sings.

Sharad is silent.

'Moreover,' says Kapadia, 'The bullet flew into the mosque-cum-temple when there wasn't so much as a hint of a Muslim nearby.'

'Don't delude yourself. For ages, pirs and maulvis have been rolling out prayer rugs and offering namaz there whenever they passed that mosque,' shouts Sharad.

'What world do you live in? There are pujas happening there now. A police unit's also on duty there; they remove their shoes and report for duty. It's already become a temple.'

'You can't just castrate it to turn it into something else,' interjects Daddu. 'Then you simply neuter it.'

Shruti is again determined that she must write—about all of this—but not a report, not a thesis, not a charming story. What rasa to choose, what style, how to write?

And this is why she can't write.

'You must give on festivals,' the maid is telling Shruti.

'Must? Meaning what?' Shruti feels angry. 'You haven't worked here a month yet, and now you're demanding something nearly every day because of the curfew.'

'But it's not my fault there's a curfew.' The maid's banging the pots and pans.

'The one before, she never made these demands. I do dislike them . . .'

'I don't make demands either.' Now she's digging in her heels. 'I'm telling you the custom for festivals.'

'We don't celebrate festivals. There's no joy in celebrating festivals when people are fighting over them. We don't celebrate them.' Shruti makes a face.

'I know what festival you celebrate,' whispers the maid. Then she laughs and looks up at Shruti. 'Eid.'

The voices from the ashram loudspeaker pour continuously into the university. Some of the teachers have started to close their windows.

A group of students is discussing the noise.

'Today I heard them talking about changing all the names. Names of places . . . They'll soon attack the name of the university!'

Professor Nandan scolds them for not discussing their studies these days—this isn't right.

'Everything's getting more separate, more distant, more devious.'

Shruti peers below to see who's speaking.

Two women are walking down the street, talking.

'I want a nice kota sari—I'll wear it in summer. A nice one— no matter how costly—with a narrow zari border, or zari with checks, not an ordinary one.'

Then they turn into the colony.

They're no longer visible, no longer audible.

Everyone is terribly anxious. More than fifty people have been killed in less than half an hour, and children were among them. Most were trampled underfoot. Regarding the rest, according to the newspapers, the medical opinion is that they died of asphyxiation.

What happened was that a crowd went with the political leaders to the neutered temple–mosque, or whatever it is, to offer namaz. Maghrib namaz. The police stopped them along the way, shot four bullets into the air and started swinging their lathis. People fled in a panic; some were trampled underfoot.

There was no need for tear gas, because after that, there was no one left.

Babu Painter says all this happened before anyone realized it. When the crowd thinned, they saw among the scattered shoes and sandals left behind in the tumult small, scattered heaps taking their last breaths, or not even that any more. Babu Painter says you can't declare such people killed in a riot.

The department members are signing a letter of complaint about the loudspeakers, prepared by Sharad and Hanif.

Nandan laughs mid-sip, at which a small fountain of tea sprays from his mouth.

'Don't the ashramites have the democratic right, eh?' he laughs as he signs.

'That's in very bad taste,' says Hanif. 'They're absurdly announcing anything they please, such as that Devi herself is delivering the honour of death to the sinners. And you're making jokes?'

'Bhai, wah, your jokes are in good taste, and your legal demands are in good taste—for the greater good! While I'm in bad taste, and I'm setting up a police state!'

There's tension.

Only the cats are coming into the streets. No one goes out if they can help it. Kapadia has phoned.

'A committee has been set up to investigate the State Reserve Police Force,' he tells them.

Cats have taken over the city. One is crossing the street, another suns herself on a parapet, a third stands at the bus stop squinting from right to left.

Daddu isn't getting up and turning off the television, but he's not watching the interviews either. He chats quietly with his glass. He stares at the glass and murmurs to himself. Now he has set it down, and his fingers, not his hands, are wiggling and telling him something.

City of cats.

In those days, in this city of ours, religion was distributed via loudspeakers, and on quiet nights, kittens cried on the boundary walls of our homes.

So many bowed their heads in shame, thinking we have created a country of demons; demons who have wiped out the sacredness of religion.

That year, gods were systematically cultivated. Seeds were planted, and teeny idols of Devi Jagadambe were placed atop them. And when the earth split, and the plant and the Devi sprouted, *Jai Jagadambe!* rang from the loudspeakers. So loudly the walls shook, as did the foundations of the churches and mosques.

Even the temple foundations shook.

Yes, bricks were smashed in our country that year, but perhaps the truth was that the very foundations of our nation shook. Clouds of dust rose, the terrified crowd trampled, sticks and stones rained down.

One such stone landed on Sharad's forehead.

I am silent.

Don't interrupt my silence. It's hard to say how much hustle it contains, how much bustle, how much copying without taking a single breath.

That's why I'm silent. But I only look silent.

Like these two, who sit before me, silently. Like these pages lying open before me, scattered and disorganized.

Now I must gather the courage to describe a scene that occurred in this place at this time. It didn't happen exactly this way, nor all at this exact time, nor in this exact location, nor was it copied down, all collected in one place in these pages of mine. But in my attempt to gather the scattered fragments of the moment, I've tried to draw inspiration from Shruti's game of collecting the laughter splashing from the divan, sometimes filling up an entire Scotch bottle, or maybe just the equivalent of an Amul butter tin, or, on special days, enormous canisters that grew so heavy you couldn't pick them up.

The house belongs to Daddu, who lives downstairs, who does not lock the door, who does not go outside, and whose village . . . But was it a village or a town, and did it even exist? No one knows. Daddu sits alone on the divan, but we must go upstairs, so I'm shifting the spotlight. Light down . . . down . . . off. I see how dark it has become. But will Daddu continue to glow like a heater element after the lights are dimmed?

Upstairs. Hanif and Shruti have been Daddu's tenants for years. Shruti was a student in the beginning and now is Hanif's wife, and a writer who writes a lot if you don't count that year. Hanif is a well-known professor, popular among students for his informal style of conversing, his knack for storytelling and his good cheer, but many of the teachers believe he's a seminar-worshipping, abroad-revering know-it-all.

Sharad, Daddu's son, Hanif's old friend, is himself well known. He speaks loudly, but he also lets others speak, and he listens, which makes it seem as though he's agreeing with them. If he becomes combative, he shares his two bits, then buries the hatchet, and that's why even his enemies join hands with him.

So this is the scene.

Laddus are being eaten, chai is being drunk. And as happens during these debates in which students are included, some tea has spilt, some laddu crumbs have scattered. Carting off a single crumb is a phalanx of ants, a tiny team of labourers.

And yes, the madhumalti vine is heavy with fragrant blossoms that entice the twittering birds, even if its leaves wither and scatter below in the yard outside Daddu's door. A cat has come in from the street and cleans her whiskers on the balcony.

Correction: a cat hasn't come, because then I'd have to chase away the birds. Which I do not wish to do.

I'm sitting at my desk ready to work.

Now let's suppose that here the voices are growing louder, more intense, jostling; the debates flow freely, just the way it happened over and over throughout that year; the fragrance of the flowers wafts in with the breeze; the cooker whistle blares; and that car drives by honking its weeping baby horn, installed by some rich brat according to the flavour of the day.

Did you suppose? Now suppose this, too, that due to the fast talking of the speakers, the ink in my pen keeps running dry, and I fear losing forever what I've been copying, right in the middle, as I endeavour to refill the ink, and so my only recourse is to sit down with the pot open in front of me, dip my pen and write. Like the scribes of bygone years!

'Why is our gaze stuck on bygone eras? Why are we so pessimistic about today and the coming days that we only look backwards, and even then, we search for symbols of alienation? Why don't we speak of Nazrul Islam, Amir Khusro?'

'Why don't we look at the expansion of the language, when words from Arabic, Farsi, Sanskrit and everyday speech were mixing together and creating a new language?'

'That's how language thrives.'

'But since the nineteenth century, Hindi and Urdu began to develop separately, no?'

'It was both things. Look at the language of Wali, Meer and Sauda, or look at Nazir Akbarabadi. Listen to the musical compositions of Adarang and Sadarang, and the prayers to pirs, Kaaji Karim, Krishna, everyone.'

'Hold on. Wait a minute. Listen to this. It's an old composition. Bhimsen Joshi's singing. Listen:

sumiraun tero naam
jiiv diya sab sansaar
he kaaji kariim
araj karat ibrahiim
mere to maula
tujh bin kaun nistaare
sumiraun tero naam

We remember your name
you created the world, you created creatures
oh, Qazi Karim
Ibrahim begs of you
that truly, oh, master
without you I have no one

who can give me salvation
and take me across the sea of life
and so I recite your name

'To the point that many of the colours and images we now use regularly are mostly from that time when our mixed culture was created. Colours like mehndi, rani pink, firozi turquoise; patterns like chintz and lahariya embroidery . . . Who knows what actually remains from before, from the Vedic tradition?'

I'm writing continuously, and I have another clever idea—this is not stolen from anybody—I won't write the names of those speaking the dialogue, and I'll leave out the quotation marks. So much ink, so much paper, so many moments I save.

We humans often make one particular mistake: we believe the fact that something that has occurred is proof of its inevitability.

That it was meant to happen.

But isn't it possible the reason why it happened no longer exists?

Were there no other factors that might have brought about different results?

And then why didn't something different happen? Couldn't they have done something else?

I want to raise the question of women as an example: Right now, women aren't as successful as men in many fields. Haven't you heard this is due to their limitations? Meaning women are like this, that's why it happened.

Because there's so much hostility; that's why it's happening; that's why it had to happen.

There is hostility, sir, we can't deny that. There are also vested interests, of course, but there's so much hostility, sir.

And the hostility's getting more oxygen.

Not just oxygen, it's also getting plenty to eat and drink. How easily people ignore the things we have in common. Even the media doesn't pay attention.

Look, sir, all the mullahs in the world are going mad, Muslims are banding together, helping each other out, even here . . .

And those not banding together—there's a price on their heads—and in our country at least, not much effort is put into protecting them.

Also, it's clear that the progressive Muslims are speaking from a joint forum, not as Muslims.

And why are you accusing the mullahs of being aggressive, when the pandits and priests are doing the same thing? Religious extremism exists in every religion, but there are also those who speak against it.

Sir, our education system is flawed, it has made us forget how religion flows in the veins of the people; we think we're liberal only if we ignore religion.

You're making a huge mistake; you're dividing things into the wrong categories. On the one hand, we have religion and extremism, and on the other, those who are educated, liberal, agnostic. But these things can exist side by side in the same person. Not all educated people are agnostics, nor all uneducated people illiberal, nor all Hindus and Muslims extremists.

All the same, most Muslims are like that, educated or not . . . there's so much backwardness . . .

That's enough talk of Muslim backwardness. The government also wrongs them greatly.

You're right. It does wrong them. And that brings out their communalist natures and becomes a way for the government to absolve itself of the onerous responsibility of fulfilling their basic needs in life, just giving them the sop of special recognition for their community.

This is too much, sir. Must we come up with the cure for every one of their problems? Are we responsible for everything? Is it all the fault of the Hindus?

No, but the Hindus are more at fault, because they're in the majority.

Enough, enough. Are we still going on about what Nehru said, that the majority has more of an obligation to prevent the poison of communalism?

How can you not believe that? The poison that spreads throughout society blends into everyday life and begins to look ordinary, like the natural order of things, so much so that it no longer seems like poison, while the community feeling of the minority stands separate, unnatural, distorted, loud and visible. Spotting it and attacking it becomes much easier.

We've been looking for the causes forever. And whatever they've been doing forever, they're doing it even more now, and more aggressively.

It's a lie that one community kept demolishing temples to convert everyone to their religion, while the other community was completely tolerant, arms outstretched, and just kept welcoming everyone. Communities aren't divided into black and white, nor is truth, nor is society.

Forget the welcoming bit. Want to know how much Hindus stick to their own? Go abroad and you'll see.

Are we only secular if we bad-mouth Hindus? Why do we only bad-mouth Hindus?

We do the same for Muslims, but we must follow different parameters for each.

Oh, the majoritarian thing again.

That too. But more. For example, do Hindus have to prove all the time that they belong in this country?

Listen, I'll play you a Begum Akhtar recording where she says over and over, 'Our country, that is, Hindostan.' Why does she need to explain? Is there any doubt?

They've given rise to doubt with their tricks.

But we started it with our suspicions. Look, if they worship Mecca and Medina, is that treason? If the Hindus of Mauritius consider Kashi a pilgrimage site . . .

All Muslims consider Pakistan their be-all and end-all.

All? What nonsense! You'll find many who don't have anything to do with Pakistan, and even if they do, they don't see any opportunities for themselves there. And those who see them in Pakistan or in Kuwait . . .

But Hindus and Christians also see opportunities in the Middle East. And as for America . . .

For all of you now . . .

. . . not for all of us . . .

. . . well, anyway, for many like you, it's become the be-all and end-all. Does that bother you? Everyone dreams of a better life. They go get a green card and later become American citizens, but even then, we're proud of them.

Not us.

Well, many. But if you say Muslim, or Pakistan, then everyone starts whining about nationalism.

Why are you whining?

If Hindus say the Constitution is bad and burn the tricolour, we say they have the right to criticize, but if Muslims do something similar, they're the enemy of the nation.

Arre, bhai, take it easy.

This is a friendly debate.

I know. But that's a double standard.

Here, have another laddu.

Oh! Your hair smells of ghee.

Ghee is good for hair; it turns it black!

Heavens, no! Why would I put ghee in my hair? I use coconut oil.

But then how come? The truth will out. Smell.

You've eaten a lot of laddus; you must have wiped your hands on your hair.

Yes, laddu has the same smell.

It must have risen from your belly and found whatever empty space it could and arrived there, and now it's coming out of your head.

Ha ha ha!

Ha ha ha!

Well, you got rid of your anger by making us look small, so we'll put up with it. Please accept our gratitude.

We Hindus have always been tolerant, my darling, and have expressed our gratitude.

First of all, don't call me a Hindu, and second of all, stop saying *always always*.

Ha ha ha!

Now you're getting angry? Like your Hindu sisters.

But, sir, we just said this as a joke; but sir, people seriously believe that Hindus should feel angry.

Look, ji, even for Hindus, in this age of modern change, the opportunities are shrinking and uncertainties are growing, so they're getting frustrated with whomever they must share their prospects. They don't want to cede any ground at all.

It seems from what you're saying that the Hindus are the villains and the Muslims are just scapegoats.

Oh, and also, the scapegoat theory . . .

Arre, I hope Shorty Josh isn't listening!

Ha ha ha!

But all joking aside, the things we're saying put the bad guys on one side and the innocents on the other. That the Muslims are getting all the beating. The Muslims are innocent, they're just backward; that's why they don't try to mix with the rest. If they fight, they've been incited, so they're innocent. But isn't this an injustice to us Hindus? Their mindset has also emerged from their circumstances. You say yourself the illusion of reality is also an important reality. In every situation it seems to the Hindus that they themselves are the minority, not in terms of numbers but in terms of real power.

Now you're talking like these ashramites . . .

But are all the ashramites crazy? I also want to ask why we're repeating only those things about the Hinduists which they say hysterically, aggressively, madly, badly, rudely, giving them a bad name. So, what I'm asking is . . .

Speak, speak, don't hesitate, we want an open debate.

I forgot. If I remember, I'll say.

Fine, but I do want to give one answer to the question about why we speak only of the hysterical things the Hinduists say. Because when they don't say such crazy things . . .

Then, too, they show malice towards Muslims.

It's possible, but the path to friendship and dialogue isn't closed off there. There are various views, but there's always respect for humans, and the philosophy of live and let live. You and I are both humans, after all, right . . .

Shall I recite a sher by Ghalib? Daddu told it to me:

Bas ki dushvaar hai har baat kaa aasaan hona
Aadmi ko bhi muyassar nahin insaan hona

How difficult it is for each thing to be simple
Even for man, it's not easy to be human

Wah!
True!
It's not easy to be human. Beautiful.
It's great you didn't say wow.
Can I write it down? Will you recite it again?
How difficult it is for each thing . . .

Thing or *task*?

Hmm? *Task* maybe. Or *thing*. I'll have to ask.

Fine, I'll ask him when I'm leaving.

But, sir, I still don't understand. Hearing the same things from all sides makes me dizzy. If you'll permit me . . .

Don't ask for permission, go ahead. We're all just trying to understand.

I didn't mean you, so don't take it the wrong way, please, but Muslims have made no effort, they just keep apart and mistrust . . .

That's not correct. There are also those who live side by side with others . . .

But less so.

Hindus, too, haven't made much effort to reassure. They've added to the suspicion. If both sides meet more, if there's open dialogue, there'll be fewer misconceptions, and . . .

I keep getting angry when they cheer for Pakistan.

But how many cheer? Okay, maybe some excited kids feeling wilful or combative—they might cheer sometimes. But how big a deal is that?

Listen, the concept of national borders is rather strange. They cannot divide people. Listen, once I went to the border in Rajasthan. On this side was Tharparkar Road, on that side the village of Tharparkar. The jeep climbed a sand dune, and I was shown where the border was from the Border Security Force watchtower. Aha, so this is the border? This is Hindustan, and that's Pakistan!

And Bishen of 'Toba Tek Singh' died right in the middle.

Such a muddle. We live this side; that side is supposed to be our enemy. But they're our relatives! How to deal with them as friend and foe at the same time!

All the same, I would say that the Muslims are perverse and seem determined to get beaten.

Yaar, what the hell are you talking about?

You don't mind, sir?

No, speak. So, they're trying to get themselves beaten up?

Any excuse and they pick up a stone.

All over the world, riots begin this way. When minorities feel insecure, they ghettoize themselves, and whenever they feel alarmed or hostile, they pick up a stone. But that's not the real beginning. The humiliation and anger they feel at being sidelined is already there. That's how it begins.

See? There you go again, making them look innocent. They're just reacting. Nowadays, that's exactly what the Hindus are saying, that they're simply reacting.

But that's a lie. No such thing has happened to the Hindus.

What are you trying to say?

That there's so much that's wrong, and it's neither entirely the fault of the Hindus nor of the Muslims, and nor is confrontation the solution. Both must be on the same side as one team and try to iron out their differences.

All these arguments seem so hollow. No one takes us seriously.

Forget about no one. Do you even take yourself seriously? If not, then first sort through the confusion in your own mind. Exercise your discernment. Is there a difference between a Muslim like Hanif and a Hindu like Sharad?

What do you mean?

There isn't, but at the same time there is!

Amazing. Then I'll just keep quiet.

No, don't keep quiet. Focus. Isn't there a difference? Why is there a greater difference between them than there is between two Hanifs in two different locations? Imagine a Keralite Hanif and a Lucknawi Hanif. Or how about the difference between Prince Hanif and low-caste Bhangi Hanif? Or the difference between a Bhangi Hanif and a Bhangi Sharad?

But these differences . . .

Might it be your own prejudice that makes this difference seem so great? To me this is more . . .

What if they're from one place, but educated, and recognized as belonging to different religions?

Yes, such a Hindu and such a Muslim will be similar . . .

No, sir, what I was saying got lost again. I wasn't talking about the two of you, but of those living that side. Over there, sir, I feel afraid going into the Muslim neighbourhoods.

As do they, coming to your side.

All the same, they know that there's no such danger for them on our side, like . . .

Yes, this we must admit. Perhaps they're simply more prone to violence.

Because they're accustomed to halal butchering.

True, I once went to a halal butcher. Not the slightest hesitation when it comes to bloodletting.

They enjoy killing. I'm not saying that, but that's what people say about them.

Bhai, wah, then the doctor community must be the most bloody of all, always hacking people up, corpses dripping blood everywhere, they must love it. In that case, it would surprise me if any doctor were a vegetarian.

And how about those women who won't kill lizards or cockroaches? They must be so soft-hearted, such delicate natures.

But surely you've heard they set their daughters-in-law on fire, then stand back and watch the show? They burn them alive.

What connections you're making!

Arre, baba, I dropped my cup!

Why are you speaking so hysterically?

Hysteria. I have something I'd like to say about that, but you'll have to be quiet for a moment. Let me wipe this up.

You tell; I'll do it.

Okay, leave it, I'll do it later.

No, I'll do it. You tell please . . . the ants will come.

I'm copying it all down, I'm copying it all down.

Okay, look over there . . . that's it. I must have put it in the small bucket, thank you. Yes, hysterical. Tell me, why are women diagnosed with the sickness of hysteria more than men? Because their limited freedom to make choices and advance causes frustration and suffocation. Men can achieve that with greater ease. I'm speaking generally; I'm not bringing up the finer points yet. Men appear cultured and peace-loving because they get what they want without fighting. But women have to fight every time, and it makes them look all monstrous and shrill. Now if a man begins to shriek and allege exploitation, won't it seem ridiculous?

Women must scream to get anything. Men scream when they lose.

Now you're going a bit far . . .

Generally speaking, this is the issue. It's the same with Hindus and Muslims. Generally. All these things have to do with weak vs strong groups.

Muslims are entirely communalist.

So are Hindus.

But in one case it comes from insecurity and fear, and in the other, from strength and egotism. One must look at the differences between the two kinds of screaming. Both need our understanding, but if we have sensitivity, then we'll sympathize more with the weaker side.

We're sensitive, but they aren't.

They, meaning who?

The Muslims . . .

But we're not Hindus or Muslims.

I'm not.

I am but not that kind.

Like what?

Like them. Who live over there. Who start riots. Who cause bloodshed.

Do you know what riots are? Shruti rises. The real riots are happening there, where the blood flows.

Suddenly everyone falls silent, like when all the shops shut their metal shutters at once at the start of a curfew.

When the moment has passed, everyone begins to scatter. The students are saying bye, the teacups are being gathered, and downstairs, at Daddu's place, Bade Ghulam Ali Khan is singing *Hari om tatsat* on the radiogram.

Who knows what Shruti meant when she declared that the true riot occurs there, where the blood flows.

And my pen continues to write: *there, where the blood flows.*

And, oh, good people, here too it flows, in our veins, beneath this thin skin of ours!

Humans disappeared from the streets and cats took to wandering about in the open. Then we'd lie low in our houses, panicked, surrounded by the silence of cats. There was an unfamiliar hubbub that year that began to unnerve us. Bits and pieces lay strewn everywhere, many of which were invisible to us. Everyone was picking up whatever fragments they liked, fitting them together, creating myriad stories. We feared this could mean no story was true. Then all the bits would fall silent, lying scattered about us.

The ashram stood at the centre of it all: us on this side, them on that. We were told there had always been two categories, Hindu and Muslim, and even today these two were distinct: Hindu and Muslim. We never believed that, and we insisted that there were always many kinds of Hindus and many kinds of Muslims, as there are today; go look over there. In the centre, the ashram, over here, us, over there, all of them, all sorts of Hindus and Muslims.

It wasn't as if when things happened, we didn't understand that the *those-people* and the *over-there* theory should be rejected. But before we could reject it and crush it and throw it away, those people, who were not that far away, but rather peering out from under the skin of the over-here people, crushed these people.

But then.

But then a lot of time passed, and that year became the past year, and looking at it from this distance we had the illusion that the whole thing was perfectly clear to us, as though we were the viewers and that year was painted on canvas.

But a year that's sunk into the crevices of history will become nothing more than a skeleton. All we can do is pull it out and pair it with its former flesh and appearance, and imagine what sort of attire had clothed it in that era. Creating one more story.

But why not look at it differently? Why not accept that, contrary to what we assume, that year has not yet passed, because we've dragged it into these next years, weighing them down? If so, then what? Then this story, which has been forged from the buzzing of the radio, TV and newspaper, but also from the shrinking silences between them, belongs as much to those who died as to those who did not, and not just to those ones but also to these ones, and the dead play as much of a role as the non-dead. If so, where will it all lead?

And I fear that perhaps those ones had existed within us before as well, and perhaps that year is still happening and has not actually passed at all.

Yes, I know I've fallen silent again.

But no, I'll not remain so. I'll keep copying.

Let me just touch these pages for a moment as I copy down the sights from home, the department, from here, from there.

Every day finds Shruti, pen in hand. She's attempting to write what she has in mind, and that has brought everything to a standstill. But she sits down as usual, her home as her office, at 9.30 a.m., and stays there until five, except for a half-hour lunch break, staring at the madhumalti, pen at the ready, distraught.

'It's not happening,' she complains to Hanif.

'Then write something else,' he suggests.

'Are you managing to write anything?' she asks, incensed.

'Truly,' says Hanif, 'these days are ruining any chance of work.'

And then there's so much dust flying about that it sneaks through the cracks of closed doors and spreads through the house. At which the maid also stops coming, but now it's not because of the curfew but because of the coconut she bought to make chutney, from which had emerged a stone idol of the Devi. Now she's busy running neighbourhood prayer meetings and promising to erect a small temple to the Goddess. Let the dust fly. That isn't what she says. That's what I say, after seeing piety there, dust here.

Professor Nandan is combing his moustache with his fingers again. He turns his head to one side, grabs a particular hair, snips it with his teeth.

A number of voices have joined to observe that there are those in this so-called important department who have not written a single article in years.

'And you'll force them to sit here morning to night and write books?' jeers Sharad.

'Listen . . .' Hanif smiles.

'A story?' asks Urmila without much enthusiasm.

'No, this is the absolute truth, word for word . . .' says Hanif, placing his hand on his heart and speaking Sanskritized Hindi.

'He's speaking so much Sanskrit, is our Hanif Miyan!' Shorty Josh observes to Nandan, like it's an inside joke.

'At one university, a rule was made that those who have written no books shall never be promoted to the rank of professor. But there was one scholar—I won't tell the name; he's still living and is now a professor—who was upset because he was determined to become a professor no matter what. So listen to what he did. The gentleman went to the National Archives, had a Xerox made of an old official file, gave it separate chapter names, divided it up, then sent it off to a press and had it printed as a book!'

Everyone guffaws.

'This is no laughing matter. It's a thinking matter.' Hanif is also laughing. 'Rules and regulations are no joke.'

Nandan makes another *snip* on his moustache.

'Friends, allow me to waste just a bit more of your precious time,' continues Hanif, growing more theatrical, 'by presenting another tale. There was another gentleman . . .'

'Also a professor?' chuckles Sharad.

'Indubitably!' replies Hanif in Urdu.

'You're showing off your Urdu, Dr Sahib!' Shorty Josh cries.

'I heard that, Josh Sahib. If you keep searching for Sanskrit and Urdu, you'll be deprived of the deep matter I'm relating to you. Please do lend an ear. The gentleman of whom I speak was going to Calcutta to interview for a position as a professor. What to do, poor thing: over the course of his journey his suitcase was stolen. It had contained the press copy of his forthcoming book, which he needed to submit to his publisher. On top of that, the thief had also snatched the notes for his next book. Now this sounds like a special case, no? The interviewers were not cruel. They accepted the gentleman had written two books, and . . .'

'. . . he got the professorship!' cries Sharad, smacking his lips in delight.

'Why wouldn't he?' asks Hanif. 'Everything according to the rules.'

'Two books . . .?' asks one research scholar.

'. . . that have yet to enter this world!' laughs Hanif. 'And now for one tiny, ant-sized . . .' He holds up two fingers as if to smush an ant. '. . . final tale.' He turns towards Shorty Josh. 'This one is true, word for word. A third hopeful held a seminar, compiled the seminar papers, made himself the editor and published the whole thing, and that became his book, and thus he was deemed a professor.'

Snip. Nandan fells another hair.

'Daddu, you're laughing for no reason,' says Shruti.

'Ask her why she's writing all this. And if you don't know how, what will you write? She doesn't know her ABC, and she's gone off to write the entire saga? What? Encyclopedia Devi Ashramika? Hahaha.'

Daddu's laughter seems to inflate balloons that float about the room.

'If you don't understand it, why are you going after it? Let go of the poor thing's tail. Communalism is a cat, whose tail you wish to grab to make it dance. But what is the cat doing? It's just wandering about in the street. The cat is a free animal. Vain and joyful. Belonging to no one. If it can't be captured by anyone else, how can it be captured by you? Arre, leave the poor thing alone. Even if it comes to your house, so what? It will just eat the mice.

You won't learn how to catch mice yourself. Ha ha ha, the poor thing can't even catch mice, but she has big dreams. You sleep. Come here, I'll pat you to sleep, the way your mother did when you were a baby. Then dream you've captured a cat!'

How amazing is Daddu? The room has filled with balloons.

'Everyone must learn how to weave stories from you.' Shruti is charmed.

'That's what I'm saying, but of course you must change the topic.'

Now Daddu is turning the divan into a balloon!

Sharad and Hanif go together to explain to Nandu why they're against the new rule dictating that everyone must sit in the department from morning to evening. It would simply stifle the soul of the department. If people need to work, a work atmosphere will make it happen for them, but you can't force anyone to change. Change should come from within, not from piling on rules. This will needlessly create an atmosphere of suspicion.

'But people are getting suspicious,' explains Nandan. 'Some people are getting more leaves, while others are hunkered down here from morning to evening.'

'But you're here right now,' says Sharad. 'After you leave, they'll use this rule to oppress people.'

'Sycophancy will set in . . .' adds Hanif.

'What can I do?' asks Nandan. 'When absolutely everyone's demanding this . . .'

What Professor Nandan does not say is if the rotation continues, he'll have to leave his chair. Professor Nandan says he's been in bad health, and that 'the wife is also ailing', which is why he's thinking of stepping down and handing the headship to someone else.

When he hears about this, Daddu shrieks with laughter.

Sharad is sitting in the jeep with Kapadia for the procession. The police have given strict orders: no cassettes, no cursing or discourteous shouting. The procession in the Devi's name should proceed respectfully.

A massive crowd has gathered. People shout, *Jai Jagadambe! Jai Jagadambe!* which is neither profane nor rude.

'Processions even here?' asks Sharad.

The jeep advances. One can hear voices chanting softly:

Let's all make India great!
Demolished mosques are in their fate!

'Hey!' thunders Kapadia.

Two officers immediately jump down, brandishing lathis. More voices are audible:

Jai Jagadambe
Devi, your glory is boundless
See us through our troubles
Jai Jagadambe

'What rascals,' says Kapadia, turning to Sharad and laughing.

The procession enters Naya Bazaar. A barber, razor in hand, leans over the lathered face of his customer. He stops mid-shave to watch the procession. Suddenly a young man comes running from a gali screaming, 'Help, help! The Muslims have killed someone! Help, help!'

Knives pop up like balloons. The crowd runs into the gali, out of the gali, screaming. Colours fly. Yellow. Red. Purple.

Why do I smell the stench of a hospital?

The slogans have changed.

'Fire!' commands Kapadia.

Then he makes a phone call.

Three corpses are carried from the gali. One is the old fakir.

'The one who wore a long cloak and carried a brass begging bowl; you'd often find him standing there,' says Shruti.

'Boys will be boys!' quips Kapadia. He has come to the house. 'A few of them were sitting at the dhaba laughing and calling out, "Allahu Akbar, you're a dirty wanker!"'

'Yaar, are you even listening?' asks Sharad with annoyance.

But Kapadia has downed three pegs, and though they were prepared by Daddu, he seems to have grown weary of using his ears and is now running off at the mouth.

'. . . I'll take you to the hospital, I'll show you the Hampi ruins . . . I didn't cry like this when my father died . . .' His speech is slurred.

'Yaar,' counters Sharad, 'you know about the attacks of the sultans on Ram Raja, but not about how Achyut Ray brought in Bijapur's Ibrahim Adil Shah to oppress his own people, nor about how when Ram Raja attacked Ahmad Nagar, he smashed mosques, despoiled women, picked up Qurans to . . .'

But Kapadia wants to say his piece. 'Don't you feel upset when you see smashed temples?' *Slur slur.*

'The history of Vijayanagar is the story of a power struggle, in which sometimes a king would ally with a nawab . . .'

'Didn't the beautiful artwork fill your heart with love?'

'Hampi isn't even Hindu. It's the Indo–Saracenic style, so there are also Islamic features that . . .'

'What things we made . . .'

'. . . include medieval examples.'

Suddenly, Kapadia gets angry. 'I'm fed up, Sharad Miyan, fed up! You people can't stop teaching history. But who are you trying to teach . . .?'

'. . . yes, who?' asks Sharad, also fed up.

'On duty, Kapadia doesn't take sides; that's also the truth,' argues Sharad. 'It's we who want to know everything. For him, none of this is necessary: scrutinizing, expressing, reassessing, asking about the outcome . . .'

When Hanif doesn't seem to agree, Sharad reminds him, 'You yourself were telling the students how many levels of relations and emotions there are in this society. When someone from a low caste, like a Shudra, paints a picture of a god he cannot worship in a temple; just imagine what will come out when he's painting: joy, anger . . .'

'Okay!' Hanif admits defeat and smiles. 'But this concession is the artwork of three pegs!'

'I'm asking why you're getting most upset of all. Come now! If the department goes to hell, let it, but they're not sending you personally to some hellish place!' jests Daddu.

'Daddu, you too!' cries Shruti.

The divan's acting like it's drinking Horlicks!

'All right, bring them,' Daddu motions to Shruti to rise. 'Bring two glasses for these jihadis. Bring one for yourself as well. Now you must be partaking as well even if you try to hide it from me. No, no! Don't be afraid, your Daddu's very liberal! Take a vacation at my department whenever you want, whenever you want, come to class here! Drink whatever you wish!'

'Drink as much as you wish!' laughs Hanif.

'Dole, your Daddu is a true feminist; run and grab a glass for yourself as well. I believe in male–female equality! She's truly silly, this girl, but listen, I too believe in equality! Right?'

His laughter is high-pitched.

'No, I won't take any,' laughs Shruti. 'But I will accept that you believe in gender equality. You're calling these men silly too, like me!'

'Ah ha ha ha! She's getting sharp.' Daddu's delighted, funnelling all the world's sharpness into his sparkling shrieking bouncing.

'Truly I consider all three of you equally ridiculous.'

'Daddu, besides you, who else is sharp?' Shruti is showing her sparkle too.

'Professor Nandan!' he responds immediately.

'Trivedi is happy with our communalism report,' announces Shorty Josh cheerfully.

'This is what's happening.' Sharad punches his fist in the air. 'All Hanif Jaidis have become Hanif Zaidis.'

'Why are you dragging me into this?' objects Hanif.

'Not you. I'm giving your name as an example,' snaps Sharad.

'Why my name? Even when the students come, you give my name as an example . . .'

'Why have you started reacting this way when you hear the word Muslim?' asks Sharad with surprise.

'Why give such examples?' agrees Shruti. 'Speak normally. Yes, so all Muslims are becoming one, and . . .'

'And . . .' Sharad stops, unsure. Should he be annoyed or continue? '. . . all Hindus are one,' he continues. 'The Gulams of Rajasthan and Gujarat are becoming Ghulams, and in Lucknow, Aligarh, people are madly switching their Js to Zs. I don't know why he shies away like this.' Suddenly he begins to berate Hanif again. 'Now I'll hesitate to call you Miyan Bhai. If you won't take a joke as a joke, then . . .'

'Jokes don't always turn out funny,' cautions Shruti.

'Jokes are a sign of good health. Everyone keeps pulling each other's legs. The subject makes fun of the ruler, one caste of another, the Lakhnawi of the Dakhni . . .'

'The man makes fun of the woman, and when she doesn't laugh, he says she's humourless!' retorts Shruti. 'If a joke makes both parties laugh, it's a joke, otherwise, it's an insult; it's disrespect.'

'So I'm disrespecting him?' Sharad again punches his fist in the air.

'Why have you started punching your fist in the air like the ashramites?' Hanif suddenly bursts out laughing.

'Me? Like them?' Sharad is offended.

'Now who's humourless?' Hanif goes from jesting to grave.

Those not obligated to undertake family planning are growing stronger and reproducing like insects. They create their own marriage laws and need only say 'talaq' three times to divorce, so they can keep changing wives throughout their lives, or keep four wives at a time, and when they destroy the virtue of women from another community, their elders give their blessings and say, 'You will enjoy a good fate, my sons,' and they slaughter cows . . .

'Who wrote that?' asks Shruti.

Hanif looks down at the newspaper: '*A Frightened Citizen.*'

'But it sounds more like *A Jealous Citizen* to me!' Sharad smiles.

'Sharad, are you laughing?' teases Shruti.

'No, I'm just reading.' Sharad picks up the book in his lap and shows it to her: *The Invention of the Real.*

Hanif sticks his head out from behind the newspaper. 'Listen to the last line: *And if we rebel against all this, we're told there are other such religions and that you people are being communalists.*'

'So by enumerating the faults of these ones, they prove the virtues of the other religions. This is today's math, Shruti,' remarks Sharad with astonishment.

'Sorry, Hanif,' he says. 'But this is something different!'

I'm stunned and start writing.

'. . . our uncle placed that sword before the gods at our home altar. He says even today that it bears the blood of Muslims.'

Then he adds, 'Sorry, Hanif Sahib!'

Who's this? I stop copying for a moment to discover he's a professor from elsewhere, sipping tea in the staffroom.

'. . . we can't lecture those who experienced Partition. Those whose homes, land, everything ended up over there . . .' He's speaking to everyone, but now and again he looks over at Hanif, as though he's speaking only to him. 'So many times I've yearned to go see for myself the descendants of whoever seized our ancestral home. It must be home for them now. But it's still a piece of our hearts.'

Even Sharad glances at Hanif as though he's waiting for him to speak. Then he himself speaks: 'There are heart-pieces scattered over here as well.'

'Yes, yes.' The stranger professor looks morose. 'What has this hatred to do with us now? We're educated, we and you have remained this side, we're all in same boat; together we'll live, together we'll die.' He's again looking only at Hanif. He's laughing. He's whispering, 'But those Muslims who can't understand this, we'll line them up and set them straight. We too are hot-blooded. We're Sindhi, a cut above the Pathans! Don't know about you.'

Now he's looking at Nandan.

It's not curfew; it's some kind of game! Here we go again.

I feel a sense of temporary relief when I ascertain I'm well stocked with ink.

'What happened?' ask Hanif and Sharad, peering in through the glass door.

Daddu is reading something aloud to Shruti. He stops.

'What happened?' he asks.

'Maybe it's on the evening news.'

They come inside.

The two of them are arguing.

'Why did you keep quiet?' asks Sharad.

'Why was he talking to me alone, not to the rest of you?' Is this Hanif's question or his answer?

'They probably have swords on display over there too. And Hindus there are lined up so they can be taught a lesson . . .'

'Why are you getting so defensive?' demands Hanif.

'You became weirdly quiet,' retorts Sharad.

The two of them continue to argue.

They argue all the time.

'Why are you being so aggressive?' asks Hanif, angrier.

'Make up your mind: Am I defensive or aggressive?' snaps Sharad.

It seems Kapadia has crossed the three-peg mark yet again!

'Put an end to cricket in these two countries. It always increases the danger of rioting,' he says.

'Why are you bringing a fight between two governments into a game?' asks Shruti.

And how does this strike Kapadia?

'It's not just a battle between two governments. They say, this is no game, it's jihad . . .'

'Yaar, the fiery temper stays on the field of play. Afterwards, all are friends,' explains Hanif.

'And in some areas that spirit of friendship grows,' adds Sharad.

Kapadia has fallen silent.

Maybe he hasn't had three pegs!

'We should explain this to people,' he says, his tone changed.

'Totally,' replies Sharad happily.

'Cricket matches will keep happening . . .'

'Yes.'

'. . . and soon they'll create a new Pakistan.'

'Totally,' says Sharad before he has registered what Kapadia has said.

Then he shakes his head in astonishment. 'No!'

When the curfew siren sounds, everyone quickens their pace.

'Menopause?'

Shruti, Hanif and Sharad all begin to laugh hysterically when Daddu suggests this metaphor.

'Him and me.' Daddu lifts the edge of his dhoti to wipe the stars of laughter from his eyes. 'This is our menopause. Our days are coming to an end. We've already done whatever we could. Written books. Travelled.'

'Had children. The department is his baby!' laughs Shruti.

'Had children. That baby of his. These three babies of mine. Now there's nothing left for us. Whatever happened is in the past now. The days ahead belong to a new generation. Imagine our state as all of you pass us by, one after another.'

'But at first he was the furthest ahead,' laughs Sharad.

'Yes!' The divan begins to bob along with Daddu. 'Now they're inviting this guy to Oxford, he's getting book prizes, he doesn't care about Daddu and Nandan Sahib, us two lonely guys! Just as Faiz says:

> *Phir koi aaya dil-e-zaar nahin koi nahin*
> *raah-rau hoga kahin aur chala jaaega*
> *ab yahan, koi nahin, koi nahin, ayega*
>
> *Oh, my aching heart, has someone come? No, it's no one.*
> *Must be a wayfarer, on his way elsewhere.*
> *Now no one will come here, no one at all.*

'Ha ha ha ha!' Daddu expands and bounces upwards. He crows with maniacal laughter. 'Now I can't go anywhere myself, but I can stop you! Arre, have some mercy on us.'

The prime minister will meet with the mahant of the ashram. The city government has installed workers nearby. Hot tar paves the streets and women labourers sit by the sides of the road, down by where the river sometimes flows, toasting thick rotis on clay tawas.

It's the season of riots, the season of curfews, the season of people losing their minds. The season of wreaking havoc, for Hindus, for Muslims.

Three have died.

Now the tally of the dead has increased to five.

According to the latest news, eight people have been killed.

There's a curfew in the city, and the army's doing a flag march in sensitive areas.

One hears that a modern flyover will be built across from the ashram. It will be called the Jagadambe Flyover.

The situation is tense but under control.

The members of the department have got special permission to do a peace march. Babu Painter has said they'll print advertisements for it in the newspaper, inviting the like-minded to join.

Now it's being debated whether Hanif and a few of the Muslim students, such as Musheer and Taslima, should march in front with their peace posters, or all the way in the back.

I was following them around, taking down all they said, heard, saw, but I also started to fear it was just the same thing over and over. Always the same flavour.

Then there'd be more riots, then another curfew, then things would relax a bit. Then there'd be another interfaith meeting and another peace march.

We were always the same people marching, messages of peace on banners held high, flanked by rows of policemen. Those peering down from their windows regarded us with silent contempt, and we averted our eyes when we saw one another, because even to us it seemed this would make no difference. It was all so pointless.

As though that year itself was pointless. Everything about it was pointless: everyone simply re-enacting the same drama, all our roles already established. You'll kill again, you'll die again, you'll be photographed again, you'll write words of goodwill, you'll sit apart and not get involved in these squabbles, you'll open the door and say, 'I'm not coming unless they bring up the Kashmir problem,' and, no matter what you hear see read, you'll continue to believe that only Hindus have been killed and only temples have been demolished, and you'll only open your mouth in order to say this.

Statistics were pointless. History itself was pointless. For our benumbed brains, numbness had become pointless. Reactions to news of bizarre forms of looting, killing and rape had been reduced to *uffo, tsk tsk*, and were also pointless.

The mob of spectators called the peace march a joke and burst out laughing.

Late at night, Shruti awakes. She shakes Hanif lightly, and the two of them begin to talk.

'As though nothing is shifting at all, everything is right where it was, no one is changing. Somewhere within the layers, behind the arguments, hidden in the depths, lies that point which is the root, that one solid thing, untouched by argument or the air surrounding the riots. An untouched, self-satisfied point, where Hindus and Muslims have been against one another since who knows when.'

'They have been though, that's all there is to it,' says Shruti.

'You will completely ignore us.' Hanif holds her head in his hands.

'Us?' Shruti looks at him attentively. 'Who is us?'

'Us is not them,' he says after some thought.

'You believe that?'

'You don't?'

They lie close together and go to sleep. And everything that happened that year keeps on happening.

'I'm telling the truth,' Sharad says to Hanif. 'Kapadia has forbidden any policeman on duty from wearing a tilak while doing police work.'

The pigeons continue with their cooing, beaks shut.

'All right, quiet everyone. Hanif will now tell me why he doesn't want to become head.' Daddu waves his hand to stop everyone's chirruping.

'Forget it, Daddu. First of all, I'm afraid Nandan will be able to jerry-rig this process to keep it from happening before his retirement.'

'Yaar, it's a university rule, not his own personal decision,' interrupts Sharad.

Daddu again holds up a hand to silence them. 'Okay, let's take it as a given that he can do such a thing. But then, after two years, your number will still come up. What I want to know is, if he can't get his way then, why wouldn't you agree?'

'I'll say I'm not available,' replies Hanif.

'But Daddu is asking why,' Shruti reminds him.

'Look, Sharad became a professor one week after me; making him the next head will be no problem. What I don't want is for Mother Nandan to tell me how to do every little thing: bathe the baby like this, dress it like that.'

'So he won't nag if it's me?' asks Sharad.

'You can humour him . . . you don't tell stories!'

'The mama–baby–ayah syndrome,' laughs Shruti.

'Menopause syndrome!' declares Daddu. 'Would it be possible for the department to retire along with Professor Nandan?'

And without waiting for their laughter, he begins to bounce.

Shorty Josh comes rushing in.

'Someone pulled the emergency chain to stop a train travelling through a deserted area just outside our city! Many men were murdered and women attacked.' He pauses and looks over at the women, then says, 'They raped them with iron bars.'

Everyone trembles and cries out. Sharad is about to say something. But he's shaking and keeps quiet.

Shruti opens the gate and enters. She's about to go straight upstairs when the downstairs door opens. She starts and turns.

Daddu is standing there.

'Arre!' Now she's even more startled. One never encounters Daddu at the door. 'What's wrong, Daddu?'

He stands there calmly.

'Where are you coming from?' he asks. It's a simple question, but not simple, because Daddu has got up to come and ask it.

'I was at the library, Daddu.'

'Yes, yes.' He shakes his head. 'Show me your new books.' He smiles and turns back, but he doesn't seem completely at ease.

Shruti laughs and answers, 'They're completely new writers. You wouldn't understand them! I also took out that Tagore book you were reading to me in Bangla. Now I'll read it in English! I'll be right back.'

By the time she returns, Sharad and Hanif have also arrived.

'Who was she, Daddu?' they ask.

Daddu chuckles. 'It must have been Shruti Sen. Arre, she's a loony Bengali. She used to visit a long time back, then she became a renunciant or something and disappeared somewhere in the Himalayas! Actually, I was in the bathroom when the phone call came. Nankau picked it up. He said, "It's Shruti Memsahib, she says she'll call again, she says she's not feeling well." Ha ha ha!'

He bounces lightly, like a tennis ball.

'So did she call again, or not?' asks Hanif.

'She didn't. So then I called you. I'd forgotten all other Shrutis besides this one. When you said you'd just seen her, she was writing over there, then I realized that other loony must have called. Where the devil did she appear from? The amazing thing is how everyone in the world with the name Shruti is a loony!'

But really, there's only one person in this world who seems like a loony right now, and that's Daddu!

People are greeting one another. Hello hello.

'Wah, Head Sahib, this is a totally new look! The achkan looks wonderful on you.'

'Ha ha ha ha!' Professor Nandan laughs coyly and blushes. 'I just felt since the world isn't changing, I should change myself.'

'That's the truth. Let's change ourselves. That's the only way to change the world.'

There seem to be more ashram vans now. Today, two stop in front of the university. One can make out the Devi on the bonnet from far off. She has the calves of a fleshy war maiden and wears a laangh-style sari. Her fiery eyes glitter like embers, and her loose hair rises skywards as though cavorting with the clouds.

Shruti and Hanif are also sitting with Kapadia.

'Everything's already happened now,' he's telling them. 'People are fed up. They're openly giving us the names of the troublemakers from both sides. If the government showed any strictness, they'd keep all the religious types at home. That's what needs to happen. Anyway, this time the Muslims have taken quite a beating. Wasn't I telling you, Sharad? Khojas, Bohras, people who don't even fully consider themselves Muslims, they've also been attacked. The cruellest of men will weep. They've attacked helpless people, and they're asking why are you killing us; we're Memons . . .'

Sharad laughs and says, 'But you said Muslims are so arrogant, they're so aggressive, they've created another Pakistan right here . . .'

Kapadia smacks himself in the mouth. 'Yaar, I was born a bloody loudmouth! But now I also see it, to tell you the truth. I'll tell you one thing,' he says, turning to Shruti. 'You're a writer, you must understand such things. Not everything people say is thought through. There are many of us, yes, me too, who just babble on, say things they've heard, picked up from here and there, whatever ideas come to mind, right or wrong, about society, without thinking about them. Where would people get new ideas, after all? They just say the same old things, all that stuff just keeps popping out, right Daddu?'

Suddenly he doesn't seem so bad to Shruti.

Now he's speaking to Hanif: 'Anyway, you're a completely different type. If you ever go meet with those Muslims, you'll be extremely disappointed. They crawl about like bugs in their closed-off mohallas, but they're still proud to be descendants of nawabs and badshahs—princes and kings. They intend to rule, or nothing. They're no less at fault for poisoning the atmosphere. Now it's even the case that well-to-do Muslims and Hindus are getting afraid and leaving mixed neighbourhoods. If the enlightened people leave, where will they go? Anyway . . .' He glances at Shruti. 'Have you people thought of getting your own home at all?'

Shruti wonders: Where would they live? What would that be like? Suddenly she begins to loathe Kapadia.

Daddu sits alone swaying to the sweet sounds of Baul music when the dhobi opens the door and enters. Daddu removes the record, leaves the room and returns with his diary.

By now, the dhobi has unwrapped his bundle, and arranged shiny starched piles of clothing all over the sofa and the divan. Daddu has opened his diary and sits among the piles. The dhobi lists each item, and Daddu ticks it off: three dust cloths, four pillowcases, two petticoats, seven sheets . . .

Many people are delighted when they see the page in the newspaper advertising the programme that is to take place at the ashram. That very evening there will be a showing of the old film *Jogan.*

'Nargis is in it, and Dilip Kumar,' says Urmila.

Bombs have exploded in a few places; more bombs have been found in other places. Sharad and Shruti have come to see. People are lamenting.

'One woman's gone mad. Her one-month-old baby died,' a woman tells them.

'It's good you didn't bring *him*, otherwise people wouldn't be able to speak openly . . .'

Shruti opens her mouth, but Sharad gives her a look, and she keeps quiet.

'We never hurt them. What did our women and children do? Look, look, it's in their blood . . . the tendency to kill and cause misery . . . all they want to do now is increase their numbers . . . they want to kill Hindus and have more babies . . . please believe me: we're the ones declining, our numbers will decline.'

'One of theirs is equal to ten of ours. That's the math.'

'Now do the math to see who's in the minority,' laments Shruti.

'See, only the two of us went and people spoke openly,' he says. 'Sorry, what I mean is . . .'

'Why do you keep saying sorry? I know what you mean,' snaps Shruti.

In the evenings, there's a hint of darkness, and the lights of the ashram fair suddenly illuminate, casting their brilliance all the way to the bridge. The darkness then wanders about, hiding in the lanes beyond.

The gaze with which Shruti fixes her pen is so piercing, it seems to become a splinter that sticks in the pen.

Or else it's her mind that's got stuck!

No, it isn't just that her mind is paralysed; it's that her pen has a life of its own and moves of its own accord. When the pen sees the mind has turned into a block of wood, it swings into action, and when the mind is restless, the pen lies still and plays dead!

Why, Shruti?

And why, pen? Are you ungrateful for your nice, expensive ink?

Shruti is explaining something to Daddu; he feels he's explaining something to her; Hanif and Sharad silently hold their glasses as they listen to the two of them and wait for Daddu to get up to go to the bathroom.

Shruti is saying, 'So then, some shopkeepers, some devotees, the entire family, are all part of this plot. Everyone's coming together to craft a lie.'

'No, never,' says Daddu. 'Did you feel your cleaning lady was lying? No, right? That wasn't a lie. For her, the Devi truly came. To liberate her family. Those people are worshipping the goddess with pure hearts. It's not a conspiracy at all!'

He stands up to go to the loo.

'Now this is pure,' jokes Hanif, examining the whisky bottle before handing it to Sharad.

'How so?' Shruti is annoyed.

During tea, there's discussion of how the university has started hiring fewer job applicants from other states.

'There's no actual rule, but look at the other departments and see what's happening,' says Urmila. 'The geography department allowed a post to lapse. When they couldn't find a candidate from here, they didn't hire anyone.'

'There's trouble with outsiders sometimes,' Shorty Josh observes wisely. 'They have no roots here; they don't have the same commitment. What do you think, Professor Nandan? Is that wrong?'

'Both scenarios are possible. Not all outsiders are bad, nor are all insiders good.' Nandan jerks his head and loses his grip on his moustache, which leaps from between his teeth. 'Our department wanted to take the best, from wherever they came.' He motions to Hanif and Sharad and a few others.

'But isn't it our duty to advance the good people from our own state?'

'All that's in Hanif's hands now.' He smiles. His moustaches quiver as though they are falling into the gap of his smile. 'There will be two appointments under his headship. He'll know what's best to do.'

'Oh, no, no, no, do not lose any sleep over this.' Hanif laughs mischievously. 'I am not available for the headship.'

'Why should I lose any sleep? Are you going to do something shady? And why won't you become head?' demands Nandan.

'The senior-most is supposed to become the head . . .' explains Shorty Josh.

'But there's no such rule, is there? So then what? Because now we undertake every task by the rules!' Hanif is in the mood to annoy.

'Why? Are you not available because you're making plans for long foreign stays?' asks Nandan, his anger escaping his control. He trims a hair from his moustache in celebration. *Snip.*

'My dear friends, I desire not my own good but the good of the department!' Hanif's tone is cheerful.

'Arre, since when?' parries Shorty Josh.

Is Hanif offended? But his tone is teasing. 'No, actually, I'm thinking only of my own good. You must have heard that tale, Josh Sahib, the Sanskrit one! That a rishi—right, Sharad, what was it? A rishi saw a wounded mouse in the road and felt pity for it, so he turned it into a handsome prince. With time, the prince grew very wicked—a mouse will always do mischief! And ultimately, he began to annoy even the rishi. One day the rishi had had enough, and cried, *Punar mushak bhava! Become a mouse once more!* And the prince turned back into a mouse!'

Laughter bubbles up here and there.

'Wiped out in a moment; neest-o-nabud,' laughs Hanif.

'If it's a Sanskrit tale, why are you sprinkling it with Urdu words?' chuckles Shorty Josh.

'Because it's an Urdu-style tale, from the Sanskrit,' suggests Sharad.

'So what?' Hanif is also laughing. 'Here we lounge in English, drink in Urdu, lie down in Sanskrit, die in . . .'

'Stop! Stop!' laughs Urmila.

Everyone's laughing, but they're laughing at one another. No?

The ashram is a place of worship, a festive place, a place of flashing, blinking lights. Whether or not there's a Nargis film on, even if there's nothing on at all, just as long as the curfew's not on, everyone's having the time of their lives over there.

Sharad and a few other members of the department are going by train.

'Bye! Be careful,' says Shruti. Her eyes are fearful as she speaks.

'Arre, what do I have to fear? I'm from this community,' replies Sharad, but now he's looking fearfully back at Shruti.

'This guy isn't like that, not completely. Otherwise, would I sit in your home, Hanif, and say this?' Kapadia slaps his chest.

Hanif falls silent at his words.

'You people just tell me this: Why is it that when I ban crowds gathering over there at one o'clock on Holi, so that no one coming or going from the mosque gets colour on them even by accident and riots don't break out, people like you pat me on the back, and say, "Wah, Captain Sahib, how secular you are!" And when I get the taziya by the temple safely, then, too, you applaud me and say, "Wah, what a secular police officer you are!"'

Now Sharad is silent too. Today, Kapadia is bent on rendering everyone speechless. 'Or else prove to me that Hindus are up to no good when they take out processions, but if Muslims do it, they only want peace!'

He is suggesting the answers to them!

'Set them both straight,' he carries on wisely, staring at Sharad and Hanif.

'Recognizing the separate problems of each.'

Someone has said this. And now Kapadia has erupted like a volcano. In fact, the lava has knocked me over.

'Did you just find out today?' the doctor asks Shruti. 'I've been giving him the medicine for years.'

'Daddu.' Shruti casts an accusing glance at him.

'All right, are you leaving, or should I chase you out?' Daddu chides the doctor, who has given him an injection and is pressing the injection site with cotton.

'But, Daddu, why did you have to keep it such a secret?' Shruti is pouting.

'Because I didn't want you to be paranoid.' Daddu widens his eyes and puffs out his cheeks theatrically. 'Paranoia. Nowadays no one is enjoying themselves unless they're spreading paranoia.'

'No,' scolds Shruti gently. 'Nowadays everyone enjoys being martyred. Everyone wants to be Jesus Christ.'

'Oh, indeed, this is true!' laughs Daddu wisely. 'Loony, how long do you intend to keep your Daddu alive?'

'Listen to this one!' Shruti looks towards the doctor and adds in a critical tone, 'You're taking things too far now, Daddu.'

Daddu laughs. 'You're the one doing that. As for me, I'm hale and hearty. This doctor's been stabbing me with needles since forever. The illness won't leave, nor yet will I!'

'Heads I win, tails you lose! So now you're hale and hearty. Look how skinny you are!' Shruti pretends to count his ribs.

'Ha ha ha!' Daddu chortles with an especially hale-and-hearty laugh. 'But I'm not dead either! Sure, maybe I'm not all that hearty, but anyway,' he declares proudly, 'I was always skinny like this, but at least I'm not a dead duck like you. Look at your face. Why are you playing dead, Mousie? Are you missing that donkey? In all the world, you had to end up with that one! He should stay at home, give his wife oil massages, press her feet. Instead, he wanders about like a vagabond. He's probably off dreaming of becoming head.'

Shruti begins to laugh, but still, she complains, 'What harm was there in telling me?'

'No harm.' Daddu smacks his lips. 'But no gain either. You loony. You don't understand such a little thing? This is a matter of breaths. One came, one went, one came, one went, and sometimes there's one that goes but nothing comes back, and that's it!' He's bobbing his head and his hands, both.

There's another discussion taking place over a newspaper report about how the city's riots are being orchestrated by the Hindu and Muslim mafia–industrialist dons.

'They get them going whenever they want,' says Shorty Josh, 'and then they shut them down when they feel like it.'

'But people who aren't in the mafia are doing it too . . .'

'When the prime minister of the country begins to prostrate himself before . . .' blurts out one student angrily.

'Religious feeling's not wrong,' interrupts another.

'Look at the new religiosity among the students,' says Urmila. 'Before coming to my class they go to the ashram and have tilaks smeared on their foreheads . . .'

'They didn't do that before . . .' Professor Nandan has his moustache hairs firmly between his teeth and is just getting going.

'But look at Kashmir, the terrible things happening there!' pipes up another student in classic Bal Thackery–demagogue style. 'Here we keep repeating *secularism, secularism*, but over there they're ruthlessly carrying off women and children. We're nurturing snakes in our midst.'

'What is this language?' Many of the teachers flare up at once. 'Have some academic decorum.'

'Go outside; you'll find out,' continues the student doggedly. 'Nothing was ever academic, nor will it be. This bookish verbosity is all whitewash. Outside everything's out in the open.' He yawns loudly and then falls silent.

'Hanif!' Shruti throws her arms around him.

'Wow!' taunts Shruti.

'Yes, wow!' imitates Daddu. 'Okay, go, get a glass, and one for yourself as well if you'll have some. What I'm saying is, I won't hit you! I'm sure you partake. Tell me, how long will you hide it?'

Shruti laughs.

'Why are you making it such a big secret?' he demands, his tone singsong.

Shruti laughs even harder.

'What do you lose by telling?' Daddu is pleased with his own joke.

'Nothing.'

'And you gain so much. A glass full of lovely drink. What do you people know! As Ghalib tells us:

Agle waqton ke hain ye log, inhen kuchh na kaho
Jo may-o-naghma ko andoh-ruba kehte hain

These people are simple old folk, pay them no heed
They believe wine and song can wipe away grief

'But what I've heard is: *He who drinks not, lives not!*'

'Heaven forbid!' Daddu raises his glass. 'Poetry has been lost to this generation. We recited poetry, you people do doggerel. Or Hindu–Muslim!'

'But you said you people did that too?'

'We were Hindu–Muslims; Hindu–Muslims didn't do Hindu–Muslim.'

They run into Professor Nandan eating puri-kachauri at the ashram fair.

'Hello, hello, this is my wife,' he says, making introductions. 'And this is Professor Sharad, and this is Professor . . .' Suddenly he falls silent and begins looking this way and that. 'I'd better not say the name out loud. Ever since the bombings, they've become extra vigilant here.'

Nandan has received phone calls from well-wishing city officials asking that the department not send their report to the newspaper, as the situation is delicate.

The department echoes with the students' endless discussions.

'Ordinary people ought to find out . . .'

'Ordinary people know . . .'

'Our report cuts through so many rumours . . .'

'This report will itself be declared an enormous rumour.'

'But we should say what we believe to be true.'

'A secular would say that!'

'I agree!'

'I disagree!'

There's one door, one window. In each hangs a curtain, from which hang children, peering out. Women's hands reach out from between the children, holding teacups or dishes of snacks.

Young men make loud declarations: 'We aren't helpless! The Arab countries will give us money! They won't give these people oil! Pakistan will shoot over the border! We've made our protective amulets, and if Allah wishes, we too can show that one of ours is worth fifty of theirs!'

Suddenly many hands burst out from behind the curtain and take the form of a small girl. 'Go away, go away!' She rushes in, pushing Hanif, Shruti and Sharad. The elders scold her. She bursts into tears. A little boy has also emerged from behind the curtain, and, finding everyone preoccupied, sets about cheerfully snacking on the namkeen and other assorted goodies.

'Now the Adivasis are starting fires,' Babu Painter has come to tell them. 'They had them touch the shrine and take a vow, then they served them liquor, gave them money and . . .'

. . . and handed them matches.

'We'll stand up for Sharad in this. After all, we want this to happen for our own sake! If a member of the family becomes the groom, then we nobodies will also rule! Oh! I shall be in the groom's wedding procession!' Daddu stiffens his collar and holds his head high. 'I want chicken and fish, a ride in the car . . .'

'But he doesn't want to become the groom!' cries Shruti.

'Who's asking him? Imagine getting a goat to slaughter and not making kebabs!' Today Daddu is bobbling his thumb.

Hanif's irritation disappears. 'You speak the truth. I am indeed being turned into keema-kabab between your son and that scoundrel Head Sahib!'

'Or between two scoundrels, more like!' Daddu chuckles at Sharad.

Sharad is also laughing. 'But you will become chair, whether you like it or not . . .'

'Whether he wants it or not, this time he won't oppose you—most of all, not you. He's anxious about reputation. Anyone could say that because you're a Muslim . . .'

'I beg your pardon.' Hanif is actually seated, but somehow it seems like he's standing as he speaks.

'Why do you always get angry the moment you hear Hindu–Muslim? That's how you'll be seen at this particular moment,' Sharad replies. Hanif and Shruti both fidget uncomfortably.

'Why are you turning the poor fellow into an exhibit,' asks Daddu, but he doesn't laugh out loud, just a slight smile, which is always hovering about his lips anyway, and if you removed it completely, he'd have to purse them and stick them out like the beak of a bird.

'Hmph, but of course Muslims would say that.'

'What do you mean?' Hanif looks dangerous.

'I don't mean,' says Urmila loudly. 'That's what people will say, if the report is published . . .'

'Let him go alone,' Sharad explains to Shruti. 'Let people speak openly.'

And another visit to Babbu Khan. He's reciting namaz, a cloth tied around his head. They stop in the doorway. His head is bowed in prayer, he hasn't fully risen yet, he hasn't even turned, and he intones, 'Is there no way, Brother Hanif, Sister Shruti? Can you do nothing? Please do something . . .'

As though this too is written in the holy Quran and is a part of the namaz . . .

'Take a look.' One has rarely seen Professor Nandan waving his hands and rocking his body in rage like this. 'What sort of revolution do we want to bring by turning everyone against us?'

He holds in his hand the slip of paper that's arrived in many departments at the university and begins to read:

> *Greetings.*
>   *The most dangerous of all are the unbelievers and the atheists.*
>   *They visit Muslims, they visit other unbelievers, and their words incite riots.*
>   *Those who are atheist, secular, humanist, self-destructive—whether Hindu or Muslim—are all despicable. They're all spawns of Satan.*
>   *. . . wherever you find them, kill them. Don't consider them your friends or helpers.*
>   *. . . secular–humanist atheists are misleading the country. The communists are sending their phony peace messengers everywhere and causing riots . . . they're teaching children their guiding principles . . . they feast on beef with Muslims . . . they mislead Hindus . . .*

Sharad snatches the paper from Nandan's hand. 'Did this come in the mail, or . . . ?' he asks glancing over it.

Many foreign sadhus have arrived in orange dhotis and canvas shoes. They wear rucksacks on their backs. They sing the praises of the Devi and carry donation boxes in their hands.

Even the city's oldest and most famous mosque has been hacked at with pickaxes: to the rear and at night. The damage was discovered the next day. Now the police are keeping watch.

Sharad is entering the mosque when a bearded mullah stops him. 'Are you Muslim?' he asks, his eyes extremely large.

'Yes,' says Sharad, but he's afraid he'll be caught making mistakes at prayer time, so he hesitates. Then grits his teeth. Then marches off in a huff.

Hanif laughs. 'You get stopped by hardliners at every turn.'

'How long will we keep forgiving the bigotry of only one side? No, really, I'm asking,' says Sharad. Shruti stares at him in surprise.

'What I'm asking is, if I come here alone, you go there alone, and we keep our high-minded speeches to ourselves, will we find out what's really going on?' Sharad stares at Shruti and Hanif as he speaks. 'If they suffer from insecurity and backwardness, then so do we.'

'We?' questions Shruti.

'Whom are you representing?' asks Hanif.

'No one,' Sharad smacks his head with a mixture of hopelessness and anger. 'But they'll think I'm representing someone.'

'Do you consider yourself a Hindu?' asks Hanif suddenly.

'Me?' Sharad is disconcerted. 'I didn't think so. When did we ever think that?' he asks, referring to the three of them as one, and adds irritably, 'Why have you started saying things like that?'

'Because you . . .'

Hanif gets up and walks away.

'Tell me, why weren't you in class this morning?' Shorty Josh is scolding a student. But I haven't come to spy on these characters and copy down his words. If Hanif or Sharad speak, I'll note it down.

But they must speak!

On the front steps, a squirrel, with a large piece of wood or some such thing in its mouth, flops its tail, chin puffed out.

By the next pillar sits a lizard puffing out its neck. Verily, it has a red double chin, but most likely this is not a sign from God.

And yet I'm laughing: one looks dangerous, the other greedy!

Oh dear, will these two ever speak, or must I simply keep going on about the squirrel and the lizard? Or should I copy down the words of Shorty Josh, who continues to berate the student? He's just said: '. . . it's the likes of you who go about causing trouble outside because you're not disciplined in the department.'

'What's that?' Shruti turns towards the balcony.

'A crying child,' suggests Hanif absent-mindedly.

'No, Hanif, I've heard it many times. It's a red Maruti playing a cassette, or a car horn.'

'Oh, really?' Sharad runs and peers over the balcony with interest, but by now the car, or whatever it is, has already passed by.

Babu Painter is prepared to have these three publish some sections of the department report in his newspaper as a long article.

'If you don't give all your names, it'll be more believable,' he suggests.

'Why?' Shruti stares at him inquisitively.

'Because we don't want people to see names from both communities and then set the paper aside without reading it, and say, oh, we already know what these sorts of people are going to say.'

Shruti is in the mood to argue. 'But we won't be speaking as Hindus or Muslims . . .'

'Oh, come now, you know you're Hindu, and . . .'

'No.' Shruti is furious. 'How can you . . .?'

'You aren't Muslim?' Babu asks Hanif.

'Me? Meaning what? Yes . . . no . . .' he falters.

'Look, Babu,' threatens Sharad, 'he doesn't say namaz every day, nor do I do puja. Now who's Muslim and who's Hindu?'

'Are all the others namaz–fasting people, or puja–bhakti people?' Babu laughs slightly. 'It's a question of names, which are a way of identifying people. And . . .'

'Give all three of our names,' says Shruti sternly. 'And let people find out who we are . . .'

'Yes, yes, Hindustani, secularist, pluralist,' retorts Babu with a crooked grin. 'The squabbling that goes on with names nowadays . . .'

'You say these terms have become meaningless,' Shruti says hotly. 'But you can't prove we don't exist. We'll come up with another name for what we are, that's separate from those other two; we'll belong to a third category and . . . and . . . and our very existence will be the proof, not our names . . .'

My hand is trembling. Truly, how can one write the language of screaming?

Hanif picks up a letter from Professor Nandan's desk. It's from his own student, who has requested permission from the head to take the exam despite her low attendance rate, which is due to her father's long illness.

Urmila and the head arc both there when the student comes.

'What will you do about notes?' Hanif asks her.

'I've borrowed them from others. I'm reading the books,' she says.

'There's no need for this. I won't allow anyone to be debarred due to attendance. How is your father now? So, you've got the notes, right? Good. If you need to ask me anything, just come by. Okay? Why turn this into an official issue?' He turns towards Professor Nandan and picks up the letter. 'So, everything's fine, now. Right? Then the place for this is in the trash bin.' He tears the letter in two and hands the pieces to the student.

'Here, you can throw it out.'

She smiles.

'Daddu don't you think____ . . .' says Shruti.

'No, I don't think____ . . .' Daddu says something else as well.

'I know he said____ . . .' says Shruti.

'So he won't have to____ . . .'

Luckily for me, Shruti can't hear either, so she stands up and closes the door.

'The madhumalti smells lovely,' she murmurs to herself. 'But these people have started to do the kirtan so loudly.'

'They've invited me over too!' boasts Daddu.

'Well then, why don't you go? You don't know anything about our vine anyway. A bird comes and sings on it . . .'

'Yes, crows are birds, after all!'

'Not a crow. Forget it. It chirps every morning.'

'Then does the poor crow not chirp? How hard-hearted you are!' There's a gleam in Daddu's eyes. 'The crow is unfairly maligned. From dawn to dusk he calls in all different voices. Sometimes *caw caw*, sometimes *coo coo*, sometimes *craw craw* . . .'

Today he's tickled by being a crow, while the divan is tickled by his laughter and begins to bounce!

Shruti's writing. Is it true the louder people sing their kirtans and bhajans or call the azan, the more true-blue they are as Hindus and Muslims? So those who are divisive are whole and pure, and those living peacefully and harmoniously are broken and incomplete? That divisive wholeness provides the benchmark?

She laughs when she sees Hanif coming.

'It's not "tatadakimasu", it's "itadakimasu"!' she tells him.

People in the department are unhappy. All of them had worked on it, too. Shorty Josh is glaring.

'But all of you were against sending it to the newspaper; you didn't want the department's name on it,' Sharad reminds them.

'Is there copyright on this sort of thing too?' Hanif smiles.

'The intention of grabbing all the credit . . .' begins Urmila.

'Nonsense,' Hanif snaps. 'There's only one goal here, to inform as many people as possible. We should publish it in ten places; we should write it in different languages.'

'You're not the sole radical here.' *Snip.* Professor Nandan tiptoes forward.

'I have class.'

Hanif departs rebelliously.

'So much arrogance isn't a good thing,' observes Professor Nandan irritably.

A wedding procession passes by with a band.

'At first I thought the ashramites were bringing out another procession,' says Urmila.

'Would they play filmi tunes?' Shorty Josh smiles.

'Why not?' Urmila laughs. 'I heard a sage with matted locks singing, *"Aaj main jawan ho gai hun / gul se gulistaan ho gai hun— today I've become a young lady / not just a rose but the whole garden!"*'

The students and teachers all burst out laughing.

'People are in a hurry for their daughters to become brides and throw sensational weddings before the fast of the Devi, before curfew,' Sharad tells them.

Nandu smiles widely. 'Ah, but there's one bride more in our midst, who's neither Hindu nor Muslim. For years, this bride has been sitting coyly at home, her veil pulled down over her face. And her name is Secularism.'

Laughter rings out again.

'The poor thing's fate is in tatters. She has no children, her household suffers, and . . .'

Hanif has his comeback ready: 'Of course, Head Sahib. We don't give our bride permission to degrade the status of an Indian woman who should be worshipped. To go outside and abandon modesty, make eyes at bigots, especially when so many tongues wag and thighs are lewdly scratched; she might be torn to pieces. She represents the decency of our home . . .'

Sharad piles on: 'Even at home, we don't let everyone see her with her face unveiled! Only in moonlight, when her face is reflected in a steel thaali filled with water, we bow to her in salutation!'

'So the touch-me-not doesn't shrivel,' a student joins in.

'People are laughing, janab,' says Professor Nandan. 'Do you have such great expectations of this bashful lady that you think she'll throw over her veil and rush into battle? What world are you living in?

This time, Sharad and Hanif go together. There will be a seminar called Culture and Society.

'All the same things will be discussed,' Shruti explains to Daddu.

'It'll be a junket!' Daddu taunts cheerfully. 'Money and liquor will flow; they'll write down on a piece of paper that this much was spent, and thus the path will be cleared for the next grant; loads of articles will be published; people will make their names, intellectuals will strut about . . .'

'Daddu, you're amazing! Are you that cynical? No faith left?' interrupts Shruti.

'I'm not cynical,' laughs Daddu. 'It's you people who are short on faith. You have no god, no guru, no path, no place to go! I have plenty of gods. I worship them all. All of creation is a miracle to me. All are gods. The mounts of gods, the signs of gods, these are everywhere! The ant, the mountain, anything you say, that is our god!'

'And the Kaaba, and . . .' Shruti continues.

'Arre, all of them. Whether it's saints, prophets or crucifixes, we press our palms together and bow our heads: pirs, mazaars . . .'

'Daddu is such a braggart,' says Shruti, but she's enjoying it.

'Do I brag or do those two? You have no idea about society or culture, but you make long speeches! You're experts at weaving a bewitching web of words.' Daddu is bobbing.

And now he's starting to weave his own bewitching web of words!

'You people don't even stop to take a breath. You keep flooding everything with words. You'll open a warehouse full of words on every subject. Not a warehouse of knowledge, mind you.'

'But that's what your generation does.'

'Of course, but a warehouse of words . . .'

'. . . is a web of entanglement!'

'Whatever you want to call it, words of every shape, every weight; empty, meaningless words . . .'

'What nonsense you're talking!' Shruti begins to laugh uncontrollably.

'Words for every pastime . . .'

'Nothing but words!'

'You make stories of words. That's what made you think of being a storywriter!'

Daddu is winking. The divan is bouncing. He's sparkling laughter.

'But how am I doing with being a storywriter?' laughs Shruti.

'Not well, right? You're unable to do it. You can't. Can a story be made of words alone?' Daddu just talks and talks. Wherever the words might turn, he follows them and soaks them in love and fun. 'As long as you people don't learn to keep quiet, if you refuse to sit apart from words for a while, how will anything get into your heads? Words, words, words! You'll shackle yourselves with words from all sides! Then you'll say, "I can't write a story." Arre, the story must have some way of moving about. Just words, all the time . . .'

'But can we live apart from words?' asks Shruti.

'Absolutely,' Daddu swivels. 'Reality exists beyond words: it's life, it's the soul.'

'Are there no words in silence?'

'Then how is it silence? Forget words. Words are an illusion. There's no calm in them, only confusion.'

'But you're using words to say that. It is I, rather, who is silent. Me, the one from this generation.' Shruti smiles triumphantly.

'Then what have you understood?' Daddu refuses to agree. 'You're not silent at all!'

'And you're not raining down words!' jokes Shruti.

'It's all an illusion,' guffaws Daddu. 'I am silent!'

But it seems to Shruti that Daddu truly is silent, though it's not actually silence; it's calm, it's soul, it's tenderness, it's affection. Even on this subject she's gathering words!

The article is coming out in several installments. Babu Painter prints them on the entire centre page.

Shruti sits at her writing desk. Her mind buzzes like a beehive. But the moment she sits down, it becomes a void.

It upsets me that she's sitting in a void with her pen uncapped.

It upsets her that the pen will start moving only if she doesn't sit.

And now she jumps up suddenly and crouches, so she's neither sitting nor standing!

'Why don't you sleep down here?' suggests Daddu.

The two of them stand up.

Shruti goes upstairs, sets the yogurt, goes to the bathroom and stands under the shower.

Then she comes out. She's in her nightie. She hasn't dried her neck properly.

Now she's putting a lock on her door.

Now she's back downstairs.

Daddu has already laid a clean sheet out for her on the bed. He's holding the pillow under his chin as he pulls on a clean case.

'What are you doing? I can do that.'

Shruti is embarrassed and so is Daddu.

'Noooo!' he says. 'A guest has come to my home. If I don't welcome her properly, I'll be disgraced throughout the village.'

Shruti has taken the pillow and secured it under her chin, but the pillowcase still won't slide on.

As for Daddu, he's taken the dust cloth off his shoulder, and he's wiping off the table next to the bed. He gets a bottle of water and a glass, and puts them there, then turns on the bathroom lights.

'You won't be scared?' asks Daddu, turning in the doorway for a moment and smiling.

At the library, Shruti learns Professor Nandan has also gone. To the Culture and Society seminar.

'Thank goodness,' she thinks. 'They invited him too.'

Babu Painter has come.

'We're getting many great reactions. Plenty of disparagement, but praise as well.'

'Meaning people are actually reading it!' jokes Daddu.

'Oh, yes, they're reading it quite a bit, Shruti Ji . . .'

Shruti is sorting through the dirty laundry.

'Why are you taking that out?' asks Daddu.

'I was thinking I'd wash it myself.'

'Have you gone completely bonkers? The dhobi's probably on his way,' scolds Daddu.

'He puts them all in the furnace, and then they come out faded.' Shruti feels indecisive; she stands and stares at the clothes.

'Sit down,' commands Daddu.

'Nowadays the dye in everything is so weak.' Babu chuckles. 'It's a good thing this weak-dyed religiosity will wash away as well! They're late getting it into the furnace!'

'Yes, Shruti, I forgot to tell you,' says Daddu. 'Someone named Maqbool Haq called, for Hanif.'

Shruti is startled. 'That's the one, right? The head of the Anjuman-e-Islam?'

'That's how it seemed to me. I asked if he wanted to leave a message, so he began to praise the article in the paper.'

'You did say, didn't you, that we wrote it too—me and Sharad?'

'No, I didn't say anything,' he responds. 'If you meet him, you can tell him.'

'Nobody's going to meet him. No, right, Daddu?'

Daddu says nothing. The shimmering drink in his glass sparkles in his eyes.

This is how we'll remember Daddu. In the light of the tall standing lamp, on the rosewood divan with the thick bedspread; thin, illuminated, glowing in the high golden light. The whisky bottle on the floor next to the lamp post: shimmer in his hand, shimmer in his eyes, he himself fair and shimmering.

'That's the horn; come look.' Shruti freezes, like a statue.

'. . . and when the time comes to divide the property, all love vanishes and bloodlust prevails?'

Hanif jumps up and comes out to the balcony. Sharad is behind him.

'What a ridiculous idea!'

A Maruti car cruises down the street crying like a baby.

They're laughing hysterically, as though they're high as kites.

'Did you two eat bhang?' Shruti laughs the moment she sees them. 'What great seminars you all have! That's why Nandu-Phandu forbids them.'

'Nandu-Phandu came with us, Memsahib.'

'Oh. Yes . . .'

'He was the one who made it fun.'

'Nandu?' asks Shruti.

'Yes, Nandu-Phandu. Exactly,' Sharad tells her.

'He had us laughing the whole way.' Hanif starts to laugh so hard he clutches his belly. 'When he told his, "You fail!" anecdote, he defeated all my stories soundly!' His face is contorted in the effort to stop laughing.

'Are you laughing or crying?' Sharad joins in.

'Behold the ninth wonder of the world! The two of you are Nandu's supporters now?' Shruti stares in surprise.

'Well, he's not a bad man,' says Sharad.

'Outside the department, he's not bad at all,' agrees Hanif.

'Yaar, in the department, too . . . He was the one that made a name for it . . . inviting people from far off, having them do good work . . .'

'Now he won't let them do it. Now he can't tolerate it, not a single idea can be had without him!' Hanif warns with a smile.

'That's possible. There are just two years left, maybe some possessiveness has crept in . . .'

'Why do you keep siding with him?' Hanif isn't laughing now. 'Understanding is one thing, enduring is another. Right, Shruti?'

Sharad looks slightly shocked. 'I'm trying to understand,' he says.

It was also true we were unable to understand why everything we'd done before, everything we'd always done and said, had now started to seem bad. Sometimes this even happened to those who themselves had been doing and saying the same things with us until yesterday. Had they changed? Or had we—and this is what we feared—started to say and do something entirely different? Something bad.

We'd begun to fear that if it seemed so bad to so many people, what we had done must have been really bad. It must have!

But what?

We began to feel alone and wonder what we had done.

'What did you say?' everyone asks the moment Hanif hangs up the phone.

'I said, yes, thank you.'

'But we heard that part.'

'Then ask, What did he say?'

'Okay, that.'

No one likes Hanif's joke.

'He said there's a great need for such thinkers and speakers.'

'And?'

'And how can we even know what Muslims have to say?'

'Was he talking about you?'

'Or about the interviews in the article?'

'Why didn't he talk to us?'

'How should I know?' asks Hanif.

'Why are you sitting there so comfortably?' asks Shruti.

'Yes, I don't like it,' agrees Sharad.

'Me sitting comfortably?' snaps Hanif.

'With Maqbool Haq talking to you,' replies Sharad.

'What am I supposed to do?' asks Hanif.

'Go water the madhumalti.' Shruti tosses her purse at him.

'With this?' Hanif smiles.

'Didn't you hear him? The sabziwallah is here.' Shruti pretends to smack him.

'I don't like him,' mumbles Sharad.

'What's wrong with the poor man?' asks Hanif.

'Yaar, the kinds of things he says, the way he makes himself out to be the representative of all the Muslims . . .'

'The sabziwallah?' Hanif's eyes widen.

'Ooh, shut up.' Sharad is annoyed.

'Oh! Someone forgot to hang up the phone. So careless,' says Shruti as she enters the room.

Daddu is watching the TV alone and laughing.

'Sala, you're getting on my nerves.' Sharad starts speaking as soon as he opens the door. 'I take your side and you . . . he . . .' He turns to Shruti angrily. As he gestures towards Hanif, he waves his hands like the wings of a pigeon—a pigeon in flight.

'What happened?' Shruti glances back and forth between the two of them.

'He's even parading his arrogance in front of the students now!' complains Sharad. 'I go around advocating for him, saying he's not bad, but then . . .'

'What are you saying, Sharad? I don't understand,' interrupts Hanif.

'What I'm saying is: Why are you always so arrogant?' He turns to Shruti and gestures towards Hanif. 'I heard he tore a student's application to pieces without regard for consequences and very nearly threw it in her face! Then he picked up the torn bits of paper and handed them to the poor girl and strutted away.'

'I did that?' Hanif stares at him in shock.

'He said, "Throw it in the trash."'

Shruti is also in shock.

'Who told you that?' asks Hanif when he manages to find his voice.

'Who did? Everyone says so.' Sharad glares at him.

'Head Sahib,' murmurs Hanif.

'You have it in for Nandu,' thunders Sharad. 'You'll be glad to know that Professor Nandan is the only one who has said nothing about this . . .'

'Yes, he's just allowed the others to say it.'

And now it's Hanif who has a murderous look in his eyes.

The phone is ringing.

Daddu isn't listening. It keeps ringing.

There's no one else to answer it. Even Nankau's gone to the bazaar.

Ring ring.

Daddu sticks his head out from behind the newspaper and stares at the phone, unmoved.

He gets up, slowly walks over, picks up the receiver but doesn't hold it to his ear. He's holding it in the air!

Someone's shouting on the phone, but Daddu continues to stand like that, holding the receiver away from his body. The same expression on his face.

And, oh, look: now he's put them both down—phone and receiver—separately.

Kapadia begins saying such things even before the third peg, as though he's just been waiting for the opportunity. And nowadays, there's nothing but opportunity! Something sparkles in his eyes when he says these things. As though he's inciting the three of them because he knows they'll blow up. No, it's another feeling: as though he wants to savour it for a little while. No, it's something else: it's as if he feels fulfilled by the hatred that rises in his heart from speaking like this.

I still remember. They were discussing a rail accident in the north one day, and Kapadia was referring to the chief minister there as an idiot—dishonest, cowardly, that's what everyone was saying. But just now, when the topic of a train collision in the east comes up, that look comes into his eyes saying this is true but also this, and this and this; and he implicates the chief minister there; he says the bastard went off to do the Haj, and although he was faulting both chief ministers, his eyes told a different story when he spoke of the Haj-going minister.

But Kapadia isn't even like that; he's a reliable police officer, everyone knows this. Sharad says so, and Shruti and Hanif remain silent, but they don't disagree, do they?

'Someone's insecure due to menopause, someone's never worked, so they're insecure, some are insecure seeing me work . . .' Hanif's laughing, but it's not a laughing laugh.

'Do you have any idea how superior and vain your tone is?' asks Sharad.

Daddu says nothing.

'I'm the same as I've always been,' says Hanif. Then he falls silent as though he no longer plans to speak.

But this too is vain and superior.

'Didn't you use to be on his side? You used to say Nandu was worthless, how jealous he was of the two of you, and your work and fame, and that he's just ageing!' Shruti cross-examines Sharad.

'I was just listening to his voice from Nandu's perspective,' Sharad clarifies.

Daddu goes after him: 'Your ears look large, like a donkey's. Why do you feel the need to listen with other people's ears? Are theirs as large as an elephant's? Bring yours over here and I'll pull at them to make them nice and big too!'

He laughs, and the three of them attempt to smile out of politeness.

Is Kapadia feeling nervous?

'No, I really do feel nervous. I have a pistol in my pocket, but you're the one who'll kill me!'

Today, the two of them are sitting in Sharad's room.

'Just now you used a fancy Urdu word like taufiq to describe your capability. You use such language because that's how your friend speaks,' begins Kapadia, who feels provoked by Sharad. 'But, yaar, don't take this the wrong way, I've got to ask. Does your friend adopt your vocabulary too?'

'Do our languages seem different to you?'

'Maybe they're not.' Kapadia gives it some thought. 'But, generally, Muslims . . . Now look, I just used an Urdu word for generally, 'umuuman, but would we say . . . um . . . sambhavna, kshamayaachna . . .?'

'Say tomorrow I grow a beard. Will he grow a Brahmin braid?' jokes Sharad.

'Will he?' continues Kapadia stubbornly.

Sharad is astonished, because now he's remembering that someone else asked him a similar question. Who? When? How has he forgotten?

Only Daddu could create an ambience of hilarity when the topic is death!

It reminds me of bouncing balloons.

'You people get frightened at the mention of a simple injection,' laughs Daddu. 'If you were villagers like me, you'd consider everything connected to modern medical science a boon! Villagers like me are overjoyed to describe the new, modern hospital deaths of our relations. We say things like: ". . . and then they poked him full of needles . . . not just once, but one in the leg . . . they put one big bottle up here and one small bottle over there . . . stuck tubes up his nose . . . stuck a needle this big over here . . . there were needle marks all over his body . . . my father lay there like that for three days . . . we just sat there, watched . . . after three days he was *off*!"'

'Daddu, you're such a liar!' The three of them burst out laughing.

'A hundred per cent true. If he could, he would proudly narrate his own death the same way!'

And with the mention of death, everything grows lighter, their laughter fills the hall like countless balloons.

What I'm trying to say about myself is that I was never under the illusion that I know or can know. I'm not here to tell anyone anything or evaluate my own opinions. I just ended up here in response to the fear I felt simmering in the air all round, and when I sensed the same air simmering in these three, I panicked. And that got me started.

Just to copy, not to explain anything.

I don't see it as a measure of my own self-confidence that I ended up writing of my own volition occasionally. Can't it be the case that what looks like something of mine could also be an outpouring from these three?

Or look at it this way: just as the three companions came together and gave rise to words, another three comrades—pen, paper and ink—came together to weave words as well!

According to Daddu, this means creating a false world, because truth lies in the silence that leaves words behind.

But my heart, even if it's insignificant, asks whether there are two worlds, both intense, and whether it's not a question of true or false, but of the two worlds and the different ways they feel.

Or maybe my heart isn't asking all this; my pen has simply taken it down. After catching one of those three expressing such things?

Forget about my heart, in fact. What I'm copying down now are the letters to the editor pouring into the newspapers, in favour of the essay one day, opposing it the next.

Certainly, I must have copied those letters down; they must be scattered around here somewhere. Or if I didn't copy them down, it's because I got tired of writing the same thing over and over; or maybe I was stingy with my ink!

But they are coming, many letters, and Trivedi has also phoned the department to ask why they're writing for the newspaper against his instructions—'This is not good. What are they doing?'—at which Professor Nandan complains that even if the articles haven't been sent from the department, everyone knows we're connected to it, and all of us have written such a report. So it's the department that's getting a bad reputation, right?

Nandan snips many hairs from his moustache and says we've done as much as we could, and that now our attention should turn back to proper department work. It is he who explains that the district magistrate has directed the university to stop allowing outside matters inside.

The constant drumbeat of questions leaves us dizzy. The university and the outside? These outside things, that belong to the city, to assessing true and false, life and death? Be concerned only with the inside matters? What things will those be that belong to the inside only and have nothing to do with the outside?

The outside has invaded the inside, but the reprimand is for not keeping the inside inside.

'For a few days,' cajoles Sharad, 'just tend to appearances. It's really a mess out there. How hard is it for you to show up from ten to five for a few days?'

'Why are you telling me all this?' Hanif looks angry.

Sharad doesn't respond. All he says is, 'I've been noticing many students behaving rudely. They don't even care about attendance!'

Sharad wants Hanif to become head. It's Hanif's turn; Hanif is his friend, so naturally Sharad is waiting for Hanif to become head. And when it seems to him not everyone is as happy about this as he is, he wants Hanif to become head even more. Why shouldn't he? But when the bickering increases, he begins to worry. Hanif should be the head; it would be unfair if he weren't. And when the teachers see how the environment is deteriorating, and they begin to say the new rules shouldn't go into effect for a couple of years, that it would be best for those holding the reins to stay put. Sharad is afraid.

We all know these things have nothing to do with the Hindu–Muslim riots breaking out in our city. How could such sentiments be present in our department?

But our faces wear a dejected look, because we've lost control of the fight. We'd be defeated in either scenario: whether Hanif becomes head or not. In either case, Hanif will no longer be Hanif, but a symbol, and that symbol is connected to the riots in the city.

The receiver lies separate from the phone again. Shruti goes and replaces it. But suddenly, she has a realization.

'Daddu, did you . . .?'

'Everyone's right here,' laughs Daddu. 'Who are you expecting to call?'

Daddu is listening, but he's not enjoying the conversation. He looks distracted.

'It's necessary,' insists Shruti, 'for good Hindus and good Muslims to meet and unite against these mad bigoted Hindus and Muslims.'

'Can't you just say "good people"?' asks Hanif.

'Why do you get angry every time you hear Hindu–Muslim?' asks Sharad with surprise.

'I also get annoyed,' Shruti says. 'That just popped out of my mouth.'

'It will pop out again and again; there's no respite from it now; we should realize that.' Sharad is getting worked up. 'Sometimes it pops out of my mouth, sometimes out of someone else's, that I'm Hindu, you're Muslim.'

Hanif winces.

'It's surprising, it's surprising,' says Sharad with surprise, 'that you act like this. As though you . . . you feel ashamed you're a Muslim.'

'Have you lost your mind?' snaps Shruti. 'It's not a question of shame for being this or being that. The shame is from the constant drumbeat about this topic. As though we're all stamped with labels, and that's the first and last thing our identity's about.'

'Well, right now, this identity takes precedence above all others,' responds Sharad heatedly.

'But I have many other identities . . .' argues Shruti.

'Are you not Muslim? Aren't you Muslim? Are you, or aren't you?' Sharad recites the words as though telling rosary beads.

The atmosphere has grown dense and heavy, and everyone wants to avoid the topic. Hanif is silent. Strangely so. Daddu is impervious. Shruti is anxious, and Sharad is speaking oddly.

I've stopped writing, to pay attention to his expressions. How peculiar he seems: upset; but as though it's necessary he keep speaking, though he's not giving any thought to what he's saying.

All the same, I should write down what he's saying.

'. . . and they'll also feel hostile that you're a Muslim. That's why I say we should go separately; then we'll find out. When they see the three of us, they tell us what they think we want to hear and suppress the rest.'

And this is where he falls silent.

Everyone is completely silent.

The staff meeting is one endless debate! What should I write down, what shouldn't I?

'There's no need to wait two years,' Professor Nandan's moustache stands smugly at attention. 'The rotation will start from now. And is it necessary to talk about what will happen after I leave? New, capable people will come up from the next generation. Anyway, what do you all think about this? Tell me openly.'

Urmila agrees that outside doings are influencing the department, and that there's more cliquishness and insolence. 'Right now, things will only get worse if we shuffle the head around.'

'First, the new head must get settled in.' Shorty Josh is thinking out loud. 'He will feel too much pressure from the current crisis. He'll suffer and so will the department.' He smiles compassionately—for the department, or for the next head, or for whom?

'Speak, please, speak,' urges Nandan.

Sharad opens his eyes.

'I just can't understand,' he says slowly, 'what you want us to say.' He falls silent. He looks around at everyone, looks at Hanif, then looks down. 'Things are done by unanimity in this department,' he continues, 'and that's what you put your signature on, Nandan Sahib. If the same will be true for the next head, then saying he'll have to face new challenges is baseless nonsen- . . . fear.'

A lecturer nods in agreement. 'It should definitely be Hanif. And . . .'

'And . . . one minute.' Sharad glances at the lecturer to apologize for interrupting him. 'If the next head can work with Professor Nandan, he'll also benefit from his lengthy experience and expertise. Yes, you were saying . . .?'

'I was just reminding everyone,' says the lecturer, 'that the atmosphere outside makes it all the more necessary that Dr Hanif take on the role of the next head, otherwise anyone can spread the rumour that because he's Muslim . . .'

Everyone interrupts, objects. Even Hanif.

'Speak, speak!' Professor Nandan says to Hanif.

All eyes on Hanif. Shorty Josh, who was about to shout, falls silent.

Hanif shifts in his seat. 'Let Josh Ji speak, then me,' he says.

Shorty Josh is already getting angry. 'I very strongly object. What Urmila just said is exactly right: we've started to let outside politics and thinking enter here.'

The lecturer who had spoken turns rather red. 'That's not what she said,' he says. 'She was talking about the students, and I was saying due to the mentality outside, the headship of Hanif Ji . . .'

'If Hanif is made head, it will only be because he's senior,' says Shorty Josh in an officious tone.

'But that's what I'm saying.' The lecturer's voice is trembling. 'In today's context, the shadow of what's happening outside falls on every decision, and that means . . .'

Now Hanif interrupts. 'Forget about outside. I'd like to say a couple of things.'

'Speak, speak,' says Professor Nandan.

At this, the urge to remain silent again overpowers Hanif, but he continues: 'Something certainly is happening in this department . . . and ever since the issue of the rotation has come up, more and more . . . I'm seeing disagreements between us . . . and they've started to seem especially . . . um . . . Some people's opinions are considered merely their personal opinions, which they hold for their own personal benefit, whereas the opinions of others are deemed to have been formed for the benefit of the department . . . I've had faith in this department . . . but now I have trouble . . .'

'When you become head, you can fix all this.' The lecturer resurfaces.

'If I become head, I'll be a puppet, and I'll be asked to sign things I don't agree with.' Hanif has lost his temper, but his voice is under control.

But Nandu's is not. 'You're making an accusation. No work is done here without the agreement of the majority . . .'

'The majority is what I'm afraid of, Head Sahib.' Hanif smiles slightly.

'You people weren't in the majority, but you were so opposed to the daily signing of the attendance register that I didn't make it a rule. I've been here many years; whenever anyone has proposed anything seriously, I've listened.' Nandu is seething.

'Look, I'll lose no matter what. What path is there for me in this debate?' asks Hanif.

'Insult to injury!' If Nandu were on Daddu's divan, what would happen next? 'So many accusations you're making, Hanif Sahib. What are you saying?'

'That I'm unable to endure this crisis,' jokes Hanif. 'Look, I don't have the kind of clout to get people to back my wishes and rustle up supporters.'

There are angry outcries from all around. 'Such words . . . such accusations . . . are not to be tolerated . . .'

'Are you done speaking?' Sharad's voice. Very calm. Dangerous. Hanif is startled.

'If you're done, then I'll say something,' continues Sharad.

'Yes . . . all I have to say is that I'm not prepared to be head under these circumstances. Even less so if I am becoming head because of my name,' finishes Hanif.

'Speak, please.' Nandan glares at Sharad.

'Now let us not deceive ourselves that the winds from the city don't reach us here; but we should also consider what's happening to us. The moment we hear a disagreement we blow up. The students are speaking out, and we're demanding rules to show them their place . . .'

'You're mixing unrelated topics,' shouts Shorty Josh, wagging a finger.

Sharad also holds up a finger. 'Please let me speak.'

'Silence!' Nandan motions to Shorty Josh.

'What's happening in this department? Qualities that used to be considered good are now labelled as indiscipline.' Sharad is on a roll now. 'We used to encourage students to take their tea with us. Now you want to put a stop to that. Why?'

'Have you seen how they speak lately?' bristles Urmila.

'And who stops them? Those who need to come, come,' says another lecturer.

'But the students know we don't like them to come. So few come now! Did we merely invite them for show, and if a couple came, that was fine, but when their numbers grew, we disliked it?'

'You too are criticizing?' Shorty Josh is shouting now.

'No, what I want to ask is how this behaviour is not for show. And those who say let them come, are they making a show of being radical? What does this mean?'

'You're the one who blows up most of all, like at the students quoting from the ashram sermons. What are you talking about?' taunts Urmila.

'That's a different matter . . .'

'Different how?'

'I'm debating them, I'm not saying get them out, don't let them come.' When Sharad speaks at length, all sorts of emotions creep into his voice: pain, anger, one thing or another.

'Why are we discussing these things?' Head Sahib wants to put the conversation back on track.

'All these things are linked,' asserts Sharad. 'Which makes it all the more necessary for us to have a head who can raise a different type of voice. It's simply a matter of voice: as far as the work is concerned, we do it together anyway. And your guidance will be needed at every moment, Head Sahib. Hanif will be the representative of our generation. Isn't that what we mean by democracy, that all sorts of voices are raised? He, too, should become head.'

'Yes, yes, of course.' Professor Nandan speaks angrily. 'The rotation has begun. It's his turn. He doesn't have the right to refuse. We're not asking him. We're telling him!' He slams his hand on the table with rage.

Shruti suddenly notices the chameleon. This is the advantage of not writing or not being able to write. She's always peering out of the window. Outside is the dense madhumalti vine, where a sparrow flutters. Beyond that, the street, where the Maruti with the dreadful or unique horn, whichever you wish to call it, races about. But now, there's a sleeping chameleon, its head protruding from a crack in the wall. Eyes open. Adapting its skin shade to the pebbly cement. As though it's simply a bit of cement snaking out. A movement on the street rouses it, and suddenly it begins to transform. It puffs out its red chin in a menacing manner. There could be poison in there. The skinny tongue has also emerged. Someone is walking down the street, towards the chameleon; the chameleon's furtive focus is on them. It slides backwards into the crack to remain unseen, but the bag of poison stays puffed, and the pointy tongue flicks just in case it's detected! But the passer-by doesn't notice it at all and walks right by. Now the chameleon re-emerges.

He's a tiny dinosaur, Shruti thinks as she watches with interest.

But, sister, do you get a better view if you hold your pen uncapped and let the ink dry like that?

Ink! Uff, ink!

Babu Painter is very happy. 'Many are angry about the reports, but the good thing is there are also sensitive people who want to know what's going on but hear nothing besides the loudspeakers. A doctor in our building was saying if he hadn't read this, he wouldn't have thought to examine the register of wounded and dead, to see which community had come to greater harm. He would have thought the number of wounded was equal in both communities, but that's only true if you simply count the names and not the actual wounds.'

'The world has changed,' laughs Hanif.

'Okay, fine, it hasn't changed,' laughs Babu Painter jovially. 'But please don't think it's entirely useless. Some questions have never been raised, and now they have been. That's important. If good people have such questions, their confusion will be resolved. Don't you agree, Daddu?' he asks respectfully.

'Yes, yes, I completely agree. Whatever you say, I agree with it.' Daddu bobs his head up and down like a tabla teacher. But he's not laughing.

No, activities at the ashram haven't cooled or decreased; in fact, they've mushroomed. Now government officials come daily, the high and the mighty, here to take darshan of the mahant. Surely there will be a picture in the paper today.

There is.

On this side of the fold, the mahant enthroned on a stool, a piece of straw stuck in his beard; and on that side, Shambhu Prakash, a famous industrialist from our city. Behind him is his wife, perhaps. Both bow to the mahant, heads lowered, palms flat on the ground. It looks as though the mahant is about to cry, 'Ready, steady, go!' and then these two will start a race.

The mahant holds out his hand in blessing. His fingers and nails are clearly visible. His hands are visible, and the rest of his body is shapeless beneath a mass of dreadlocks and fabric folds.

Actually, everyone's hands are visible, but the rest of their bodies are obscured by the clothing and the bowing.

So many hands!

Like stacks of bananas on a cart.

Two pairs of trousers stand apart. Their torsos have been cropped by the photographer. They must be policemen. The mahant dislikes devotees in uniform. So the officers must have donned plainclothes.

'Did you see today's headline?' asks Daddu.

The three of them panic. 'What is it?'

'Professor Nandan had a heart attack when Professor Hanif Jaidi seized his throne! He's lying in the hospital now, weeping.'

Daddu laughs hysterically.

People are saying there are those whose great-grandfathers' great-grandfathers had taken darshan of this same mahant.

Shruti is distracted by the trilling coming from the madhumalti vine outside.

'Daddu, are you Hindu?' she asks.

'If I'm not,' he replies, 'do you think these people taking out processions are?'

Shruti gets up and looks outside—who is making this *trill-trill* sound? It's a squirrel!

'I thought it was a bird!' she exclaims.

'Every week, orthodox tableeghi meetings take place in the mosque. They might not even let you in.'

That's Sharad.

To Hanif.

'No matter what happens, our job is to teach, not to obstruct the children's learning,' observes Professor Nandan ruefully.

'If we're silent now, they'll consider it a victory,' complains Sharad.

'Whether or not they consider it a victory isn't our focus,' says Hanif. 'If we don't speak up, our voices will be silenced. We cannot allow anyone to forget.'

'But not by destroying the peace,' adds Urmila.

'Arre,' Sharad's eyes widen, 'have the peace meeting and the peace march destroyed the peace?'

'We'll bring neither peace nor revolution if we turn everyone against the university.' Nandu is pragmatic. 'Look at the letters coming to the newspapers. It's wiser to keep quiet for a while.'

'So you're afraid?' Hanif looks him straight in the eye.

'You're not? You should be.'

At the dining table, Daddu passes a metal bowl to Shruti, an exceptionally serious look on his face.

Shruti says thank you, sticks a large spoon in it and is about to serve herself when she sees bones.

'What, bones?' she cries out and puts the bowl down. 'Daddu.' She looks over at him and laughs. 'You nearly made me spill the whole thing!'

'What!' Daddu feigns surprise. 'You don't eat meat? The wife of a hereditary carnivore behaves like a Brahmin's wife? Ha!' His laughter shoots out like a bullet.

'Amazing, Daddu!' Shruti enjoys his mischief.

'Amazing, Shruti!' he echoes back immediately.

The food is set out on the table. Shruti has made carrot halwa, which Daddu will consume with great gusto, but just a tiny portion, very slowly.

When the phone rings, Shruti pushes back her chair.

'See? The minute you put the receiver back it starts ringing. I'm sure it's something useless. Let it ring.' Daddu is munching his food old-people style, using only his front teeth.

But now Shruti has the receiver to her ear.

'Whaaat?' she hisses. 'Who's this!' she scolds. 'So rude . . .'

'Put it aside,' Daddu orders as he eats. Shruti puts the receiver to one side and turns with surprise. Her face flushes when she looks at Daddu.

Daddu is crushing bits of food together, rolling them into tiny balls. Roti and sabzi, dal and rice. He thoroughly mashes them together and pops the balls into his mouth. And now his beak is out. It's moving up and down.

It's as though Daddu believes that to talk about certain things is to pollute your tongue.

Shruti is also eating. She is staring down at her food, looking guilty.

'Why are you looking at me like that?' Sharad is taken aback and makes a face.

Hanif is silent.

'Yaar, this thing with the two of you is very strange.'

Still no answer.

'Wouldn't it be worse if we stopped telling each other what we were thinking?' persists Sharad. Still no reaction.

'I only said what many Muslims are saying themselves, that Islam is being taught less and hatred for other communities more.'

Still Hanif and Shruti maintain their silence.

'Look, this is very wrong.' Sharad's voice is louder. 'Then no one should say anything at all. You get suspicious of anything slightly different that comes out of my mouth by chance.'

'Those are words that came out by chance?' asks Shruti.

'See, now when I said, *by chance*, you gave it too much weight.' Sharad makes a face.

'Meaning we shouldn't take what you say seriously?' asked Hanif.

'Meaning don't put so much weight on every word right now. Maybe no one's sure what they're saying or hearing.' Sharad looks helpless.

Two fruit-sellers' carts have been set on fire in front of the university. One belonged to a seventy-year-old woman, who, as Babu Painter's newspaper said, was confronting some youths, crying, 'Kill me, go ahead and kill me, you servants of Allah, kill me too, hellworms!'

Sharad and Hanif are standing on the second storey of the library, looking down at the street. They see burnt tires and what's left of the cart. A thin stream of smoke rises from a filthy heap on the ground.

'We're the minorities,' says Hanif, standing by the madhumalti.

'You mean Muslims?' Sharad stares at Hanif with surprise when he hears him say this.

'Fool.' Hanif is extremely annoyed. 'I mean people like us.'

'Who are neither Hindu nor Muslim . . .' adds Shruti, gathering up dried flowers and yellow leaves.

'What are we called, then?' Sharad's voice is muted.

'It could be that what we're called is *wrong*, since we give rise to suspicion. Maybe someone will think of an appropriate name, but if it's wrong, that doesn't mean we don't exist . . .'

'What are we then? Where are we . . .'

'We belong to a third category,' interjects Shruti. 'And we are not so few . . .'

'A single swallow does not make a summer,' interrupts Hanif.

'But of course, swallows don't exist in India!' laughs Sharad.

Anwar Bhai is explaining that many girls have stopped coming to his school. 'One thing is,' he says, '. . . people don't feel safe any more.'

'Please, come! Arre, how can we let you go! Come in, please. Come, here's the house.' He's introducing his family, who each greet them in turn.

In response to one, Shruti touches her forehead in Muslim greeting, but says namaste; to another she presses her palms together, but says hello instead of namaste; to a third, she says adaab, her hands hanging at her sides.

I want to laugh, but she looks tearful, perhaps due to this jumble of hands here, words there!

News has spread in the department that Hanif screamed that he refuses to become a dummy head; he must be a head who's able to make decisions on his own and do as he pleases, to rule them all, as his forebears once did.

I myself did not realize how messily I was copying things down, but it had started to seem as though what had seemed to be— that there was a city, and that these three were in it—sometimes became these three, and the city in them. I had thought that these three were a picture and the city was their frame. But it wasn't that simple. Nothing had stayed that simple. What had been in the picture one moment would in the next become stuck in the frame, and as if that weren't enough, the thing that was the frame would begin moving and coming apart, and the picture itself would go still and rigid. Could anyone understand all this shifting and drifting? If you can imagine that, the fluid frame and shifting changing picture, sometimes the frame moving, or else the picture, then you'll understand: that was us that year, lost, befuddled. Or it was a deepening silence amid a constant din that was us that year. Or deafening thoughts besieged by a gathering stillness were us that year. Like true fatalists, we waited in fear for the gathering stillness or the constant din to come and devour us all.

A Muslim factory has burnt down. The fire spread and reduced to ashes the polythene factory next door, which was Hindu. The two neighbours, and with them many other Hindus and Muslims, stand bereft.

'We're not enemies.'

'No, no, that would be impossible. This is the mischief of outsiders.'

'Yes, from over there . . . the fire was set from over there.'

One bystander laughs like a madwoman.

'If you light a fire, both will burn,' she cries. 'If you light a lamp, both will shine.'

One of her front teeth is missing. She is laughing so hard spittle drips from her lips.

I see the anxiety that darts across Hanif's face with the swiftness of a snake, then coils up, tail thumping, when Shruti says, 'But at our house, only one person is Muslim, my husband Hanif.'

Babu isn't angered by Shruti's anger. He listens to her patiently. He is not even offended when she accuses, 'You make a living off printing certain things in your paper to make it sell, and people now consider those things despicable, but if you write something like *Muslim dogs*, they'll grab a copy.'

'These are all clichés,' says Babu Painter. 'The puja supply shops at the Dwarka temple are Muslim, but their merchants are forbidden entry. Muslims make the kites in Gujarat for Makar Sankranti; in Jaipur, Muslims fashion the sacred threads of Brahmins; and the Patuas of Bengal who paint Hindu religious icons are all Muslim. People are bored of reading such articles and ignore them now . . .'

'Nevertheless, we must keep telling these stories,' retorts Shruti. 'If not today, then tomorrow people will hear . . .'

'And please don't feel contempt,' says Babu. 'It's simply a matter of making a living. That's only possible by selling newspapers, and people want something beyond that, something besides that. The fact that Hindus and Muslims have had close ties for generations . . .'

'So you won't print our essay?' Shruti glares at him.

'These close ties are like agreements forged between enemies for the sake of livelihood. This was how they came to make a living.'

'Doubtless,' says Hanif, with a sidelong glance. 'It's a question of making a living even when the Muslim shops have filled with Devi calendars!'

'To fear or fight for one's bread . . .' Babu is about to say something more when Shruti looks at him with annoyance and says, 'You also think this way.'

'Don't disdain. This won't work,' says Babu clearly. He indicates some lines in the article and says, 'These things about the ashram . . .'

Before he can finish, Shruti bursts out angrily, 'It's true. Forbidden, totally . . . for Muslims to go there. They don't say it, but they believe it. They ask your name at the slightest suspicion. You can ask Hanif . . .'

Hanif smiles faintly. 'Yes . . . the name . . .'

Babu is upset for the first time. 'Please try to understand, Shruti. One must be attentive to what one can say and the way things are now. We must open people's ears, not close them. They're simply not prepared to hear what you have to say against the ashram. First off, they'll be angry. Our mahant is a major leader. From your perspective, you can speak against him fearlessly . . .'

Now Shruti loses her temper.

'From your perspective, Babu, you can fearlessly say, *don't speak*, because you're situated on the side which flows with the majority community. Whereas I . . .' she stops, thinks a bit, then says, '. . . secure, well-off me, I feel the breeze from the other side too, maybe just lightly, but it's terrifying, nonetheless. It's left people badly shaken, though at our place, there's only one Muslim, my husband Hanif . . .'

Hanif looks uneasy.

'. . . but what's happened is that whether I speak or anyone else speaks, I've begun to hear with their ears, and, like them, sometimes I too end up fearful and . . .'

'You don't appear to know that I'm Muslim,' interrupts Babu.

My pen freezes, just for a moment.

These three don't go to the ashram for many days. It's become old hat! The same old ashram, fair, sermons, mosque, curfew, *Jai Jagadambe*, murder–mayhem.

'Why does he do such things? As though everyone in the department's hounding him.' Sharad has one complaint after another.

'The things Nandu was pleased with yesterday annoy him daily now. Why?' complains Hanif.

The two of them are determined to speak at once. This one that one which one how am I to write anything down!

'So what if he said that? He said it very politely. He even told all the ladies to wear saris as much as they could . . .'

'His department is being disgraced by people wearing kurtas with trousers!'

'Yaar, a bit of strictness will fix the growing laxity . . . sometimes you have to tighten the nuts and bolts to keep the machine running.'

'The world is being set straight by tightening me!' laughs Hanif bitterly.

'And then, see, again . . .' Sharad complains, 'everything that's happening is happening to him. He takes everything like a personal blow and overreacts, even though he knows that because of his name these days, this . . .'

'As long as things keep happening because of my name— Hanif—I should be left alone.' Hanif grits his teeth.

'How can he do that?' Sharad asks Shruti. 'Demand everyone leave him be for a specific period?'

'Just leave me alone!' Hanif gets angry.

'If the two of you don't quiet down now, I'll tell Daddu where all his liquor is going,' warns Shruti. 'You're fighting so much.'

When Daddu returns from the bathroom, they start to discuss the tile roof.

We ourselves have no idea why we're so worked up, why it is that when Hanif calls himself a Muslim it's no big thing, but if someone else says it, he gets annoyed. Why Sharad, who wanders about the city and says on his return 'Yaar, from the illiterate you expect it', but why do even the educated speak against Muslims? And why, when Shruti sits, pen uncapped, ink drying, does she suddenly stand and angrily brandish her fist in the air, with only the flapping sparrow making its nest as a witness, then pick up the straw that's fallen from her face and fling it towards the madhumalti, crying, 'Go, go nest over there!'?

'Why is it like this? Think about it,' Sharad asks. Think about how Shruti used to say that if the educated and the uneducated are both like this, how besieged Muslims must feel. But Sharad would say, think about what it means that the educated and the uneducated all believe the same thing. Does this mean what's been happening is all a justification for their beliefs?

Hanif keeps quiet at such moments now. Like the silence that spreads after the metal shutters slam shut at curfew.

But we were truly unable to understand, and we'd begun to squabble among ourselves.

'You should stop going into the city alone,' Shruti tells Sharad angrily.

'Why but?' retorts Sharad. 'Those who think differently from us, if we don't listen patiently and respectfully to what they say, how will we know there are people who are different from us?'

'But respect is becoming a form of tacit agreement,' says Shruti.

If Shruti were to go and look up close, Sharad thinks sadly, she'd see that those are people too, not faceless terms which have been injured and killed!

Maybe so much sympathy isn't a good thing, thinks Shruti. All these people are human, but even so, we should never consider their viewpoint innocent, since it doesn't recognize humanity.

'And you, why are you silent?' Sharad periodically gets irritated during such discussions and turns to Hanif to scan his face as though maybe there's some secret Muslim emotion hidden there.

Actually, in this atmosphere of doubt and suspicion, we'd unconsciously begun to disbelieve one another. While speaking out against the tendency of imbuing names with too much meaning, we ourselves had started to do it. We'd begun to speak as though, in truth, only two identities remained, and everything was either Hindu or Muslim.

Everything had become Hindu–Muslim, every colour, every word, every salaam–namaskar, achkan–dhoti, even green and yellow. A bookstore had Saraswati in the title, but now the owner with the Muslim name cut the goddess out. A restaurant was called Mughal Mahal, but now its Hindu owner was searching for a more Hindu name in the ever-shrinking dictionary.

Arre, everything was being labelled!

Countless similes, sayings, rumours were being killed off, and seized from ordinary people and taken off where someone was sprinkling them Ganges water, nazr ki shirini, Charan Amrita, or Aab-e-Zamzam.

That year, we began to accept the rules and definitions laid out by those whom we considered wrong.

It was a stubborn year; a year which was determined to divide everything, every colour, every word, every person into Hindu and Muslim. So much was taken from Hindu, so much emptied of Muslim that what was left was neither Hindu nor Muslim, nor was it any of us.

Babu Painter has returned. As he's leaving, Sharad says khuda hafiz and embraces him.

'What is this you're doing? So sappy . . .' Hanif is angry.

'The way he was speaking, I felt tearful,' replies Sharad. 'Hugging is ordinary over there, anyway.'

'Why can't anything be simple for you?' snaps Shruti. 'Now you're telling us about the ordinary things Muslims do?'

'Yaar, you're the ones who won't let anything be simple. These days you study every gesture and write a long thesis about it. Will no simplicity be left in our time?'

Professor Nandan is sulking.

'I had forbidden any writing for a few days. Now I'm being forced to answer too many questions.'

Shruti and Hanif stand next to the sabziwallah's cart at Daddu's gate.

'Should we get brinjal?'

Hanif scowls. 'There are other vegetables too.'

'And everything's so expensive. You make a face at the mention of every single vegetable and then you say, "I don't make a fuss."'

'How do I make a fuss? I eat everything.'

'By making a face,' snaps Shruti.

'But I do eat it.' Hanif stares at her. 'Here, let me look.' He touches the vegetables on the cart. 'How much for the guar beans?'

'Fifty rupees a paav.'

'This is what they call a fusspot . . .' Shruti is irritable.

'I'm not fussy.'

'Those with fussy thoughts are called fusspots,' retorts Shruti. 'We'll take the eggplant. Give us eggplant, bhai. Half a kilo. You'll eat bharta, won't you, spicy?' she asks in a critical tone.

'I eat everything . . .'

'Take more veggies, behin ji,' suggests the vegetable seller as he adjusts his clanking scales.

'Why?' Shruti stares at him apprehensively. 'Bhai, don't weigh it with a jerk like that.'

'No, behin ji. Here, take this.' He picks up another small eggplant and places it on the scale. This makes it jerk and clank again.

'Why?' asks Hanif. 'Aren't you coming tomorrow?'

'Who knows whether I'll be able to come tomorrow or not, sahib ji.'

'Is there going to be trouble somewhere? Who told you?' asks Shruti in a single breath.

'Who can tell about trouble nowadays? But a storm might be brewing. Look to the east, so many clouds.' He gestures towards the sky.

Sharad has encountered a tall White woman in the lanes where he walks alone.

'Are you writing about the riots?' he asks.

'No, I'm collecting domestic artwork by women.'

'Oh,' says Sharad.

Her name is Beverly.

'No, not about the riots,' she adds with a shiver. 'I don't like riots.'

Sharad smiles disdainfully and thinks, wow, what a thing to say, as if anyone likes riots. But his laughter changes as it reaches the corners of his mouth, as if to say, so this is naivety, that thing we no longer possess.

Trivedi is also unhappy that some members of the department have been publishing articles.

According to an irritable Nandu, the authorities are telling him, 'People are going around making mountains of molehills, citing you as a reference.'

On one level this is correct. Everyone is exaggerating more and more, especially those to whom something has happened. Now the one who was gang-raped and got eight stitches is saying fifty people attacked her! When a large crowd arrives in the mohalla to loot and such, they're tallied up as though people are less concerned about saving lives and goods and more about getting an exact tally of the rioters! There were fifty! No, five hundred! No, five thousand!

But these are not mole hills. They're actual mountains!

And anyway, the disagreements make the accounting the main point, rather than the reality of the rape itself.

'I'm telling you, right?' says Shruti scowling. 'It flew away from somewhere near the madhumalti, and it was definitely a swallow.'

'Why are you bothering my daughter?' jokes Daddu. 'If she says so, believe her. Yes, yes, you are right, my dear.' His cajoling voice turns theatrical. 'It was definitely a swallow.' But he isn't saying *swallow*, he's saying *swellow*, amusement shining in his eyes as he gazes at Shruti. 'I saw it too. Sálim Ali was standing next to me, and he saw it too. He was the one who told me.'

Sharad and Hanif both grin.

'Why Sálim Ali? It was the swallow herself who said, "Hello, I am a swallow."'

'You think I'm lying?' Shruti is offended. 'I'm saying, I saw it.'

'Yes, yes,' cajoles Daddu. 'I saw it as well. It was this big.' He holds up his hands in the air, far apart. 'It had horns on its head . . .'

'Daddu.' Shruti smiles.

'It had a long beard.' Daddu continues with his drama.

'Is it possible it was you, Sharad?' asks Hanif, backing Daddu up. 'Perhaps you went upstairs and perched on our vine to tease Shruti?'

This twist in the tale drives Daddu crazy with laughter.

Shruti laughs too, but then she says, 'Don't believe it if you don't want to. But it was definitely a swallow. Actually, there were three of them. They're called ababils. They have a split striped tail this long.'

'Aha, and you also have a tail,' says Hanif looking at Sharad. Daddu bounces.

'It comes in winter,' says Shruti, ignoring him. 'And you told me,' she turns towards Sharad, 'there were no swallows in India.'

Sharad shakes his head. 'Well, there are definitely no swallows in Indian summer! Or else change the saying. Say, *a single swallow does not make an Indian summer.*'

'What you mean,' corrects Hanif, 'is that a single swallow does not make an Indian winter!'

Daddu bounces slightly higher. 'But she's seen three!' he cries.

'So have you!' smiles Shruti.

'Arre, yes, I saw three. With these very eyes.' Daddu holds out his hand and lightly touches Shruti's eyes. 'These eyes bear witness.'

'But, Daddu, have you not heard that story? The one where a gentleman gets everyone to believe everything he says in his capacity as an eyewitness? If you want to know Akbar's views about mangoes . . .'

Daddu begins to bounce all the way to the ceiling. 'Which he found out by eating mangoes with Akbar! Hahahaha!' Now he's bouncing up again and again. What if he stopped mid-bounce and stayed suspended above?

Hanif doesn't finish his story, but he laughs, 'Yes, for everything he says, yeah, so-and-so told me himself, or so-and-so was sitting right there too! Even if so-and-so's been gone for centuries!'

Daddu laughs and laughs, then stops, then laughs again, then stops. 'Look, Shruti, he's annoying you. He's a real rascal, he thinks you're an idiot. Why do you live with him? Why don't you listen to me? Pack up your things and come down here; we'll chase Sharad upstairs—he's also a right scoundrel—and you and I will live peacefully down here . . .'

'You're annoying me too.' Shruti pouts.

'What?' Daddu's mouth and eyes widen. 'But I'm taking your side. I'm telling everyone I saw a swallow.' Suddenly he whispers, his eyes sparkling brightly, 'Tomorrow, we'll tell them a kangaroo came and sat on our madhumalti!'

The room begins to fill with laughter, it fills and fills, reaching such a velocity that it's pushing us outside; this is what Shruti thinks amid the guffaws, and she imagines the laughter spreading like a solid substance.

'But the maulvi's gone for good! What difference does it make to have this discussion, whether they separated the head from the body or cut him into four pieces, or threw out the head and burnt the body, or robbed his house, or just killed him, but didn't rob the house? Arre, what I'm saying is whether you believe they didn't cut him up at all or that they cut him into a thousand pieces, it doesn't really make a difference. The maulvi's gone for good, finished and done for.'

Daddu is explaining at length as though they'll have trouble understanding. The details must be picked apart. His beak has emerged, and he's waving his hands around.

The moment they enter the ashram, some holy women surround Beverly and separate her from Sharad. There's a large tent for the white foreigners to sit under.

Sharad is forced to sit elsewhere, with his fellow countrymen. The crowd at this tent flows outside to sit in the sunlight.

The sunlight probably bothers the foreigners, so there's a table fan, and everyone stays under the tent. Many foreigners don't even know how to bend their knees, so chairs have been arranged for them, but several are also seated on the durrees spread out on the ground.

The people of the country we inhabit flow through the ashram like the Ganga. Under the tent, on the durrees, over the ground outside.

The mahant is saying: '. . . our culture is liberal, not narrow like
other cultures. This is a Ganga–Jamuna culture, many different
streams flow together . . . Europeans and Americans are horrified
at the cultural decline and rise of materialism in the West and
have come to Ma. Ma's affection and tenderness are boundless . . .
Jai Jagadambe . . . victory to the motherland . . .'

A teenage girl sits with her parents near Sharad. She wears
a V-neck kurta and a shalwar. A holy woman stops when she
sees her.

'You don't have a covering? No odhni?'

She says something to another holy woman, and I write down
what I manage to hear: 'Mahant Ji Maharaj will now distribute
prasad.'

No hubbub arises. Everyone is extremely peaceful. Someone
hands a folded shawl to someone else, who puts it in the holy
woman's hands, who slowly covers the girl's V.

'Mutually cordial behaviour . . . cultural refinement . . .'
Mahant Ji continues his sermon.

'Understand anything?' asks Sharad as he takes Beverly over
to the festival shops.

'No.' She's flipping through the pages of a design book.

'That's why I like you,' laughs Sharad.

'Look, you didn't behave well.' Sharad is arguing.

'She's Professor Nandan's student. I have nothing to do
with her.' Hanif is also arguing. 'And she's completely empty
up top.'

They park their scooters and go inside arguing.

'Truly, who do you think you are? You think everyone else is
an idiot!'

'Why is he watching my every move so closely lately?'

Daddu pours tea into two cups, and adds one spoonful of sugar for Hanif and two and a half spoons for Sharad, and now he's slowly mixing in the sugar.

'Now this too?' Sharad picks up his cup. 'If you do strange things, won't people talk?'

'People will talk even if I do nothing.' Hanif picks up his cup as well. 'Stories are circulating saying absolutely anything about me.'

'What's wrong?' asks Shruti.

'Paranoid on top of that.' Sharad picks up a spoon and begins to stir vigorously. 'Is there a conspiracy?'

'There is.' Hanif is also stirring.

'What are you two talking about?' asks Shruti again.

'You seem like an idiot to me,' says Sharad. 'Everyone's prepared for you to take the headship . . .'

'No.' Hanif cuts him off. 'They're finding fault in everything I do so I'll seem wrong. And then have me loudly proclaim that I don't want the headship!'

'Oh, wow! Now you're being forced to say you don't want to be head,' taunts Sharad as he dissolves his sugar.

'I'm being forced to proclaim it.' Hanif is also angrily dissolving the sugar.

'Tell us too,' demands Shruti, annoyed.

'Do you not show pointless anger at inappropriate moments?'

'I did before, too. Now it's being gossiped about. He doesn't want to leave his chair, especially not for me.'

'Oh, and you're such a great being!'

Sharad stops stirring and starts dipping his spoon up and down.

'It's the head that's such a great being, and he's scared of me.' Unconsciously, Hanif has started to copy Sharad's movements. He, too, begins to stir his tea differently.

'What's this? Daddu and I are here as well. Tell us too . . .' demands Shruti bitterly.

'There are two sides to everything. He loves his chair, but he truly thinks you're vain and insolent. You clash with absolutely everyone without trying to understand; you're not diplomatic!'

'Why just two sides? There are many sides to everything, but here, all the sides are aspects of the same thing: he wants to keep control of the reins.'

'He's handing them over to you . . .'

'He doesn't want to, but if he must, he'll malign me in the process . . .'

Tea and sugar are being vigorously mixed in both cups.

'Are you trying to churn your tea into butter?' demands Shruti.

'Come, come, I'll make you another.' Daddu smiles.

'No.' Sharad looks down at the cup, then swallows the contents in one gulp.

Obviously, Hanif does the same!

Maqbool Haq has called again. He is inviting Hanif to speak somewhere.

'Tell him no.' Sharad motions at his side.

'No.' Shruti is waving her arms around like she's mute, trying to convey the idea of *no*.

'No,' says Hanif. He tells him he's busy for the foreseeable future.

The moment he hangs up, he snaps, 'Let me have a conversation. Ask him where he's inviting me? To speak to whom?'

'But why is he inviting you in particular?' asks Shruti.

'Anywhere Maqbool Haq invites you, you can't go,' cautions Sharad.

It's believed the bomb that exploded in the mosque was from the stockpile of weapons the Muslims keep hidden there, and that it was an accident.

'Who knows? Anything's possible.' Sharad is looking at the newspaper. 'These days there's no telling. But if Muslims are stockpiling weapons, that's not a good thing,' he adds, after some thought.

'They are stockpiling weapons,' says Hanif.

'What else should they do? Some may feel this is the only way,' adds Shruti.

'I don't like it.' Sharad is thinking out loud. 'Should we even view these activities with sympathy?'

'Don't presume our sympathy means we're saying it's okay.' Shruti glares at him.

'So then, when Hindus say all of them have only one way of doing things . . .'

'Sharad, can our own discernment tell us nothing? What are you trying to accomplish?' Shruti fumes.

'How long will we keep repeating the same things?' he snaps. 'You . . . do you have any opinion?' he asks Hanif, irritated.

'I want to know your opinion,' says Hanif. 'I don't like your manner.'

'What don't you like about it?' asks Sharad, getting angrier.

Hanif is silent. He's thinking. 'I don't know,' he says.

All of us have become either Hindu or Muslim.

Once this hall was filled with colourful balloons. But they weren't real balloons; they were bobbing bubbles of laughter.

Our gums open wide to create laughter, but not the sort of laughter that used to bubble into balloons and float about.

Gathered in a large hall at the camp is a group of women who have fled their homes and neighbourhoods in fear.

'Nothing happened where they live,' Kapadia is telling Sharad and Beverly. 'They just got scared. The camp is being run by their own community. Please come,' Kapadia calls out to the women, and some elderly bearded men come along as well.

'This one has come from abroad. You can tell her.'

The same stories are being told. Forgive me, my pen is rebelling on its own. It's fatigued from writing the same things over and over.

It won't write.

Not even my ears will listen.

This is very wrong. Don't let closing your ears become a habit.

'Even when she goes to relieve herself, she wears a sari,' an old man explains.

'See,' whispers Kapadia in English. 'We've freed their women from the constraints of purdah!'

When the record finishes, Daddu gets up himself, removes it from the turntable and switches off the radiogram.

'See?' he says to Shruti with a smile. Although I realize what he really means is, *hear?*

'Why does she weep for this body? Did you hear what he was singing?

bhola man jaane amar meri kaayaa

dhan re joban sapne si maayaa

My innocent heart believes my body is immortal
Wealth and youth are a dream-like illusion.'

He touches his glowing skin, and says, 'Coming and going is
all . . .'
Oh dear, my ink has spilt. Oh no.

'Zindagi kya hai anaasir men zuhuur-e-tartiib
Maut kya hai inhiin ajza ka parishaan honaa.'

'What is life but all elements meticulously ordered
What is death but the disturbance of these elements.'

'Do you know,' he asks after closing his eyes and waving his
hand in the air, 'who wrote that? Pandit Brij Narayan Chakbast!
Now what do you think?'

I hear people have started calling the part of the city on that side
of the bridge *Pakistan* and this side *Hindustan*.

I've also heard loudspeaker sales have doubled, tripled,
quadrupled. I have no trouble believing this because my own ears
bear witness: when the city lanes aren't cloaked in silence these
days, they're ear-splitting!

People also say when the aarti is blasted from the ashram
and the temples, the azan echoes back from the minarets of the
mosques just as loudly.

Whatever the case may be, many of us fear both sounds.

News is that guns and bombs are being stored in the home of Rais Mahmood Bidiwallah in the city.

A college girl walks ahead of Sharad and Beverly. She is pushing her bicycle while balancing a large sheet of chart paper across the handlebars. She has long fingernails painted in playful pink.

'Look at her toes,' says Beverly.

Her toenails are just as pink. Or maybe magenta?

'There's a tyre mark on her foot, look,' Beverly points again.

Truly. Now I, too, can see. The tyre tread pattern has been imprinted on the girl's foot.

'You would notice that.' Sharad smiles. 'Please know this is not a traditional domestic design! It's completely insignificant.'

'The ones here must be of a different design.' Beverly is thinking about women's drawings.

'You're probably also wondering where I'm taking you,' adds Sharad apologetically.

'I do want to know. I don't know anything,' says Beverly.

'That's why I like you,' replies Sharad, smitten.

'You just insulted me!' giggles Beverly. The girl walking ahead turns and smiles.

'Hi!' says Beverly, looking her directly in the eyes.

'So far your storm hasn't come,' says Shruti as the lauki is weighed.

'Where do you bring the vegetables from, bhai?' asks Sharad.

'From the village. Please believe, Babu Sahib, we only earn two paisas. We bring them from twelve kilometres away and sell them in the city.'

'Are there Muslims in your village?' Who knows what Sharad is thinking when he asks this?

'No, not out by us, but wherever there are, they're bad,' the sabziwallah answers carelessly.

'What do you mean?' snaps Shruti. 'Do you know my husband is Muslim?'

Hanif smiles, but with embarrassment.

The sabziwallah is also embarrassed. 'Oh, but Babu Sahib is different. You're educated people. I don't say it, but people say the Turks . . .' he whimpers and falls silent.

'People talk like this, casually, without even thinking,' says Sharad as they return inside. 'Just out of habit. These things have no meaning for them.'

Hanif is holding some sort of leafy green. He pauses as he gathers it up. 'Don't just dismiss it like that.'

Sharad also stops.

'If we look for meaning in every single thing, then all things will point to that one thing. Look, there are so many factors, they all float about and get picked up casually, and ordinary people say absurd things unwittingly. This vegetable seller has nothing to do with Muslims, he has no leisure to think beyond scraping together two meals a day.'

'Yaar, that sounds like something from a film dialogue,' laughs Hanif, but he's annoyed too.

Sharad is now intent on defending himself. 'It's complicated; there are many strands. So complex . . .'

'Is this *complex* a new word you've learnt? Everything is so complex that anything we understand is wrong?' snaps Hanif.

By then, all three of them have gone inside, and one continues into the downstairs house and two continue upstairs carrying their vegetables.

The ashram van is coming. The Devi in front.

Beverly wants to ride in it.

Now the van is moving.

Sharad whispers, 'I don't mind sitting here with you.'

'Then don't call me an idiot again,' Beverly whispers with a laugh.

'Who called you an idiot?' objects Sharad. 'You're devoid of prejudices. You don't know what any of this means, or that means.'

'I'm not an idiot, but I don't know anything.' Beverly enjoys the whispering.

'Beverly,' Sharad pats her affectionately, 'why don't you understand? You make weighty topics seem so innocent. Light. Blameless.' By now Sharad has begun to look at her indulgently.

'I'm empty, I know nothing, I don't understand, and you're saying it like I should take it as compliment!' Beverly laughs softly. But she takes Sharad's hand in hers and bounces it as though she's made even his hand light and airy!

The other people sitting in the van enjoy watching them. Beverly is completely unaware, Sharad feels a bit self-conscious, and the driver adjusts his rearview mirror so he can see them too, because why should he be deprived?

Daddu is disappointed when a woman on the television, dressed in a silk sari with zari border, announces the film will be broadcast late, following a message from the governor.

'They've ruined it,' he complains, and switches off the TV.

'It seems more people have died,' says Sharad. 'So our Miyan Bhai, our governor, is standing by to make a statement.'

Shruti starts and looks at Hanif, who has just entered holding a trowel. When he goes to the kitchen to wash the dirt from his hands, Shruti takes Sharad to task. 'Why do you keep randomly calling Muslims Miyan Bhai?'

Sharad is startled. 'What do you want me to do? Say it more purposefully?'

'Just tell me why.'

Sharad is annoyed. 'Not saying it would be purposeful too.'

'Then why don't you say Hindu Bhai?'

'For the Muslim governor?' jokes Sharad.

Daddu smiles faintly and begins to flip through an issue of *Filmfare*.

Hanif returns, wiping his hands with a handkerchief. Then he rubs them on his kameez.

'Don't talk rubbish,' Shruti scolds. 'When a Hindu Bhai is elected, then . . .'

'Rubbish?' Sharad explodes. 'Hanif,' he says, his tone suddenly harsh, 'come here a minute.'

'I've already come.'

Hanif sits down.

'Please sit here. Some things need to be decided right now,' declares Sharad.

'Then say something.' Hanif looks impatient.

Sharad is silent.

Hanif stands up for some reason.

'Why have you started behaving strangely?' roars Sharad. 'I feel almost scared around you now.'

'I can't do anything about that.' Hanif sinks back into the sofa.

'Enough is enough! Why can't you?' Sharad is whining strangely. 'Give me some reassurance . . .'

'Reassurance! What sort of reassurance should I give you? That I'm a patriot?'

'Enough is enough, Hanif, enough is enough.' Sharad is enraged. 'You twist everything I say so badly, I . . . I . . .' He begins to stammer.

'Shut up . . .' Hanif grits his teeth.

Daddu closes *Filmfare* and puts it to one side. The pressure of his fingertips has left light oil marks on the cover. He looks at each of them. He wants to say something. He smiles.

'Arre, fools,' he says, 'why are you growling like owls?'

I am immediately struck by this: fools that growl like owls! But there's no time to enjoy this amusing metaphor.

Daddu continues: 'Stick out your chests like men and settle this the hands-on way. The film is off. Push the table to one side, the akhara is ready and so are the two spectators. So . . .' He smiles at Shruti. 'Do you know how to whistle and hoot and such?' he asks.

'Yes, that sounds fine.' Sharad stares angrily at Hanif for a moment, then smiles at Daddu. 'I'll give him such a thrashing, he'll forget his arrogance.'

'And you'll come snivelling back to Daddu.' Hanif laughs out loud.

'Don't glare like that,' cautions Sharad.

'What are you going to do about it?' Hanif stiffens.

Shruti looks first at Daddu and then at the two of them.

'Uffo, will you really do this, like children . . .?'

'I am a child.' Sharad emphasizes the *am*. 'I have a clean heart. This guy is the old man. He presses everything between his molars and chews on it; chews and chews, but won't swallow, won't spit it out.' He pretends to chew his cud like a cow or buffalo.

'Stop it, stop it!' Shruti clutches her stomach laughing.

'It's all simply because I affectionately used the phrase "Miyan Bhai".'

'Arre, baba, then say Miyan Bhai as much as you need to; go ahead and say it!' laughs Hanif.

'No. Now I will say only Professor Bhai or Intellectual Bhai.'

'Say Ineffectual Bhai,' suggests Shruti.

And Daddu finally has an excuse to bounce!

Shruti is writing:

Sometimes it was we who turned ourselves into Hindus and Muslims; sometimes it was you.

Shruti stands for a long time by the madhumalti. Occasionally she turns to look inside, then buries her nose in the flowers.

No, she looks inside once, then she buries her nose in the flowers once, then back inside, then buries her nose! The funny thing is there's no fragrance.

Shruti won't accept it. To her there is a fragrance, but burying her nose again and again, and inhaling to draw in the fragrance has given rise either to a fragrance or a delusion. Who knows? Whichever you prefer.

Whether the fragrance is real or the delusion, no one has asked, but I've written it all down.

It's funny that she's deluded, that she thinks, I'll make it happen, I'll pull the fragrance out, but not that it will come from the natural qualities of the flower.

And what shall we say of the flowers? Cheerfully unaware? Vain? They'll radiate whatever fragrance they're supposed to, no matter how much Shruti buries her nose in them and strains her lungs, because what she's forcefully inhaling comes from her heart.

The madhumalti's fragrance is such that whenever it wishes, it can waft all the way to the street. But not if Shruti wills it, right?

She sticks her nose in the madhumalti again, and inhales. Then she looks inside, then inhales, then inside. Kapadia has come for a visit. He's inside, and he's talking continuously.

Daddu says he just talks a big game; just because he says crazy things doesn't mean there's anything bad in his heart. He'd never actually do crazy things.

He's a man you can trust, thinks Shruti.

But Shruti doesn't like the things he says. And such things they are! He was laughing and saying, '. . . poor guys, if they hadn't once ruled, today they wouldn't be so doomed!'

But Daddu says Kapadia's speech has no meaning; it's just words; it's all show; it's bluster; it's a make-believe world. His heart belongs to a separate world which bears no relation to his spoken words.

'If I consider you an idiot but call you brilliant,' says Daddu, 'is there any link between my heart and my speech?'

Shruti smiles again and buries her nose in the flowers.

Daddu will say anything. He'll spin tale upon tale, following each one wherever it may go—here, there, every which way, tearing it down, letting it flourish, bouncing with it.

Shruti laughs out loud. Then she peers inside. Kapadia is seated; he's yammering on, but now he doesn't seem so bad, because he's falling within the glow of the lamp that hangs over Daddu.

Daddu and the scene around him shimmer.

Shruti goes inside.

Beverly has: a camera, a small tape recorder and Sharad. Sharad takes her frequently to the city's galis and lanes. He's often recognized. Many people are drawn to them when they see the tape recorder.

Those who wish to speak, do so at length. They lean over and stick their faces right next to the tape and project loudly, as though they're standing on stage. Their voices sound unnatural. Mechanical, like the tape.

The way things work with the tape is that the words that come out of the first speaker's mouth are repeated by the next speaker as though it's a lesson they've memorized by rote or are rehearsing. The scattered words take on the solid form of a single story and attain the substance of truth from continuous repetition.

Professor Nandan is obsessed with the idea that articles like this are giving the department a bad name and thus interfering with their aims.

'As sociologists, we cannot take a superficial view. It's necessary to temporarily halt writing on these topics and take time to ponder.'

'No one disagrees, but we should also remain alert to daily developments,' says Sharad.

Hanif is silent.

'Today the Hindu seems to be the attacker, the Muslim his prey, but it's not as simple as that. Due to the complexity of the matter, we need to look at it layer by layer . . .'

'This complexity argument is being introduced to justify bad behaviour . . .' interrupts Hanif.

Everyone falls silent at his sudden outburst, as if they're not sure what to say.

It's Nandan who breaks the silence, laughing. 'Well, at least you spoke!'

Hanif is silent, then he too laughs.

'You made me.'

The room is silent except for the sound of tea sipping. A couple of teachers leave to do their work.

'Dagdu, are you trying to kill me? I'm a long-time diabetes patient,' complains Professor Nandan as he sips.

'This much is true . . .' Sharad stops mid-utterance, lost in thought, then continues, '. . . that we shouldn't make the error of over-simplification. If they . . . twist and break . . . the past . . . for their own communalist views . . . do we not . . . do the same . . . for our secular . . . or what have you . . . ideology?'

Hanif and many others stare at him in surprise. Perhaps no one expected to hear such words coming from Sharad's mouth.

'What if we too are creating a false history?' he clarifies.

Hanif gathers up his papers noisily. There's a rustling sound.

'Please expand a bit,' says Nandu with interest.

'We go around saying Hindus and Muslims used to live harmoniously side by side. Do we actually know that?' asks Sharad.

'Were we not living harmoniously?' asks Nandan.

Hanif stands up to leave. Nandan looks up at him.

'What do you think, Hanif? Is there merit to this?'

Although there's nothing special about this question, Hanif sees something other than simple attentiveness on Nandan's face, and this makes it impossible for Nandan to stay calm, as though he's more interested in reading Hanif's emotions than having a discussion. And he's also slightly amused that Hanif's very best friend has gone against him on this topic, making Hanif feel trapped.

'We know there were conflicts, and we know there was also amity, even if we don't know all the details. So why not bring the amity parts to the forefront?' Hanif retorts.

'But should we hide the conflicts?' Today Nandan is forced to speak his mind! Shorty Josh is on vacation, and Urmila is at an arts faculty meeting.

'We do pick and choose. Some things we put front and centre. This doesn't mean we're falsifying by leaving things out. There were conflicts, and we accept that. But why should we bring them to the forefront? Why don't we stop them? If there was amity, and there still can be, why not encourage it? Why not consider conflict deadly and oppose it?'

Professor Nandan has fallen silent. If he could speak, he'd say, 'Huh?' because Sharad has returned to his old tune.

'That's not how it happens,' he means to continue but then stops. 'Dagdu!' he calls out and begins giving him instructions.

How I wish I were a painter right now!

In the centre, a huge mountain of garlic. Countless fingers dance over it. Reaching out from the long sleeves of women's garments. The curved cloves, the swiftly moving fingers, the tiny, peeled piles and the fluff of the garlic paper dancing about in the air and over the floor.

This is a flock of displaced women.

Sharad's nose smarts, and his head spins from the sharp odour.

'As though it's the scent of a community!' he declares to Beverly and rushes outside.

At the entrance to the ashram the guard stops Hanif.

'You can't go inside.'

Hanif looks offended.

Shruti even more so.

Hanif sees this and puts his arm around her.

'Someone must have found out.'

'Daddu, I was thinking . . .'

'Arre re re!' Daddu pretends to be shocked. 'You've started to think too? But then what will happen to the godliness of God?'

'. . . that . . .' Shruti laughs but then turns serious '. . . that I haven't completed any work this year.'

Daddu's listening.

'When I published a story, I got letters that said, "You're writing obscene stories now."'

Daddu laughs.

'After that, I didn't send anything I wrote anywhere. I didn't do anything, Daddu. I've done nothing this year.'

'Those two ineffectuals haven't written anything either?' asks Daddu.

'Just the department report and the article based on it . . .'

'Now, don't deceive me.' Daddu's head is wobbling, as if to say, *caught red-handed!* 'Even I understand the difference between a report and research. Nobody's applied themselves or done any work.'

Shruti is a bit tearful.

Daddu smiles. Then he, too, looks serious. He must certainly find it difficult to appear serious. He must feel pain from his veins tensing up, and then he lets go and relaxes. Now his head is bobbing again. 'No point regretting when the birds have pecked the field of seeds,' he teases.

Shruti feels sad.

'Arre, loony,' Daddu consoles her. 'I'm here. Right, you silly donkey? Why are you worrying? You just have to write a story, not become a boss in Dr Nandan's regime! Come, give me your hand, and let me write with it. I won't tell anyone. Everyone will cheer, *Shruti Shruti Shruti!* Tell me, how many stories do you need to write? I'll write as many as you say. One, two, fifteen or twenty, a thousand, two thousand. Ha ha ha ha,' he shoots off firecrackers of laughter, but today Shruti is in a mood. She smiles sadly as she taps the arm of the sofa. Daddu's crackers fizzle.

He arranges his dhoti. 'This appears to be a very serious situation. It's become a question of life or death. Come here.' He pats the spot next to him on the divan. Shruti stands up and walks over.

Daddu places a hand on her knee. 'If you do as I say, you'll write a wonderful, fresh, exciting story, the subject of which will be anything but this.' He waves his hands around in the air. 'This is what's destroyed you all.' His face and speech are full of mirth, but the divan is calm. 'Write a story about monkeys, or cats, or the circus, or anything, just don't write about this!' Now he takes his hand from her knee and waves it in the air with a *no, no!* gesture, laughing in that same oddly calm way.

'We didn't do all this reading and writing to get trapped . . .' Shruti, too, gestures widely. ' . . . in all this.'

'Look at my hair, it's gone grey trying to convince you.' Now Daddu's smiling happily.

Both sit quietly.

Slowly, Daddu's lips transform into a beak. Ever so slowly. And when the beak has emerged completely, turning Daddu into a bird, he looks up at Shruti.

'This is our ill fate that we're going through a period when nothing can be simple and beautiful. This scream you're hearing, it's just a scream, not a real voice. You tell me, if you scream madly, will that be Shruti's voice, or will it be the one in which you soberly speak? Don't lose your voice . . .'

Just then, the door opens.

Darkness has fallen. Hanif is seated before the same low table where Shruti writes, staring outside. The balcony is out there, where the madhumalti has grown dense. In the darkness, the lights of the room and the table and chairs are reflected in the glass door, and the vine outside is not visible. The breeze rustles.

Hanif listens quietly. 'Listen,' he says to Shruti. 'What a strange sound. Could be fire, could be water, could be wind.'

'But it's the wind,' Shruti tells him.

I hold the notebook in my hand and weigh the pages. They have a pleasing weight. To have done so much feels magical! Of course, it's not my doing, although the copying was my idea, and the labour of writing it down is mine alone.

Shall I caress the inkpot?

No. What if it falls?

There's been no curfew for some time. Whether or not there is one right now, there will be one soon. I do not like the game with the ink.

But I badly wish to touch it.

A strange obsession!

Shall I just dip one finger and touch a mere bindi's worth? Should I apply it to my forehead? I'm startled at my own thoughts.

Now people like us must think all the time: If I do this, does it make me Hindu, or Muslim?

If I blink: Hindu, or Muslim?

Is Hanif telling fewer stories?

But Daddu isn't laughing less. Just now, Shruti filled six buckets to the brim with laughter!

But he's not telling fewer stories, is he?

Sharad sits outside on the veranda with Beverly. Hanif comes out with half a bucket of water. 'Oh, hello!' He didn't know these two were sitting out here. He reddens slightly, wondering if it was a mistake to come out.

Sharad blushes at his blush. He wants to say something casual.

'Ah, so you've taken that out after so long?'

What? I wonder as I write it down.

'What?' asks Hanif as he waters the madhumalti.

'Your Pathan suit.' Sharad points to his outfit.

'What are you talking about? I wear this every day from evening on,' replies Hanif, avoiding eye contact.

'But I haven't seen it before.'

'I'm sure you have, but now, in your eyes, I look different,' says Hanif. He waves goodbye and goes in.

Sharad puffs on a cigarette.

After a little while, he says to Beverly, 'Do you see how it is?'

'I didn't notice anything,' says Beverly.

'He got annoyed.'

'I didn't think so. Yes, he did pause for a moment because he was wondering if we might not want anyone coming out here,' adds Beverly.

'That too. I was also a bit embarrassed, but he got annoyed.'

'It didn't seem like that to me . . .'

'Well, you don't know about all this . . .'

'See? Now you've started again with me not knowing anything,' laughs Beverly.

'I mean about these things . . . the thing I was talking about . . .' Sharad clarifies.

'About the Pathan suit?'

'Yes, the Pathan suit, as though he was offended by what I said.'

'I didn't think so.'

'What's the big deal if I said "You're wearing a Pathan suit . . ."?'

'It's not a big deal.'

'I wear one too. He knows that.'

'You're misinterpreting.'

'He thinks everything's an insinuation.'

'I don't think so.'

'And I don't even like how he looks in a Pathan suit.'

'Plot twist!'

'But I wasn't insinuating anything. Some clothes look good on a person, some don't.'

'Okay, why don't you put yours on so I can see how you look?'

'I'll look Pakistani.'

Beverly looks up at him, but he's smiling.

'I don't even understand jokes like that,' she says seriously.

'Arre, don't be an idiot. I was just joking.'

'You're calling me an idiot again,' she laughs.

'But that time I wasn't joking.' Now he's serious.

'Which time?' she asks after a pause.

'Why did I just remember that now?'

'What?' asks Beverly, a little afraid.

'I only remember such things when I'm with you.'

'What things?'

'No, I remember them all the time.'

'Tell me.'

'But I only just understood,' he says, as though speaking to himself.

'What?'

'With you.' He stamps out his cigarette on the ground.

'Sharad . . .'

'When news came that a group of women had been raped . . .'

'When that train was stopped?'

'. . . I desperately hoped they weren't Hindu women.'

It's evening. Shruti is watering the madhumalti. Suddenly the sabziwallah comes running on to the street pushing his cart. At full gallop. *Rattle rattle*. A potato rolls off the cart in front of the house. An enormous yellow-tinged mass appears between the earth and sky. Shruti cannot think straight.

'What's that?' she asks.

All at once, the sinister blazing colour blankets everything. She turns quickly to go inside as the whirlwind of dust picks up speed, faster and faster. Two bicycles lazing on the street tumble like leaves. Doors and windows bang shut. Things crash about upstairs.

'Hanif!' Shruti screams at the top of her lungs, and runs. The two of them rush to close all the doors and windows and slam paperweights atop the flying books. There's dust everywhere inside the house.

'Where's the torch?' yells Hanif. Just then the lights go out.

As startled as I am, I've grown so accustomed to copying I don't even stop in the darkness.

Now everyone's sitting downstairs, where the storm can't reach.

Daddu stands up slowly and, with measured steps, walks over to the dining table, from which he fetches a candle and matches.

Outside, the dust storm rises in terrifying swirls. It's everywhere. Inside, Daddu leans over the stone fireplace. He drips wax on to the mantelpiece, so he can stick the candle there. As soon as it's lit, a shimmering golden glow illuminates his face, casting on the wall behind him a deep flickering shadow, four times taller than he.

Such a dust storm, no one can go outside. Even the curfew is terrified, and has run off to hide, like a frightened sheep.

'I heard a loud cracking sound in the night,' says Shruti.

'You're writing another story!' teases Daddu.

'You didn't hear it?' she asks Sharad and Hanif.

'In this downpour?' Hanif looks at her as though she's lost her mind.

'Maybe a tree fell,' suggests Sharad.

'It was a tree,' says Shruti. 'It must have been the old tamarind in the colony.' She looks sad.

'But the madhumalti's okay?' asks Daddu. He's not laughing, and his seriousness isn't an act.

'What could happen to it? It's constantly raining leaves, *pitter-patter, pitter-patter*, filling the front yard with trash,' says Sharad.

'Why are you always criticizing?' Shruti is annoyed.

'The snakes will climb it and sneak into your house. Then you'll come to your senses,' laughs Sharad.

'Birds come to this madhumalti, not snakes. Didn't a flamingo come from Siberia this year?' Daddu turns towards Shruti.

'They'll come, just you wait,' she laughs. 'Just wait for this rain to stop.'

'*Pitter-patter, pitter-patter*,' repeats Sharad.

'But what a rain it was! Amazing, sahib.' Hanif speaks with wonderment.

'*Pitter-patter, pitter-patter,*' says Sharad.

'It came all of a sudden,' says Hanif, as though describing a miracle.

'And now it refuses to stop,' adds Shruti irritably.

'What! But I thought you loved the rain?' counters Daddu.

'Yes, but not all these other things—when there's no electricity, no milk . . .' Shruti pouts.

'No telephone,' says Sharad.

'No liquor,' says Hanif.

'What?' Daddu quickly looks down at the base of the lamp. There are two bottles. 'We still have some.' He sighs with relief.

'But only that much,' says Sharad.

'This will last months.' Daddu smiles.

'If only you drink it,' jokes Shruti, winking at Hanif and Sharad. 'But the dhobi won't come, the sabziwallah won't come, nor the newspaper, nor the mail . . .'

Daddu is unworried. 'I like the rains as long as I don't get wet, that's my one condition.'

How could the divan stay quiet in this weather? And so, it begins to bounce stormily!

Naked electrical wires lie scattered about. A few people have been finished off this way.

I feel so happy when I see my stock of ink. But then my heart begins to pound with anxiety. In this weather there's no question of going out to get more.

Whilst I weep over my ink, everyone else is crying because the water pipe has burst, and the water will soon be cut off.

I'm the one who sees Sharad and Hanif standing against the wall outside the gate under an umbrella. Shruti has put a bucket under the roof pipe so it'll fill with rainwater by morning. And Daddu . . .

Daddu glows like always. Who knows if he's had the good fortune to bathe as he usually does, but nonetheless!

'If they can't fix the connection, a tanker will bring water,' Sharad tells them. 'Kapadia has got the phone fixed.'

'Beverly says the river's overflowing,' Sharad tells them after another phone call.

'The river?' Everyone laughs. The map says a river flows beneath the bridge in our city, but none of us say that.

'Yes, the river. She's saying dead animals are floating by. Even buffalo! I'm thinking of putting on a raincoat and going out to watch.'

'That's hardly a thing to watch!' laughs Daddu. 'You people will never change.' He shakes his head disapprovingly.

A sliver of sunlight has appeared. Trees have fallen. When Sharad and Hanif arrive in the department, the clean-up is already under way. Some areas are thick with dust and others drenched in rain.

'It took only four days to end up like this,' complains Urmila, pressing the edge of her sari over her nose as she dusts off her books.

'The Muslims couldn't cause any trouble for an entire week!' laughs Dagdu as he beats the floor with a grass broom, barefoot, his pajama rolled up to the knees.

Sharad and Hanif are walking towards their offices.

'As soon as we get here it all starts again,' says Sharad.

'I'm fed up with it,' mutters Hanif.

'Even the workers speak without thinking . . .'

'See you,' says Hanif and goes into his office.

Either he didn't hear or he doesn't want to talk about it.

I've bought a whole lot of ink at once. Now I don't have to worry so much if I copy down useless things.

Daddu is inside with the waves of music. He's also talking to himself.

Shruti is busy gathering up the storm-drenched flowers and leaves. The string holding the vine has loosened with the damp. She's thinking as she tightens it.

Hanif appears at her side.

'May you live long,' she chirps happily. 'I was just thinking of you and hoping you'd do something about this . . .'

'. . . like tie it up with wire instead. I was thinking the same thing myself. I'll go get some.' Halfway there, he turns. 'Do you ever think of your humble servant when you have no tasks for me to perform?'

'Hmmm . . .' Shruti pouts, cat-like.

He brings the wire and fastens it up carefully.

'Careful, careful,' he warns. 'It'll fall.'

'It's no longer a vine; it's become your baby,' teases Shruti.

'That's why I don't want Nandu-Phandu's baby,' quips Hanif.

'And mine?' Shruti pouts.

Hanif climbs down from the stool. He taps her cheeks gently. 'It's not the right time,' he says softly.

'Come, let's go inside,' she says after he's done and put back the stool. 'Daddu's busy talking to himself.'

'We'll go in a minute,' he says.

The two of them hold hands and gaze at the madhumalti. Inside, Daddu puts on more music and chats with himself. He knows Shruti and Hanif are outside, but he waits for no one, nor does he account for his time in terms of anyone else's comings or goings.

This is simply Daddu's way: if someone wants to talk, they can go ahead; if they want to stop, stop; want to sit quietly, just do it. Sit by him and he'll twinkle like a firefly in the night sky.

'Today he sat quietly,' Sharad complains to Shruti.

'He didn't tell me what happened,' says Shruti.

'Nothing happened. The same things happen over and over, but he used to make good arguments and show people the flaws in theirs . . .'

'He showed them over and over?' asks Shruti.

'That's not what I meant. What happens is, there shouldn't be rumours. Like right now . . .' Sharad searches for the right metaphor. 'Right now, it's like everyone's shining their flashlights at him at once.'

'If he doesn't feel like speaking, why should he?' she demands.

'He can't be so touchy.'

'Touchy?'

'If he stays silent, they'll say he's acting funny.'

'Why do you stay silent when he talks?' asks Shruti as she dumps all the salad on to Hanif's plate.

'I don't like all these questions about my silence,' snaps Hanif.

'But I'm asking,' begs Shruti.

'What are you asking?' he asks affectionately as he tosses his greens.

'About that . . .'

'It's because he talks strangely. He's begun to speak like the real issue isn't that I'm Muslim, but that I'm not Hindu.'

'Hanif.' Shruti covers her plate with her hand.

'My teeth will hurt. This is a grave injustice; you gave me too much.' Hanif leans over and dumps more salad on to Shruti's plate.

The green leaves fall on her hands.

'When the likes of Dagdu speak, they do it without hatred. He lives happily among Muslims,' Sharad is saying.

'Then why did he speak like that?' asks Beverly.

'Differentiate, Beverly, differentiate.' Sharad has taken on a teacherly mien. 'Over there too, people must be saying, that was fine, the storm came, but the Hindus didn't cause any trouble. Everyone's created an abstract category, where the people over there,' he gestures into the distance, 'cause trouble, create chaos, but when they come among real people they live side by side, in friendship, with a sense of belonging and civility.'

'So all the enmity is abstract?' she asks.

'It is . . .' Sharad begins.

'Swords don't cut in the abstract,' snaps Shruti. 'What dangerous things you're saying. You're ignoring real tragedies befalling human beings by saying "it's abstract". When Dagdu's abstract thought blows up, the attack will be on something real. And then Hanif . . .'

'Dagdu will never see Hanif as a Muslim.' Sharad shakes his head.

'Hanif too . . .' insists Shruti.

'Never Hanif, never,' interrupts Sharad.

'He wouldn't consider him a Muslim?' asks Beverly.

'Not like that, not a real one.'

'The real one is a reactionary,' laughs Hanif bitterly.

'Why don't you ask me? I know everything,' suggests Daddu playfully, 'about the real Hindu and the real Muslim.' For some reason he seems a trifle self-conscious saying those two words. 'The braid of the one is this long.' He measures the length of a topknot braid. 'The beard of the other is this wide.' He holds his hands far apart. 'This is a beauty contest, and you people consider it a conflict! Whosoever has the longest will win! Mine's the longest! No, mine!' Daddu narrows his eyes to raisins and begins to laugh. 'Let both wear the crown: you are the true Hindu, and you are the true Muslim!'

Being with Daddu is a brand-new experience for Beverly. She's finding it great fun.

'But, Daddu, there's only one crown,' she says.

'What's that?' Daddu's eyes widen, they twinkle with stars, but the very next moment he finds the solution. 'Why don't *you* wear the crown and sit on the throne!' He laughs uproariously. 'And tie all the braids and all the beards together. And then throw the bastards in the air!'

'A braids-and-beards contest!' Shruti laughs.

'They'll bounce up and down, and everyone will pull on the braids and the beards of the other. Then . . . yes . . .' He's impressed by the progress of his own story. 'Then . . . out will come the true Hindu and the true Muslim!'

Daddu-isms.

Of course, no one went to Daddu to solve a problem. That is, they didn't think to themselves, okay, today let's go talk about the true Hindu and the true Muslim with Daddu. In fact, one couldn't even talk to Daddu like that. When he spoke, he didn't consider the meanings of the things he said. They were mere rainbow-coloured bubbles bursting from the warmth that surrounded him at all times.

One simply went to him to sit in that ambience, to laze, to smile. To gently delight in those bubbles.

And to bounce! When not just bubbles but a ruckus erupted, and the divan sprang to life. But whether it was bubbles or commotion that surrounded Daddu, the glow of his warmth always remained soft and golden; it never transformed into a sharply crackling fire. It was an invisible, pervasive energy: simple, dignified, warming. Those who entered his orbit felt a peaceful sort of freedom course through their veins. Besides Daddu's guffaws and the bouncing of the divan, there was no feeling of excess.

It was for this that one entered his orbit of affection. Not to speak out or to learn something. Daddu couldn't teach anything in the traditional sense. So no one could learn Urdu from him or writing or singing, or even drinking! He explained nothing in the usual sense. In fact, he couldn't even tell his own life story.

Everyone would just sit in his company. He might be reading, or eating, or watching TV, or listening to music, or silent, or bouncing, but he was always radiating a gentle warmth. Those who didn't know all this said there was nothing happening there; that the conversation made no sense; that it was a waste of time.

What to say except that such people didn't belong there?

If Daddu were here now, he'd say they don't know how to soak up the rasa in life, or how to be alive; they're dry, crumbly people; they're trapped in some tiny shrunken place.

Don't misinterpret: Daddu's right here . . . But where is he? Is that him?

Sharad and Hanif have started to argue a lot. They're doing it again right now.

Sharad is angry.

'Either you stay silent or you speak scornfully. Anyone who doesn't think the way you do is wrong! So much scorn . . .'

Hanif is also angry.

'All this sympathy with all different points of view . . . Where is it taking you? You want to become a part of everywhere you go. You'll bow down to all, but soon it'll be those others peering from inside you, and you won't even recognize yourself.'

'If you're going to stick in your heels so far, be so stubborn, what'll you learn from anyone? What you know is everything! You just stay right where you always were. You learn nothing about anyone. As though everything's frozen in place, nothing new has happened . . .'

'All you do is whine,' growls Hanif. 'How can you sympathize with a view which in its very inception is disrespectful of others? How can you even listen to that?'

'You consider your opinion the truth. The perspective may seem disrespectful, but whatever pain lies behind it, whatever realities, those things aren't offensive . . .'

'Behind every opinion—offensive or not—lies true pain. So then what?'

'Opinions aren't the beginning or the end.'

'Better to call them wrong from beginning to end, and then talk about something else; otherwise keep quiet.'

'Like you! That makes people wary. The silent cunning community isn't saying anything. When they finally speak up, it'll be to announce jihad.'

'You haven't gone mad, have you?'

'I'm not saying this about you. I'm saying it about Muslims "as a community".'

'Giving my silence as an example?'

'See, that's exactly what you do. Exactly what you do.'

'See, that's exactly what you . . .'

These two have fought in the past, too, but nowadays this is the only topic, and they've also begun to yell. If they see Daddu coming, they shut up. Otherwise, they just keep yelling.

The two of them sit silently with Shruti.

'What's this that's happened?' reproaches Shruti. 'If even you two can't talk to each other, what's the point?'

No one breaks the silence.

Then they do.

'He won't listen to anyone.'

'I won't, or you won't?'

'It's such a small thing,' says Sharad. 'He doesn't understand everyone's searching and not understanding clearly. When they make attempts, things pour from their mouths: rumours, distortions. Once they've emerged, they repeat them, but it's not clear they believe them. What I'm saying is, whatever they may be stating, there's still an ongoing inner processing that's taking place. Yaar, there's a great distance between unswerving belief and utterance. You take utterance as conviction. But in this case, everything's in flux.'

'Maybe what he says is right,' says Shruti. 'Sharad, you're becoming literary.'

Hanif smiles. 'We know, but we ask.'

Shruti laughs when she sees him smile.

'What crazy nonsense are you putting together now?' laughs Sharad.

'A story! Listen,' says Hanif. 'This was in the olden days. A thakur sahib mounted his horse and set out for another town. His barber followed him on foot. They'd only just left the village when the thakur sahib turned and asked the barber, "Arre, Gangadin, where is my horse?" The barber said, "Sarkar, you're riding it." The thakur sahib immediately responded, "Of course. I knew that. But all the same, one should ask."'

All three collapse in laughter.

'But what's the moral?' asks Sharad, laughing.

'The horse is Islam or Hinduism, to which nothing is happening, and it's the thakur and the barber who are busy worrying,' says Shruti.

'The moral is whatever you think it is, take from it what you wish,' says Hanif.

A police van with a loudspeaker is touring the city:

> *Do not believe the rumours.*
> *Nothing has happened to the drinking water.*
> *Call this number to get correct information.*
> *Do not believe the rumours.*

Everywhere you turn, there's an uproar.

Boil water before drinking it.

Jaundice has broken out.

The Muslims allege that their water tanks have been poisoned.

The Hindus allege the same.

Photos appear in the newspapers of water flowing through the streets.

One newspaper says the streets are flooding with household tank water, making it dangerous to get jaundice patients to the hospital.

A picture in another newspaper shows canals instead of streets. 'The City is Turning into Venice', reads the title.

Shruti sits silently, but her pen is carefully capped.

She begins to laugh and picks it up.

If she writes, she'll uncap it.

She's silent, again.

But what's this? She's speaking to herself? Has she adopted Daddu's habit? Murmuring to herself and shaking her head. Nothing clear is coming out.

'Hanif!' she yells suddenly. A *yes* comes in response from the bathroom.

'Am I Hindu?'

No answer.

'Whether I like it or not, I'm Hindu?'

'Maybe,' says the voice emanating from the bathroom.

'Sharad too?'

'Yes.'

'You?'

'No.'

'Are you Muslim?'

'Yes.'

'But not me?'

'Shruti.' The bathroom voice laughs.

'I'm more like Sharad, less like you?'

'There's probably some strand you two share that matches,' says the bathroom.

'And you don't have that strand?'

The bathroom is silent.

'I'm a woman,' she says.

'I don't know.'

'What was that?' Shruti calls out again.

'I was speaking of Hindu strands, not about the woman part,' the bathroom retorts whimsically.

'My father was Punjabi?'

The bathroom is silent.

'Was he or wasn't he?'

'Of course he was, baba.' The sound of running water brackets the voice.

'My mother was Banarsi?'

'Yes.'

'Then how many strands are there in me and Sharad, but not in you?'

The bathroom door opens, and Hanif comes out in an undershirt and a pair of shorts, towelling his damp hair.

Shruti stands. She narrows her eyes and says, 'Why should I sort through every one of my strands? Whatever I am, I'm complete. Why should I declare one particular strand to be the real me? If I pull it out and display it separately, will it remain a part of me or transform into a separately dangling limb?'

She holds her fingers together in the air as though holding up a loose strand, which is connected to no body, swinging lifelessly.

'Why are you standing up, and why are you scolding?' Hanif approaches her, laughing.

'I'm scolding because why won't you wear a bathrobe! If you come out practically naked like that, you'll catch a cold!'

'Arre re re, don't scold!' Hanif stops her. 'You please write, I'll get the clothes myself.'

Shruti sits down with a thud, and quickly uncaps her pen and begins to write. Flowingly:

Why should I separate each strand, each colour, from my full identity? Whatever I am is beautifully robust in my consciousness. Why should I forcibly awaken it, choose some aspect of it, abandon others? In doing so my soul contracts. The dignity of my self shrinks. Its diversity, its simple, beautiful form is ruined. Making this bit hazy, darkening that bit, pulling this way, suppressing that way, we are distorting, contorting our own forms and degrading them.

'I won't,' she says to Hanif irritably.

'Now what?' he smiles.

'I am liquid. So I flow? I am light. I am a wave. What can you do?'

'Nothing, nothing.' Hanif ducks, as though he's being attacked.

'If they pull out some tiny bit of me and hold it up and highlight and crystallize just that, why should I accept it?' she asks sternly.

'You're looking very stern right now,' laughs Hanif.

'I'm averse to stern, narrow definitions,' laughs Shruti. She picks up the sheet of paper from the table and proceeds to tear it to pieces.

'You wrote something? No, no, no! Why are you ripping it up?' Hanif races over. Shruti smooshes the scraps together and rushes over to the dustbin, her eyes fixed mutinously on Hanif. Suddenly, a book falls to the floor with a crash. Before she can stop herself, she grazes it with her foot.

'Oh, noooo.' She picks up the book and touches it to her forehead. 'Is this action Hindu or Muslim?'

She turns to look at him, her head still bowed.

'The university doesn't want to give anyone leave at this time,' says Sharad, coming to sit in Hanif's office.

Hanif's face darkens. 'It's not so much the university as this department. Now it's starting to behave like the other departments.'

'Well, they're worried about courses. If all the teachers keep going off to conferences, how will the courses be completed?' Sharad is trying to persuade Hanif.

'How many are going? And how many are going from here?' retorts Hanif.

'If anyone else were going besides you, Professor Nandan would forbid them too,' argues Sharad.

'I agree. It's wrong all the same. Why this zealotry when the work's getting done? Why the need to tighten the grip?'

'Other departments are getting annoyed; they think our department considers itself a big deal.'

'So they're being appeased?' complains Hanif.

'We can't just cut ourselves off from everyone else.'

Sharad is sulking. Hanif stares silently out of the window. The palm behind the neem sways. Its large leaves flap like flags.

'I'm going. If they want to grant leave, they can do it; if they have to cut my wages, they can go ahead . . .'

'Don't do it.'

Sharad is upset.

News spreads of bombs exploding at four locations in the city. There's static on the radio, and then they pick up the BBC.

A school bus has flipped over into the 'river'. A bomb exploded on the bridge and many children were injured. Some died.

The colony residents are gathered outside Daddu's gate. Children, wives, servants come out by turns to join the crowd. Shruti, Sharad and Hanif are also there.

'There were always riots. Over there—not here—but such barbarity? Such tiny children, in nursery school.'

'Where are you talking about? It's wrong of us to be so liberal. None of us could be so cruel.'

'Riots, killings, both communities do these things; but this type of barbarity, Ram Ram Ram!'

'Arre, they still won't stop. See their nerve. Their special status has made them perverse.'

'But who set the bomb? No one knows yet.'

'Don't be an idiot. Everyone knows who's doing the bombing.'

'My daughter's so scared she wanders around closing all the doors and windows.'

'Now you're not safe even if you hide at home.'

'That's right, who knows, maybe even under our own window . . .' At this many of the other people laugh.

'Oh, come now, stop it, such fancy words! How long can we avoid calling evil evil? There's a community of Hitlers among us. You know, don't you, what sorts of things Hitler did? He'd throw babies in the air and shoot at them. He'd hold tiny children upside down and tear their legs apart like this.'

They're saying this to Hanif too, perhaps with that popular refrain in mind: *not you, of course.*

'Look in the fridge, if there's any sabzi, take it,' Daddu says to Shruti.

Hanif and Shruti, out for a walk in the colony, overhear one person in a small group walking ahead of them saying that Hindus have taken up violence because Muslims have spread hatred and resorted to bomb throwing and so on, so of course Hindus would start feeling hatred for them.

'Will they ever stop?' asks Shruti.

Hanif shakes his head silently.

'If we say something, they'll say you just want to speak against the Hindus. As though we're advocating on behalf of bomb throwers.'

'. . . so they're saying, mm hmm, just use a scarecrow instead . . .' says one of the people.

'Why don't you go be a scarecrow yourself!' jibes Hanif under his breath, his words not reaching the people walking ahead.

But Shruti's laughter does. One of them turns to look.

'Truly . . . a scarecrow . . .' Shruti covers her face to laugh as though the person ahead might tear her laughter to shreds.

The people who had stayed silent when there was violence everywhere were now crying out: 'See who they're siding with? We know all about you people and your favouritism! See how those people responded! Bombs!'

Hanif refuses to visit the families and neighbourhoods of those who've been killed.

'This isn't right,' Shruti and Sharad both say.

'Why? Why isn't it okay now?' he yells. 'You yourselves said if we don't go together people will speak more openly.'

The department is closed.

The newspaper came today. The ashram has made a huge donation to the hospital. They're not allowed to take out processions these days.

Daddu is making up a tale in which everyone is sitting on a swing, but instead of enjoying themselves they're fighting. And then what will happen?

'They'll lose their balance and fall, and then they'll get hurt, won't they? If it swings this way this much, it'll swing that way the same amount. If they fall, they'll get injured or die, as long as they refuse to sit together and hold hands. Will their problems be solved on the swing?' he asks, trying to laugh, but no one else joins him, nor does the divan budge.

Kapadia is very busy. 'I must run immediately,' he says. He drinks his tea quickly. 'What's happening is bad. What's happened is very bad,' he says. 'How can we explain that to people? They won't understand. What's happened is very bad.'

He puts down his teacup, stands up and starts looking for his glasses. He has taken out his car key. The glasses are next to Daddu. He picks them up and hands them to Kapadia.

'Backlash is another fear. The worst part is those people have lost sympathy; not even you secular types are able to keep up your secularism any more. How to explain to them? There's so much fear. It's very bad.'

Sharad sees him out.

As he starts the engine, Kapadia says, 'Tell me some time, you teacher–writer types, how we should respond.'

The department is deserted.

'If you want, you can stay here a few days,' Sharad tells Beverly.

'But bombs could explode anywhere!' she laughs.

'Come, I'll take you home.'

He stands up.

'No, I'll be fine . . .'

'Let him take you,' says Daddu.

Yes, there's been a string of bombings.

The sales of loudspeakers must have gone up because the police have also begun to use them quite a bit. Their announcements echo far and wide. Not so much announcements as warnings:

Warning: do not touch unclaimed items.

If you see a suspicious parcel, immediately inform the bomb squad.

Do not let children wander around alone.

If you see anything lying about unattended—toys, radios—protect yourself and keep children away.

At railway stations, bus stations, buses, trains, ticket counters, every which way, posters scream *warning warning*.

'What if you open a letter, could there be a bomb in the envelope?' asks Shruti.

In jest, but there's no jest in my fear. When I'm dipping my pen into the ink, I think, who knows, who knows, the bottle could explode when I open it!

People have grown fearful of bombs. We don't know which places to avoid any more. Nonetheless, some people still go away for a few days to stay with friends and relations.

When holidays are declared in schools, children throw their hands in the air with glee and shriek *Jai Jagadambe!* and the parents say, 'In our day we studied; nowadays there's just expensive school bags and curfews and strikes and riots, aah.'

But on the other hand, we're not afraid. Everyone knows they'll die someday, but who really believes it? One minute we'll be a walking-talking-thinking being, and the next, we'll be like that table and chair! We'll be even worse than that; flies will buzz around us, worms and bugs will eat us, and we'll rot, completely unaware.

Also, despite everything, we're still far from over there.

There's a curfew. Children are playing cricket in the galis.

Sharad is showing Beverly the city.

'All this burnt down. The fire spread to the shop next door too. They've completely redone it.'

'Over here people tied rubber tyres together and set them on fire.'

'Many people died here. There was only one escape route, but the rioters came in that way too. Women were injured jumping off their roofs at the backs of the houses.'

'Look, the walls are still black.'

Now that's what I call sightseeing!

There's a light on in the seminar room. A research scholar is reading out her paper. It's a very long paper, and she's reading the entire thing. The pages tremble in her hands. Sometimes she slides forward completely in her chair, then she leans all the way back.

Professor Nandan looks around to see who's there, who's not.

'Where's so and so?' he asks Sharad, at his side. Sharad's head is resting on his hand. He starts at Nandan's question. The pen falls from his hand, and his glasses slide off his nose. He laughs awkwardly and pushes his chair back to search for them. Hanif laughs.

'Aunty, aunty!' The girl from next door runs up to Shruti, breathless. 'They've got lauki and brinjal and unripe bananas. Do you want any?'

Women emerge from their houses with thalis, baskets, bags and surround the vegetable cart.

Shorty Josh is buried in his shawl, but his voice emerges excitedly. It could even be said to be scolding. He's dressing down a research scholar.

'Even if you were at this university, you were in another department. So what if you were at this university?'

The researcher is about to respond when Sharad arrives.

'What is it, Josh Sahib? Trying to escape the cold?'

'I feel no warmth. It's freezing.' Shorty Josh raises a hand in salutation. 'You went too?'

'Many people went,' says Sharad. 'Hanif was speaking.'

'That's what I'm saying. He should have informed the office. More people may have wanted to go. Talk times should be determined keeping in mind the schedules of people here.'

'Miyan, why are you feeling jealous?' Sharad gives Shorty Josh a whack. 'Research scholars organized it; an informal conversation between a few people.'

Shorty Josh waves a hand of warning and says, 'Look, lots of people are saying, this is informal, that's informal. This whole department has become informal. Why is there an office if none of the decisions are made here?'

When he sees Hanif, Daddu folds up the newspaper and hands it to him.

'You read it, Daddu.' Hanif hands it back.

'There's nothing to read. You take a look. Maybe you people will find something.'

The colony residents have banded together and hired a Nepali watchman. They've heard Nepalis are very honest.

They close their eyes peacefully when they hear the *tap tap* of his stick moving by their houses at night, and then, as the *tap tap* recedes, they open them again.

We don't feel a thing any more when we read about bizarre types of rioting and killing. We've read the headlines with unseeing eyes many times, then folded up the newspapers and put them away.

Urmila covers her nose with the edge of her sari.

'Such a foul odour was coming from the hospital morgue,' she tells them. 'There are many unidentifiable corpses; no one will take them away. The killers should be given the punishment of standing in there for five minutes, all their bravado will melt away.'

'Don't say such childish things,' says Shorty Josh. 'Shall I close this window?' he asks. 'It seems I'm feeling the cold most of all.' The corner of his shawl has dipped into some dal or sabzi, and the turmeric stain hasn't gone away.

'Yes, it is childish,' Urmila agrees. 'But maybe if we sent the police there, they'd start doing their jobs better! Have them pick up the corpses and move them.'

Some people snicker.

Professor Nandan snips at his moustache. 'It won't make any difference to anyone,' he says. 'No one feels any horror at these scenes any more.'

'And we're going around giving lectures and believing people are changing,' Shorty Josh flips his shawl over his shoulder.

'There's no point in lectures or articles any more.' Nandan waves his hand. 'People are getting suspicious of university types more than anyone else. They have a low opinion of the university.'

'One wind blows in the university, another in the rest of the city,' says Urmila.

'I don't know what response to give,' complains Nandan. 'Everyone asks me. What are you saying now? Are you still repeating the same things?'

'We should keep quiet for a while, it's for the best . . .' ventures Shorty Josh.

'. . . but then they ask, Why aren't you people speaking? Why are you silent now?' Professor Nandan is upset. 'We can't support all this, and we've criticized enough.'

Sharad is silent, and so is Hanif.

'Otherwise, everyone should eat here,' decides Daddu.

Shruti gives the scooter a kick before getting on. Hanif grabs and wiggles it. Sharad walks over to them and laughs.

'Afraid of bombs?'

'No, bhai,' Shruti laughs. 'Maya was saying a snake slithered out from under her scooter, right when she was starting it.'

'From under the scooter?' Sharad's eyes bulge.

'It was coiled somewhere inside,' explains Shruti.

'Oh my God.' Sharad puts his hand on his chest. 'In this weather?'

Hanif guffaws. Shruti blushes and says, 'It was an after-the-rains thing.'

'And we're scared today!' Hanif gets on the scooter. 'Have a seat,' he says.

'It's good to be careful,' says Sharad. 'I'll also wiggle my scooter a bit.' He smiles and puts on his helmet.

'Everything's been decided from the start,' mutters Hanif.

There's not a single couple on the shortcut bridge.

'If they say don't write, don't speak, don't go, obey this law, that law, they're not saying it themselves; the good of the department is saying it, the betterment of education is saying it, the greater good is saying it.'

There used to be such romance on this bridge!

'And if I say keep quiet, or if I say speak, or if I say don't follow such rules, then I'm being selfish . . .'

'Hanif, we shouldn't go this way any more.' Sharad is jumpy. 'But nothing will be achieved by simply opposing,' he adds.

Hanif looks around. The trees cast dense shadows. Above chirp hidden birds. It's a lovely atmosphere: romantic, bewitching. But so deserted.

Beverly sits quietly, but Sharad is quarrelling.

'I don't know why she's not talking. If you see it, you'll understand. This is a very different type of cruelty. Modern bombs and weapons smuggled in . . . people who form gangs and go on killing sprees can't even compete; they die too. It's hard to imagine the horror. You press the remote and walk away cheerfully eating peanuts, as bodies scatter behind you like broken toys . . .'

'But we also . . . we also . . .' Shruti stammers. 'Hanif, you tell!' she cries.

Yes, more bombs have exploded.

'You go to sleep.'

Hanif is reading in the other room with the light on.

Later, when Shruti's eyes open suddenly, everything's dark. She feels around on the bed. Then she sees him in the dark. He's just sitting there, perhaps looking out of the window.

'Hanif,' Shruti calls out. 'What are you doing?'

'I just turned out the light. I'm coming.'

Later that night she still hears him moving about.

Kapadia has sent a jeep, but Hanif doesn't want to go.

'He's obeying Nandu. He's asked us to abandon all this for the time being,' says Sharad, snickering.

'Don't joke, Sharad,' snaps Shruti.

'No, really.' Sharad frowns. 'He's getting a new project on migrant labourers. Now he'll have to go into those areas. We've already done whatever we needed over here . . .'

'Absolutely don't go,' jokes Daddu. 'I also forbid it.' He looks at Beverly and smiles. 'But you can go.' He narrows his eyes and examines her closely. 'Yes, yes, you can go.'

'But why?' laughs Beverly.

'Arre, because you're a foreigner. It's not like you have to live here. Take these three back with you. Then they can be involved in these matters from a comfortable distance. Will someone please tell me why people living here are always going over there? There's nothing left for them!'

His laughter fizzes.

The jeep driver arrives.

'Sir, Kapadia Sir has said that . . .' he begins.

'Yes, let's go.' Sharad and Beverly stand up.

'I won't go either,' says Shruti.

'You go. Why not . . .?' Hanif looks angry.

'I'll get some work done too.' Shruti glares.

'Go, go.' Daddu waves his hand. 'Before he gets tempted. I cannot understand the interest you people have in all this.'

Shruti begins to laugh.

'Why are you laughing?' asks Hanif calmly, though he's irritated.

'I'm laughing at Daddu's beauty contest! When all the braids and all the beards are bound together, and a great hullaballoo arises!'

Daddu looks pleased.

'If one falls, the other falls too. Dragging each other down. How must they look?' Shruti laughs as she imagines this. 'Their clothes torn off; the pandit and the mullah both naked.'

'No no no no,' Daddu stops her suddenly. 'Then that is absolutely not right. Not even the gods can shame the naked! No one can beat them. There's nothing the naked are shy of doing. Not even the gods can shame them!' He repeats in jest: 'Not even the gods can shame the naked!' Then he begins to say it over and over. 'Not even the gods can shame the naked!'

Our city filled with those whom not even the gods could shame that year.

'Then we'll both go; we'll go in first class.'

Hanif looks at her, dumbfounded. 'Do bombs not explode in first?' He closes one cupboard and opens another. 'It's just an hour and a half. One can easily get seats in second. They don't have much money for travel.'

'Then why are you going?' Shruti makes a face. 'You're the one who has to worry the most!'

'Okay, enough. Stop making senseless objections.' Hanif sticks his head back in the cupboard. 'Remember—there was that one article—"Fundamentalism and the Secular State"?'

'No one's going from the department, but . . .' Shruti is fuming.

'No one else was invited. No one's telling you to go either.' Hanif flips through papers and books. 'Where did that article go?'

'I'll go,' insists Shruti. 'No one's even listening, but you have to give speeches.'

'You don't even want me to go where people are prepared to listen to me?' Hanif stands up. 'Stop trying to come with me . . . all this nagging.'

'Out of my way; let me look.' Shruti pushes him aside. 'Secular secular! Around here no one wants to take even one breath that's not religious, and you go . . .'

'Why are you saying that as though secular means against religion?' Hanif also squeezes into the cupboard. 'It's better to keep religion separate.'

'No one will understand. No one will understand.'

Shruti sticks the article in his face.

'Do you see the difference?' Sharad asks Beverly. 'Right now, if these were Muslim camps, then we'd be given a fully prepared list. Who died, who was wounded, who's missing. There's no comparison between their organization and ours, in terms of discipline and skill.'

'Don't talk like that,' snaps Beverly.

Sharad sits reading in his room. The light's on, and he's wrapped in the quilt.

But he's not reading, he's staring into the void.

He hears the *tap tap* of the chowkidar.

He's possibly asleep with his eyes open. Who knows what time it is.

Daddu comes in.

'Go to sleep,' he says.

'Hmmm.' Sharad's eyes move a little. Then he lies back with a thud.

Daddu turns off the lights.

'It rarely happens like that,' Hanif explains to Shruti on the train. 'Don't be paranoid.'

Shruti looks truly terrified.

'Look once under the seat in a detached way, then look in the front and in the back to make sure there's no packet or bottle or box or transistor lying around.' Hanif leans down and looks. Shruti also peers around, but anxiously.

'Make it seem natural.' Hanif turns to her. 'As though you're glancing down to see if there's mud stuck to your shoes; if you should shake them.' He stands up and brushes off his shoes.

The woman sitting across from them is laughing.

She holds out her glass and says, nodding towards the bottle in Hanif's lap, 'Please give me a little water.'

Hanif opens the lid. The woman's arm is sheathed in an endless succession of glass bangles. He looks up. She covers her head with her pallu.

But, I'm Musl-... he begins.

'If you're so worried about losing your dharma, then don't touch me,' the woman scolds.

Shruti and Hanif both blush.

Today, not Hanif and Shruti, but Kapadia and Beverly are eating downstairs. Daddu is busy with his mashing. He smushes the carrots and peas, then pops them in his mouth. Kapadia is busy with his talking, freeing everyone else to focus on their meals.

'I'm going to lock up all the hooligans for a few days . . . the Hindu hooligans too . . . then things will stabilize. Discipline's needed, but it's just that we fear . . . they stoned that collector in Bihar to death. Some powerful people are hooligans, but I'm not the type to get scared . . . beat the bastards . . . I'll die doing it. I'll become a martyr . . . Muslims never just die, they become martyrs—shahids. Have you noticed, those bastards use the strangest words . . . Nowadays Hindus don't just die either, they're sacrificed—balidaan! Hear that, Daddu? The Islamization of the Hindu religion! The mahants of the ashram are fasting . . . The way those kids died, people are even more riled. Advanced technology giving them brand-new ways of fighting . . . there's a huge reaction against it . . .'

Sharad speaks up as he takes a bite: 'But bombing's also a reaction.'

'That's a later thing.' Kapadia sucks on the stuffed brinjal— bharvaan baingan—like he's sucking soup from a bone. 'The Hindus' outrage is the true reaction. They felt like, How long have we endured this? Forgive them because they're illiterate, keep quiet because Nehru said so.'

Beverly stops eating. She wears that look of innocent curiosity that appears every time she hears something new.

'So is the real reaction that one, when the Hindus reacted against the Muslims and Nehru? Before that . . .'

'So what?' Kapadia has entirely devoured the brinjal. He wipes the masala paste sticking to his fingers on the roti lying on his plate. 'Is the first one the real reaction? Why should the Muslim reaction be called the first one?'

'It's the old riddle of the chicken and the egg! You'll be repeating it till doomsday!' cries Daddu, fizzing with laughter. Streams of air escape from between his teeth.

He has cleaned his plate. He gets up and leaves.

The rule at Daddu's house is that whoever's done eating may go wash their hands; they're not expected to sit at the table and wait for everyone else to finish or try to accompany them and eat at the same pace, until everyone's final morsel falls into their mouths at once.

'Everything's a reaction,' says Sharad.

'So? The mistake . . .' Kapadia taps his spoon.

'. . . has been made by the person who did wrong. Whether in his reaction or . . .' suggests Beverly.

'Everything's a reaction. We should get rid of this whole reaction discourse . . .' says Sharad.

'But it's helpful for understanding . . .' says Beverly.

'. . . but not for forgiveness . . .' concludes Sharad.

'Yaar, you edumacated people!' laughs Kapadia as he stands up.

In the nation's capital, a new political party has been created. It's called the Akhil Bharatiya Vir Dal. The ABVD.

Some members of the department have sent an announcement letter to the vice chancellor requesting the rotation system be put on hold for the next two years in view of the deteriorating situation in the city and the university.

Some members haven't signed it.

'I can't understand,' says Shruti. 'Tell me why.'

'Will only our department be disrupted by the rotation?' retorts Hanif.

'Sometimes you say you don't want it . . .' mumbles Shruti.

'I absolutely don't want it,' says Hanif.

'If it's a matter of someone else . . .'

'If it's a matter of someone else doing it, why would I object?'

'It's fine if he stays until his retirement. Here's your milk.'

'Why? I already drank it.' Hanif pushes the glass away.

'Arre, careful.' Shruti picks up the glass. 'You already drank some? But I just boiled it.'

'I drank yesterday's.'

'But nothing was left from yesterday.'

'There was.'

'You're forgetting.'

'Can't you forget?'

Hanif goes into the bathroom.

Shruti searches for a milky glass or cup among the dirty dishes. She knocks on the bathroom door.

'Why are you lying?' she asks. 'Try to remember. If you do, tell me; then come out and drink it.'

There's a student chapter of the ABVD at the university. They've invited the ashram Mahant to be chief guest at their inaugural meeting.

When death looms, who thinks to fear it? Can't you die of fear itself?

Which happened that year. They say many who didn't die in the riots died of fear.

They said the victims implored their attackers when they came . . . a Muslim . . . with a dagger . . . a Hindu . . . with a trident . . . Help! Help! Don't kill me . . . I'm Christian . . . Help! But I'm Bohra . . . son, I'm like your mother . . .

There are garlands of marigolds, red roses and periwinkles at the ashram. A smell fills the nostrils. Not of flowers. A suffocating hospital stench. The smell of colours.

Red–yellow–purple smells.

'Differentiate a bit between home and office. Otherwise, why shouldn't we let our children come here to do their homework?' says Urmila.

'Whose family comes here to do their work?' asks Sharad.

'Oh, maybe none do . . . But the department is for the department members, yes?'

In the newspaper, there's a picture of many mahants sitting and fasting. Long, matted locks and straggly beards. Right in the middle lie three of the most important mahants in a semi-conscious state. Doesn't this look like one of Daddu's beauty contests!

There's a sign at the school gate which says in red letters:

HINDUS AWAKE! SAVE THE NATION!

Inside, there's a dirt floor which looks like it's swept and cleaned daily. The children sit on the ground. They're divided into separate sections of varying sizes. Classes are in progress.

'No, no, don't stop anyone,' Shruti, Hanif, Sharad, Beverly, all speak out.

An Adivasi student of Hanif's is showing them his impoverished district.

The director says, 'Do stay and watch the film. The government sends the children free films to watch.'

A government development officer arrives. He explains how much money the government gives to make films for children's education, sprinkling a bit of English into his speech.

This is a very poor area indeed. The children are fed at the school, that's why their families send them here. No Hindus visit, nor Muslims. These are all things the students tell them. But the Christian priests have been coming for years.

There's an area with mud walls and a red-tiled roof. This is where they run the film projector.

All the classes have stopped for the films, and the tiny children march proudly inside and sit down.

Many of them look about four or five years old. The girls wear their hair in two braids looped to the sides of their heads and fastened with bright-red ribbons. All of them peer from the corners of their eyes at the city dwellers seated on the girls' bench along one side of the room, especially the foreigner.

The reel whirrs, and the film begins.

'There are three films,' the government officer explains, turning towards them.

The white spots of the old print dance on the screen as the reel rolls.

In the first film, Chacha Nehru is shown taking a stroll with his grandsons, Sanjay and Rajiv, affectionately holding their hands. Then he's walking in a garden, examining the flowers. Then he's feeding a Pomeranian in his lap. Then he's standing with Mountbatten. Then he's playing cricket very badly.

Whirr whirr, the reel turns.

In the second film, foreign doctors in green masks and aprons are gathered around an operating table, holding scissors, knives, needles. The person lying on the table is being given a new heart. The camera focuses directly on the open chest and the beating heart. It is bright red, bloody—raw flesh.

The third film is a long song, performed by Nargis, Sunil Dutt and Prem Nath. The music rises to a crescendo in the middle of the song, and then the mayhem of riots appears on the screen. People are dying, fleeing, screaming, killing; there's destruction, everyone's eyes are bloodshot, the screen is soaked in the blood of trampled bodies. Suddenly the smiling actors materialize from out of nowhere and begin to sing. Everyone holds hands warmly.

Jai Jagadambe! whispers Sharad.

Sharad and Beverly are in a rickshaw. They've taped a great many interviews and taken numerous notes. Wherever bombs have exploded.

'Say what you will, Beverly,' says Sharad puffing on a cigarette. 'If you look up close, all that remains are the daily troubles of human beings.'

'What was it like to see that woman, hmm?'

'I felt angry.' Sharad tosses out his cigarette.

'At whom? At the woman?'

'No, at those who put her in that condition.'

'That's very dangerous. Never throw them out without extinguishing them first.' Beverly turns and looks back, as though she expects to find sparks or fire or smoke!

'It's so horrible,' some people are saying. 'At least when Hindus were doing it, one knew which places to avoid. Now there's no way of knowing where they'll come from; they could be anywhere.'

'Look at what goes on nowadays. With the kind of money they have, there could be rockets, missiles, anything.'

'Have you ever wondered . . .'

Seeing Hanif and Sharad coming, the colony residents fall silent, but Shruti has been standing there all along. Won't she tell?

And me, and my pen?

These days, there's a new project in the department.

'Do you know,' says Professor Nandan, 'that people have come up with a theory of germ warfare, and they're wondering why there were more illnesses in Hindu-majority areas?'

It appears he's only talking to Sharad and Hanif.

'The greatest number of hepatitis cases occurred among the hut dwellers. Migrant labourers. A lot of filth spread after the rains, and the drinking water and sewage are now mingled.'

And did anyone ask him, if they were going to spread germs why they didn't do it where they could shut down businesses and do some serious damage to the country? They found only this insignificant city to attack?

'But they're more interested in the part of the theory that says this is a Muslim plot.'

Perhaps he wants to advance the importance of the project in their eyes by saying *theory-theory*? Or does he want to show them how the department's still humming along? See, it hasn't shut down! Articles, conferences and speeches continue apace!

Shruti feels around on the bed. It's empty. The room is dark. She reaches for the bedside switch and then recoils guiltily. She tiptoes noiselessly into the living room. It's a moonlit night. Hanif stands on the balcony. He's bathed in the haze of moonlight. The

madhumalti flowers hang by his side like clusters of stars. Shruti
watches him secretly from behind the door.

The ashram has purchased the land next to the castrated temple–
mosque. They will build a school there.

'I'll submit it, but the editor will remove it,' says Babu Painter.
'Don't stop writing, but let's wait a bit.'

When the two of them enter, they see Daddu's glass on the table.

'He must have gone to the bathroom. Do you want some?'
Sharad asks Beverly.

She refuses.

They go straight into Sharad's room and sit down. Sharad
is silent.

'What's wrong?' Beverly examines his face, which is
extremely sad.

Sharad looks back at her. She's a tall, thin, delicate girl. Her
eyes sparkle with a mosaic of purple and green. Sharad stares at
her intently.

'Beverly . . . what I'm seeing . . .' he says haltingly. His throat
feels constricted.

'Yes, it's very painful.' Beverly's soft face fills with compassion.

She looks down. She looks up again at Sharad. She rests a
hand on his shoulder. Of sympathy.

Or support.

'Sharad, thank you. Thank you for showing me all this.'

We can't say such things, thinks Sharad. 'Thank you for showing me all this.' People would take it the wrong way. I'm forced to think about everything I say. 'Thank you, for showing us so many torched houses, so many half-burnt corpses.' He adds this bit of dialogue in his mind and smiles.

Beverly's hand feels smooth, like butter or cream. Soft and round.

He touches it lightly. Her head is bowed, revealing her long, smooth neck, like the curving stem of a flower. There's a dark line down the middle. Sharad runs his finger down the line. He strokes from top to bottom, to the soft mound at the top of the backbone. 'How soft this bone is,' he says. The sights in the galis and hospital weave about him. He feels tearful.

Out of curiosity, he presses the skin on Beverly's shoulder for a moment, then pulls away. It leaves a dimple that begins to fill after it's released from his touch, like a cushion; then it turns yellow, then red the very next moment. Then the red, too, begins to disappear. Beverly softly strokes his hand.

Sharad feels close to tears. If she speaks, I'll weep, he fears.

'No, we can't go in the ashram van.' Shruti is arguing out in the street.

'It was empty, there was nothing else . . .' Sharad makes a face. 'We're taking so much stuff . . .'

They've done loads of shopping.

'Go to Pakistan or Qabristan! Die!' someone shouts.

All four of them jump. They turn angrily in the direction of the voice.

Three women in burqas are walking nearby. Three youths have just passed them on a motorcycle.

'They were talking to them,' observes Sharad pointlessly.

'Why have you started giving clarifications?' asks Shruti.

'Nowadays he clarifies for everyone!' Hanif walks ahead, carrying the bags.

'It's not like the other side doesn't shout obscenities,' retorts Sharad, to his back.

The back stops. The head resting on it turns. 'How many have you heard? How many have these two heard?'

'So if we haven't, that's proof?' Sharad is annoyed.

'They probably do, but not so openly . . .' suggests Beverly.

'Don't say anything; you don't know.' Sharad gives her a light smack.

Hanif has gone into a shop up ahead.

'Now when I'm out with him, I feel stifled,' Sharad tells Shruti. 'There's no knowing what will offend him. He'll pick on me.'

'You're right,' Beverly piles on. 'You show sympathy only when the other person seems helpless, innocent, desperate, if they scold, then . . .'

Shruti follows Hanif into the shop.

When the two re-emerge, they're carrying a bucket with three brooms in it.

'What did I say to him that annoyed him and made him walk away?' growls Sharad.

'You said it to me,' Beverly replies. 'Because I opened my mouth.'

'Are you really that cold, Daddu?'

Daddu gets up and shuts off the heater.

'What to do? If I turn it on, I feel hot; if I shut it off, I'm cold!'

'Daddu, I'm going to write a story,' says Shruti, sitting down. 'Not about all this, just a story.'

Daddu smiles and quietly shakes his head. He recites:

'Saavan ke baadlon ki tarah se bhare hue
Ye vo nayan hain jinse ki jangal hare hue.'

'Full, like the monsoon clouds
These are the eyes that coloured the jungle green'

Then he asks, 'Tell me, what language is that song written in and who wrote it? You don't know, do you?' His hands sparkle. 'Ignoramus, they happily mixed Hindi and Urdu; it's a poem by the Muslim poet Sauda.'

'What?' Shruti stares dumbfounded.

'Yes!' Daddu's hands dance. 'Will you write a story like this? You can't write anything. Your boat has sunk!' he cries, laughing.

'Has not.' Shruti smiles.

'Okay, I'll accept your *has not*, but you've made my job harder. Must I teach you your own language now?'

He returns to his books and becomes engrossed. At some point, he exclaims, 'Arre, what do you people know? You recognize a thing by its exterior, but the insides have disappeared! Here.' He picks out a book. 'Listen.' He flips the pages. '"*Sajan, tum* . . ." Listen.'

'I'm listening.' Shruti sits up straight.

'Sajan, tum mukh setii ulto naqaab aahista aahista.'
'Darling, lift the veil from your face, slowly, slowly'

'Amazing, Daddu!'
'Now listen to the second line . . .'

'Ki jyun gil se nikastaa hai gulaab aahista aahista.'
'As the rose emerges from the earth, slowly slowly.'

'Wah wah!' He nods with pleasure.
'Sauda?' Shruti asks.

'No, that's Wali. They're both from the eighteenth century. Good God, you people know nothing!'

A bomb was found in the picture hall.

Hanif comes up behind Shruti and puts his arms around her. 'Okay, baba, I told a lie. I didn't have any milk!'

Shruti laughs. 'But why?'

'Just because.'

'Because why?' Shruti bores into him with her eyes.

'It wasn't even about the milk.' Hanif touches the madhumalti lightly.

'It offends you, yes?' Shruti turns his face towards her stubbornly.

Hanif starts.

'You don't want to become the head because Nandu will harass you, but if they cheerfully cut you out and proceed as though you're not worthy, then . . .? Right?'

'It's natural to feel a bit offended,' agrees Hanif calmly. 'Whether I don't wish to do it is another matter, but his wanting to . . .'

'But, Hanif, you do know what people are like right now, and he has to leave the chair.'

'But, Shruti, every Tom, Dick and Harry gets the headship in the rotation . . .'

'If the plan was to attack with germs, they would have chosen something more lethal than mere jaundice! Muslims are not so naive.' Shorty Josh laughs at the stupid rumour floating around.

'You all can just leave me alone.'

'Then I won't go either,' Shruti says.

'Why are you doing this?' Hanif makes a face.

'Why do you feel guilty?' asks Sharad in an affable tone.

'Yaar, sometimes you yourself forbid me from going. Now I'm saying I'm not going, and you're saying, Let's go.' Hanif frowns.

'Maybe you shouldn't go. What if people get angry when they see you?' Shruti adds after some thought.

'Why would they make him a target? Okay, let it be.' Sharad feels a bit uncomfortable when he sees Hanif's expression.

'But you go, Shruti. No one will say anything to you,' encourages Hanif.

'They won't say anything to you either.' Sharad wants to reassure him, but he doesn't have the courage to speak up. Hanif is making him feel strangely tense.

Daddu, it seems, hasn't moved from his spot. Books with old bindings lie open about him as he recites couplets to himself and then offers words of praise, also to himself.

'*Shab-e-khalvat men gul ruu sun / khitaab aahista aahista*,' he recites.

'Meer?' asks Shruti, putting the receiver back on the phone properly.

'Stunning! It means: . . . *trysting at night with the rose-visaged beloved / whispering, softly, softly*. No, Wali again. Now that man could write.'

Shruti is thinking. She wants to say, Hanif, the street where I can walk fearlessly, but you walk fearfully, that street has changed for both of us; that street has infected us both like it's a curse.

'I'll write a good story, Daddu. Not about any of this. Really,' she says.

'Oh, wah . . . !' says Daddu. 'Amazing.' He's reading again. Meer. Aloud:

> *'Aafaaq ki manzil se gaya kaun salaamat*
> *Asbaab lutaa raah men yaan har safarii ka.'*

> *'Who has ever safely left this world?*
> *Every traveller is robbed of all belongings along the way.'*

'Doesn't your liberality melt away when you see their pain?' Sharad asks Beverly.

'I'm hardly a Hindu!' she replies.

Shruti knows Hanif isn't asleep, even though his back is turned and it's dark. She can't help it; she reaches out and places a hand on his shoulder.

The encouragement and empathy flowing from that hand distresses him. He feels his soul contracting. He wants to push the hand away. His anger throbs beneath the hand. The rest of his body has no sensation, as though there's no skin there, it's just an open wound that Shruti is pressing.

When advertisements appear on the TV, Daddu goes to the bathroom, or fills his glass, or picks up the newspaper. Right now, there's an advertisement for trucks: *What curves, what smoothness!* A woman stands in front of a tire.

There's another advertisement, for constipation relief: a woman caresses her body from below her breasts to just above the thighs. This is where constipation lies!

'Daddu isn't watching. Did you notice?' Sharad asks Hanif and Shruti with a laugh.

If we don't look away in disgust when we see naked pictures, what will happen? The nudity might enter our bloodstream, and without even thinking about it, we could fall prey to horrible, naughty, vulgar thoughts.

Daddu always looks away.

'Why wouldn't I want to tell you?' asks Hanif.

Hanif and Shruti are holding hands, taking an after-dinner stroll in front of the house.

'It's not because I fear for my personal safety . . . I'm fine . . . but I fear becoming part of this vast infamy, this vast hatred, this perversion . . . I . . . I've become linked with all that,' Hanif says softly.

'But those are other people.' Shruti doesn't want to accept the premise.

'I've become linked with the idea of Islam,' says Hanif.

'Wrong,' retorts Shruti heatedly.

'Try to understand, Shruti,' says Hanif. 'Just think quietly for a moment. All this that's happening . . . my . . . my . . . Muslimness has been foisted on me.'

'But it's them . . .' begins Shruti.

'The us/them theory is too simplistic: saying what's happening is happening over there, that those people are doing it. We're separate, we're clean, we're something different. But is that really true?' Hanif's words are flowing now. 'Is nothing happening inside us? Is it all happening outside?'

These days it gets dark early. It's foggy up ahead; the streetlights are enveloped in a smoky haze.

This is a time for sacrifice. The mahant's voice comes from above, an akaashvaani, broadcasting through the loudspeakers: *The Devi asks for accounting from the idol-destroyer and the cow-devourer . . . we must cleanse the stain . . . only then can we return to the bygone era of peace and non-violence.*

Sharad and Beverly are standing on the university campus, and Sharad is translating.

'But don't think all the holy men are hypocrites and swindlers,' he says. 'Perhaps we don't even understand religious fervour. Yes, possibly it's anarchy, and societal prejudices have inflamed them. And the extremist element is also jumping on the bandwagon. But temples were indeed destroyed, and that's bound to upset them. If these people don't feel that way, who will?'

With Beverly, Sharad feels a new kind of freedom. He can say anything around her. He won't be accused of becoming a Hindu partisan for saying this thing, or of going over to the Muslim side for saying that. He can be supportive of Nandan or forgiving of Kapadia.

'They're talking about their fatwas. Have they seen ours?' laughs Sharad. 'The fatwas of the seculars! What are things coming to when one must watch every word before speaking! People swoop in to tell you the meaning! You're just not allowed to express the confusion in your own head!' he rants.

'This is such an intense phase you all are going through!' exclaims Beverly.

'Can any Indian say such a thing? They'd be immediately declared wicked!'

'It's just like the churning of the ocean. Everything topsy-turvy. Where will it all go and how? What form will it take? Oh!' Beverly wears an expression of wonderment, as though it's all a miracle and she's surrounded by enchantment.

'I can say such suspect things to you without feeling guilty. But out there . . .' Sharad makes a face. 'If I say they've acquired modern foreign firepower, suddenly I'm anti-Muslim, and if I say the Hindus are going through a phase of uncertainty, I've become pro-Hindu.'

Suddenly he feels sorry for himself.

Beverly pats his hair affectionately.

He's absorbed in his thoughts as she softly caresses his hair. He's afraid if she speaks he'll burst into tears.

'Beverly, I love that you don't know these things already, that you're learning them with a pure heart. You can say ridiculous things. You can say dangerous things. Beverly, I can say anything here.' Sharad's eyes glisten strangely.

Beverly caresses his eyes. Suddenly he grabs her hand and kisses it recklessly. He presses it to his cheek, covers his eyes with it, then kisses it again. He grasps it tightly and continues to speak.

'Beverly, even I don't know what's in my heart; why I feel more sympathy for one person than another. I don't know. The words come first, the thought comes later, the reason later still, if at all. If he felt more sympathy for the women in burqas, would he say it out loud the way I would? I can't even understand why

I go around yelling, *We are one!* and then feeling doubt, and wondering, *But are we?*

Beverly doesn't know how to stop Sharad's outpourings. He stops speaking, lets go of her hand and fixes her with a devastated glance.

All the world's desolation is reflected on his face.

'Beverly,' he whispers noiselessly. He holds her hand again, gently, both hands, and covers his face with her palms. I can't see if he's weeping.

'Sharad Sir, can't you be the speaker? What if there are problems when Hanif Sir speaks?' A student is talking to Sharad and Hanif, who are sunning themselves outside the department.

Meaning, Hanif, you keep quiet.

What I see: the well-wishers saying, *Please speak!* But the enemies are also saying, *Please speak!* The well-wishers are saying, *Please keep quiet!* But the enemies are also saying, *Please keep quiet!* The same words. How easy it has become to misunderstand. To get jumbled.

Here's how the scene unfolded:

When the first stone is thrown, Sharad simply raises his hand and says, 'Wait.' And keeps speaking. Perhaps that's how it goes: when a stone is thrown, we become fearless in the moment, prepared for any outcome, and our words begin to flow.

When Sharad raises his hand, the students who had stood to chase the stone-thrower sit down quietly.

'Please think.' Sharad lowers his hand. 'When people respond to a disagreement with stones, we should realize we've come to a juncture where no one will be able to stop the decline of our culture if we don't wake up now. This is our last chance. If we can't do it now, we'll fall silent forever. It'll bring us to a social order in which a stone decides our actions.'

We already sit there prepared for anything, because the air crackles with tension, but all the tension seems ludicrous until the stone is thrown. We ourselves are embarrassed by the way we glance about furtively, unnerved by the stiff, starchy air. Fear, my friend, lies over there, and stones, my friend, lie over there! We're ashamed of our fear.

When the stone is thrown, we feel even more ashamed. Our hearts begin to pound as though we're embarrassed by our own cowardice. Many look at someone else in the audience and smile weakly to rid themselves of this shame. As though we're giving this insignificant stone excessive significance if we look too serious, and we'll come to consider ourselves martyrs!

Shruti's heart begins to pound; she, too, makes eye contact with the woman sitting across from her and smiles. As though the stone is a joke, and she knows it too.

The students who jumped up to pursue the stone-thrower control their emotions when Sharad, looking wise and calm, signals not to do anything, to sit down again.

And then it's as though the train of words, which was trundling along and had stopped in its tracks with a jolt when the stone was thrown, begins to hum along again at a nice clip.

'You call yourself Hindu?' asks Sharad, gently heating up. 'The practice of debate lies at the root of the Hindu religion and culture. Don't you people know the traditions of khandan–mandan, of refutation and elaboration, or doctrinal debate? Does Hinduism follow one single belief? In fact, there are many. And this will always be the case. But what will remain of the great Hindu religion you're all so worried about after you've rendered it stiflingly mean and narrow by extracting all its culture, tradition and dharma?'

Everyone is sitting in the community hall. Not a single Muslim has come, aside from our Hanif Jaidi. The hall is lit with tube lights, and the carpet bears the stains of countless bare feet. The mic is plugged into the wall, its wire extended over to the stage. Although it's not really a stage, just a white sheet.

The same questions are being raised in this town as in other places, and this is why people have come to learn something from Sharad's lecture.

They are mostly middle-aged couples. The men sit cross-legged, the women with their saris properly arranged, knees angled to the side. A small band of children leans against the doors or squats nearby.

'Let's ask questions, give answers, debate. But throwing stones?

'There should be a uniform code, but not because of our hostility. Right now, there's no kind of uniform code. Hindus have their own code, which doesn't contain complete uniformity. Authority has been given to popular but antiquated customs. A maternal uncle and niece can marry in some Hindu communities in the south; a wedding can be effected among some Hindus without even taking the seven rounds about the sacred fire; Adivasis and clans have their own customs; there are unmarried unions; and we don't get upset about any of it. How many traditions must be eradicated in this country according to the new thinking that one code must be followed? Where should diversity be preserved, where should we leave it be? These things won't be decided through animosity but through friendly debate, with all stakeholders involved.'

It was the last such gathering of that year. After that, there was an uproar about such events inciting violence, that they must be shut down, and so they were.

'Islam is not some sort of mass-production factory,' Sharad had said into the mic, 'from which every person emerges as a model of the same narrow-minded, reactionary, confrontational cultural and religious thinking—where only our names are different.

'And consider this, for any topic we discuss—the problems of Assam, Punjab, the Northeast—we speak of numerous factors: government, terrorism, frustrated social classes, etc. Why do we never discuss similar factors when it comes to Muslim communalism?'

'It's necessary,' he had continued, 'for orthodox people to feel trust and kinship, whether Hindu or Muslim, or any other religion. Their frustrations, their mutual distrust should be solved with expressions of humanity. No one here is foreign, or non- . . .'

'Shut up, non-Hindu!' challenged a loud, boastful voice.

This was when a window was broken with the second stone.

Three stones were thrown at that meeting. The police had to be called, and right when people were shouting, *Let him speak! Let him speak!* Hanif got up, took the mic and spoke as well.

'The non-Hindu isn't me; it's you,' responded Sharad to the second stone. 'I'm Hindu. And as a Hindu, I can't remain silent. My culture is capacious; it's linked with religion but also forged from other sources. You cannot hijack the term Hindu and dismiss me. You're not Hindu. You're partisans of Hindutva, a philosophy which has been stagnant for ages. There's no such stagnancy in Hinduism. No tradition stagnates at one unchanging point.

'You can't even see your own shortsightedness. I'm not against religion, or modernism, or Indian culture, or the uniform civil code, or any of these mutually conflicting factors. These are all moving pieces, changing with the influence of time and society, and we must come together and make an elegant whole of them.'

At this, some fiery youths walked out of the hall shouting, *Jai Jagadambe!*

Sharad's voice was inaudible over the din.

'I entreat you to maintain tolerance and control,' implored the student who invited his teachers to speak. 'Listen first to the speaker. You may openly ask questions, but please don't be rude.'

'But we must ask where we're heading. Nowadays, we must first press our palms together and beg for tolerance before we open our mouths; tomorrow . . .'

And now Hanif stood up next to the student and began to speak.

'Listen, please, everyone. We keep making false starts. We keep going back in history, searching for crimes. What I say is, let's start from right now, right here, from today, with positivity.'

Whispers spread through the meeting: 'He's Muslim . . . His name is Hanif.'

'Yes, I am a Muslim, and I'm saying all the same things Sharad's already said. I'm calling for reform among Muslims as well as among others. I'm speaking out against the closed-minded elements of all religions. I'm speaking out against the Hindus and Muslims who have made religion so hateful, those . . .'

With a scream of 'Shut up, non-Hindu!' the third stone sailed in. And hit Sharad on the head.

Hanif only got as far as *from right now, right here*, because the starting point for the audience was that he would not be forgiven.

Sharad needed first aid. The gathering dispersed.

That was the last such event that year.

Such events were no longer possible because of the way in which our city had already been divided.

Our city was not half-Hindu, half-Muslim; it had become half-non-Hindu, half-non-Muslim.

But when stones are thrown, our passionate utterances filling the air suddenly deflate and fall silent, as though not stones but hot wax has been flung and now hardens on our lips.

Hanif has fallen silent.

Even Daddu looks upset.

And I, who sit with pen uncapped, have grown frightened: What if everyone ends up just sitting like this with their mouths hanging open? Then my ink will dry up. If I try to draw the pen across the paper, will it simply be air writing?

'We heard Muslims threw stones at you and ruined your meeting,' say people in the department.

'What!' Sharad exclaims, flabbergasted.

Shruti opens the door when the maid rings the buzzer. The maid proceeds into the kitchen with her sari hiked up and tied around her waist. She's scrubbing the pots and pans furiously, *bang crash bang*, making lots of noise.

Shruti sits cross-legged and sways back and forth like someone singing bhajans. Truly. But there are no bhajans playing in her mind, something else is, because swaying like this is what she does when she's thinking.

'Please shut the door after me,' the maid calls out. 'Sahib isn't here?' she asks when Shruti comes.

'Didn't you know . . .' Shruti begins to say with a smile.

What she's about to say is that the university has opened again and that he's giving a lecture right now. But she panics at her own phrase: *Didn't you know* . . . As though some tiding of misfortune hovers before her, like, *Didn't you know . . . yesterday in a traffic accident, he . . .?*

'Why do you ask?' Shruti asks uneasily.

'Because he was here yesterday,' answers the maid carelessly. She slips on her sandals on the stairs and goes below.

'I heard there was also a fire there!' Kapadia grins. 'Trouble follows them wherever they go!'

Daddu is silent but scowling.

'Does Nandu-Phandu feel less insecure?' asks Shruti, breaking the silence.

'The insecurity of the powerful goes away only when they regain power. We'll see,' says Sharad.

'Daddu what is the exact meaning of tadipaar, this type of banishment?' asks Shruti.

When Daddu sips his drink, the light shifts on his throat.

'Dole, that . . .' he begins.

'Do you know over there . . .' Sharad drowns him out, speaking of some other department. '. . . so-and-so,' he's speaking of a senior lecturer, 'had wanted to submit an objection to such-and-such's appointment in writing? He resigned from all committees and wrote a complaint letter to the VC. But when the rest of the people in the department threatened to serve a show-cause notice, he retracted his complaint.'

'But why?' asks Shruti.

'When there are qualified people here, why have you selected someone from outside?'

'Hmph! Today,' Hanif sneers, 'he was forced to remain silent. Tomorrow he'll be considered a martyr for the very same reason. He'll become a hero.'

'. . . on the temples.' Daddu continues his explanation to Shruti.

'He shouldn't have spoken. Tell your friend not to expose himself to danger needlessly,' says Beverly softly.

'Danger?' Sharad laughs loudly. 'Did you hear something that frightened you?'

'Don't laugh.' Beverly stands up. 'Are we going to ignore danger until someone gets stabbed?'

'Stabbed?' Sharad laughs again. 'Us?'

Beverly is tying her shoelaces, and her face shows signs of annoyance. 'I wish I could stab you myself to make you more aware.'

'Beverly.' Sharad pulls her to his side. 'Don't worry. I do get afraid . . . Don't stare at me like that.' He looks sad.

Beverly also looks sad. The cries of children playing in the colony float into the room.

'I'm ashamed, Beverly,' apologizes Sharad. 'Don't leave me like this.' His voice trembles with anxiety.

'You were speaking so well at the gathering. But here . . .' She can't finish.

'When there's an attack on the minority, I'm prepared to lay down my life on their behalf. I come running again and again when the minority needs encouragement. But why do we go out of our way to avoid ever saying the minority has done the slightest wrong?'

They both sit silently. Perhaps unwittingly, Sharad finds himself repeating what he's said before.

'I'm very ashamed.' He stands up agitatedly. 'We feel so guilty for being in the majority that even when we see another in the wrong, we ourselves feel ashamed . . . But why? Beverly,' he says fearfully.

Beverly pushes his hand away.

'But let me speak.' There are tears in his eyes. *Don't leave me*, he wants to say.

Professor Nandan has had pots of flowers set out on the department steps.

He's planning to request a computer from the Special Assistance Review Committee.

The pots are planted with large marigolds ringed by chrysanthemums. Their yellow hue sparkles distinctively.

Hanif is typing something in the department.

'This is not the time to give a talk and become a hero,' he hears Nandan saying.

'For how long will we ignore Hindu sentiments? Muslims do it, we do it too. Name me one Muslim who considers the welfare of Hindus.'

'And our own world-famous progressive Muslim only looks after his own welfare, of course,' says Urmila.

Hanif glances over at Type Babu. Is he listening too?

'What's happening is an affront to Hinduism. But we won't accomplish anything by alienating them. We'll just end up more isolated. Oh, what's that you're doing?' Nandan's tone has changed.

'You've never tried eating them?' asks Urmila gleefully.

Hanif walks out of the office. Urmila has broken off a marigold blossom, twisted off the yellow petals and popped the small white seed into her mouth.

'I was worried the girls would pick the flowers to tuck in their hair, and here you are snacking on them,' laughs Nandan. When he sees Hanif, he nods slightly and climbs up a step with a *snip*.

Hanif looks around. Bright-yellow petals lie scattered everywhere, even outside the rubbish bin in the corner.

Nobody finds it interesting that a photo of Sharad with a Band-Aid has been printed on the third page of the newspaper.

There's a letter to the editor today:

> *Sharad's and Hanif's statements were fantastic. In this day and age, we need courage such as theirs. It's a good thing these people live far from the areas of knifings, riots, bombings, so they can fearlessly speak out on all sorts of topics.*

Daddu sits on the divan, trimming his nails with a clipper. Half his body is turned sideways, allowing the morning sun to illuminate his hands. Sharad is chewing his lip. Daddu smooths his nails with a file and blows on them.

An anonymous letter has arrived in the department mail.
Now outsiders are teaching us our religion! it reads.

The cabinet to the right of Hanif's desk is crammed with books. To the left there's a window, and outside, a set of stairs. Anyone who passes by on the stairs is reflected in the glass of the cabinet. A woman is walking down the steps with her child.

'Is that an office, Mamma?'

'Yes, it is. Shhh!'

When Hanif looks up at the cabinet, he makes eye contact with the woman. Both quickly avert their eyes. When she's gone, he pulls the curtain across.

He can hear Sharad lecturing his class: 'Who told you most Muslims study in educational institutions such as Nadwa and Darul-ulum? They study in many different Islamic schools that offer modern courses of study—English, maths, science. And who says only extreme Hindu-haters come from institutions like Nadwa? Are only enemies of Muslims coming out of the Hindu gurukuls?'

'Ohhh, sir!' cries a girl, deeply affected.

'Listen.' Hanif knows this speechifying tone of Sharad's all too well. 'In no religion is just one school of thought followed. Where one teacher might make a conservative argument, another will teach the opposite. Take the question of the fatwa. Fatwas are not the purview of a single religious leader; many can make them. One leader might say that in the Quran this has been said about women, but then a different verse from the Quran might say something else. Syed Ahmad Barelvi said India is Dar al-harb, or a place of war, and now India is not under Muslim rule, so everyone must depart; but then a different fatwa comes down declaring there's no need to depart, because this country is Dar al-aman, a place of peace.'

'Ohhh, sir!' the same girl cries out.

'Nor is it true that fatwas can only be given in terms of Sharia and Hadith. Fatwas have their own politics as well. In every religion, in every era, both voices arise. This is our political choice: Which voice do we choose to listen to? What is it?' he stops to ask.

Hanif pulls the curtain shut again. He sits in his chair, wondering if this man can be trusted.

Daddu is saying people have always had savage natures. Cycles that demonstrate their essential savagery recur.

'Just imagine, the heady freedom of such madness!' he exclaims to Shruti. 'Imagine the moment when those people who were yesterday just like you and me turn into savage beasts!'

The look in his eyes frightens Shruti.

'And tomorrow it'll happen to you and me too.' He waves his hands dismissively, as if to say, *What's the big deal?*

'If you wish to escape the beasts . . .' Now he's teasing Shruti. '. . . then lock yourself up in this room with me. I'll hang a picture of wherever you want to travel right here and teach you how to travel while sitting in one place!'

Shruti smiles.

'But if you try to interrogate those beasts like that good-for-nothing husband of yours does, you too will be ensnared. You'll have to talk to them the same way they do, and no one can win that way. They can't just come and give you a kick, and you say, "You bloody non-progressive!" You must also lift a leg and kick them back.'

At this, Daddu lifts a leg. Not for kicking but for stretching, because when he laughs he stretches out, and this pleases the divan!

'But we must fight back,' says Shruti.

'Arre, baba, then fight, na. But wait till they're like you and me again!' crows Daddu with a laugh, but his laughter stops abruptly.

Two letters are printed in the newspaper today.

One says:

Apologize. You agreed to speak at the gathering so you could tear Hindus apart. Are you spreading knowledge or atheism?

The other says:

We're all sheep.

'Why did you feel the need to speak?' Sharad asks Hanif.

Although when Beverly said she was frightened, he laughed.

'Should we reply?' The question arises from the band of students and teachers in front of the department.

It's getting colder, and people feel the urge to hop from one foot to the other as they soak up the sunlight.

'Place, population, environment, all create either meekness or violence,' says one girl.

'Like us,' replies a boy angrily. 'We'll get our revenge.'

'On whom? For what?' The girl is also angry. 'I should burn you because your ancestors made my ancestors commit sati?'

'Don't you talk please, mem sahiba,' retorts the boy with annoyance. 'Someone who thinks it's okay to dishonour women will feel nothing at a temple being desecrated?'

'What's this!' Many teachers and Sharad, and even Hanif, scold the boy.

'Please don't speak, sir! A man like you, who could dishonour a girl student he should have viewed as his own daughter . . .'

Hanif is stunned.

'A response must be written, a stern one,' says Sharad.

'I suggest you just quickly finish the course. Everything's going fine right now,' says Professor Nandan, campaigning not to ruin the year for the children.

'No, no, there's no need for you to do a talk for Haq. Have you been commissioned by the government to fix all things Hindu–Muslim?'

Sharad also feels worried when he looks at Shruti. 'For one thing, there was no need for you to speak; you're Muslim after all.'

'Everyone already knew my name,' Hanif points out.

'Then even more so. And on top of that you started bad-mouthing Hindus.'

'And what were you doing?' Hanif is enraged.

'Yaar, there's a difference between you and me. How long will we ignore it?'

'You're resorting to that now?' exclaims Shruti.

'This is no sentimental idealism . . .' Sharad tries to explain.

'Sharad,' Shruti says anxiously, 'that thing we keep saying we are, has that become sentimental idealists? If so, it's unwavering and beautiful and true, and it'll be our motive for living, and we are numerous . . .'

'Shruti.' Sharad comes forward and grabs her hand. 'There's been a tragedy. It's true we are one, but it's also true that Hanif and Sharad have come to have two different meanings . . .'

Hanif is still silent. Now Shruti and Sharad are too.

Daddu is gesticulating and speaking, but Shruti's mind wanders. She can hear Hanif walking around upstairs.

'One minute,' she says.

She rushes quickly up the stairs. The door is unlocked. She turns the handle and goes inside.

Hanif sits in the chair, his face turned towards the madhumalti. A thick book lies open in his lap.

She softly shuts the door and tiptoes back downstairs.

Daddu is saying something else, when again she hears the sound of pacing from above. Amazing.

How can she say *one minute* again. She's in a quandary.

'. . . we'll also do that which is enjoyable,' Daddu continues.

As soon as he rises to go to the bathroom, Shruti jumps up and goes upstairs. Hanif is still sitting as he was before. Shruti stares in astonishment.

'What?' he asks testily.

Kapadia has phoned to say today's article was written by a retired high court judge, a great devotee of the ashram's mahant.

'You should definitely send a letter to the editor,' says Babu Painter, who has also called.

Daddu sits silently. Nankau has come to show him a bill. Daddu examines it carefully, asks something, then adds it up. He reaches out and picks up his wallet from the table, gives him a Rs 100 note and lies back on the divan.

Recently, Daddu has turned the divan so that it won't look outside even by accident. If Shruti calls out for him to look at the madhumalti, he must turn his head.

He sits silently.

The other shop is by the bridge.

No, I push that thought aside. All this is Daddu's mischief, when he mentioned in conversation that they're just like us, those people, they just sometimes go through phases.

This shopkeeper is very young.

Surely he didn't use to regard everyone—women, elders— with such a haughty gaze. Nor did the tips of his moustache point straight up, Rajput style. He seems utterly unaware of that thing we call fear.

But why am I afraid then?

I simply must go there now, for ink.

Or maybe it's because I see how shaken Shruti is when she hears about the accusation against Hanif violating his own student.

She feels a sudden rush of fear, anger and shame all at once. The student revealed the place of women in all the different debates and arguments: Hindu vs Muslim, barbarity vs civilization, moral vs immoral, nowadays vs back in the day. A temple, that is, a place of worship, which a human or a devil, that is, man, could worship or destroy . . . could enact their Hinduness or Muslimness upon.

What will become of women? Shruti thinks about what that student said, and she scares me.

Sharad and Beverly's answer comes in Babu's newspaper. The title of the letter is written in boldface letters:

Religion or Racket?

Since when has free debate been a bad thing? Since when has debate in educational institutions and between teachers and students been immoral? It's astonishing there's even a question of shutting down debate, yet no one asks about the ashram meddling in universities via their loudspeakers and devotees! Are they spreading religion? Are they teaching the great Hindu religion? No one knows where the ashram is getting all its financing from. Perhaps the Goddess rained down gold in the blinking of an eye?

Below the letter are many signatures, gathered by Beverly and Sharad. Nandan and Shorty Josh have not signed. Hanif and Shruti have.

Suddenly, letters are published in every newspaper, either for or against the gathering and what was said there.

Such a small town, such a small gathering!

'Don't pick it up. Just put the receiver to one side,' Daddu scolds Shruti.

Shruti writes something, tears it up, throws it away.

I pick it up and copy it down:

Outside = naked
No outside matters inside the university.
Outside = Hanif

'If the little things go away, then what will remain in our life, specks of nature that we are?' asks Shruti fearfully in the dark.

'Why are you bringing up nature?' asks Hanif. 'The big things are consuming everything now.'

Beverly and Sharad are again sitting in Sharad's room, chatting.

'Does it seem to you what people are saying has no meaning?'

'I had four operations in three years,' Beverly tells him. She lifts her T-shirt to show him her scar, with the obliviousness people from White countries have about their bodies on such occasions. 'I had kidney stones. I had an operation.'

Sharad lightly touches the part of her waist she's bunching between her fingers.

'People speak without knowing the meaning of their words,' he says. 'If you tell them the meaning, it turns out that's not what they're really saying.'

'It was okay for a few months, then there was more pain, and the stitches came undone,' Beverly tells him.

'They don't know what's going on, and they open their mouths and make sounds.'

Sharad removes Beverly's hand from her waist and replaces it with his own.

'Then there was another operation, but after a few months the stitches came out again. My insides started coming outside.'

Beverly puts her hand back on her waist.

'From inside? From where? On what diet do they subsist, these sounds?'

Sharad gets up and begins to pace.

'Then I went to a plastic surgeon.'

'Where does all this prejudice, this animosity come from?'

He's pacing back and forth, wrapped in a shawl.

'Since then, I've been fine.'

Beverly pulls her T-shirt back down.

'But there must be many among us who only open our mouths because we're worried, who only speak out in solidarity. Is that the first time we hear that inner voice? Then we think: Was this what I meant? Only then can we change our voices. But isn't it a good thing that what's inside is coming to the fore? If we feel afraid when we see our own faces, will we change them? Is that something we can change?'

Now he's standing in front of Beverly.

'You didn't listen to a word I said,' complains Beverly. She pokes him.

Sharad kneels before her. Now they're of equal height.

'But you didn't either.'

'Sorry.' Beverly makes the sign of the cross.

Sharad copies her and says, 'I'm sorry too.'

They sit face to face. Suddenly, he feels overcome with emotion. 'I only like you,' he says.

Beverly holds out her hands, and he takes them in his, then gently lets go.

'You're the only one in this city . . . otherwise I'd flee.'

Sharad looks at Beverly and wonders how you can be so close to someone and so far at the same time. His eyes hurt from staring at her. They're turning red. They look bloodshot with fatigue. He's tired, very tired, and wants to rest his head in Beverly's lap. He wants to say, Let's go get married.

He stands up suddenly.

'What people are saying, it's all meaningless,' he repeats and starts pacing again.

The loudspeaker over there blares so loudly that the department members stand in the corridors listening to it every day.

'This sounds like a new voice,' says Urmila.

'Is it a man or a woman?' laughs Shorty Josh.

Today the moral values, democratic authority, wealth and unity of
85 per cent of the Indian population is in danger. That means the
entire country is in danger . . . Mother India is calling . . .

Quite a few students have climbed on to the roof of the canteen
across the way to peer down towards the ashram. They're up to all
sorts of shenanigans, as is the way among students.

When they hear the ear-splitting cries of *Jai Jagadambe! Jai*
Jagadambe! a couple of enthusiastic students break out their disco
moves.

A brief letter has arrived in the department mail:

Tell Hanif to apologize.

There's no postage stamp, no seal, and it's typed.

Professor Nandan is furious. 'Who could have done this? It
didn't come by post.'

Shorty Josh, too, is shaken. 'This was posted after the
department opened,' he observes.

'Why do you say that?'

'Because the letterbox is inside the main gate, which is locked.'

'Yes, I hadn't even thought of that.'

'Then it must be from someone here? Or else a student or an
administrator,' says Urmila. She adds softly, 'Look among those
who come wearing a tilak . . .'

'No one becomes a communalist just from believing in
religion,' scolds Sharad.

'They could be worried for their religion. They might have
felt their religion was insulted by the letter that came from us,'
says Urmila.

'We weren't insulting anyone's religion. We were writing against the mischief that's occurring in the name of religion,' retorts Sharad heatedly. 'Why did you sign it then?'

'Well, certainly not to get people riled up,' replies Urmila, feeling annoyed at the look he's giving her.

'Nobody's getting riled up,' says Sharad ruefully.

We had become despondent. We were isolated. We'd be lying if we said we were ever the sort of people who wanted to leave the comfort of our homes and go out and fight for revolution in the streets.

We were fond of our small personal circles. We were just ordinary people, devoted to an ordinary life. We simply wanted to pursue our work. Keeping our private spaces private.

But that year, no space remained private, not even for protected, well-off people like us. There was no longer any guarantee that any of us could go on living a simple, anonymous life.

Our hearts obligated us to emerge from our spaces, but those others forced us to come out, to explain ourselves, state our names, pull down our trousers and show who we really were.

Hindu–Muslim, Hindu–Muslim: this was the refrain.

If we said both were present in us, we were ridiculed.

Meaning when Shruti said it, she was ridiculed.

When Hanif said it, there was disbelief, but also joy, that, yes, a Muslim can become a non-Muslim in every respect, but he'll always remain a non-Hindu!

Who knows what was left of us.

There was a steady drumbeat on the streets announcing majority insecurity. At which we came out and demanded to know what insecurity.

When they said, 'Now we'll have a Hindu nation,' we came out again and asked, 'When were we not a Hindu nation?' but without this rejecting of others through hatred and pride.

And when people on the streets demanded to know what we'd accomplished by being secular, we jumped up and asked, 'When were we ever secular? You don't just become secular by saying you are.'

But then we began to think about those multiple streams that had flowed within us from the start, whether anyone wanted them there or not, whether there was a Hindu nation or not, whether they were secular or not.

Who knows what we were.

But whatever we were, perhaps our mother was secular and our father bigoted, and that's what made us double-headed hydras.

'Now what will happen?' ask the people in the department.

'What should we do now?'

'Let's have a meeting and publicly condemn this act.'

'Let's send a letter to the newspaper.'

'It was just some childish prank. Doing such things will only give importance to whoever did it. Don't pay attention.'

'If we address every little thing, we waste valuable time and give such matters too much weight,' agrees Nandan.

'Perhaps it's wrong to immediately slot everything into this camp or that camp,' says Sharad. Nandan nods in agreement.

It's possible they're not assenting to the same thing.

Daddu sits alone with his beak out. He doesn't see Shruti enter. His eyes are downcast. His hands are still, but his fingers wiggle like a spider's legs. His lips move as he mumbles an entire conversation with himself.

'Come, come!' he cries happily when he sees her. 'Go get another cup. Two cups!' he calls out when he hears Sharad's scooter.

'Tell me, what news of the outside world?' asks Daddu. He's assessing the colour of the tea as he slowly pours in the milk.

'The news isn't good,' says Shruti. Daddu is silent. 'No, the news is not good.'

Sharad shares an update on the brouhaha in the department. 'There's only been that one anonymous threat. But one cannot keep silent.'

Daddu is gloomy. 'But what will you accomplish by speaking out? This hatred runs very deep.'

Sharad and Shruti both stare at him silently.

'Sometimes it seems like it's all the doing of some idiotic child who will just go silent on his own. Sometimes it seems like it's precisely our thinking so and keeping quiet that's encouraged him, and he's no longer a child but a demon, growing larger and larger,' says Sharad hopelessly.

'Yes,' Shruti agrees. 'I don't understand how it is that we're making it grow if we aren't paying attention. But also, when we are paying attention, it expands?'

'It's none of that. It's not about some child becoming a demon. These are simply the flames of hatred fanned for centuries and never allowed to cool,' declares Daddu.

'Daddu, what are you saying?' asks Shruti, upset. 'Only yesterday you were telling me about your Dadi . . .'

'Yes, I was telling you about my Dadi . . .'

Daddu stands up, adjusts the waist of his dhoti, then sits back down and puts up his feet.

'What did you tell her?' asks Sharad eagerly.

'I was talking about religion,' says Daddu. 'But that had nothing to do with this.' It seems like he's about to hold forth, but then he keeps quiet.

'It won't do not to respond,' says Sharad. 'First of all, this is about Hanif; and second of all . . .'

'This is not just about Hanif,' interjects Shruti helplessly.

'Run! Run!' shouts Professor Nandan. A furore has broken out. Students and teachers pour from the classrooms.

Dagdu and Type Babu arrive panting. They're dragging a teenage boy by the kameez.

'It was him!' they cry.

The boy is frightened.

'I don't know anything. I'm telling the truth. I just deliver newspapers.'

'Yes, he does, he brings the newspapers to the library,' a few people agree.

'You know! Please save me!' implores the boy. 'I didn't do anything. They beat me so hard.' He begins to cry. There are finger marks across his face.

'Watch it . . .' growls Type Babu, raising a hand.

Dagdu zealously grabs the boy by the collar and growls most impressively.

'Let him go,' says Head Sahib.

'Oooh, I'll smack him again!' cries Dagdu. But he lets him go.

'We were screaming after him, and he was running away.' Type Babu feels like a tiger on the hunt.

'Where did you get these?' Nandan holds up a thick packet of papers he's just ripped open.

'I don't know . . . they . . . those people . . . outside the bank... . . . they were standing next to the peanut seller . . . they said, when you deliver the newspaper, put this in too . . .'

'Haven't you heard the police cars announcing from gali to gali to beware unknown persons and things? Are you nuts?' scolds Shorty Josh.

The boy's eyes fill with fear and alarm.

'You mean a bomb . . .?'

'Let him go.' Nandan turns away.

'But what is it?' people ask.

Head Sahib hands the packet to Urmila and walks away. It's a collection of flyers for distribution. Everyone picks them up and starts reading.

||*Jai Jagadambe*||
The Miracle of the Devi

A priest was conducting a puja at the Devi ashram temple. Suddenly a snake appeared. When he saw it, the priest assumed it to be a nag devta, a snake deity, and bowed down to it. Just then, the Devi appeared and spoke thus: Listen carefully to what I say. This snake is one of those who take birth on earth from time to time to debase the religion of the people. You must kill them. Whoever does so and prints and distributes 2000 of these pamphlets in my name will find his wish fulfilled within twenty-four days, but he who puts it off for tomorrow will experience something horrible after twenty-four days.

So saying, the Goddess took thirty-six steps back, turned the snake to ash with the intensity of her gaze and vanished. Upon hearing this news, a man from Bombay had 1000 pamphlets printed and distributed. He didn't allow snakes with the faces of men to enter his home, upon which he won a lottery worth 62 lakh. A rickshaw driver from Dhanbad had 625 pamphlets printed and

*distributed; after eight days he came upon a pitcher overflowing
with gold pieces. Similarly, an unemployed youth refused to hide
the seditious snakes in his home and was thinking of getting the
pamphlets printed when he got a job. One man ripped up the
pamphlets, believing them to be false, and continued to feed milk
to the neighbourhood snake, upon which his son died. A merchant
from Agra was given this pamphlet to read, but then, after careful
consideration, did not print or distribute it for an entire month; at
which terrible things befell his business and, in addition, his wife
died. Later, a resident of Babultara narrated this message to four
other people, and together the five of them had 1500 pamphlets
printed, after which they identified the snakes in their midst and
had them taken away, and within one hour they reaped benefits
worth thousands of rupees. Now they are building a Devi temple
in their village.*

*Thus, we beseech all of you readers to spread the word in faith
and identify the snakes, in order to protect dharma. In this way,
you will reap miraculous rewards.*

Shout Jai Jagadambe!

Victory to Jagadambe!

The department echoed with the rustling of pages slipping and
falling and passing from hand to hand.

Everyone is eating downstairs. The wild grasses in the front yard
shine like a mesh of fine wires in the light rain. Nankau brings
in the rotis one at a time. Every time he places one on someone's
plate—whether Hanif's, Sharad's or Shruti's—he asks, 'Should I
bring more after this?'

'Keep making them for now,' grumbles Sharad. 'Why are you
bringing them out one at a time?'

'Because they go stale. So many leftovers,' he mumbles as he walks away. 'And then Daddu will scold me. But I don't care, I'll keep making them.'

Daddu's beak moves as he eats.

'Why are you silent?' Shruti asks Hanif. She kicks him lightly.

'I'm not.' He's busy eating.

Daddu turns the empty jar of pickles completely upside down. A tiny bit of oil and spice slowly drips on to his dal.

'Sorry, thank you, please, we don't even know how to say all this . . .' Sharad is muttering about the department. 'I was reading a microfilm and people nearby were talking. Or not so much talking as being noisy and goofing off. Hanif, what are you thinking?'

Daddu glances at them.

Hanif starts. 'Oh, sorry.'

'This one knows how to say sorry,' smiles Shruti.

'What are you thinking, bhai? Really, you look very serious, like a pufferfish!' Sharad purses his lips and puffs out his cheeks.

'Nothing, nothing.' Hanif opens the container of rotis and takes one out, at which Daddu pushes everything over to him—sabzi, dal, chutney.

'Are you feeling all right?' Sharad looks at him attentively. 'You look upset.'

'Something's the matter,' agrees Shruti. 'Are you thinking about that pamphlet?'

'Don't be silly,' snaps Hanif. 'There have always been such pamphlets. Chain letters.'

Then maybe it's the *apologize* thing . . .' suggests Shruti.

'Leave me alone, will you?' explodes Hanif. 'Is there nothing else left to think?'

Shruti is startled.

Daddu continues to eat.

Everyone is silent now.

Daddu finishes and goes to wash his hands. He leaves the room without looking at anyone.

Shruti's face is red. 'Screaming in front of everyone. It's such bad manners,' she says.

'Because you keep after me,' grumbles Hanif.

'Then why are you sitting there looking so grumpy?'

'Who's grumpy? I was eating. I felt serious. Must I continuously laugh like a lunatic? I was thinking about something.'

'You were thinking about that.' Now Shruti is a pufferfish.

'Here we go again . . .' Hanif rolls his eyes.

'That's what you're thinking about all the time. You connect everything to yourself, as though everything that's happening is happening to you.' Shruti is tearful. Angry, too. 'On top of that, you don't even know how to say sorry,' she adds childishly.

'You were just saying he did know that,' corrects Sharad in a futile attempt to get everyone laughing.

'But he doesn't know how,' buzzes Shruti. 'He thinks only of himself. He has delusions of grandeur and thinks the whole world's after him.'

'You're doing this on purpose.' Hanif's voice is calm, but it also contains a note of warning. 'You're goading me; you want to fight.'

'See, see how he's speaking?' complains Shruti. 'Something inside him is making him act like this.'

'Something, Shruti,' says Hanif in a dangerous tone, 'is inside you, that's making you go to great lengths like this. What I'm saying is . . .'

His chair tips over as he stands.

Just then, Daddu returns and sits down on the divan.

'Do not attribute every fleeting emotion, every stray word, every shift in my sleep, every little thing, to a single source of disturbance.' Hanif's voice is muted as he rights the chair. 'Will you allow nothing to stay normal for me? If you won't, you too will turn me into a stranger.'

'Ah,' says Shruti softly, though she still feels heated.

'Why are you still making rotis?' Sharad scolds Nankau loudly.

'Now it's only safe where there aren't any Muslims,' declares Dagdu.

'But why do the riots always happen where the Muslims are?' asks a student who has overheard him.

Professor Nandan smiles. 'No surprise there!' he declares.

'Indeed, no,' says Hanif softly.

Everyone starts at the sound of his voice. Then they all laugh a bit too loudly.

I saw the silence enveloping everyone. I knew we each had our own separate silences. We avoided one another's glances. We avoided one another. We who were the true minorities, members of that third category of people which contained both Hindus and Muslims, and others too; even we avoided one another's silences.

A cool breeze rustles the leaves. The topic is being discussed in the staffroom.

'The letters keep coming. But you say we should keep quiet?'

'If we give them too much attention, we turn the focus on them.'

'But we have to write. Then the focus will be on what we say. There are people like us, but they're not finding the language, they're not finding the slogans . . .'

'Let's reveal the secrets of the ashram on posters . . .'

'We shouldn't mention the ashram . . .'

'Religion . . .'

'We shouldn't mention religion . . .'

The room is growing cold, but there's no limit to these issues.

Shruti is telling Beverly what Daddu told her. He'd said he was never taught about religion by mullahs or pandits. 'It was my dadi who taught me,' he said. 'In those days, she was reading religious texts. There was a book for children on the life of Prophet Muhammad, which she read to me. It described Muhammad as a messenger of peace who silently endured all the crimes against him in Mecca. After he won Medina, he returned to Mecca and forgave all his enemies.' Daddu said when he grew up, he found out that Mohammad had indeed announced a general forgiveness but also had a few enemies killed off. All the same, he was a messenger of peace and compassion, right? Generally speaking, his was a path of forgiveness, no?

'Daddu was also telling me it was his dadi who told him stories of Ram and Krishna and Jesus and Moses,' Shruti says to Beverly.

Hanif sips his tea. Sharad smokes a cigarette.

'Daddu, please tell.' Shruti is sitting with Daddu. He's rubbing his hands together by the heater. His hands glow, as though generating a warmth of their own. 'Last night I dreamt about your dadi,' she says.

'My dadi, yes,' he says. 'She lived in another city.'

'Not in the village?' smiles Shruti.

'A suburb, like a village,' says Daddu.

'Was she religious?'

'Yes, and so were we. The kind of religion children follow.'

Daddu is digging up threads from his memory. 'For Diwali puja, we'd get flattened rice, batashey and toys. On Dussehra, tableaus would be brought out in processions. On Janmashtami, we would decorate displays commemorating Krishna's birth. We'd gaze upon the gods and get excited about prashad, firecrackers and toys.'

'And what about Eid or Muharram?' asks Shruti, because this is how we think: if we veer towards Holi and Diwali, then next we must turn to Eid and Muharram.

'There were many Muslim homes, near Dadi's mohalla,' Daddu explains. 'When I used to go there, I would play, eat, drink with them. You know . . .' Daddu climbs on to the divan and puts his feet up. He's waving his hands about. 'When Dadi passed away, I stayed a whole year with the family of a Muslim friend of hers, so I could take the high school exam. She was Dadi's best friend,' he explains.

'In that house,' continues Daddu, who has returned to his childhood, 'they prayed five times a day. If they were keeping the fast, they'd wake me early for the sehri . . .'

'Did you keep the fast too?' Shruti is listening intently.

'No,' he waves a hand. 'I'd eat the sehri treats, then get breakfast at eight o'clock, then lunch, then I'd eat the iftari with them after sundown.' Daddu laughs. 'For us children, religion meant food, playing, a holiday. That's the reality of religion, entire neighbourhoods meeting each other for different kinds of celebrations. The rest of the religious rituals, the puja, the namaz, that's everyone's personal business, you can do it all day or not at all . . .'

Daddu is speaking as though prayers and such are dispensable in religion. No, that's not what he's saying. What he's saying is, it's not something to get all worked up about. 'Those who feel the need, press their palms together and say their prayers, do whatever they have to, then come out and enjoy themselves with other people.'

'You've never done puja?' Shruti is acting like she's interviewing him.

'I have.' Daddu is laughing at himself, the hero of his own story. 'Once I fasted for Janmashtami, but I continued to take fruit and water.' He waggles a finger. 'And many times, many, many times; time and again,' he adds for emphasis, 'I would go to the Varah Ji temple in our town. And do you know, I did not realize the god Varah is a pig? I didn't even notice what the idol looked like. I'd press my palms together, take arti, be happy . . .'

'And with Muslims?'

'Look.' Daddu has entered a rapt state. 'A procession carrying the taziya used to stop in front of our home and stay put until our dada came out. Once he emerged, the procession would continue with Dada at the head.'

'Religion.' Daddu says the word *religion* like he's cracking a whip, and then he becomes Daddu again, today's Daddu. 'It's not this hullabaloo. What we are flows in our veins, Hindu or Muslim to the core, yet strangely unmindful of it, not all this shouting and carrying on. Religion,' Daddu cracks the whip again, 'gives people a lovely way to feel bound together with their different customs: one prepares a gujhiya, another cooks sevaiyan, my grandfather carried the taziya, my uncle saluted Ram in the Ram Leela. Bigotry isn't part of religion. It's about dominance.'

Daddu is silent for a while, his eyes shining.

'I was a fool; you people are probably wiser,' he says suddenly. 'I didn't recognize gods, but I was a devotee. And one Muharram, I nearly sent that family a "Happy Muharram" card!'

'And did you?' laughs Shruti.

Daddu looks at her and retracts his beak. Then he begins to laugh uproariously to himself.

'I don't know whether someone explained it to me or what, but at the last minute, I didn't send it!'

Both are laughing heartily. Treating the divan as they used to.

It's that phone call again:

Your mother is a bitch. Your wife is a bitch.

I don't like that ink seller. Every time he picks out an inkpot for me, he stares at me with a suspicious smile, touching a finger to his temple.

Apologize, demands a new letter in the paper, with many signatures. Daddu recognizes some of the names. He says they're prominent citizens in the city, devotees of Devi.

They're saying their religious sensitivities have been hurt, as have they.

Today, another letter has been published saying we must get rid of the renegades in our religion. And we must get rid of the outsiders.

Today's letter carries a whiff of a threat:

Apologize. This is a legal crime. Under section 295 of the IPC,
Hanif Zaidi has hurt the religious sentiments of the people. There
should be a case against him. He should be arrested. A warrant
should be put out in his name.

Riots.

Similar events ensue.

Then more riots.

Sharad is teaching a class. Quickly. The students in the back row
have their feet up on the chairs in front of them and their caps
pulled down over their eyes.

'Were you marked present?' roars Sharad. 'Nothing's keeping
you then. Go home and sleep.'

The students stand up. The lecture continues. Quickly.
The students stand up and stamp and drag their heels as they
walk out.

Sharad stops. The students in the front turn to watch those
departing. The lecture continues at a rapid pace.

A new letter says the ashram has been dishonoured.

The rioting is under control, but ongoing.

Tension has spread throughout the department.

People are laughing and saying, 'They've gone nuts.'

We're listening to the bhajans coming from the ashram. The city is on edge.

Back to the refugee camp.

Hanif isn't going? This is the Muslim camp. Doesn't he know?

He still won't go, even though he knows?

Many students are frightened. Letters arrive daily. Posters have gone up all over the university. Something must be done.

'Our teaching is done for,' mutters Nandan.

'But, sir, we can't just sit quietly,' cry the anxious students.

Everyone is saying the same thing, that civilized people like us have gone too, they've gone with the wife and kids and picked out things to loot before burning down the shops.

'It wasn't looting, it was a party.'

'They measured their feet and took shoes.'

'They picked up matching blouse pieces.'

'I saw it with my own eyes. I can see the street from my window. My neighbour's son came with a Maruti. I saw him loading it up with stuff.'

Shruti feels like crying, but when her tearful voice reaches her lips, the words that emerge are scorched: 'Why do you stay silent? Everything's all about you. What will people think, what must they already think?'

You can see the fires in the city from here. Sharad stands alone by the madhumalti staring over there. The red sky is in full bloom, punctuated by clouds of smoke. The rest of the sky is purple.

Daddu sits silently.

And again, they go, they listen, they speak.

Sharad, Shruti and Beverly are looking at an album full of information, and proof of the dead and wounded. The proof is offered in the form of full-colour photos. The camp children lean in, staring at the photos of bloated bodies soaked with blood and tar. They look over this shoulder, they look over that. Burnt, maimed, half-dead, grisly bodies.

Shruti is upset.

'Let's send the children outside,' whispers Beverly.

'Yes, they stripped me,' the women tell them.

'I hid in a trunk.'

'The police came, but then they left.'

'Yes, they did that to her . . .'

'Ten times . . .'

'Stitches where she pees.'

A woman in a velvet wrap stands near them. She begins to weep.

'We used to give the children expensive fruits every day. We put Krackjack and glucose biscuits in their tiffin carriers, and now we have to cook for all the people in the camp . . . Our community is a different subsect from that one . . . Here, most people are from that one, when money comes, they . . . they . . . Look, the woman standing over there, she says, first our group should get it; them—that's us—later. Please write down how much damage we've suffered, what our home was worth . . . Please write it down . . .'

At her insistence, Shruti takes out pen and paper. Beverly touches the woman's shoulder and explains in her broken Hindustani, 'Sister, we're not from the government. We can't distribute money. We can only write reports for people to read and learn from . . .'

Shruti feels deflated. She thinks, Why can't I say things simply like her? I behave like it's theatre and I'm playing a false role. I don't even know how to meet them, talk to them. I'm just acting. She feels undone.

The students take out a procession. They start from the university and pass by the ashram, then the courthouse, then the newspaper office, then return and stage a sit-in outside the vice chancellor's office.

The sunlight illuminates their posters:

Stop the libelous ashram!
Open debate is our motto!
Down with yellow journalism!

'This time, Shruti,' says Daddu, 'they've really gone too far.' He's shaking his head like he can barely believe it himself.

'You're the one who says people go mad.'

'Yes.' Daddu is looking a bit outside, a bit inside. 'People don't go crazy. They're already crazy! Culture, traditional mores—these are just outer layers of their attire: beneath that they're the same primeval, rapacious, wild beings.'

Shruti fears the look on Daddu's face.

'They feel free to kill anyone, do anything, loot anything. It's not violence for them. They rejoice in being drenched in blood, they dance in delight when they burn someone alive, and the more they do it, the more they get high off the stench of corpses, and find God in the screams of their victims . . .'

'Daddu,' Shruti can barely get the word out.

At this moment, Daddu resembles a vulture. Maybe he's trying to laugh but is unable to do so.

'And then?' he asks. The light in his eyes has gone out. 'Then they return to normal. They put on their civilized clothes again.'

Shruti feels frightened. A question comes unbidden to her mind: What if Daddu is one of those who have returned to 'normal'?

A horrifying thought.

Horrifying thoughts are plentiful these days.

Babu Painter calls.

'Don't alienate the press just now,' he warns.

Daddu is watching a programme on the television. He's also perusing a film magazine. Beverly, Shruti, Sharad, Hanif are seated around the dining table.

Beverly says, 'If Babu won't publish it, I can get it printed abroad. There won't be a restriction on it outside.'

'Outside,' says Shruti.

'What?' asks Hanif.

'Another outside,' says Shruti, feeling alienated.

'Listen,' says Sharad. He reads the letter from the ABVD aloud from the newspaper:

> *These are the people spreading communalist poison. We come to the university to study, but politics is forcing its way in here as well. Until now, we always considered ourselves Hindustani, but they're forcing communal thought on us. They're misleading students and turning them against religion . . .*

Daddu says something. Everyone turns towards him, but he's watching TV, engrossed.

What I hear is: Oh, God!

So I write down: *Oh, God!*

Oh, God!

Kapadia comes by.

'Don't speak against the ashram to the students. They have major officials backing them.'

'The whole thing will get complicated. We shouldn't apologize, but we should explain we weren't saying any such thing, and we should bury this thing right here.' Professor Nandan is anxiously uprooting his entire moustache.

'Everyone's after us, advising us!' replies Sharad excitedly.

'It's a very dangerous clause, Professor Sharad.' Nandan looks very upset. 'We don't want any trouble at the university; we need to get on with our work peacefully.'

'There's no need to grovel and beg forgiveness, but a polite clarification . . .'

'That's what I'm saying,' repeats Nandan.

Shorty Josh wraps his shawl tightly. His zeal seems to have cooled.

'But for what?' Sharad is livid now. 'Why is there even a question of apologizing? If we explain ourselves to them, people will say we were wrong, that we admit that. We don't even have to talk to them.'

One girl jumps up to express agreement. 'If a mad dog barks, why should we respond? Especially to acknowledge a mistake?'

'You would want to stay away from the mad dog, wouldn't you?' asks Nandan impatiently.

'We'll kill it,' suggests another student.

'You can't. There isn't just one. And they're mixed in with the ordinary dogs, so you won't be able to tell them apart . . .'

'So?'

'So we must protect ourselves.'

'Meaning apologize!' Sharad looks terrifying.

'Meaning . . .'

'Hanif?' asks Sharad.

Hanif remains silent for a moment. Then he says, 'Up till now, we've debated about where the roots lie, what's tradition, what's historical fact. Now the entire issue has been reduced to *Apologize, why, don't apologize, why not, have we done wrong, have they done wrong.*'

'That's not an answer,' explodes Sharad.

'I don't know what the answer is. Whom should we address if they're not even listening? If we speak separately, then to whom . . .?'

'Don't rant,' says Sharad.

Hanif falls silent. 'Daddu.' He suddenly smiles. 'Sharad's father. He says, "Not even the gods can shame the naked!"'

The excitable student gets up and writes in chalk on the hall blackboard: 'Not even the gods can shame the naked!'

There's a picture in the newspaper. An overturned scooter. A helmet lies nearby, and a dead person in rumpled jeans lies sprawled in the middle of the street. Dark liquid flows from his body, forming a pattern. On the edge of the pattern lie two screwdrivers of different lengths.

Why does the ink guy act like this? Does he mean to frighten me? Again with the finger on the temple and the head thrown back as he lifts his eyes in a rebellious gaze. What's his name?

Which . . . which . . . community is he from?

One hears the vice chancellor has decided not to continue with the two-year rotation system.

Shruti slips a dressing gown over her nightie, goes downstairs and knocks on Sharad's door.

'One minute,' says Sharad when he sees her. He disappears for a moment, throws on a kurta and a sweater, and returns.

Shruti hands him the newspaper.

'What's this?' He glances over it.

'Here.' Shruti points.

I see:

Letter to the Editor.

Sharad's eyes dart back and forth, then he begins to read aloud:

The charges we levelled regarding the misappropriation of funds are baseless. We retract them.

He looks astonished, and reads on:

We ask forgiveness.

'What?' he cries.

We truly know nothing about religion. We know nothing about the Hindu religion.

'What's this?' he explodes.

'Look at the rest. Look at the signatures,' says Shruti.

There are three names:

Nandan, Urmila, Sharad.

Sharad turns sharply, opens his desk drawer and brings a sheet of paper to Shruti.

Shruti begins to read silently.

Sharad reads aloud by her side:

It was not our intention to hurt any religious sentiments. We believe in freedom for all faiths. We made no charges regarding misappropriation of funds. How can we retract charges we did not make. That's baseless. We did not make accusations of dishonesty about money against the ashram, we only observed that there was a large amount of money flowing in and asked for an accounting to be made. Where is it from? In view of the greatness of Hindu religion, we also asked if what is being propagated is Hindu dharma. If so, we truly know nothing about religion or Hindu dharma. If our questions have hurt anybody's religious sentiments, we apologize. It was a misunderstanding, and we entreat them to understand what we are saying. If the claims about religion that are being made are true, then we truly know nothing about it, and we know nothing about Hinduism.

At the bottom of the letter is also Hanif's signature.

Now Hanif has come downstairs as well.

Babu Painter has come too.

'These are the editor's cuts. I saw them myself only today.' He's talking very loudly on the phone. Hanif, Shruti, Sharad—all stand about.

Just then, Daddu emerges from his bedroom. He notices everyone crowded around, but the only indication he gives is a slight change in his gait. Without looking at anyone, he walks right by and sits down on the divan.

Shruti takes the newspaper from Babu's hand and hands it to Daddu.

There's an edge to the wind. Darkness quickly falls.

One has rarely seen Professor Nandan so agitated. His voice is hitting the highest register.

'We've already said what we're going to say. Before we even opened our mouths people already know what we'll say. It's no longer a department but a spectacle.'

Nandan wants this so-called 'chapter' to end right here.

'The more we push it, the further it will go.'

'Are we pushing it?' asks Hanif softly.

Everyone else is completely silent.

It is Nandan who speaks at last. 'All we do from morning to night is draft letters to the editor.'

'*Subah hoti hai shaam hoti hai
Umr yun hi tamaam hoti hai.*'

'*Morning to night
Thus passes a lifetime.*'

Daddu recites with a sigh. He smiles affectionately, but his eyes are troubled.

'What should we do about it, Daddu?' asks Shruti. She, too, feels troubled. 'Writing holds no meaning,' she adds.

*Na sataaish ki tamanna na sile ki parva
Gar nahin hain mere ash'aar men maani na sahi*

*I have no desire for praise, nor expectation of reward
If my verses hold no meaning, so be it*

'Understand?' asks Daddu slowly and melodiously. 'Loony! For years even Ghalib's contemporaries misunderstood him, but he kept on doing his thing. *If my verses hold no meaning, so be it.* He who understands not is ignorant and not discerning. But he was

Ghalib. Who are you! You are nothing, and there's no meaning in your writing!'

'But there is! How could there not be?' pouts Shruti.

'Is there now?' challenges Daddu. 'Is there meaning in these things? Who knows! You people are the type who write things down, read them yourselves and then offer your own praise!' He begins to laugh but there's no mirth in the laughter.

'If no one else praises, one must do it oneself,' chuckles Shruti in the same mirthless manner, her reactions to Daddu's words following a well-established pattern.

'Yes, yes.' Daddu shakes his head. 'You don't write poetry, but you certainly have the manner of a poet. Beat your own drum! There was a famous Persian poet called Maulana Rumi, listen to what he said:

> 'Man nadānam fā'ilātūn fā'ilāt
> Shi'r migoyam bih az qand o nabāt.'

> 'I know nothing of rhyme or meter
> Yet I compose couplets sweeter than sugar or candy.'

'Understand, loony?' He laughs again. 'But in order to recite a sweet verse, you must choose a sweet subject.'

'But how can I, Daddu?' smiles Shruti. Her voice is shot through with worry.

Daddu has opened his mouth to speak. Perhaps he's about to recall a new couplet, but just then the door slams open. Sharad and Hanif enter. It looks like Sharad has come running. He's panting.

'The student union has passed a resolution—to dismiss . . . to dismiss . . . Hanif from the university.'

Daddu's mouth drops completely open.

'Dismiss?' asks Shruti, stunned.

'Dismiss!' repeats Sharad. 'They've gone mad!'

'How can they do such a thing?' Daddu's voice suddenly emerges as though it's come unstuck.

'They can't do that,' says Sharad, throwing himself into a chair. 'It's nonsense. The student union doesn't even have that authority.' A thousand expressions make their way to Sharad's face. 'But witness their audacity. They've gone mad, completely mad,' he seethes. 'It's not even a question of removing, they don't even have that right at all; but look at their . . . their audacity! Look at their audacity,' he repeats. He's astonished. 'We'll turn them all out,' he cries. 'We'll expel them . . .'

'But why did they do this?' Shruti is in a state of shock.

'"Get rid of the one spreading communalist poison." That's what they said. They've gone mad.'

Sharad's voice has changed. If I didn't look up, I wouldn't recognize him. When I look down again to write, my pen is shaken by the sound of their hearts beating with anxiety in all of their chests.

With the off-season rain it grew colder, and when the water had to be released from the dam, the so-called river filled to the brim.

The only thing being discussed today: Hanif.

Wherever you look, it's him: Hanif.

In the paper as well: Hanif.

Shruti looks up when she hears the sabziwallah's call.

'Can you go get some, please?' she asks as she sinks back under the quilt. There's no movement coming from Hanif's direction. But suddenly it occurs to Shruti that the sabziwallah might have heard the news.

'You go,' says Hanif.

I see Daddu replacing the receiver properly on the phone. Then he goes and stares out the glass door.

'Well, it's good the vice chancellor immediately put out such a stern statement.

'He's put it exactly right:

> It is not the responsibility of the student union to employ or dismiss anyone at the university. Professor Hanif is internationally respected, and the university is proud of him. The audacity the student union has shown by announcing this absurd opinion is reprehensible, etc.

'Good,' says Sharad, folding up the newspaper. 'Our letter will come soon. It's necessary.'

'Do you see that bird?'

'The sparrow?'

Hanif looks up from his tea.

'No,' says Shruti, 'Hush shh shh shh shh. It's something else,' she whispers. 'It hasn't come before.'

The bird is small and hops not on the branches but on the leaves. It's a shade larger than the leaves. As though it's a leaf itself. When it hops, the leaves dance.

'How light it must be.' Shruti is filled with wonder. 'It's standing on a leaf.'

'Raindrops make the leaves tremble like that too.'

A few days before, Hanif was sitting here in the rain staring outside. It had seemed bizarre how you couldn't see the falling drops. The separate leaves would suddenly flip completely and hang vertically.

'It's not even scared. We're sitting here, and it's hopping about, unaware of us,' whispers Shruti. 'Don't move, don't move, it'll fly away.'

Hanif gently puts down his plate.

'Shall I find out what it's called?'

Shruti is in the process of standing up softly.

'No, sit for now.' Hanif stops her. 'It'll fly away. Observe carefully, find it in the book later.'

'Okay, let's observe.'

The two of them begin to examine the bird.

'There's a black beak, not too pointy, a white belly, a soft brown back . . .'

'There are black stripes along the edges of the wings.'

'Black eyes.'

'A white spot on the tail.'

'Smaller than a sparrow.'

'I've written it all down.'

'You're writing it down? Great.'

'It's not afraid, I wrote that.'

'Great.'

'The edges of the madhumalti leaves are turning yellow. I wrote that too,' says Hanif, his hand stopping.

'What?' For a moment Shruti doesn't understand. 'Okay.' She smiles. 'Great.'

'So what bird was it?' smiles Hanif.

'A yellowing-leaf-edge-hopper,' replies Shruti.

'She flew away. Ooh, she flew away.' Hanif is relaxed now. He loudly pushes back his chair and stands up.

The two of them stand on the balcony gazing at their vine. There are new green leaves below; on top, yellow, drying, mature leaves, eager to drop.

'Feels like a bad omen,' says Shruti.

'When you're depressed anything feels like a bad omen,' says Hanif, pulling her close.

Shruti stands silently with her arms around Hanif for a while, then says, 'I'm becoming more superstitious these days.'

Hanif presses her arm with his. 'It happens.' He rests his head on her hair. 'I recall a story about this . . .' he says.

'Tell, tell!' chirps Shruti unnaturally. Hanif looks up.

Unnaturally, yes. As though such occasions rarely arise— don't let them pass. I try to remember when Hanif last told a story, but by the time I remember, he'll have started this one, so I let go of the past and busy myself with copying.

'A boy used to live next door to me—I don't even remember his name—but I used to visit him on a daily basis. At some point they were holding a wedding there, and all his relatives arrived en masse. Someone, maybe it was his aunt, his chachi, had come to take part in the wedding and fallen gravely ill. She was so ill the doctor lost hope. There was a great panic, but what worried my friend's parents most of all was the possibility that a death in the family might force them to postpone the wedding. Therefore, they approached one of the special wedding guests, a tantrik, a holy man, by the name of Bhonpa Baba, and clasped their hands together, begging him to intervene.'

'Bhonpa Baba!' chuckles Shruti.

'Don't worry, beta, said this Bhonpa Baba.' Hanif imitates the tantrik's manner. 'The wedding is tomorrow. I shall stop Yamraj, the God of Death, for forty-eight hours.'

Shruti laughs more. Her laughter is also unnatural.

'But my friend's parents were still not entirely free of worry, so they also requested of another spiritually realized soul who was a guest at the wedding to please keep Yamraj away until the next day. Everyone called him Lala Ji. Well, Lala Ji gave the same assurance. So now, what do you think happened next?' asks Hanif laughing.

'Did she die?' clucks Shruti. 'She didn't die?' She begins to laugh, wide-eyed. 'Is it a lie?'

'She didn't die,' says Hanif. 'The wedding took place. Chachi didn't die. Not then, not now. She was still alive a few years ago.'

And now Shruti laughs heartily, but it seems less for the story and more for joy about something else.

'It's not over.' Hanif presses her face lightly with his palm. 'When Chachi and her husband learnt what my friend's parents had done, they were quite offended. Nothing can stay hidden for long in a joint family, and they found out that when the shadow of death lay near Chachi, these people were more concerned about the wedding arrangements! And in addition, they were also angry at Bhonpa Baba and Lala Ji, demanding to know why they promised to hold Yamraj off only for two days?'

Shruti is laughing loudly now.

'So the husband said, I'm Brahmin; I hereby curse Lala Ji, so he'll fall ill before he can return to his home from the wedding.'

'Now you're making it up.' Shruti glares.

'No, you must believe it. Lala Ji had only made it as far as the station when he was struck with diarrhoea!'

'Hanif!' Shruti laughs out loud. 'So why did they spare Bhonpa Baba?'

Hanif has his answer ready. 'They said that since Bhonpa Baba was a tantric, they feared him, and so they swallowed their anger. But Lala Ji belonged to an inferior caste, as he was a mere Baniya!'

'Poor thing, you're making up stories like Daddu now . . .'

'Next time, I'll introduce you to those people. Chacha has died, Bhonpa Baba's also gone, but Chachi's probably still around.'

'So there was no bad omen,' says Shruti affectionately. She taps a yellowing leaf, and it falls. 'Are you tense?' she asks, looking down at the leaf.

'Are you?' asks Hanif, looking at her.

'Sharad was asking,' she clarifies.

Sharad says Nandan was the one to appoint Hanif in the department, so don't forget that; don't make him the villain for no reason.

'Why would he bring him in and then not want him?' he asks Shruti, because Hanif doesn't want to talk.

'But then why is he bothering him?'

'He doesn't even say anything . . .'

'Then why is he letting others do it?'

'Yaar, how's he supposed to make them shut up? He's human, not a god.'

'How did he do it before?' Shruti asks. 'Did no one speak out before?'

Is that an answer or a question?

'No one's saying . . .' Sharad begins.

'Then who is? Is it a wave? A current? Hmph, Daddu-type talk!' says Shruti, as though Daddu speaks nonsense! Which is what she usually says, but not in the negative way she's speaking right now. 'But you used to be with him,' accuses Shruti.

'But it's he who's no longer with me,' snaps Sharad. 'The strange things he says . . .'

'But he's not saying anything at all.'

Is Shruti supporting Hanif, or is she complaining?

'But it's a talking silence, a weird talking silence.'

Sharad is definitely complaining about Hanif.

'His silence is like this! And Nandu's is like that!'

Now Shruti is complaining about Sharad.

'So you won't sign?' Sharad asks straight out.

A research scholar is having people in the department sign a statement against the student union proposal.

'It's not a matter of my signing or not signing; whether one does, or all do, it's the same thing,' says Nandan, with a look of displeasure.

'So you won't do it?' asks Sharad, staring at him.

'What does it matter if I do or not? I'll do it,' says Nandan. But he doesn't. 'Now, please, that's enough of that. Why give so much weight to excitable children doing stupid things? Our work . . .'

'This is our work,' interrupts Sharad. 'Will you sign or not?'

'Oho.' Professor Nandan looks harassed. 'There you go again. What does signing matter? Whether I do or not. If you say so, I'll do it, but please leave the department out of it.' He presses his palms together, almost as though he's begging.

Sharad snatches the protest letter from the student and walks away. Everyone is left speechless. Before anyone can understand what's happening, Sharad has gone stamping off.

Everyone sits downstairs by Daddu for a long time. The divan does not bounce even once. Finally, Daddu smiles and says, 'Go, now, sleep.'

And I will say there's a chill wind.

They're awake. So late at night.

Now such letters appear in the paper daily.
One:

> *This issue is not about just one Hanif; it's about all of us, it's about the poisonous atmosphere in the city.*

Another:

> *Our institute condemns the audacity of the student union.*

Sharad hands the newspaper to Shruti.

It must be close to daybreak, because they're both asleep, and these days they're always asleep at this time.

Today, there's a letter in the newspaper that says:

> *Hanif Zaidi has brought this on himself with his vanity and combativeness. He's started bringing politics into the classroom, and he's giving lectures against the Hindu religion. Do we send students to him for higher education or to learn how to riot?*

Shruti hands the newspaper to Sharad.

There's a photo in the newspaper of the vice chancellor and the head of the student union smiling together, like in a toothpaste commercial, and shaking hands. Underneath, it says that the vice chancellor advised the students to buckle down and study hard, so they can do a good job running the country in the future.

Hanif stares at the picture.

'I've heard,' says Shruti, 'that the river has completely filled under the bridge, from the release of the dam water.'

'Yes, you can see it from the department,' replies Hanif.

Once they go to sleep, I'll be done with my copying for the night.

Oh dear, oh dear, oh dear! Uff, I dozed off. I was having such a terrifying dream: the river had flooded, and now it was not water rushing beneath the bridge but ink. It rose on all sides, pulling everyone into its inky flow. We thrashed about, desperate to escape, as the flood pushed the riverbanks further away. I felt so alarmed, not knowing which way to go! I needed ink, I needed to refill my pen. But where to go, which way, which way? I was so frightened. What if I drown swimming anxiously about searching for ink in the ink?

Daddu is looking at the newspaper. Nowadays, one always opens it up to the letters-to-the-editor page first:

> *This is the bayonet which will finish off all the progressive elements . . . What a sinister joke it is that those who oppose communalism are accused of spreading it . . .*

Daddu finishes his tea and heads to the bathroom with the newspaper.

It's obvious there will be trouble wherever there are Muslims.

This is a line from a letter to the editor. The department members express worry, laughter, dismay at this. Two people are silent, of course: Hanif and Professor Nandan.

'Look, Daddu!' says Shruti, pushing up the arm of her sweater.

Daddu pats her arm: the skin is rough.

'It must be dryness. Use some of my oil.'

'No, Daddu. It's some sort of icky skin condition. Look how it's broken out.' Shruti's worried.

'Don't worry, my dear.' Daddu pats her arm. 'Worrying won't make it go away. If you want, I'll call for that doctor.' Shruti looks jumpier at the thought of a doctor. 'Try using my oil for a couple of days. If it doesn't get better, we'll think about the doctor,' he says when he sees her expression. He wraps himself in his quilt and sits on the divan in front of the heater. 'Anyway, that rascal lives right in the middle of the city on that side. Who knows how long it'll take him to get over here! Nowadays it's better if you don't need a doctor.' Shruti is silent, so he adds in a serious tone, 'Don't be scared, I'm just joking. Nothing's wrong with you.'

Shruti is quiet, but she wishes Daddu would say meaningless things like before and scream with laughter. That the divan would really bounce. That she could go and sit by his side. That the two of them could bounce all the way to the ceiling.

The editor has published another letter:

> *We should take note of the fact that only our Hindu comrades have apologized . . .*

'Let's write a response to this one!' suggests Sharad bitterly. 'Yaar, forget it!' replies Hanif, annoyed.

Where's Beverly? This question occurs to me because I catch Sharad thinking about her. What keeps happening this year is that when Hanif is angry with Sharad or ignoring him, Sharad doesn't speak up, consciously or unconsciously, and then he holds a grudge and starts to feel very much alone. At such moments, Beverly's friendship is a great support to him.

Kapadia has been telling them about the state of the city. As soon as he sees Hanif, he stands up and warmly shakes his hand. Daddu, who's been carefully listening to everything, stands up and goes to get a glass for Hanif.

'Nowadays you're the only thing anyone's talking about.' Kapadia speaks warmly to Hanif, who nods mechanically in agreement.

'He's the one they're talking about,' agrees Sharad. 'No one says anything about the ashram. On top of that, there's not even talk of taking disciplinary action against the student union.'

'What are you saying?' Kapadia takes the glass from Daddu and measures out a peg for Hanif. 'We're sitting on naked electrical wires here; you want to blow the fuse, not cause an explosion! Let the thing subside. Right, Hanif?'

Daddu, who's again listening to everyone carefully, looks away, but Sharad, Shruti and Kapadia have all turned towards Hanif.

'What should I say?' Hanif is startled to find all eyes on him.

'What? Is it nothing to do with you?' Sharad blurts out thoughtlessly. He's beginning to lose patience with Hanif's aloofness.

'Bhai, it's not just about me.' Hanif feels besieged. 'How can they hurt me?' He's playing the hero.

He's started acting like a martyr, Sharad thinks to himself with disgust. 'None of this is bothering you?' he asks angrily. 'They can't get rid of you, but all this harassment, picking your name from so many, removing it from the signatories, forcing you into this grotesque debate; it's all a witch-hunt.'

Whose side is he on? wonders Shruti.

'But if we dismiss it as silly students up to mischief, won't we be ignoring the truly sinister mentality that's gripping so many?' she asks Kapadia. 'We'll only make it worse . . .'

'If we notice it, we'll be acknowledging its existence.'

'But it does exist.' Shruti feels unsettled.

'But . . .'

'But what?' asks Daddu. As each person speaks, he bends forward, opens his eyes wide and listens as though with his eyes.

'But . . .' Kapadia starts and turns towards Daddu. He doesn't know why, but he can't decide what to say next. His brow is furrowed, as though he's searching for a way to break through this impasse. He begins to laugh. 'Bhai, they have divine power. What do you have? Human power? Who's stronger?'

No one laughs.

Sharad takes out a cigarette and matches, and asks, 'And where does your strength lie? Is it in goddess-less places, hmm? Like with us, or in the old city mosque, or in opposition to Babu's newspaper.'

He's getting carried away, thinks Hanif, looking down.

Kapadia is sulking now. 'We don't spare hooligans from any side.'

'We know what the police do.' Who knows why Sharad is dragging the police into it.

'You have no idea, Professor Sharad.' Kapadia waggles a finger. He's offended. 'We show equal strictness to the hooligans of both sides. Neither the entire police force nor the entire government is evil. Under TADA . . .'

'Countless Muslims are under surveillance,' Hanif suddenly blurts out.

'Hindus too,' retorts Kapadia loudly. 'We're not letting up on terrorists one bit . . .'

'You're not letting up on terrorism. But do you catch any of those who are directing the riots—the big shots who do all the dirty work, whose names everyone already knows? They know no one will capture them. Does a terrorist have this much confidence?' explodes Hanif.

'So you want to give them that?' Kapadia is obstinate.

'Hanif didn't say that,' says Daddu, looking upset. 'He's saying so many Muslims have been killed openly, but their murderers, although known, haven't been captured . . .'

'Daddu!' Kapadia cuts off even Daddu. 'Let me tell you something. I've been doing police work for a long time. Try to understand what I'm saying. It's thanks to the police that today me and you, and Muslims like this one, are safe. If we step back

even once and allow a free-for-all, the Hindus will be decimated.
If we don't stop them . . .'

'Oh, come on!' Sharad laughs. A shiver runs down his spine,
and he falls silent.

Today there's not just a letter but an entire article. It's about
how the Muslims worship at the altar of foreign aid, and the
government worships at the altar of the Muslims, and Islam
worships at the altar of bigotry.

So much has happened, I feel tired, and here's Daddu, still
unaware of the outside world, but reading the newspaper. What's
happened to him?

A phone call asking if everything's okay.

'It's embarrassing that letters have come from far-off places
condemning the actions of the student union.' Sharad is looking
down as he speaks in the staffroom. 'But our department, where
our own colleague is the victim of a witch-hunt, has not been able
to raise a single voice.'

'Don't overreact,' scolds Hanif.

'Witch-hunt? Who where which? Around here, sahib, there's
only a hero!' Shorty Josh walks out laughing.

At the deafening collective cry from the ashram of
Jai Jagadambe, a flock of birds flaps into the sky.

'It was either a striated finch, which is shikari muniya in Hindi, or
a tailor bird, which is called phutki,' says Shruti, flipping through
the pages of Sálim Ali.

'What?' asks Hanif.

'Nothing.' She falls silent.

It seems like Hanif wants to say something. He looks at her. Then he looks away. As though he's about to speak.

'Oho,' he says.

Many letters are arriving by mail:

We were saddened to hear . . .

Are you okay?

'What should I say?' Hanif grits his teeth.

The two of them are getting their scooters out. The students are acting rowdy outside the library. It has been many days since the curfew was lifted, and everyone wants to finish their work, as long as things are okay.

'So what you want,' says Sharad icily, 'is for the student union to be punished?'

'They should know this isn't a game, whether they did it out of ignorance or for some other reason. They need to be discouraged from ever doing it again . . .'

Hanif starts his engine angrily.

Why is he putting me in the position of explaining? Why is he putting me in the witness stand? wonders Sharad, but before he can understand, Hanif has whizzed off.

When Daddu gets up in the morning, he finds Shruti sitting downstairs.

'Arre, our Dole's even forgotten how to smile and laugh.' He sits on the divan and grins. 'Now, what can Daddu do? Tell me, where should I take you? The circus? The fair?'

'Anywhere.' Shruti smiles slightly. 'Let's leave this place and go somewhere.'

Daddu smiles. Shruti pours his tea. He picks up the cup and begins sipping, and recites:

Rahiye ab aisi jagah chal kar jahaan koi na ho
Ham-sukhan koi na ho aur ham-zabaan koi na ho

Let us go and live in a place where there's no one at all
None to talk to, nor speak our language, no one at all

Shruti suddenly feels tearful.

Daddu is silent. Then, in the same tone, he adds, as though he's reciting further lines from Ghalib: 'Take me now to the village, now only the village is best, take me now to the village, now only the village is blessed. No fighting, no harm, let's stay there, and farm.'

Shruti bursts out laughing.

'Arre, don't laugh,' says Daddu. 'Then that serious intellectualesque face of yours will be spoiled.'

'But why can't intellectuals laugh?' asks Shruti.

'If they start laughing, they'll look like imbeciles. Can anyone look like an intellectual with a gaping mouth, protruding teeth, squinting eyes?'

She laughs more, and he says, 'Okay, at least close the doors and windows so the wind won't blow in and make that expression stick. Then what will become of your serious, impressive face?'

Shruti gets up laughing, and she would have sat down next to Daddu on the divan and poured one more cup of tea, but now the divan has become an intellectual!

The students have come again.

'Sir, this is so rude, in today's letter . . .'

Hanif serves everyone chai. Shruti crisps roasted black gram and puffed rice in mustard oil, then sprinkles the dish with chilli and black salt, and sets it out with the tea.

Kapadia has come upstairs with Sharad.

'What an artistic home,' he remarks as he glances around.

He drinks some coffee and is getting ready to leave when he turns and says at the door, 'If you ever need anything, day or night, let me know.'

'Why did you bring him here?' Hanif asks Sharad after Kapadia has left. It seems this, too, has made him angry.

'Maybe he was asking you not to be offended by his shouting that day,' guesses Sharad.

'Nonsense,' says Shruti.

'He's not worth forgiving.' Hanif scowls.

'Is anyone worth forgiving in your view?' snaps Sharad. 'He just wants to alienate everyone,' he says, seeing how upset Shruti looks.

They learn in conversation that Beverly has gone to Nepal and will soon return.

Hanif, Hanif, Hanif! There's been drama. All the drama boils down to one name. I sit on high alert, pen at the ready. Now I must keep copying, I must keep at it.

Daddu is completely focused on the film *Gandhi*, which is playing on the television.

Shruti says, 'I'm thinking I'll put a small desk downstairs, right here . . .'

'. . . and then you'll write!' exclaims Sharad.

'. . . and then I can see the madhumalti from here,' retorts Shruti.

'What was the name of that bird you were mentioning the other day? A flowerpecker? Yes, so you're one of those, only for writing!'

Shruti makes a face.

'Penpecker!' Sharad puffs out his face and points at her.

'Why do you alienate everyone when there's a crisis?' Shruti is getting annoyed.

'For sure your miyan has been telling you stories.' Sharad stares with surprise. Then he makes a face.

'Why are you dragging him into it?'

'I'm not dragging.'

'Leave him alone.' Shruti is extremely annoyed.

'Not even he is okay with that,' chuckles Sharad.

Just then, Daddu, completely absorbed in the film, begins to guffaw. 'Hahaha! Godse has made himself the bad guy for nothing. He wasted all those bullets in his pistol. The old man would have died on his own! He'd never have had the stomach to see all this.'

Suddenly he falls silent and sits back with his beak out.

A procession of ashram devotees passes Sharad and Hanif on the street.

'Let them pass.'

The two of them stand to the side propping up their scooters. The ashram van has arrived, with the giant cutout of the Devi on the bonnet. The woman sitting in the van wears a saffron garment and speaks in a searingly loud voice.

'Is there something wrong with the mic?' asks Sharad. 'My ears are burning like they're stuffed with chilli peppers!'

The woman's shriek draws near:

Our environment has already been polluted, morality has declined, we are unable to draw breath without fear and suspicion . . . When some part of the body begins to rot, what must one do? To keep the rot from spreading to the rest of the body, one must cut off that limb and throw it away. Otherwise, all of society will rot.

Her fist vibrates as she clenches the mic, and the crowd cries out, *Jai Jagadambe!*

Sharad opens his mouth to say they've lost their minds, but he's repeated that sentence too many times, so he shuts it again.

The ashram van has stopped up ahead, and an enormous crowd, crashing like the waves of the ocean, swarms around from the street, the roofs, motor rickshaws, even trees, their palms pressed together.

The mahant descends from the van with a divine smile. He's blessing the crowd. The woman who gave the speech steps down behind him. The people press forward and garland them with roses and jasmine.

Cries of *Jai Jagadambe!* echo throughout. People race behind the van. They can still hear the woman's voice, but the individual words are now indistinct.

'Amazing,' begins Sharad, but suddenly he has the sensation that he's never before understood Hanif as a separate entity from himself in this way, he's never felt a distinct shame for him. He's started trying to explain and clarify to him, with the intention of comforting him. They had always stood apart from the crowd as one, influenced by a shared anger or shame. Today he sees and hears everything in two separate ways, first with his own eyes and ears, then with Hanif's.

Sharad feels annoyed at Hanif as he considers this. This jerk has been keeping his mouth shut, he thinks. But the shouting of the mullahs is even more terrifying than this. He feels his own thinking is correct.

Now, too, Hanif sits silently. Sharad and Shruti speak at length with the students.

A strange letter has appeared in the newspaper today. The writer claims to have met Hanif Jaidi once at a dinner, some fifteen years ago. Reading of his activities now, his memories of that dinner have been refreshed, because at that time as well, Hanif Jaidi had said strange things and had shown support for Pakistan.

Sharad is annoyed with Hanif for keeping quiet this long.

'You'll have to respond,' he says.

'What should I say?' asks Hanif irritably. 'I remember neither the dinner nor the conversation.'

'Try to remember. You must have said something . . .' Sharad begins.

'Why should I remember?' Hanif's voice trembles with rage. 'Why should I respond?'

He picks up the tray, goes into the kitchen and slams it down. When he returns, he picks up the newspaper and throws it on to the bookshelf. Then he flings off his socks.

'Stop it!' yells Shruti. Everyone freezes.

'Can't you put things down gently? Must you slam things around?' she scolds. The students look embarrassed.

Hanif carries his chair inside without saying a word. The students follow suit.

'You drag your chair. You slam your stool, you stir up all kinds of dust like a wild creature . . .'

The students start clearing things up soundlessly.

'Stop it.' Hanif stands with his feet firmly planted before Shruti.

'You stop it,' she says, still seated.

The two of them are still as statues. The students and Sharad are all frozen mid-action, trying to think of what to do with the dishes, stools, anything.

Should I leave all the others behind and follow only Hanif? If he's silent, should I ink his silence in bold letters? Should I draw a thick line around them? If he laughs, should I underline that? Should everything he does be written in bold? If he stretches, if he sneezes, if he sniffs the madhumalti, if . . .

'You still won't speak?' Sharad waves the newspaper in front of Professor Nandan's face.

'I saw.' Nandan is sitting calmly. 'Everything's already been said.'

'It says if someone like Hanif is made department chair, then . . .'

'Don't lose your head, Sharad,' reprimands Nandan. 'Everyone knows Hanif isn't like this. If someone writes a letter to the editor, his headship doesn't disappear. Hanif doesn't turn into what they say he is . . .'

'It's not a question of Hanif . . .' says Sharad, gritting his teeth.

Just then, Hanif passes by in the hall. 'Why does he have to come out right now?' he mumbles. Nandan also sees Hanif.

'These letters are supporting a common belief that being Muslim is a synonym for being a communalist.'

'And the other letters?' Nandan snips at his moustache with his teeth, grimaces and spits out the hairs. 'The ones insisting that Hanif is great, he's nothing but the best?'

Sharad sits down in a chair, livid.

Nandan looks at him for a little while. Behind his head, in the window, a squirrel darts to and fro. Nandan speaks gently. 'He's your friend. You're panicking. Don't turn one person's case into a cause.'

Sharad stares at him wordlessly.

Nandan feels encouraged by his silence. 'I have to consider the entire department . . .'

'When it's a question of the secular image of the department, Hanif will walk at the front of the peace march as a symbol, but when it comes to the headship, he'll become an individual . . .' observes Sharad morosely.

Shorty Josh suddenly speaks, and I realize he, too, has entered at some point and sat down. 'The headship isn't connected to his present crisis; it's to do with his overall behaviour,' he says.

'And is the present crisis connected to his headship?' Sharad asks this softly, but his eyes are blazing.

'Don't be so clever!' cries Nandan. 'You're calling the one who can galvanize the entire world behind him a victim? If it were one of us, we'd long since have been defeated.' Nandan's eyes are blazing.

He's standing by the gate. Short and muscled, a huge black beard melting into his black garment, long hair, red eyes. In his hand a pair of large iron tongs.

Is he a madman or what?

He's not looking at anyone.

He's holding up the tongs at a strange angle.

Bhonpa Baba?

Fear.

Should we be afraid or not?

'But this is not a good thing,' says Shruti. She's already said this three or four times.

'But what can we do? That's how people are.' Daddu sits cross-legged, hands clasped, upset.

'Because of this guy the department faces a disaster,' says Sharad.

'Hanif, if you roll in the mud, they'll raise you like a flag, but if you hold your head high like a flag, they'll roll you in the mud,' laughs Daddu.

Hanif laughs, but it's not real laughter.

Actually, Daddu's laugh isn't laughter either.

'Hanif, they were saying, "Hanif . . ."' starts Sharad heatedly.

'Yaar . . .' Hanif turns to him in anger. 'I've had enough. I don't want to hear what your people have said about me any more. What had to happen happened. Now drop it!'

Everyone is silent. Shruti shrinks back. Sharad sulks.

Daddu swirls his glass for a while. It is he who breaks the silence.

'Yes, stop all this. Let's talk about nice things,' he says. But no one says anything.

The department is empty, but Sharad is sitting in his office. The water tank on the roof is being cleaned. They've turned on the faucet, and the water cascades from the upper storey to the ground below, like a spring. The sound lends a strange desolation to the dark winter evening.

Sharad dials Beverly's telephone number.

'Beverly? Welcome back! How are you?'

'. . .'

'No, I'm at the department.'

'. . .'

'Oh, great. Good for you.'

'. . .'

'I was busy with all that.'

'. . .'

'Don't say it like that. Who told you that?'

'. . .'

'There's no reason to be afraid.'

'. . .'

'Not you too. . .'

'. . .'

'So you have some idea of what's going on in the city . . .'

'. . .'

'But . . .'

'. . .'

'Really? You tell me. Is that something we should fear?'

'. . .'

'I want you to tell the truth, so I'll stop dismissing my own fear. If I allow myself to fear, I can do something . . .'

'. . .'

'But that's just it. It's not simply a question of him alone; he's also forgotten everyone but himself.'

'. . .'

'What injustice?'

'. . .'

'No, not right now.'

'. . .'

'I'll just go home.'

'. . .'

'Beverly?'

'. . .'

'I like helpless, beaten people.'

'. . .'

'I'm focused on trying to save them, I'm prepared to die for them.'

'. . .'

'When they show their teeth, I feel angry.'

'. . .'

'It's possible. Feeling guilty can inspire me like nothing else. I become oblivious to everything else when I'm uplifting the fallen.'

'. . .'

'Then I don't like it. They've already fallen . . .'

'. . .'

'No, I'm fine.'

'. . .'

'How am I playing the martyr?'

'. . .'

'You . . .'

'. . .'

'No, not today.'

'. . .'

'Yes.'

'. . .'

'Maybe.'

'. . .'

'Okay.'

'. . .'

'No, no.'

'. . .'

'You also take care.'

'. . .'

'Right,' says Sharad and hangs up. The waterfall continues to tumble outside.

The ashramites have created mobile hospitals. Devi in front, van in back, doctor and compounder inside.

Someone has written on the wall of the ashram:

We laughed and took Pakistan
We'll die and take Hindustan!

Sharad notices Hanif on the upstairs balcony. Hanif also sees him, but he leans over oddly so he can't be seen in the semi-darkness.

He's sitting up there feeling like a martyr, thinks Sharad irritably. Wrapping himself in his solitude like a blanket! Sharad cocks his head to one side.

Shorty Josh calls in the band of students staging a sit-in outside the head's office. The head reads their petition and promises to send copies to the vice chancellor and the dean.

For the moment, there's calm in the city, and the ashramites are holding peace gatherings. In our colony, too, one can hear devotees singing the kirtan.

A neighbourhood family, with whom they share a passing acquaintance, is making the rounds to say goodbye.

'What's this? You didn't discuss it with anyone, you just straight away packed up your things?' complains Shruti to the wife.

'We don't fear for ourselves, but these tiny children . . .' The man leaves it at that, so his wife continues.

'You hear about murders and rapes every day . . .' She, too, leaves her sentences unfinished.

'But nothing happens here,' states Shruti confidently.

'But look what's happening with Hanif Bhai.'

'Oh, yes, but that . . .' begins Sharad.

'Now even those doing the saving are unsafe,' says the wife.

'We have our own people there,' says the husband.

'Look, things will get better,' says Hanif.

'Khuda hafiz. Goodbye.'

'Khuda hafiz.'

When a truck packed and loaded with the family's things drives by, the three of them watch desolately from the window.

Nowadays, Daddu inspects the mail himself and sometimes even tears up an advertisement or an envelope. Then he squishes the torn bits together, stuffs them in a plastic bag, wraps it up tightly, throws it in the trash bin in the kitchen and returns to the divan.

'Look!' says Professor Nandan, slapping the students' petition on Sharad's desk. 'The students are upset, and demand to know why the department is being turned into a forum for politics and communalism.'

Sharad picks up the document.

The grass is being trampled in a battle between elephants . . . this
is impeding our ability to study . . .

'Who's behind this?' asks Sharad, looking up.

'I'll tell you what's behind it: this obsession you have with
putting Hanif on a pedestal!'

These words have been boiling up inside Nandan for some
time. Finally, they burst forth.

They learn from Kapadia that a hit list is being posted all over the city.

'This is the work of terrorists,' he says, looking at Hanif.

Hanif is sitting up straight, but his soul contorts, and he
recoils as though he's been marked.

'They're Hindu terrorists,' says Kapadia.

Hanif and Shruti both look at him with surprise.

'There's no reason to be afraid. Live well. Have fun!' says
Kapadia as he's leaving. 'Call me immediately if you need me.' He
looks at Hanif again.

Shruti stares at him fearfully.

It seems to Hanif as though this police officer's gaze has stuck
a label on him announcing his name and religion.

Like other city dwellers, I too wish to say that there was nothing to
fear. It's just that when a few incidents occur far off, terror spreads
throughout the city.

But is the terror truly intangible, and are the incidents the
only truly concrete things? Do those who didn't die or won't be
killed have any presence in the tale?

And consider this too. So often we've felt afraid for days and days. But did anything happen? Nothing at all. The fear rose, then fell away. Just like today: it's risen but it will fall away.

'We don't find your jokes amusing.' Shruti slams down the phone.

'What's this? Why are you getting angry?' asks Daddu.

'He says if Hanif the hero is smart, he can have it both ways.'

'Quite right.' Daddu smiles slightly.

'He insists on making jokes, but not everyone thinks they're funny. He keeps calling Hanif a hero like that,' complains Shruti.

'So what can you do about it?' Daddu seems sad. 'Every single thing is said a thousand ways. Laugh.' He laughs. 'Show intelligence. What he's saying is actually correct.' Daddu motions towards the phone. 'If he were smart, he'd run for office and become an MP or something. There's still time. I'll give him a few slaps. Then we'd all get together and scream bloody murder, and he'd resign, and after that a message will come straight from the capital saying, "You have been respectfully nominated to the Rajya Sabha. Please grace our parliament with your presence!"'

Shruti is silent.

'What? Don't you like my joke either?' Daddu looks annoyed.

'People are probably talking exactly like that,' says Shruti.

'I bet they're saying nothing at all. That idiot can't even make himself head.'

'That's good.' Shruti smiles now.

'Yes, yes.' Daddu wobbles his head. 'You like it. Idiots are what you like, but that means you should also like Kapadia.'

'Why does he call every single day?' muses Shruti.

When a call comes from Babu Painter, Sharad turns his back to
Daddu and whispers on the phone. Then he whispers softly to
Beverly. Daddu's eyes are on Sharad's back.

Maqbool Haq has asked someone to interview Hanif.

'You shouldn't have agreed,' Shruti tells him. Hanif is
silent.

'It's a question of your reputation.' He's still silent. Shruti
becomes agitated. 'You sit around like a turtle with your head
pulled in, and now suddenly you've switched to playing the tiger,
but it's for the wrong Muslim.'

'And do you know what the others want?' Hanif breaks the
silence. 'They want me to say, "I'm a Muslim and I shall remain
a tortoise."'

'Come in.'

Daddu is carefully wiping off the table with a cloth. Right,
left, right, left, and again, then top to bottom. He's dampened
one side with the cloth. First, he wipes with that side, then the dry
side. The wet table sparkles, but a moment later, it dries and the
shine dulls. Like stripes of shadow and sunlight.

'I was waiting for you to come. I have a task for you.'

'Tell me.' Shruti reaches for the dust cloth.

'This I'll do. You need to do the other things. I'd forgotten
Lallan is coming today with the children, and I've given Nankau
the day off.'

'There's no food prepared?'

Shruti goes to the fridge.

Daddu follows her.

'Well, there's this leftover dal. There's some sabzi.' He opens the chapati container by the gas. 'There are six parathas,' he says, counting them. 'There should be some yogurt.' He's stuck his entire head into the fridge and is searching.

'That's not enough.'

Shruti also opens the cover and looks inside.

'I forgot, otherwise I'd have had him make more,' repeats Daddu.

'It's no trouble. I'll just make a few more,' says Shruti promptly.

'That's what I was thinking,' says Daddu. 'Put some onions and tomatoes in the dal to stretch it and make some rice.'

'Now you go sit down.' Shruti looks at her watch. 'I'll make it myself.'

Daddu's expression of relief reveals how worried he was before.

'Both of you eat here too,' he calls from the divan.

After some time, he comes to the kitchen door.

'Oh, why are you kneading the dough?' he asks. 'You could have just made rice.'

'It's no trouble.'

Shruti stands on tiptoe wrestling with the flour.

'Shall I knead it?' asks Daddu.

Shruti sighs and laughs.

'So you think I don't know how?' Daddu also laughs. 'In the village I used to toast big thick rotis—tikkars—on the dry dung fire.'

'You did everything in the village!' laughs Shruti. She presses her lips together. By now the dough resembles rubber.

'Oho, you're making fun of my village! It wasn't at all difficult to cook then. Cooking's only difficult in cities, where people want such fine, thin chapatis, and pulau, and sparkling basmati. We used to make gulaithi! Or we used to take dal, pour it in the pot and drop balls of dough in it, then leave them to cook on the cow-dung fire.'

'Oh, like baati.' Shruti is collecting the rolling pin, board and chapati pan.

'No, silly, not baati, this was . . .'

'Where are the tongs?' asks Shruti, searching around.

Daddu joins the search. Both clatter the pots and pans.

'Maybe Nankau doesn't use them,' suggests Daddu.

'My hands will burn,' explains Shruti as she bends over, searching behind boxes.

'I'll make them,' says Daddu, stuck inside a cabinet.

'You'll make them with no tongs, no fire, not even flour!' laughs Shruti. 'Just hang up a picture of food for Lallan Uncle, then he can have your kind of dinner!'

'What's that?' Daddu gets it a moment later. 'Not all people can digest like that. You've got to have digestion like me for that.'

Shruti flips over the puffing roti on the pan and looks around.

'What sort of an Indian woman are you? Our women are delicate, but they make rotis without tongs.'

Daddu opens the fridge.

'Will they be in there?'

'Who knows?' he laughs. 'It seems Nankau is aiming to become the queen of all chapati warriors!'

'Well, I'll be a coward. I'm going to bring some from upstairs.'

Shruti turns off the gas.

When she returns from upstairs, Daddu is standing in the kitchen with the tongs. 'They were hanging right here. Right above the gas!'

'Here?' Shruti looks at where they were hanging. She also holds a pair of tongs.

'I noticed them right after you shut the door,' says Daddu.

'You could have yelled,' she retorts, but just for the sake of it, since Daddu never yells, not in his manner, not in his speech nor in his anything. Pitch-perfect, beautiful. High octave only in music. But if a high octave came from elsewhere, Daddu would lower his gaze. If it came from him, he'd commit suicide.

No, no shouting, no ranting, no stumbling, nothing high-pitched, none of this for Daddu. Except for in the world of his laughter!

'Something's happening to him.'

Beverly is at the department. Sharad says this to her.

'There must be.'

'Not like that.'

There's something in Sharad's voice that I'm not catching.

'Maqbool Haq? But you're the one who addresses the ashramites so respectfully as bhagwan.'

'But I don't let the bhagwans into my house!'

Daddu opens the mail. He's reading the hit list. His eyes dart back and forth, and then he looks up, towards the upstairs flat. He tears up the paper, balls up the scraps and walks into the kitchen. The paper is yellow.

When Sharad hears the scooter, he goes to the glass door. Daddu's eyes are on his back. Sharad quickly puts on his coat, and says, 'I'll be right back.' He goes out after Hanif.

'The hit list is nonsense. A childish ploy to cause fear. Don't pay any attention,' Kapadia is saying as Shruti enters.

'What?' She's alert now.

'A couple of names are fabricated. There isn't even anyone by the name of Sohail Usman in this city!'

'The ashram . . .' Sharad looks at Shruti and falls silent.

'The ashram has no role in this, the ashram is oblivious. These are others who are hiding behind them. If there weren't an ashram, they would take inspiration from elsewhere. It's an excuse, Sharad, an excuse.' Then he looks at Shruti as well. 'We should all stay alert nowadays. But not to worry,' he adds.

Shruti's throat feels constricted. She wants to ask something, but she doesn't have the nerve.

'Daddu . . .' she begins when she sees him approaching.

Kapadia looks from one to the other with surprise.

Haq comes by to ask Hanif to speak at a gathering.

'Don't go,' says Shruti.

'I'll definitely go,' says Hanif.

'Yes, you should go,' says Shruti after a moment.

'I'm thinking of not going,' replies Hanif.

Amidst it all, we fear for Hanif, but we also don't really think anything will happen to him.

On the other hand, did we ever think what has happened to him would happen?

We often don't accept that something's happened to him. I'm just telling you what people say. People say, and Shorty Josh says with a laugh, that Hanif is not so important that anyone would get a reward for doing something to him. There are many separate factors at work: a religious storm swirls in the ashram; in the department all that's been attempted is to follow a few rules. And why does Hanif not consider anyone but himself? And look, he too is shouting slogans. So is it any surprise if someone's offended? And listen, what's being said to him alone, that he should apologize, and the death threats that have been printed, those things aren't being said just to him but to all of us, countering our same tired secular slogans, but his name looks a bit different, so his name is used to curse us all.

'We're all getting targeted because of him,' remark some people in the department ruefully. 'He'll be beaten and pull us down with him.'

But some say he's a hero! He's lapping up all the attention! He's the talk of the town!

Today I see Sharad sliding a list of emergency numbers under the phone, which Daddu reads after Sharad leaves the house.

You can see the neem tree from Hanif's office. Its yellow leaves float down and fall on Urmila and Sharad. Hanif goes to the window and sees the two of them laughing together.

'Come on, make a bet,' Sharad is saying.

'Which side are you on?' asks Urmila, holding out her hand.

'Whichever one you aren't!' says Sharad, shaking her hand.

Smoke still rises from a pile of ashes nearby. The gardener has gathered the dry leaves and burnt them.

Hanif doesn't like it, whatever it is. For good or ill, the department people are talking about him, and Urmila didn't even sign the letter.

Yesterday afternoon, a crowd broke into Mustafa's home, locked his wife and elderly mother in a room, and stole watches, jewellery and money. Then they smashed a bunch of stuff and ran. No one knew who it was. Maqbool Haq is on the move. He gets out of a long car with four others and meets with Hanif in the department.

Seeing them standing together, Sharad thinks of the word *gang*. He sees Urmila looking at him and starts up a conversation.

Shruti steals downstairs.

'Sharad,' she calls out.

Sharad is bent over his desk writing something.

'Oh, come in, Shruti.'

He stands, pulls up a chair and removes a pillow.

'Nothing's wrong, is it? Being afraid is ridiculous, right?' Shruti speaks haltingly.

'Of course. Shruti, they were just kids . . .'

'But these letters. Kapadia . . .'

'The hit list is nonsense,' says Sharad with disgust. But as he speaks, he seems frightened.

'It is, but . . . his . . . name . . .' Shruti speaks haltingly. 'Why hide it from me?' Now she feels angry.

'Meaningless stuff.' Sharad dismisses the whole thing with a wave of the hand. But he looks truly worried. He opens his mouth but then shakes his head as though banishing his own worry. 'Hanif's an important man! Haven't you seen how many people support him? Friends, strangers? Can anyone touch him? Whoever has the nerve will be wiped out.'

'Don't speak like the others. Saying he's a hero even if he's being destroyed.'

'No, no, no.' Sharad shakes his head so much it's like he's forgotten to stop. 'No one will let that happen. So much publicity . . .'

'Does he want it? Like this? Whose side are you on?' demands Shruti.

Sharad is silent. He holds out his hand. Shruti looks indecisive, then gives him hers.

'Are you scared?' she asks, detached.

'Yes, maybe,' he replies, looking down.

'The thing is . . .'

'Just say it.' Beverly eggs him on, but irritably.

'. . . that he's begun to seem like an odd sort of Muslim,' says Sharad.

'Go say that in the mirror and see how you look,' snaps Beverly.

Everyone seems weirdly suspicious, but my suspicion cannot be unfounded. That ink seller truly does press a finger to his temple and stare at me like that. And this time he held in his hand a *Jai Jagadambe!* pen purchased from the ashram.

Two shiny stars and a half moon have appeared in the pink sky. There's no breeze. The silence echoes sadly.

Sharad stands by the madhumalti for a long time. Daddu, Hanif and Shruti sit on the other side of the glass door. He knows the moment he goes inside, Hanif will stand up and walk away.

He's joined the Haq gang but dares glare at me! he thinks.

The three of them are looking down, but Daddu's head is bobbing. He's handing Hanif the bottle and speaking. Hanif measures pegs into two glasses.

Sharad's heart swells by turns with love and hate for Hanif.

Hanif leaves for the department alone now, he thinks.

Once they'd returned home on such a twilit evening, Hanif had got off his scooter and said, 'I'll be right back.' And then Sharad had also said, 'I'll be right back.' And both had practically run outside, through the gate, to pee against the boundary wall!

Fool, I used to be your friend! he thinks sadly. And then angrily: You're inside, sitting in my home, and I'm the one scared of appearing before you?

Someone has stuck the yellow hit list to the wall of the department in the middle of the night. Hanif's name is seventh on the list.

'How ugly,' says Professor Nandan to Sharad as they walk up to Hanif. 'Some idiotic children again.'

When he gets home, Sharad approaches Hanif again. Shruti is also there.

'It was posted in the department,' Sharad tells Shruti awkwardly. It's as though he feels frightened of Hanif. Hanif is silent. What should one say on such an occasion? 'It's nothing,' he adds in an artificial manner. 'It's been posted all over for a while.'

'I know,' says Hanif.

Shruti and Sharad start.

'Why didn't you say something?' asks Shruti.

'Why didn't you?' retorts Hanif.

'Where did you see it?' Sharad looks wretched.

'Maqbool Haq showed me.' Hanif looks away.

'Don't meet with him,' argues Sharad. 'Tell him . . .'

'You're an idiot.' Hanif is irritated.

'Yes, yes, say that, say you're an idiot. Tell him you can't meet . . .'

'I'm saying it about you.'

'Yes, I'm an idiot too,' snaps Sharad with a flash of anger. Then he subsides.

'Then keep quiet,' cautions Shruti, alarmed.

'And how does one do that—keep quiet?'

Sometimes we feel like the perpetrators, sometimes like the victims.

Then the Devi drinks the proffered milk, and those who had not believed before begin to believe now. Two proofs of the Devi's miracle have spread throughout the city: one, that eyewitnesses are saying it happened; and two, it was on the BBC.

Shruti says she wants to install a grille over the window on the upstairs balcony.

'It will look bad,' scolds Hanif.

'Sliding.'

'But there's already a sliding door.'

'But if you open it and go in the other room,' says Shruti, 'the langurs can break in.'

'Langurs?' Hanif stares at her in disbelief. 'I've never seen a langur here, and Daddu's house is open day and night. Do you want to put up iron bars everywhere?'

'You people are quick to scoff.' Hanif sometimes says something brief like this before getting up to leave a gathering. 'If they've actually offered up litres of milk, the Devi has surely drunk it, otherwise you'd see it flowing across the floor of the temple.'

He says this and departs, but Nandu is pleased.

'If something is true for such a large number of people, it really is true in a certain sense. We're too quick to rattle off terms like self-hypnosis, blind faith, bogus mass hysteria, and dismiss them, but this entire country is ecstatic, and one fears saying this to you, and even more so to your friend Hanif . . .' he says affectionately.

'But he's the one who said it,' Sharad reminds him.

'One fears,' continues Nandu, 'saying something to you two, and then your coming after us and calling us cowards and appeasers. Laughing off phenomena like this milk thing . . .'

'But he's the one who said it.'

'The two of you aren't the only radicals. A lot of thinking and understanding is called for. I can't write quickly like before. But does it make me a radical or a show-off to say that the Devi absorbed the milk? This is the truth of pure devotion.'

Nandu takes a bite of his moustache.

'What do we say, what do you hear?' asks Sharad.

'You? You haven't said anything at all. It's your friend who's controversial!'

This time he points to his right temple with his right finger.

I feel terrified. He can't be doing it for no reason. Is there nowhere else on this side of the city to buy ink?

They're BA students. Fourteen of them. They've asked for permission to be removed from Hanif's section starting this semester, and to be allowed into Professor Nandan's and Urmila's sections.

Today, Hanif's face has darkened. Shruti doesn't know what to say.

'Why?' she blurts out. Then she looks at him fearfully.

'There must be some reason. Someone must have goaded them into it. Maybe they don't like my lectures. Or maybe they're scared of me.'

Hanif's voice sounds changed. Guarded.

Shruti slides over to him.

He looks badly shaken. He starts to turn away from Shruti. Then he turns back and opens his mouth. Then closes it again.

'Did you write anything?' he asks after much thought.

'Yes,' she says haltingly. '. . . Hanif . . .'

'Bring it here, show it to me.'

Hanif holds out his hand thinking what she wrote is right next to her, but quickly withdraws it when she tries to reach out to him instead. She goes and gets her papers. He grabs them. His lips tremble. His eyes fill with tears.

'Hanif,' weeps Shruti.

Now it's Hanif who's sobbing, babbling.

'. . . students . . .' is what I hear, and no matter how many times Shruti reaches out to him, he pushes her away.

Dust flies everywhere. I sit with my manuscript. Instead of writing I blow away the dust. But it always flies back.

Nothing's happening at all Just some people from the department averting their eyes when they recognize Hanif by his trousers as he descends the stairs. Or by his shoes. Meaning they recognize him. Hanif.

Sometimes something happens in the middle of something else, after which everything else changes. Or maybe we only consider something changed when we start to see it? He was exactly like this when he was a child, and we used to laugh at his mistakes and say, *Oh, he's just a child*. But now he has grown up and still making mistakes, as adults do; only now we can't laugh and say, *Oh, he's just a grown-up*.

We'd all grown up. The city had also grown up.

It was a strange time. The pace of life had been upended, but somehow this had become a synonym for the right way up. And this was how we recognized everything, meaning not standing on our feet but standing on our heads, even if we were standing up straight, the ground would be the air, and the sky the ground.

The city was both bustling and busted. Today a storm, tomorrow respite. Who knew what the next day might bring!

Even so, we eagerly awaited tomorrow, or if not tomorrow, the day after.

Eagerly awaited, or feared? In truth, our fear was for tomorrow; today was a blessing, today nothing happened. And if not tomorrow, then the next day. What had flowed in our veins before now came bursting from our wounds, which were still ordinary scrapes. But who knew what would flow from them tomorrow?

And the next day.

Far off, bayonets are at the ready. When they turn, they'll be aimed at us, and they'll be aimed at you. At every disagreement.

They'll be telling everyone what to do, what to sing, what to teach, what to write, what to wear, what to eat.

I was thankful to remain in the background. No one could reach into my darkness to stop my hand. But for how long? This was my fear. But everyone feared. Avoiding the gaze of their own fears.

On top of that, these three had begun to fear one another. Not like before, when there was still scope for skirmishing and truces. It was strange now.

I remember Sharad seeing Haq and his comrades surrounding Hanif: he wasn't just annoyed but also afraid. If something were to happen to one of them—and nothing has happened to him; look how quickly they band together—could we ever be like that?

Hanif was also frightened of the accumulating questions in the department, finding in Sharad the echo of those questions, finding him laughing and talking in their midst. In the end he's the one who must become head; they will make him the head. So where do I fit into all of this?

Both of them were scornful, but in truth they also feared. We'd begun to fear both ourselves and others.

Shruti feared the tearful voice that emerged from her own mouth with the crackle of hate. She feared Sharad's questions, Hanif's silence, her own reactions.

And I feared that these three had collectively changed the problem. The curfew in the city, the ashram processions, the violence, the arson, the attractions of the new 'temple': Had we left all these behind in the newspaper and become too immersed in ourselves? In criticizing one another, in staring at our own faces?

It also occurred to me that I should stop copying. Hanif sits alone and desires with every fibre of his being to cut off that part of his body where Shruti lays an encouraging hand. Do I have to write about that aspect of that year? Or this: that Shruti laments, *he's hiding everything from me*, even though nothing so dire is happening. And isn't what's happening to him happening to me? Or this: that Sharad is saying to Beverly, 'Don't become like the rest, there's so little space left where there's none of that. Not you, too?'

And the department people who'd begun to ask those same questions that one has tired of hearing, sometimes with a smile, or annoyance, or deep seriousness, such as, 'After all, isn't it worth thinking about why the riots always happen where the Muslims are?' Which they ask like questions, although they aren't really questions, but answers, their own and everyone else's.

Without trying to understand, I sit here, restless copying my occupation, but again and again, I find myself frightened of those sights and words.

No, that isn't it. I'd begun to fear these words and sights which I was copying down were the outer layer, a thin crust, and that tremors were occurring beneath them, which in reality were changing our city and us, and which were completely contrary to what was apparent.

So was I just copying down a big lie? This was what I feared.

But no, I didn't stop, because distinguishing between true and false wasn't a decision I was prepared to make. And if that year was false, and these words a sham, then this tragedy, too, belonged to our city alone.

Now, whatever one may say, at least my hands were not paralysed like the hands of these three. When one is to copy down not oneself but others, then perhaps some vitality can remain.

The way before, when they wrote all the time, they weren't as fearful, and they could still focus on the outside world and other people.

So I kept fearing, but I also kept writing.

The breeze has stopped, and the dusty city-wide pollution hangs suspended in the sky. The sky, which buckles beneath the weight of winter. Descending straight into our beings.

Kapadia calls.

'Don't worry. But all the same, don't wander about alone.'

Maqbool Haq calls.

'We'll respond to bricks with stones.'

Beverly calls.

'Do you all want to come and stay in my flat for a while?'

Sharad has, without telling anyone, removed one of the two names on the name plate from the outside gate. Daddu watches him from inside, through the glass door, but Sharad does not know this, because he glances up at the balcony as he slips the plate into his bag and zips it shut.

Hanif is missing.

Shruti stands on the balcony squinting towards the bridge, then looks down at the gate and glances up and down the street.

Periodically she goes and stirs the carrots and milk stewing over a low flame and scrapes the sides of the karahi to push the halwa into the middle.

Hanif doesn't go to the department on holidays or curfew days any more, but she still thinks it's possible he's simply gone there. Although nowadays, Hanif goes only to teach his classes, then comes straight home to do his reading and writing. But all the same.

She pulls a chair out to the balcony and sits down.

Should I go downstairs? she wonders. But Sharad's scooter is in the garage, and she fears that if he sits with her and Daddu downstairs he'll stir up a tempest and make her more scared, so she won't go.

But Hanif doesn't do such things.

She feels panicky.

On the other hand, what does he do nowadays that's the same as before? She comforts herself with this thought. For a long time, she just stirs the halwa. Then she goes and stands on the balcony again.

A strapping boy in tight pants walks haughtily down the street. He throws back his head and glances up at Shruti. A faint but lewd smile plays about his lips. He walks on, but keeps turning back and smiling that smile.

Shruti is stirring the halwa again. She feels annoyed at how slowly it's cooking and turns up the flame. It begins to bubble, the hot steam hitting her face.

She returns to the balcony. The boy has reached the end of the street and is about to turn the corner. He grits his teeth, throws a fist in the air, pounds his chest and turns into the colony. Shruti reads in his demeanour a cry of *Jai Jagadambe!*

She sniffs the halwa and returns to the kitchen. The high heat has almost completely evaporated the milk. She quickly beats it with a slotted spoon. Then she pours in some sugar. She thinks,

I'll taste it for sweetness, so she blows on a small bit in a spoon to cool it and brings it to her lips.

Right at that moment, a random thought occurs to her: Here halwa is being devoured; over there, who knows . . .? She stops mid-taste, lip and tongue randomly sticking out the tiniest distance from the spoon, but she dismisses her childishness and tastes the sweetness. As she sprinkles it with cardamom and almonds, she begins to fear openly.

Shruti writes a note. *I've gone for a walk.* After taping it to the door, she walks slowly down the stairs and out to the gate, though she continues to fear Sharad might see her.

It's dusk. She wanders all about the colony for a long time. What if he's sitting in the park? He hasn't walked over towards that hill, has he?

An extremely old man is walking down the steps from the park. He rests the tip of his cane on the street below and leans over it, in the process of lifting his feet to get down the steps. His entire body trembles, as does his cane. Shruti reaches out and holds on to his arm. He looks fearful but steadies himself and is able to descend. He mumbles something and perhaps smiles tremulously before proceeding on his way with unsteady steps.

As she watches him, she doubts he can even see where he's going. Should I ask him his address? she wonders. The old man props his cane against a red letterbox and stands there shakily, like a shadow in the darkness. First he turns his head, then his whole body, as though blindly searching. Shruti watches him enter the gali.

She smiles and wonders: Shall I go into the house to see if he's back? Then I'll come back here and see if that old man was able to get home!

Hanif is in the flat.

'You were gone so long,' she says softly.

'I went to get the scooter serviced,' he replies calmly.

'You could have said where you were going,' she suggests.

'I did, I told the maid.'

The scent of halwa wafts into the room, with a wave of cardamom.

'I made carrot halwa,' laughs Shruti. Her throat feels constricted as she laughs.

Professor Nandan has told Hanif once more that the rotation must continue and he's next. It's clear from his words that this is merely a formality, and he has no expectation of Hanif saying yes.

The strange thing is that even though he anticipates his answer, he feels the need to insist on performing the whole ritual.

'Come now, enough is enough . . .' he pleads. 'Now drop it; enough of this attempt to flee your responsibilities . . . Aren't you obligated to us all? Like a wayward boy brought back on the straight and narrow by agreeing to a marriage? He he he!'

Hanif glares at him with loathing.

'Why are you playing the role of the villain?' he asks.

Nandan is shocked.

Some ashram priests have entered the colony to perform a puja at someone's home. Prasad is distributed to all the neighbouring homes. Cardamom pods, flowers and slices of coconut wrapped in red and yellow muslin. Daddu sets it on top of the fridge.

'Why doesn't he want the entire episode forgotten?'

Nowadays Sharad only talks to Shruti when Hanif is not there.

'When the hit lists stopped coming, he started openly hanging out with the Haq gang!'

'Haq drops by sometimes, but Hanif doesn't go anywhere with him,' says Shruti tearfully.

'His name is already mud. Does he want it completely destroyed? Doesn't he know what poisonous things Haq has written in his newspaper?'

'That's not him, is it?'

They both stand at the sound of a scooter. Sharad quickly slides on his mojari slippers, goes to the door, then spins around like a top emptying the ashtray into the kitchen dustbin under some scraps of paper and peelings, pressing the rest of the trash on top of the ashes and washing his hands. After which, he makes like a rabbit!

Daddu has gone outside to get the mail. He rips in half the saffron flag stuffed in the letter box and throws it outside the gate. It's made of paper and wood, small.

He comes back inside and searches for something. He peers under the table, then squats and, as though rotating on a pulley, searches below the chairs, behind the sofa. Then he stands up and rushes to the bedroom, where he leans over and looks under the bed. He searches behind all the doors. He pauses midway as his eye travels to the corner of the veranda outside the glass door. He goes outside and picks up the broom.

Now Nandan comes to chat with Sharad in his office instead of summoning him via intercom the way he used to.

There are no disagreements anyway, since Sharad's stopped giving speeches and writing articles. This is not exactly by design, but speeches happen when someone invites you and articles happen when Babu prints them. Babu has received strict orders not to print such articles, and he himself agrees.

'If Hanif wants, he can stay at my home. Of course, everything will be okay. We're all in this together,' says Babu.

Actually, Nandan has told Sharad if he's very afraid Nandan could set him up at the university guesthouse, but Sharad hasn't told Shruti this.

It's a joke, isn't it, that we're afraid? At some moments, we fear a noise, at others silence! Over time, letters have come, then they've stopped, phone calls have come, then they too have stopped, even the hit lists posted everywhere on walls are starting to fray. We felt fearful so many times that year, but then we calmed down, grew accustomed to the fear, to seeing and hearing such things. We couldn't sleep. Then we could. This happened many times, but all the same, now and then we felt afraid. Perhaps it's helplessness— we knew the fear would depart again, but as long as it stayed, we'd have to feel it. We were frightened!

Shruti fears going out at night.

Hanif fears going out by day.

When Sharad goes to bid Beverly farewell at the station, he suddenly feels empty inside. As though he has no friends left.

'I'll miss you,' he says.

'And I you,' says Beverly. She gives Sharad's leg an affectionate tap with her knee.

Some other year would she have been my girlfriend? Sharad asks himself.

'I could only talk to you,' he says out loud.

'That's because for the most part, I don't understand anything!' Beverly strokes Sharad's shoe with hers.

'With you, all the obstacles, all the filth, all the complications, all of them melted away, and I became lighter.'

'You became? But I'm still here, I haven't left yet.' Beverly bursts out laughing.

'Beverly, I can't even express what you mean to me,' says Sharad tearfully.

'You Indians are very emotional,' teases Beverly.

'Another stereotype!' laughs Sharad.

'Write,' says Beverly.

With you I was able to speak outside of stereotypes, thinks Sharad. But will I write to her? he wonders, after he's settled her in the train and stands on the platform.

The whistle blows.

'Any magazines?' he asks from the window. 'Shall I get you some fruit?' He's walking alongside the train. 'You have water, right?'

He waves.

Shruti writes something and laughs.

> We're not secular, we're secural. We only say so much, to make sure we remain secure, so our privacy won't be invaded, so we don't get shot!

Don't tell cynical jokes, she tells herself.

I don't know what she's sat down to write. But she did say—didn't she?—that she would write something else besides all this.

Sharad feels a twinge when he sees Hanif at his office door.

'Hello, come in,' he says, feeling as though he's never said such a formal *come in* to Hanif before.

'When is your term starting?' asks Hanif from the door.

'The VC's probably sent a letter,' Sharad tells him.

'It'll take one month, two months more?'

'I think it'll be soon.'

'I'll put in a request for sabbatical then.'

Hanif is about to turn away when Sharad's tutorial students arrive. Sharad doesn't want them to see that something has changed between him and Hanif.

'Righto! See you later, man!' he calls out jovially.

As soon as Hanif leaves, he feels angry he had to put on an act like that.

I'll tell you something strange. The department people have begun to talk like the ashramites.

No, I said that wrong.

They're not talking like the ashramites at all, not with their bigotry, or their passion. The department people are intellectuals, and they're saying intellectual things, but the things they say bear an uncanny resemblance to the things one hears over there.

I'm saying this because when Sharad has debates with his students mimamsa-style, I listen with pen and paper in hand, and I hear these people questioning what they've said until now, and their questions are the same things the ashramites present as answers: Are all communities alike? Don't the core differences of their thoughts influence their behaviour? Is our sympathy unidirectional? Can so many people be totally wrong? Et cetera, et cetera.

I'm astonished when I hear this. Not astonished—dumbfounded. Is this the only difference between those and these? One group expresses the words in the form of an answer, the other a question?

Where do we find ourselves? Have we moved forward? Or is this a circle, and we've just returned to the starting point?

I'm stunned that these people have turned out to be so naive, so backward, so blind, despite how proud they are of their intellects—it's their job to use their brains, after all. How could it take this long for them to understand what those people, the people of the city, so many of them, have unconsciously understood and believed from the start?

It began to look like what those people were explaining from their subconscious minds, these ones have picked up in their conscious minds and now repeat, except with a question mark at the end. But isn't this question mark simply a formality arising from their intellectualism? Tomorrow the question marks will be removed, and *these* will become *those*.

The incredible part is how long it takes the thinkers.

But I also fear we've been so foolish, we're only now understanding what all of them already understood. And that's enough to bring all our self-confidence crashing down.

When Sharad comes in, Hanif goes out to the balcony.

'You're undoubtedly safe here,' Sharad tells Shruti. 'But there's no harm in being safer. Beverly's left her key. I have her flat for six months. Foreigners live around there.'

Hanif steps inside. 'Sharad, stop giving us ridiculous advice.'

'It's impossible to have a conversation with you.' Sharad doesn't sit down. 'I've heard there's something's going on at the ashram, some disturbance among the mahants themselves. If riots break out . . .'

'If it comes to that, we'll decide what we need to do,' says Hanif, putting him off.

'You don't think of anyone but yourself,' snaps Sharad. 'Think of Shruti.'

'I don't need you to tell me that.'

'Shruti, you think about it,' says Sharad, turning to her.

'Don't scare her,' warns Hanif, glaring at him.

Sharad leaves.

Shruti is examining the madhumalti. What would I do, she wonders, if a band of hooligans were to break in right now?

It's good Hanif isn't home, she thinks. Could I jump down? She assesses the distance. If my bones didn't break, I'd be able to run out and warn Hanif.

She laughs with embarrassment at her nonsensical thoughts.

Actually, the city is calm. Nankau buys mounds of peas from the vegetable seller every day and fries them with ginger and green chillies to serve with tea. Then he sprinkles them with lime and coriander leaves. Whoever's fated to sit by Daddu that evening will discover that tasty peas are also in their destiny!

Sharad can't stop coughing. He's clutching his scooter, coughing.

'Put on a muffler. Gargle!' Shruti calls down.

Daddu's doctor has come. Daddu gets up immediately and takes him into his bedroom. He refuses to let him speak in front of any of them!

'He stays with you and me for five minutes,' Hanif says to Shruti. About Sharad. 'He hangs out with Nandu and what he calls "Nandu's egrets". Once he's head, he'll have to work with them, right? He'll have to, won't he . . .?'

'But he says you stay apart,' Shruti tries to add.

'. . . whatever he says,' he interrupts.

How small that year made our world.

'What?' asks Hanif, a bit irritated.

'That's what I'm talking about,' says Shruti. 'You get annoyed just hearing his name.'

'Then why are you defending him?' snaps Hanif. 'Why are you telling me he does everything out of concern for us? I know that.'

'Even so?' Shruti looks at him with surprise.

'Even so,' Hanif says and then falls silent. Far off, there are ominous sounds like the striking of kettledrums. 'Shruti, that guy,' begins Hanif, 'doesn't even trust what he himself has said. He keeps talking because he's been saying the same things his whole life. He doesn't even believe his own words.'

Hanif now feels angry at his own struggle to explain. Shruti waits.

'If someone were to attack me tomorrow, he'd jump heatedly in the middle, bear the brunt himself and start shouting at the attacker.'

'Even then?' Shruti looks more confused.

'Even then. Because he would do it out of habit, not faith. And another thing . . .' He falls silent again.

'What?' asks Shruti, growing impatient.

'I'm telling you.' Hanif glares. 'And now it also seems like when he's panicking at his lack of faith, he goes overboard, as though that will make it return.'

'We all feel muddled.' Shruti doesn't want to accept what he's saying.

'Probably.' Hanif doesn't wish to continue the topic. 'But, where do . . .'—he hesitates before saying 'I'—'. . . I fit into all these questions and inclinations that have muddled him? Maybe it's something different, something like the headship that's bothering him.' Hanif's eyes are shot through with awkwardness.

Sharad has taken a walk to buy cigarettes. When he returns and enters through the gate, he sees Hanif and Shruti sitting with Daddu. He hesitates.

Here he talks and laughs, but in the staff room he'll even drink his tea without saying a word to anyone. He's probably telling a story, he thinks. He puffs on his cigarette by the gate, then grows angrier. In my own home, with my own father, he sits around like he's more related to him than me. He's turned me out!

But there's nothing he can say, because no one's stopping him from going inside; it's just that Hanif will find an excuse to get up and walk away as soon as he enters.

He can't stand me, he thinks with self-pity. What did I do to deserve this? I always fought for him. I would have made him head, too, if he could have descended from his lofty heights! But he didn't create this crisis. Sharad's empathy switches from himself to Hanif. He should know no one can stand his stubbornness, neither the department, nor the city, he thinks sympathetically. But why does he make me the scapegoat? Again, he's angry. It's also my crisis.

A couple walks by on the street and glances at Sharad with curiosity. He blushes and goes through the gate, into the front yard, where the madhumalati is. Dried leaves and flowers are strewn underfoot. Mosquitos carry out an attack from above, despite the cold.

They should have put this tree somewhere else; it's spreading rubbish everywhere. A sudden buzz of annoyance overwhelms him. You smell the fragrance above; we endure the waste below! He's angry at the dense vine. He waves to ward off the mosquitoes and hits a branch. Now he feels even angrier.

The three inside burst out laughing.

They're laughing! They don't even allow me simple joys. They've turned the joy of my headship into a crime. Yes, they have. He purses his lips in the dark. He's so irritated, he stubs out his cigarette on the branch, so it doesn't quite go out but still glows, and he smiles with childish glee as he imagines the vine catching fire.

Daddu has installed a light in the veranda. It glows, as does the full moon in the sky.

Shruti and Hanif are out for a walk. They don't go far from home. The streets are too empty, and the winter nights are desolate. A light haze covers the moon. Suddenly the haze slips away, and the moon shines as though it's been illuminated.

'I feel scared,' says Shruti, clinging to Hanif.

'At any other time, this would look beautiful,' he says, pulling her close.

'You don't feel scared?' she asks as she assesses the ghostly moon.

'I do,' he says and starts walking faster, holding her close. 'When people like Sharad say what's happening is good, in the sense that what was inside has come out into the open and now people are examining themselves and the past, asking questions . . .'

'But that's good, right? Out in the open, asking questions, seeing clearly what was suppressed inside? Then they can figure it out,' suggests Shruti, hoping to ease her fear.

'This figuring out period will harm us all. What will we do?' asks Hanif hopelessly. 'When this figuring-out period is done, will Sharad be in the ashram and I a member of the Anjuman-e-Islam?'

'You'll be murdered long before that!' says Shruti bitterly, as though she herself might do the murdering.

'Yes.' The moon is reflected in Hanif's eyes. 'And nothing will be attained by such a death, not martyrdom, nor a certificate for bravery. It won't prove the success of any campaign. It'll actually be an utterly petty, insignificant death, useless, futile.' Hanif's voice is dry, his eyes vacant.

'Why aren't you taking anything for that?' asks Daddu.

Sharad coughs as he pulls a box from his pocket to show him. He takes a pill from it and pops it in his mouth.

Shruti shuts the door behind her. As she turns, she bumps into Hanif.

'Shhh.' She puts a finger to his lips. 'Come upstairs, we'll drink tea up there today.'

Hanif is surprised, but Shruti takes him by the hand and leads him upstairs. Once she closes the door, she lets go of his hand.

'It seems like Daddu is feeling that pain again. He keeps making excuses and going off to the bathroom. If we don't leave him alone, he won't be able to stay in there.'

'Shouldn't he call the doctor?' asks Hanif.

'He must have called him.'

Hanif gazes at the closed door wistfully. Then he grabs Shruti's hand and leads her into the kitchen.

Sharad's voice floats into Hanif's office, either from a classroom or the hallway.

'Indiscipline will not be tolerated under any circumstances,' he says. Is he berating students or administrative staff? Then he starts to cough.

Nandan's voice joins his: 'You can get licorice root powder from any paan seller; it will give you some relief from that cough.'

Urmila's voice floats in: 'If you can get some betel root, that works miracles.'

Hanif recalls an amusing tale about betel root. He turns his back to the window and tries to forget it by reading the book open in his lap.

The phone is ringing. It's not yet properly morning. It seems to ring for a long time. Sharad and Daddu must be sleeping. It keeps ringing.

'Hanif.' Shruti shakes him. 'Go down and see; the door must be open.'

Ring ring. As though the phone is insisting on being answered.

'It's probably a wrong number.' Hanif turns over, half asleep.

It stops.

Then it starts again.

Now Hanif's awake too. He gets up quickly and goes downstairs.

By the time Shruti gets downstairs, everyone's awake.

'The old mahant's been murdered,' says Hanif.

'Who?' asks Shruti. 'The one with the big wings?'

'Yes,' says Sharad.

'The one who got leaves stuck in his beard?' asks Shruti foolishly.

'That one.'

'Who killed him?'

'I don't know, but it could be due to infighting.'

'This was bound to happen.' Daddu goes and sits on the divan. 'If you birth a demon, some day it'll return to swallow its parents.'

'But the elderly mahant?' asks Shruti, contemplating his age.

'Maybe they thought he was too behind the times, too slow?'

'Come, have tea. Nankau probably isn't up yet. You boil the water,' says Daddu.

'I don't like it when anyone dies or gets killed . . .' Shruti feels compassion for the deceased.

'I don't mind it,' says Hanif mercilessly. 'If you train tigers to eat humans, how long will you remain safe?'

The phone shrieks again. Sharad pounces on it.

'It's your friend Haq!' he says to Hanif.

Hanif speaks to him.

'What was he saying?' asks Daddu.

'The same. No one go out.'

'There's no question of that. No one will go out,' declares Daddu, as though girding himself for this very task!

Ring ring.
  Kapadia gives the same instructions.
  Sharad calls Babu Painter.

A huge crowd descends for the final darshan of the mahant. The police must make stringent arrangements, but no one even tries to keep people from gathering.

The event is being televised. The mahant's earthly body is loaded down with thick garlands of marigolds and roses. The TV screen shows splotches of white and orange clothing. People circumambulate the dead mahant with hands clasped.

Important people have come from the capital to offer flowers. All these scenes repeat as though the reel is stuck. The hum of the bhajans, the circling crowd, the body laden with flowers.

This, too, has been happening: Daddu has been sitting and watching for five minutes at a time, then turning off the TV and going to the bathroom or somewhere else. When he leaves, Sharad turns the TV back on.

Nankau has returned. He's bustling about, preparing dinner.

'They fired tear gas, and we ran.' His laughter is tinged with fear. 'But I did take darshan.'

The mahant's last rites take place on a sandalwood pyre. As of today, the newspapers and the government and the people on TV and the residents of the city are referring to him not as the mahant but as Mahatma Ji, the great soul.

Fear is in the air. That's why everything's closed. The police haven't made any announcements, and yet this is the mood.

Someone has fired a shot during the morning puja. An inquiry is under way. All other news pales in comparison.

The newspaper's not coming. The milk's not coming. But suddenly, Daddu opens the laundry basket and produces two boxes of condensed milk!

'So far, we have no idea,' says Kapadia. He's in uniform. He's just entered but is ready to leave. 'Now the ashram has passed into the hands of the true brawler elements. They want to infiltrate politics immediately; they want to stand candidates in the election. That's why they got into a disagreement with the Mahant–Mahatma.' He uses both titles together.

'Be careful,' he warns Hanif as he leaves.

'Oh, Daddu, namaskar,' he turns back to pay his respects to Daddu.

'Hey, Sharad, get rid of your beard. I'm not joking.' He laughs as he gets into his jeep.

The jeep drives off, leaving a trail of smoke.

The smoke leaves Sharad coughing.

There's an announcement from the police on the TV: *Don't be provoked. Stay peaceful. Don't believe rumours.* Daddu gets up and turns off the TV with a click, in his signature style. He's returning to sit on the divan when his eyes meet Shruti's, and the two smile conspiratorially. Shruti has heard a rumour, that the bullet was fired not from the crowd but from somewhere outside; that it came over the wall of the ashram.

'But then, where could it have come from, if it came from outside?' she asks Daddu pointlessly.

'Who knows.' Daddu raises his hands. 'There's the maidan on one side of the ashram, the university on the other.'

'Exactly.'

Shruti bites her lip.

There's a fear of riots. Everything's closed.

Hanif and Shruti come out to their balcony when they hear a noise. Something's happening at a nearby house. A woman, whose face they recognize, has emerged from her home and rushes after a man, screaming something at him. She's in her nightgown and her flip-flops smack the ground as she runs. When she reaches the man, she pulls at his kameez and berates him. The man is her cook. Suddenly she removes a flip-flop and starts smacking him with it. She's turning red–yellow–purple with rage.

Many people peer from their windows and verandas. Everyone returns quietly inside.

This has turned out to be the rumour of all rumours! The king of all rumours. Namely, it wasn't even a bullet, it was a bomb, which was thrown from somewhere far off.

Is it not possible to tell the difference between a bullet and a bomb nowadays?

Seeing Sharad ready to leave, Daddu asks, 'Where are you going?'

Why does it make a difference whether it's a bullet or a bomb?

Ah, but they're one hundred percent different: one is Hindu, the other Muslim!

Bad news is coming in.

We've been waiting for this since the beginning! With breath bated. Then exhaling. Gasping.

Accounts are being reported by phone of people revelling in bloodshed. And such revelries are taken from door to door.

Hindus have written in large red letters outside their homes:
This is a Hindu home.

No one has the courage to write a lie.

But what if someone enters my home and starts one of these
bloody revels, and what if my inkpot tips over? No one would
want to steal it. All the same, there's a danger! If the poor inkpot
were to tip during the festivities, it wouldn't be able to right itself.
It would be an utterly senseless martyrdom!

One hears containers are being made now which are airtight,
unbreakable, non-flammable. Maybe I could get one of those?

I'm afraid, and I squint. If I open my eyes wide, I see the
black-blue smoke billowing over the horizon. Not billowing so
much as oozing.

What is it? Is it ink?

Shruti, Sharad and Daddu sit together for a long time.

'Today I won't be able to fill a single matchbox with laughter,'
mourns Shruti.

Hanif isn't doing anything. Actually, he can't understand what's
happening. It happens; it stops happening. How long will the city
go on like this? Is this what's meant by *happening*, or is this just
getting stuck in one place?

Sharad says angrily, 'Maqbool Haq is printing rude things in his
newspaper. He's saying Muslims have separate courts because the
government courts have not protected them.'

'He's not altogether wrong,' observes Shruti sadly.

'You're forgiving him again. No one's talking sense,' grumbles Sharad.

'Enough, son,' chides Daddu. 'Is he screaming from your rooftop? Is he standing on your street?'

Sharad sits down.

'He's writing Hanif's story.'

'May he go to hell,' retorts Daddu dismissively.

When we're afraid, we feel angry.

Shruti stares at Daddu suspiciously. Today it is she who's raising a finger, waggling it and chiding him.

'Now don't you lie. He came again, didn't he? I recognized the sound of his car.'

'Arre, scolding like a granny!' Daddu admits defeat. 'Let him come to pay his daily respects. Now you're standing guard!'

'Daddu, are you . . .?' but Shruti can't even ask.

'He's not a doctor, he's a blockhead! He comes so I can cure him.' Daddu laughs off his pain.

Some Muslims have distributed sweets in celebration of the mahant's demise, which the people from the department are saying is in bad taste.

'Hanif's very stubborn,' says Shorty Josh, seeing him wearing a kurta, contrary to the new directive.

'It's arrogance; he knows everyone will dislike it. The mahant was a form of God for so many, but some were crass and distributed sweets,' frets Urmila.

Sometimes when you speak of one, you mean the whole community, and when you speak of the whole community, you're talking about only the one. This is unity in diversity!

The statement of the new leader of the ashram, the Acharya, is being read out:

In order to destroy the prestige of our ashram, a false rumour is being spread that the Mahatma was shot by an insider. We vow we won't stop until we've caught the murderer.

The students wander about like detectives.

'If anyone were hiding there, the chowkidar wouldn't be able to see them.'

'The chowkidar would never notice a thief standing out in the open; he's always napping!'

A shower of laughter.

'It was probably thrown from over there, by some accomplished terrorist.'

Sharad comes outside.

'That's crazy. If you're such an amazing thrower, why not join the Olympics?'

Someone says, 'Sir, it's also possible it was thrown with the aim of exploding it just anywhere during the puja, but it went and fell directly on the stage.'

'Well, anything can happen,' suggests Professor Nandan, who has come out after Sharad. 'But the idea that it came from here makes no sense.' He's peering far inside the ashram, where a uniformed policeman wanders about.

'I don't like any of it.' Shorty Josh has also come outside. 'That such prominent holy men should quarrel among themselves like monkeys!' He laughs. 'The religious frenzy, his criticism of other religions, none of it makes people stop revering their saint guru. If ashramites and religious folk get involved in murder and mayhem, what's the difference between them and two-bit politicians? The same power struggles!'

'You're joking, right, bhai?' laughs Sharad. 'Surely you're not hoping a Muslim murderer will emerge?'

'It doesn't have to be a Muslim, but an outsider hooligan. It can be a Hindu but not a devotee or a sadhu!'

'The likes of Haq hire hitmen to kill for them,' says one girl.

'You people watch too many films,' teases Nandan.

'What does your friend have to say?' Shorty Josh asks Sharad.

'Why do you keep saying *your friend, your friend*? He has a name and it's spoken with great respect,' snaps Sharad.

Kapadia says there are a few suspects, and Shruti's heart is in her mouth, as though she's committed a crime. She wants him to name names quickly, but she can't bring herself to ask.

'Wait, I'll come for a walk too,' she says.

'You were just saying you had to wash your hair,' Hanif reminds her.

'I'll wash it when we get back,' she says, finding Hanif looking at her strangely. 'I haven't been able to go for a walk in so long.'

'Shruti,' Hanif says warmly, 'let me be natural. You be natural too. If we fear so much, where will we go?'

'Sharad was right. As long as this is going on, let's go stay in Beverly's flat.'

'It won't come to that. If we're not safe here, we won't be safe anywhere. Uff.' Hanif is forced to say such things, though he'd rather not. 'We shouldn't allow ourselves to be so afraid. If we're always fleeing, life will become impossible.'

'It already has,' says Shruti dejectedly. 'Don't be angry.' She reaches out when she sees Hanif's expression.

'These are all things that scare us and make us feel threatened.' Hanif laces his fingers through hers. 'Mostly.' He stands up. 'I'm walking as far as the park. I'll come back soon.'

'Together we'll live, together we'll die!' Shruti stands.

'Go take a bath.' Hanif's tone is firm.

Shruti watches him from the bathroom window. A long shadow moving down the street.

If he suddenly falls, what will I do? What if someone pushes him over? She watches, terrified now, as though someone might jump into the street at any moment. I'll just keep watching, she decides, glancing down at her naked body. Until I'm able to go out.

Nowadays my pen keeps jerking, as though it's ill, or it's broken, or the ink is spoiled.

Or else everything's simply moving to this jolting rhythm.

'So was it the Muslims who finished off Mahatma Ji?'

Even though everyone knows this question is baseless, the city's begun to ask it with a smug, self-satisfied smile. Countless people have joyfully seized upon it, and once they've done so, they ask it with that same complacent smile that nourished the lie and turned it into belief, thus transforming it into an answer.

People are truly inflamed.

Truly! I saw this in a Hindu neighbourhood: a boy, must have been fifteen or sixteen, yelling, 'Football! Football! If you move, you'll be hit; if you stop, you'll be petrified!' Blood flowed in the drain. He ran towards me helter-skelter, bow-legged, holding the head of a cow with horns atop his own head. It wasn't a fake head. Unless you say the blood that oozed from it was fake, and then I'll believe you.

Everyone's now saying that the mahant, who's no more, was a true mahatma. He had to run the ashram, grow it and spread its fame over the seven seas, so to a certain extent, some sort of conflagration was inevitable, but nothing so dire. Fire is fire, greedy to swallow everything in its path. Careful! Careful! he'd said. But all sorts of people were fanning the flames, and eventually they, too, engulfed him.

The people of our city have grown fatigued, and started to say, let the party of the ashram devotees win, let them come to power, only then will we have peace, let them prove their worth. Then maybe this fire will be extinguished.

But we also fear this outcome. Even if a Hitler were to take responsibility for protecting us, life and limb, wouldn't everyone bow to him one by one? What kind of peace is that? The way the city is going, even jackals pose as lions. They hold you at gunpoint and say, stop breathing! But can you stop?

Shruti hides her fear from Hanif. She feels so alone. Hanif has told her where he's going and when he'll return, but her thoughts keep her scared.

Shruti is busy removing the dirty clothes from the basket to soak them in Surf. Hanif's kameez hangs from the basket. When she pulls it out, she smells him: his body, the fragrance of his soap, and the stench of his sweat. She stares at it for a moment. Then she puts it on and strolls about the room adjacent to the balcony.

Daddu is busily writing something. On blank paper. No, he's not adding up expenses, nor writing a letter.

Daddu writes two sentences and then crosses them out. And how smartly he cuts them. He crosses them out from the right, then his pen circles round and cuts from the left. But he's still not satisfied. Now he draws vertical lines, close together, over every letter. I hold it up to the sun and try to read it. But I can only make out one word.

'Is.'

But what *is*?

'Congratulations, Head Sahib!' announces Nandan as he enters Sharad's office.

'Don't pull my leg, Head Sahib!' laughs Sharad. 'As long as you're here, no one else can be head, however much you keep calling me Head Sahib!'

'Well, then kill me off.' Nandan also laughs.

Then your ghost will sit on the chair.

'Just break the chair.'

Both laugh heartily.

'Change your office, and soon,' says Nandan, examining Sharad's bookcases. 'Get these things shifted into the head's office, okay?' He nods warmly.

'Thank you,' says Sharad standing up.

There's a band of students outside the office.

'Go in, go in! Say congratulations, all of you,' instructs Nandan as he leaves.

Not just the students, everyone else in the department has shown up, one after another!

Seeing Hanif at the door, Sharad pushes back his chair and stands up.

'Congrats!' Hanif smiles faintly.

Sharad's eyes fill with tears. He shakes his hand and won't let go.

'Have a seat,' he says.

'I have class,' says Hanif. As he turns to leave, Sharad starts to cough.

'Sir, you should distribute sweets,' insist the students.

'What are you talking about? Distributing sweets with the city like this?'

The students are crestfallen. Nandan affectionately taps one on the back. 'Let things get better, then we'll distribute sweets all the time.'

He's truly happy I've become head, thinks Sharad. Maybe his victory in pushing aside the other one who should have had the position has eased his sorrow at losing it. He lost the chair but showed his power!

Sharad comes upstairs when he sees Hanif leaving on his scooter.

He misses Beverly.

He sits with Shruti.

If only she would ask about Beverly, he thinks. He wants to say how much he misses her, but what comes out of his mouth is, 'He's my childhood friend.'

'Yes,' nods Shruti.

'He avoids me in particular,' he laments.

'It will be fine,' says Shruti as she thinks, 'I'll be able to speak openly with him more than with Hanif.'

'I'm able to speak more openly with you than with Hanif,' says Shruti, holding out her hand.

'Yes, it's easier to speak openly with someone you're less close to.' Sharad smiles wanly. He feels as though he won't be able to speak openly with Shruti at all.

'I'm head now,' he says. 'As though I'm confessing to a crime,' he thinks.

'That's good,' says Shruti softly.

'Do you know what people are saying? They're saying a Muslim killed Gandhi!'

'People have no connection with the truth. They're applying a salve of lies to a wound, to ease the pain!'

'But who created the wound?' asks Sharad. What cause will she cite for this? He panics.

'Sorry, what did you say?' Shruti is lost in thought.

Sharad is silent in his loneliness. He misses Beverly. He doesn't want to talk to Shruti. He's wondering how to get up and leave.

Shruti's happy to have Sharad near. She wants to talk to him until Hanif returns.

'What will happen, Sharad?' she asks hopefully.

'Nothing can happen,' he replies sadly.

'It can,' she snaps. 'Something that starts somewhere at some time can stop anywhere at any time.'

'Now our reactions have become so conditioned that if something happens to that community, we say, *tsk tsk*, we say, *poor things*, and if it happens to our community, we sneer, and we say, it's happening to these ones, and that's why they're whining so much,' says Urmila.

Hanif doesn't participate in these conversations. He stands up and leaves.

Were such things discussed here before? Sharad tries to remember. What's coming out in the open here, exactly?

Hanif has reached the stairs. Sharad starts to cough when he sees him.

Dagdu brings him water. Sharad wipes his nose and mouth with a handkerchief and speaks softly.

'Perhaps in order to hide our anti-Muslim feelings from ourselves, we fill our hearts with guilt and sympathy for them, because when we say, *poor things*, we can remain pure and blameless in our own eyes. But when we see a Hindu beaten, if we allow the hysterical ranting that surges in us to come to the surface, we won't be able to look ourselves squarely in the face. Our idea of what's genteel makes hypocrites of us. What is it that I'm saying?'

'That's what I want to know,' retorts Urmila.

'But how does feeling guilty enter into this, Sharad?' asks Shorty Josh. 'One instinctively has more feeling for one's own community. Why pretend otherwise?'

'Our community?' asks Sharad bitterly. 'That was a third category!'

Shruti and Hanif are both dumbfounded when they hear a knock at the door. So late at night!

Shruti wants to say, Don't open it!

Hanif puts on his dressing gown and opens the door.

It's Sharad.

'Hanif . . . Shruti . . .' he gasps. His head is trembling. He is gripping his chest and barely able to stand.

'What happened?' they ask with alarm.

Sharad can't get the words out. Hanif pulls him inside and sits him down. Shruti locks the door.

'No . . . no . . .' Sharad is speaking in broken whispers. 'Here.' He rubs his chest. 'So much pain . . . I can't . . . breathe . . .'

His hands are cold, his forehead gleams with sweat. Shruti rubs his chest. Hanif turns towards the door.

'Call Kapadia,' says Shruti.

'That's what I'm going to do.'

'No . . . no . . .' Sharad tries to say. 'The scooter . . .'

Hanif has already gone downstairs.

'A car is better,' says Shruti.

A dog lies sleeping near a mound of ashes in the darkness. The jeep cleaves through the night at a terrifying speed.

Some uniformed orders. Some hospital swiftness. The uniform and Hanif and Shruti with the stretcher.

'Everything's clear,' says the doctor.

'That's . . . what . . . I . . . was . . . saying. No need . . . for . . . an . . . ECG,' says Sharad. He's looking a bit better.

'You have a lesion from all that coughing,' notes the doctor, glancing down at Sharad's chest. 'Just take a course of antibiotics.'

A lamp burns at the gate. Daddu. But no worries, all's well. It's still a long way till morning.

Hanif is leaning over examining his tyre when Nandan drives by on his moped.

'Creep,' mutters Hanif.

Nandan makes a U-turn and comes back.

'What happened? Does it look like a puncture?' he asks.

'Yes.' Hanif nods.

Nandan rests his feet on the ground, leaving the engine running, and looks down.

'Why don't you do this?' he says. 'Come home with me. My son will fix it right away.'

'No need to trouble yourself.' Hanif feels embarrassed.

'No trouble at all. Come sit behind me. My house is right over here. You can come to my home, right?' laughs Nandan. 'We'll drink coffee.'

'I have no objection to drinking coffee, but . . .' Hanif stands awkwardly.

'Come,' Nandan motions.

Soon, they're sitting on the lawn drinking coffee.

'Looks like you enjoy gardening too,' compliments Hanif.

'Not him, me,' corrects Mrs Nandan. 'If I ask him to look after it a bit too, he just shoves the hose on to the faucet and waters everything!'

There's a bounty of lovely flowers all around, and the red chairs are arranged attractively on the green grass. Hanif enjoys sitting in the sunshine drinking coffee.

This is the missus's baby! he thinks to himself with a smile.

'I'll be very sad to leave all this,' remarks Mrs Nandan ruefully.

'Why will you leave it?' asks Hanif. Then he immediately remembers that the headship has changed hands. Will Sharad move here? he wonders. It also occurs to him Shruti would like it here.

'It's time for me to retire, bhai,' says Nandan. 'I'll have to leave. I'm tired, Doctor Sahib. Maybe I'll take early retirement. You people can manage everything now.'

Hanif recalls a story, but he doesn't tell it. Some other time, he would have told it to Sharad. He imagines the two of them, two friends, laughing together.

This is the state of the city: it heats, it burns, it cools.

'Guavas!' exclaims Shruti, inhaling.

'I'm eating one, Didi!' calls Nankau.

'Bring some, bring some! For her too,' cackles Daddu.

Nankau brings two green guavas and two yellow ones with red spots and sets them out.

'I just washed them,' he says.

Shruti bites into one. Daddu offers her a knife, and their fragrance spreads.

'What is it?' asks Shruti. She comes outside, where Sharad stands by the madhumalti, staring in.

'It's him,' says Sharad with a peculiar air of defeat. He seems truly exhausted.

Hanif is sitting inside.

'Come on in,' she says.

'No, forget it.' He's staring hard at the flowering vine.

'Why do you avoid him?' asks Shruti irritably.

'I don't go in out of respect for him,' he says.

His gaze meets Hanif's on the other side of the door. He feels distressed.

'You go,' he says. 'Turn off the veranda lights.'

As Shruti opens the door, a wave of music rises from Daddu's radiogram.

Sharad recedes into the darkness.

'I'm being destroyed, out of respect for him,' mumbles Sharad. 'He's not a baby. Why should I treat him so delicately? Let him act his age.' Sharad feels fatigued. Antibiotics really knock you out, he thinks.

Shruti comes out again.

'Daddu's saying don't catch cold again, come inside.'

'Why doesn't Hanif say anything?' asks Sharad helplessly. 'All educated secular Muslims fall silent.'

Shruti stares at him in dismay. What's happening to him? 'Don't confuse one individual with the entire community,' she admonishes.

'The entire community is doing this. It's irritated, whimpering inside, feeling frustrated, hiding, attacking.'

'Don't mix everyone into one.' Shruti suddenly feels tired. It's all the same stuff, just different people saying it.

'We're all saying this, that the individual is separate,' says Sharad. He's scared of Shruti and hangs his head. 'I'm confused. I'll accept I'm able to see both communities the same way when I can call a Muslim a fanatic bastard with the same animosity as I can a Hindu.'

Shruti reaches out and grasps a branch of the madhumalti. It's covered in dust. She withdraws her hand.

'Yes, yes,' Sharad nods vigorously. 'I'll smoke a cigarette, then come in.' He lights a match.

'Don't smoke,' says Shruti sternly and goes back inside.

So sinister, thinks Sharad. His thoughts spin round and round like a scratched record. I'm a sensitive, middle-class-educated, polite, secular bastard! One second I hang my head in guilt, and the next I raise it, filled with poisonous thoughts.

He stares at Hanif angrily, who's sitting in the light and can't see him. Coward! He won't speak, he won't listen to any criticism. As if Muslims aren't happy when a bomb explodes and fear spreads . . .

Suddenly Sharad is filled with a desire for violence. Who says they're weak? They sit in luxury in Pakistan, dropping bombs over here.

As if in response to someone saying to him, 'No, you're wrong,' he begins to mutter, 'No, no, I'm not wrong, it's the truth.'

Truly, even in the darkness, his eyes light up with the glow of violence. They spread terror and they're smug, he thinks. He keeps staring at Hanif. He himself cannot be seen, and this gives him power.

'Creep,' he mutters. He stares hard at Hanif and smiles.

He feels at this moment he can do anything; if a riot breaks out right here, who knows, he'd be capable of anything! Anger, pain, fatigue, idiocy, all flow through him in waves.

He's about to toss out his cigarette, but then he has an idea. He approaches the madhumalti, has another thought, rejects it and takes his penknife from his pocket. He opens it up and begins to hack at a branch like a woodpecker—*peck peck peck.*

Even in the darkness of night his eyes exude a bestial madness.

This is how it was.

Where were the humans in this climate? Humans no more, they were symbols of one agenda or another. And their lives and deaths meant nothing; they were the deaths of the agenda.

The sky echoes with the sound of drums. It's turned purple. First come the Devi cutout and other idols. Then an ash-smeared holy man dancing in an opium haze, eyes flaming red, a fake red tongue hanging from his face and a small yellow loincloth tied about his waist.

Next comes the crowd: the sants and those bearing a tilak on their foreheads, all attired in saffron clothing; the youths with saffron bands tied around their heads; and the householders singing praises to the Goddess, hands folded, or striking their cymbals.

'*Gaura bhavabhaamini . . .*' they sing, their bhajans growing louder.

A holy woman stuffs a saffron flag into the gate and moves on.

'*Ripu dal samhaarini . . .*'

Suddenly, Sharad tears the gate open and rushes out.

'Devils!' he screams.

He snaps the flag in two and throws it at the crowd. 'Don't do your devil dance in front of our home, get out!'

Some youths have turned to look.

'Shut uppppp!' he yells.

Hanif comes running. He pulls Sharad in through the gate.

'Hush, hush. Come inside!' he scolds.

Sharad keeps turning and yelling as Hanif drags him into the house.

'Evildoers! You're not Hindu at all! You belong to no religion! You're a blight on the human race!'

'Have you lost your mind?' demands Hanif as he pulls him upstairs.

Inside stands Shruti, terrified.

Daddu is not in the front room.

When I look at Daddu, I can't tell what he knows. This is what he's saying: '. . . and took an ignorant step. It's not a matter of shouting slogans. Will entertainment come cheap, or will it be expensive? Clearly, there's no logical answer . . .'

All the same, Hanif usually takes his tea into his office and drinks it alone. Pigeons hidden in the casements coo, creating a drowsy atmosphere. Any voices he hears usually belong to the students. The same tired stuff. Will we ever bother to examine them properly? wonders Hanif as he dozes.

He can hear Sharad talking to a student, but they're far away. Mostly he just hears his measured tone.

'Their legal system . . . Sharia . . . a tomb on the street . . .' says the student. 'If the taziya must be taken out, then the tree must be cut down . . . religion . . . religion . . . wherever you look, there's arrogance, everyone has turned against them . . .'

'Everyone's been alienated! Are they crazy, or are we, shouting *secular secular* into the wind, all alone?' asks another student excitedly.

Sharad says something again.

'Not a single Muslim speaks out,' shrieks yet another student. 'Whether about Khomeini, Shah Bano or any issue. No matter how educated they are, they're so passive!'

Hanif gets up and leaves his office. He walks right through the middle of them. The shrieking student has a saffron cloth tied around his head.

Hanif turns to the students and says loudly, 'We've always said we belong to a third category, comprising different belief systems. Among those who have raised voices of revolt against Khomeini, Shah Bano, etc., there are also Muslims. Why do you'—he looks the saffron-banded student in the eye—'seek out only Muslims separately from all others?'

'Of course you'll defend Muslims!' yells the student rudely. 'When it comes to Hindus . . .'

'Defending one community doesn't necessarily mean opposing the other.'

Hanif is speaking for the first time in quite a while. More students and teachers sidle over to listen.

'Your religion . . .'

'I reject whichever religion commits injustice.'

'Hanif, drop it,' whispers Sharad.

'Let me speak, Sharad,' replies Hanif loudly.

He continues to speak, as the saffron-banded students glare at him angrily.

He's said such things before, but always about people over there. But now it seems that there has arrived here.

The atmosphere is off-kilter. Take the ink seller, for example. He makes a living thanks to me, but he scares me!

All that was far away, all that affected others, has become ours now, the personal story of these ones.

There's the same dust in both places, right? Whether it flies over there, or into our eyes, or gathers on the branches of our vines? And the breeze is the same, carrying the stench of corpses putrefying for centuries.

But we were not at all prepared for what happened when we scratched our skin. Here, too, the same stench rose to the surface from below.

Jai Jagadambe!

A tempo loaded with saffron-banded youths slows near the house. They fling coloured powder in the air, and one boy jumps down to stuff a saffron flag into the gate, then jumps back into the tempo.

'Arre, that's the same one!' Shruti recognizes the boy from the balcony, 'The one you'd scolded.'

'No.' Sharad pulls her back from the edge. 'That's the one who was staring at Hanif that day in the department.'

The smell of flying colours filled the air that day.

Everyone feels very much alone.

I have no faith in them, nor in myself, but I keep writing it all down. Their ambitions, their thoughts, their speech, they all spin about like footballs, rolling from this camp to that with no fixed abode.

Nandan is unhappy.

'See,' he says to Sharad, 'in times of trouble, your friend . . . he's leaving the department. He's going on sabbatical. You should find out if he means to run off to Paris or Rome!'

Nandu is saying Hanif is irresponsible.

Sharad is angry. He shakes his head sadly. 'He already ran off,' he says.

Nandu nods happily in agreement, takes a tin from his pocket and holds out a pinch of fragrant supari.

'It's come straight from Lahore,' he says.

Taak dhin dhin dhin!

Daddu's head moves to a tabla rhythm.

'Arre, children, it's the mind of man! How can you fathom it?'

Taak dhin dhin.

'These are all the antics of men.'

The heater is blazing, but Daddu has carried it in from his room. He's wrapped himself in the sanganeri-print quilt and sits on the divan looking like a tent with a tabla for a head.

Taak dhin dhin!

He wears a cap with earflaps, his eyes dance, his head creaks. A cold wind blows outside. His voice is serious.

'Now they're thinking of waging war! Why not? When he's going, he should be coming; if he's staying, he should go! What will you do? Eh?'

What could Shruti do? Hardly anything. The most she can do in her drowsy state is wait for the tent to lean over his glass for a sip, then she quickly yawns, rubs her eyes and blinks to keep them open.

'They must keep doing something. Everyone has that need, not just you and me. We need to keep talking, keep moving, to maintain the sense we're alive.'

The quilt is still, but inside it must be wiggling all over. The rhythm emerging through the *taak dhin dhin* head is strangely bewitching.

'If everyone stood together on one side, what would they say, where would they find that sensation of being alive? We'd just keep nodding in agreement. That's not necessary either. You know, agreement is quite frightening; it makes you mechanical. But disagreement, that's for humans! That's why, that's exactly why, you're over there, so I must be over here. If you came over here, I'd immediately go over there. I'd revile you; I'd oppose what you say, and then there'd be movement, and the belief that I exist, that I'm very much alive.'

Shruti is alive in the existence of her dozing movements. Her eyes keep shutting, Daddu's voice becomes Daddu's finger, which approaches her; she grabs it and goes out for a walk, wherever Daddu leads her.

'People . . .' Daddu is saying, 'they're so much more than the things they yell out, and . . .' he continues, '. . . so much smaller than that too . . .'

Shruti hears: 'Will you fear, or will you trust?' She hears Daddu asking a question.

His finger enters her dream as a comfort, that is, his voice, which is taking Shruti for a walk.

'What I'm saying is, don't fear, but don't trust either. What I'm saying is, don't even look over there. There's nothing there. It's only the wind.' Daddu's voice shimmers.

A desert on a moonlit night appears before Shruti. Huge silver dunes. Moon and wind rain down shimmering grains of sand as though between fingers.

'What's happening: it's nothing, it's only the wind. In the department, in the city. What you people are saying, so shaken, making the rounds of this lane, that lane, that's also nothing, just wind. Words of air, floating in the breeze!'

The sound of wind. On the cool sand of the desert, the soft, rustling wind. Bells ringing far off. Bells ring in the desert.

'One speaks, another listens, and they think something real has unfurled between them. But it's only the wind.'

Wind pours from Daddu's head, perched atop the quilt tent. He's like a magician, *taak dhin dhin*. Wind, wind, wind.

His voice ripples over Shruti. Now it's an ocean full of waves made of wind, which approach, billow over her and recede, filling her pockets with sand.

'It's an ocean, child . . .' Daddu is saying. 'See its vanity. It thunders at the cliff, Oh, cliff! You think you're so big, you think you're so steadfast, that you won't waver. But we'll make you bend. We'll break you; we'll crush you and swallow you up; we'll turn you to powder!'

Taak dhin dhin.

'The vanity of each is false; it's only the wind stirring up the ocean and bashing the cliffs.'

Daddu, you're crafting one story on top of another. Shruti thinks she said this. Dreams dance in her sleepy eyes.

'You people think this is all a powerful churning, that everyone's assessing their views, that centuries' worth of layers are peeling back. But this is something we can't do. No churning . . .' A hand grows from the quilt and gently beats Daddu on the head, raps on his temple. '. . . is happening up here. It's somewhere over there . . .'

The hand bursts forth again, gesturing towards the far-off sky.

'. . . and it's all wind.'

The hand has disappeared again.

'When that same air bursts from within us, we assume it's our own doing: we thought, we said, we created. What vanity, we think we thundered and crushed you. All these are games of the wind. It comes. Then it goes. This time it knocks us over, the next it uplifts us. And we think . . .'

Taak dhin dhin dhin.

'. . . that our thoughts have progressed, our zest for life has grown!'

Taak dhin dhin dhin taak.

The magician balls his fists; he intones the magic spell, and the hall fills with *wind wind wind.*

Ah, Daddu is never in the mood to hold back. Shruti now sees grass everywhere she looks. It's grown over the entire earth. It ripples and dances in the wind.

'The city you fear is nothing. Its dark galis, its screaming populace, the maze of it; none of it's real.'

The grass is growing. Its whispering becomes a song. In Shruti's imagination, it surges into a jungle, which grows denser, the branches tangling, blocking the wind.

Suddenly, she opens her eyes.

Daddu sits before her, red from the heater's warmth, twinkling.

'Should one fear what's not real? All this is fantasy. These cannibals populating the city, they're not real. Their hatred isn't real. This is merely their desire to maintain faith in being alive. They need to fill their void; they must shake off the fear of lifelessness and chase it away. Yes, the wind is blowing, and they merely flail absurdly.'

The wind has dropped away among the branches. The branches surround Shruti; they enter her, inside her grows the jungle, ever denser; it is the city, which can swallow you up, where the wind cannot reach, where breathing is stifled.

Shruti wakes with a jerk. She's completely alert. She begins to listen to Daddu with wakeful ears.

'You and I are afraid of the incidents occurring on a daily basis, but this is fantasy, not reality. Those who look like they're doing it actually are not. It's the wind, up to its antics.'

Shruti listens.

'Reality is but a quest, the eternal quest, the echoing quest in the sighing of the wind.'

There's a ripple in the quilt, a rustling.

'Forget everything,' says the magician. 'The only true reality is the quest. Everything else will come and go. That's how it is. This

horrible violence, this maddening silence, and all of us, nursing
our own egos.'

Oh, I was dreaming, Shruti realizes with a start. I saw Daddu
leading me along by the finger, and we were traversing terrifying,
tortuous mountain paths, and we'd nearly reached the sky,
where the white peaks touched the clouds. And at the foot of
the peaks, there was a lake. Extremely blue. Steam rose from it.
Daddu removed the blue with a wave of his hand, as though it
were a sheet, and under the blue sheet was a sheet of purest green.
It was amazing, and I wondered what it was called. And then I
thought: Volga!

It's amazing, I too am copying down her dream. Where did
she see all this? Did she forget what she saw? Or am I . . .?

A fantasy within a fantasy!

Daddu keeps weaving his tale.

'The real and steadfast quest. All else is a fantasy. When man
turns cannibal, he continues the same quest with violence, with
blood. That's where he sees his path, his goal, his being. In this
way he goes mad.

What's this I'm copying?

'Whatever takes hold, intoxicates. Peace, too, can be heady,
like a fever. If it takes hold, a person gets drunk on it and dances
deliriously. The wind will make him dance.'

The divan hovers a bit off the ground. The wind has lifted it
off its legs.

'This is emptiness, this is disenchantment; there's a spiritual
thirst to find meaning, which can make us turn anyone at all into
a god, feel a mad obsessive devotion.'

Daddu's eyes glint and sparkle in the golden light.

'None among us is real, nothing here is real, you may fill
all this emptiness with cruelty or with love, both are illusions;
mere wind.'

Truly, the wind has lifted the divan!

'We fear nothing happening, but then we want something to possess us, to drown us, to suffuse us, so we can forget that we're nothing, and feel we're something because of that attachment; we drown in its hue and think it's us; it's proof that we exist.'

The divan rocks lightly. First its legs lift. Then it begins to rock in the air, as though it's a boat floating on water.

'The pulsation is somewhere else, and we mistake it for our own. We give a name to meaninglessness and think we've found meaning. We create a daily routine and delude ourselves that it's something substantial. But what are you holding? The wind?'

Daddu is only a pair of eyes, but suddenly his laughter is everywhere.

'We're not living, we only think we are. Let go of vanity. What do you have to be vain about? We merely live in our own imagination.'

In the stillness of night, a desolate cry begins to drown out his laughter.

Daddu is still laughing, but the cry saturates the air. It's coming from a long way off, from the dark streets outside, and returning like an echo.

Then they hear a motorbike at the gate. And other sounds as well.

'What is it?' asks Shruti. She opens the door and goes out to the veranda.

It's a gang of youths with tilaks, their heads tied with bands of saffron.

'Where's that bastard? That dog!' She hears one of them scream over the noise of the motorbike.

'The one who calls himself our teacher—throw him outside!'

Another boy proudly stuffs a flag into the letterbox. There's an envelope in his hand.

'Give him this,' he says.

'Get out,' says Daddu, coming down from the veranda. 'Get out!' He grabs the flag and snaps it in two.

Aaiiii . . . The boys start shouting.

Suddenly the growling of the motorbike stops, and the youths open the gate and enter the yard.

'What is it?' asks Shruti, afraid. She stands in front of Daddu.

'We'll strip him, blacken his face, sit him backwards on a donkey and parade him through the city,' taunts a youth, whose every word betrays absolute confidence in his own power.

Someone spits paan near Shruti's feet, grabs her hand roughly and stuffs the envelope into it.

'Thug!' screams Shruti, shoving him away.

Hands reach out.

'Quieeeeet!' It's Daddu's voice.

'Out of the way, old man!' yell the boys.

And now, a storm.

The youths push Shruti away and grab Daddu, and the scream we hear, it's not Daddu's voice, it's something we've never heard before.

One boy shakes Daddu's arm.

'Where have you hidden him?' he demands.

'Beat me! Beat me!' cries Daddu, his eyes bloodshot. He who has no god, what else can he do? 'Will you beat your own teacher? There's no greater evil . . .'

These words bursting forth, this ragged voice, they can't belong to Daddu. Daddu doesn't sound like this. Daddu . . .

But it's he who's speaking. And screaming: 'Sisterfuckers . . . rats . . . clueless, outrageous bastards . . . cunts . . .'

These aren't Daddu's words!

'Shameless goons . . . beat me, beat me . . . beat me first . . . fornicators . . . swine . . . jackals . . . hijras . . .'

With a roar the gang falls upon him. They crush him and fling him like an arrow shot from a bow. Daddu goes flying and falls in the dust next to the madhumalti vine with a thud, his limbs tangling with the vines, pulling them down with him.

A set of pink gums studded with two rows of teeth falls separately.

Only I see Shruti fall begging at the feet of those kids. They disappear with an ear-splitting revving of the engine. Then complete silence.

Daddu lies face down. His dhoti has climbed above his thighs, and his bare, skinny knees lie exposed in the dust.

Suddenly he stands, pushing Shruti's hand aside. He rushes into the house, swift as the wind.

His face and clothes are smeared with dust.

The pink gums of his dentures lie below the madhumalti. They look like a lump of horrifying flesh.

And this is when my pen falls from my hand.

Shruti picks up the dentures, goes inside and washes them off. She wipes them dry and goes to Daddu.

Daddu has changed his clothes. He's washed his face. He's lying on the bed with his back to her.

Shruti places the dentures by the bed and stands there, watching his back. She stands and watches for a long time. Nothing happens.

The dentures stay where they are.

Daddu had fallen silent. In that moment between standing and falling, the whole world spun once, and everything flipped.

Daddu had sealed his lips.

The pen slipped from my hand. When Shruti picked up the gums, I also picked up my pen, but I wasn't able to write any more.

Fantasy! That's what Daddu had said. How to copy down fantasy? How to present it? In what form? This whole problem, of reality and fantasy, extends beyond form. The ink has taken a form and continues to splatter beyond it, its appearance every which way, the form growing formless.

Daddu's silence has descended into me.

I, too, have realized he will speak no more.

We were scared, of the new machismo, the new religiosity, the new antics.

No one saw Daddu falling besides me and Shruti. Did Daddu himself even know what happened?

When he fell, Shruti's heart broke. Walking upright was the measure of his self-respect, and the way he fell would have destroyed that for anyone.

He used to say he was a hundred years old, and everyone would laugh. But when he stood after his fall, he truly did look that old. When he stood upright, he was a beautiful straight line, redolent with mustard oil, feet on the earth, sky above his head. When he fell, he was dragged into the dust, pressed below the sky, face smeared with earth.

And when he stood, his dentures fell. Shruti picked them up, washed them, dried them and placed them on his bedside table.

And there they remained.

Only I saw her fall at the feet of those people, or these people, or whichever people they were, begging them to leave Daddu alone.

This, too, was a fragment that moved along in an orderly fashion, until suddenly, one day, it collided with another fragment, and then there was an explosion, and everything scattered.

I'll stop here for now. Even if my pen doesn't want to. Sharad and Shruti sit before me, the divan reflected silently in their eyes. The divan is silent, as is the splattering laughter, and yet . . .

I have borne witness thus far—isn't copying also a form of testimony? But just one last thing: I hereby testify that the laughter, too, left the divan and sailed up, up, up, and there, in the darkened sky, it took the form of a kite, and its string, well, it must be somewhere around here . . . Is it here? Where is it? Over there?

A Note from the Translator

January 22, 2024. I'm out for an early morning stroll in Bombay. Storefronts flutter with a profusion of saffron-colored flags celebrating the consecration of a new temple to Lord Rama in the far-off city of Ayodhya, in the state of Uttar Pradesh. I love this color. A bright orange yellow. The color of mango lassis and tangerines; of strips of light in sunrises and sunsets and flames in a cozy fire. But here I feel no warmth. I shiver, because I remember when Babar's Mosque was demolished by an angry mob of Hindu nationalists brandishing just such flags and the horrifying violence that swept through Muslim communities in the aftermath. And although I am an American, I have spent decades reading all about the 1947 Partition of India and Pakistan. I have taught university classes on the subject and translated five Partition novels. I know the devastation that is caused by nationalism and narratives of majoritarian vulnerability and what happens when a minority is othered as an enemy within. The Subcontinent is not alone in this respect, and nowadays, though red is another color of warmth,

I shiver as I walk down my own street in Vermont and see the gigantic red Trump sign billowing from my neighbor's front porch.

This book takes place during a year not specified, in a city not named. But the year definitely bears a resemblance to 1992, and the city is not unlike Ayodhya. Or maybe not: I have had arguments with people from various parts of India claiming that it is obviously about *their* city, in such and such a year. Therein lies the power of the narrative, which painstakingly documents the breakdown of society with the rise of communalism, a term that connotes communes and communal harmony in the West but is used in the Subcontinent to describe sectarian bigotry and violence. Geetanjali Shree's writing is preoccupied not just with the Partition and communalism, but with the invisible partitions that are constantly enacted in a fissured society.

The notion of what is one's own and what is other is constantly and subtly redefined throughout *Our City That Year,* so that page by page, sentence by sentence, divisions form and allegiances shift. This is often witnessed through conversations our unnamed narrator eavesdrops on, usually entering midstream, so that it is difficult to ascertain what has been said before (which poses a challenge for the translator, who must guess or reconstruct what went on before to make sure the conversation will gesture in the right direction).

In *Our City That Year,* there is one foreigner, the clueless white graduate student Beverly. Beverly specializes in knowing nothing at all about what is going on, and thus provides the opportunity to other characters, who are failing to write about what they see (especially Sharad), to explain. She enters a cacophony of ongoing conversations as a blank slate—until she's not—and starts taking sides when the characters bicker and hold views more complex than her initial vacuous pronouncement: 'I don't like riots.'

I, too, was once a clueless white foreign graduate student in a north Indian city during a year not unlike the one portrayed in the book. I knew nothing, until I knew something, and then quite a lot, enough to translate this book and internalize its lessons, not just for India, but for other fissured societies: America, Palestine, Korea, and so many more. *Our City That Year,* a novel intensely specific to a particular time and place, also belongs to a profusion of times and places. And as you, the reader, walk down the lanes and roadways of this city, deafened and blinded by endlessly spewed propaganda, you may be reminded of other cities and other nationalisms, and perhaps this will cast a fresh light on the fissures and cracks spidering through your own environment, and you will dream of a day when orange and red and any other colors can be reclaimed for the broadest possible palette of meanings.

—Daisy Rockwell

Translator's Acknowledgements

Many thanks to Geetanjali Shree for entrusting me with this important translation and answering all my nitpicking questions. I am grateful to our many editorial teams: Manasi Subramaniam and Vineet Gill at Penguin Random House India; Kristen Alfaro, Julia Sanches and Mayada Ibrahim at Tilted Axis; and Gretchen Schmidt at HarperVia. Thank you to my wonderful agent, Kanishka Gupta, for all you do. Two people aided me immeasurably when I was deep in the trenches of this translation: Vaibhav Sharma, who helped me navigate some very tricky bits of broken dialogue and idiomatic references, and Aftab Ahmad, who patiently went over every Urdu couplet with me (with some assists from Musharraf Ali Farooqi as well!). Shukriya also due to my Persian teacher, Muhammad Ali Mojaradi, who gave invaluable assistance for the Rumi quote. I am thankful for the patience of my husband and daughter, who must put up with my obsession with words and their meanings day in and day out. To my three cats, Jenny Linsky, Princess Leia and Madama Butterfly, who contributed tirelessly to this project; words cannot begin to express my gratitude, which is okay when you think about it, because they wouldn't really be useful anyway. Aftab, my shareek mutarjim, supporting me through thick and thin, this translation is dedicated to you.

Here ends Geetanjali Shree's
Our City That Year.

The first edition of this book was printed
and bound at Lakeside Book Company
in Harrisonburg, Virginia, in March 2025.

A NOTE ON THE TYPE

The text of this novel was set in Adobe Garamond
Pro, a typeface designed by Carol Twombly in 1990.
She studied specimen pages printed by William
Caslon (designer of the original Caslon) from the
mid-eighteenth century. The original Caslon en-
joyed great popularity; it was used for the American Declaration of Independence in 1776. Elegant
yet dependable, Adobe Caslon Pro shares many of
its best qualities, making it an excellent choice for
magazines, journals, book publishing, and corporate
communications.

HARPERVIA

An imprint dedicated to publishing international voices,
offering readers a chance to encounter other lives and other
points of view via the language of the imagination.